The Mooncusser

A Novel

by

H.P. Dunne

A Write Way Publishing Book

The Legend of the Mooncussers

"...the name Mooncusser seemed perfect to me, since men skulking in and out of the place probably preferred the obscurity of the dark. But the original Mooncussers had been more evil by far than any gambler, drinker or whoremonger, which is probably why Dot changed the name to Ireland by the Sea.

"Mooncussers were land priates who used trickery to lure unwary captains onto the treacherous Barnegat shoals, then picked clean the wreckage that washed ashore. On dark or foggy nights, they would hang a ship's lantern, like the one in Dotty's bay window, around the neck of a horse or mule and create the look of a vessel riding at anchor by walking the animal slowly back and forth on the beach. Ships on an Atlantic crossing, bound for New York to the north or the Delaware harbor to the south, would try to hug this shore, but the captain who let himself be guided by the Wrecker's Light would find himself aground and breaking up in the vicious surf before he knew it. A few such incidents were all it took to start the legends..."

"The Mooncusser is Billy Joel's River of Dreams, set to literature."
—**Gregor Barnum**

Other books by H.P. Dunne

Fiction

Daughter of Darkness
The Dead of Autumn
The Mind Mending Machine

Non-Fiction

To Love and Work
One Question That Can Save Your Marriage
(La Question Qui Sauvera Mon Mariage)

*Dedicated to the spirit
Of Mary Galvin Waggaman,
Woman of gentle humor and quiet will.
And to her children and grandchildren.*

Copyright © 1994 by H.P. Dunne

Write Way Publishing
3806 S. Fraser
Aurora, Colorado 80014

First Edition; 1995

All rights reserved. No part of this book may be reproduced in any form, except by a newspaper or magazine reviewer who wishes to quote brief passages in connection with a review.

Queries regarding rights and permissions should be addressed to Write Way Publishing, 3806 S. Fraser, Aurora, CO 80014

ISBN: 1-885173-03-2

1 2 3 4 5 6 7 8 9 10

Book I
C's Knot

Book II
McSea

Book III
Appearing Now for the First Time in America

Book I
C's Knot

Chapter One

C is my name. With no period. "C as in ocean," I liked to tell attractive women, back when I was young and handsome, and thought these were traits to be cocky about. "C as in vision," I used to say, and in hindsight, the irony of that quip is enough to bring a tear or two. Would a man of vision have let the down-sizers blind-side him the way I did? I don't think so.

The day my boss told me the company had decided to give me a package, I simply emptied my desk, like the good soldier I'd always been, and closed the door on a career of nearly twenty-seven years. It was too early to go home, so that same day I rented a partitioned cubby at a place I'd heard about where I would have access to the kinds of office equipment and clerical back-up needed to launch my re-employment campaign. Within two days I had turned myself into a one-man, one-client employment agency, and during my first three months I mailed out thirteen hundred and eighty-two resumes, each with a personalized cover letter. For that effort I got back sixteen polite form letters that said, in so many words, "thanks for your interest in the so-and-so corporation, but please get lost"; what happened to the other thirteen hundred and sixty-six became the raw material of nightmares, although that is of no consequence now.

Here in my rented cubby I am provided a desk, a chair and a phone; the notebook computer, with Windows and a nifty solitaire game, is my own. Somewhere in another office, or maybe in another part of the city, a lady named Jill, whom I've never met, answers my calls by saying, "Mr. Shackleton's office. No, I'm sorry, he's in an important meeting." Meanwhile, back at my company, voice mail hints that I'm on special assignment and gives out my new phone number.

I am too full of bitter despair and self-loathing these days to work at finding a job, so instead, when I tire of solitaire, I treat myself to movies in my head, street-gang showdowns or my first sweet moments of passion among the dunes on the Jersey shore. In this way I've enjoyed a few bloody but victorious rematches with the guy who broke my nose and handed me my only Golden Gloves defeat, way back in the olden days of the early sixties. And a half dozen times now, as I've drifted along inside my mind—this is hard to admit because it sounds so nuts—I have found myself at the bow rail of an ocean-going schooner, the kind of vessel you see these days only when the tall ships come around. The salt spray that explodes up past the bowsprit is so real to me sometimes, my eyes almost feel its salty sting. And the air is actually frigid on my face. Several times over the last few weeks I have caught myself shivering and squinting and blinking, and then smiling at the wall of my cubby the way I imagine people in mental hospitals smile. I am sailing west, judging from where the morning sun glares through the winter clouds, but my journey seems to be without destination, which is fine with me since in my craziest moments I suspect death by treachery awaits my arrival.

I try hard not to think about where I've come to and how little the future holds, but beyond my day dreaming I can think of little else. If this is where striving and dedication lead, I ask myself, why should I bother? And that kind of shameless self-pity invariably starts me ruminating about injustice and higher purposes and other useless stuff.

According to one of the world's most conspicuously successful and supposedly best-run corporate entities, I am no longer of use. Indeed, I am worse than useless. Why else would they be paying me so handsomely to go away? My mistake, I've recently concluded, is that I chose to labor on the wrong end of the elephant. It was my calling, or so it seemed in the early days, to be the one who came along behind with a large shovel and broom, making things tidy. And it was easy. And fun. Although I see now that I should have been out front giving the beast his voice, since the ones who rule are those who presume to speak for these inanimate entities that dominate us. Next time around, I've promised myself, I'll be the guy who says things like, "It's what the company expects from you," or "you owe it to the department." That sort of thing.

All our lives, it seems, we are kept in line by the supposed desires and demands of one monolithic entity or another. You owe it to your FAMILY, to the CHURCH, to your TEAM, the SCHOOL, the FRATERNITY, the COMPANY, the COUNTRY. And, purple hype aside, the sword of exclusion hangs over our heads to keep us loyal.

The last thing my boss said to me, right after he told me that "the company decided yesterday to give you a package," was that I would one day realize "on this day the company did you the biggest favor of your life."

The company decided? Give me a fucking break!

The company did me the biggest favor of my life? Who are we kidding here?

The company is a bunch of legal and financial documents, real-estate holdings, inventories, production machinery, data-processing equipment and office furniture. It can't decide a thing. The ones who decide are a bunch of suits, white guys, mostly, with a smattering of color and an equal smattering of women. It's the old drama of the INs versus the OUTs, the same that ruled the elementary school playground and the halls of high school. As always, the INs set up the rules in order to make themselves more IN, and always at the expense of the OUTs.

We had been friends for twenty two years, my boss and I, our careers linked like mountain climbers. The last thing I said to him was, "How 'bout them Mets, Marvin?" (At the time the Mets were struggling to stay out of last place.) Which reminds me that in truth, the last, last thing my boss Marvin said to me was this: "Shit! Season's in the crapper anyhow. Oh, well. There's always next year."

Lunch is now my one meaningful activity, and I devote myself to it with the zeal of a corrupt politician in danger of being voted out of office. I rotate my way through a shrinking list of potential eating companions, which includes a few key journalists whose favor I used to curry as part of my work. And once a month, on the second Friday, I get together at noon with my three closest friends.

Republicans separated by a few hundred thousand in monthly income, we four have always presumed homogeneity, but, truth be told, we are alike now only in superficial ways. Except for Jason Sargent, a kind and sensitive brain surgeon from Columbia Presbyterian, we are too self-absorbed to notice the changes life has put us all through, which is one reason we assume that we still have much in common. Any one of these men could have been enduring the same hell I was and I would not have known.

On September's second Friday, I went early to our usual place and by the time Brian Cox arrived, a second Bloody Mary was before me, looking, I hoped, like my first. As always, Cox milked his journey through the bar for all the attention he could get. His famous voice boomed across the room as he called hello, by name, to someone at a small, dark table in the corner.

The couple there cringed behind their menus.

"McWilly!" he shouted, pounding my back as he sidled in beside me. "What a pain in the ass this celeb horseshit is," he added, in a hoarse whisper, as he gave the drinkers up and down the bar his hundred-watt smile. Then, leaning close, he said: "Guy in the corner's a VP at the Peacock. That's the president's secretary he's with." Cox's laugh exploded through the room. "I fucked her last week," he said, loud enough to be heard by the first dozen drinkers on either side of us at the bar.

Brian is a television star who gives away cars and cash and dream houses and washer-dryer sets and refrigerators and TVs and trips to Hawaii. He has for a dozen years now been the MC of an insipid game show that comes on each weekday morning at ten, having been taped the previous afternoon. For some reason he thinks it makes him special.

Jason Sargent arrived next, and once again Cox's voice rang out above the din as he called Jason's name.

"Gotten into any good head lately, Doctor?" Cox asked. Because he knows how this line grates on Jason, Cox uses it every time they meet.

These two are as different as men can be. Jason is substance, Brian nothing but style. Jason is precise, alert and curious, hesitant until he's absolutely certain. Cox is impetuous, self-absorbed and brimming with empty bluster. On the golf course, Jason Sargent lines up each putt, regardless how short, reading the flow of the green from every angle while we three, and several holes of golfers behind us, wait; Cox bangs balls off trees and rocks until one of his shots happens to roll into the cup. Amazingly, they have the same handicap, slightly lower than Bill Kern's and about ten strokes higher than mine.

Jason Sargent has the lean body of a devoted runner, and I suspected this monthly ritual was the only lunch he allowed himself; it was, I knew, the only time he missed his session on the indoor track at the New York Athletic Club. Sincerity, self-discipline, intellect and a stunted sense of humor were the man's outstanding qualities. Sargent's dark curly hair was thinning in front and worn close. He dressed conservatively, today's ensemble being a light-brown suit with a burgundy tie that had tiny light-blue amoebae crawling all over it.

In contrast, there was a casualness and an approachable, ex-athlete's softness about Cox, who wore Levis today, neatly pressed, penny loafers, a silk shirt the color of rose wine and a gray-blue houndstooth jacket.

Sargent gave Brian his humorless, thin-lipped smile as, without a word, he turned to me.

"Have you been in hiding, C William?" he asked. "It feels like weeks. I call, but you're always in a meeting."

no inflection. "And this," I added, holding up my Bloody Mary, "is the first drink I've had in two months. Well, no. The second." (There was no point lying unnecessarily when it was so often necessary.)

"And your work goes well?" Jason asked.

"Dr. Spin," said Cox, his tone walking right to the edge of nastiness. "Fucker could put a positive spin on Hitler's Grand Solution."

Brian has been jealous of me since high school, and his steadily increasing wealth and fame have never seemed to tip the scales even a fraction. NBC pays him an obscene weekly salary for use of his wavy black hair, his gleaming teeth, his booming voice and his knack for making his handsome face appear astonished, perplexed, wowed, chagrined, dubious or delighted, on cue. I think he'd trade lives with me in a second, but I can't begin to understand why.

If I let myself think about it, which I rarely do, it amazes me the way a relatively recent electronic invention has turned this quite ordinary man into royalty. His are the empty talents of a carny huckster, although I have to admit he's gotten better-looking each year, with his steel-girder jaw and his professional quaff and dye job, his twinkling blue contact lenses, sparkling capped teeth and smooth, well-tanned, twice-lifted skin. No one remembers that Brian Cox once ran the hundred in 9.8 seconds, in football equipment, and had aspirations of diving for sunken treasure in all the world's oceans. I'd be surprised if *he* remembered.

Cox ordered a wine spritzer, Sargent a Polish Spring on the rocks with a wedge of lime, and while we waited for Bill Kern, my two friends and I spoke about the Mets, who were a disgrace, and the Giants, for whom there was great hope. Then we turned to the stock market, where, unlike me, they both had considerable sums invested.

"It's neither bull nor bear," said Cox. "It's a squirrel market, insane ups and downs, with everyone protecting his nuts."

Cox had a habit of passing off stolen lines as his own, probably as a consequence of relating to the world through a TelePrompTer; I thought I remembered Bill Kern saying the same about the market two or three weekends back when we were all out on the golf course, but I didn't say anything. In fact, for the sake of friendship, I responded with a laugh.

Bill Kern arrived twenty minutes late, as usual, his suit coat over his arm, a hard shell briefcase in hand. In the case, I knew, was a cellular phone and a "notebook" computer with built-in fax, along with the paperwork on at least three multi-million-dollar deals, a skyscraper to be bought or sold, a corporate buy-out to be leveraged. I could feel Kern's energy before I heard his voice, although that may have been my imagination, which did seem to be getting a bit out of hand.

I admired Bill Kern, and several times I have wished I was more like him. Actually, there's more to say on this subject, but it'll have to wait; for now I'll simply admit that over the last twenty years there have been several occasions when I have saved myself from being manipulated or controlled, cheated or even shanghaied into marriage, by the simple tactic of envisioning Kern's face and pretending to be him. He is a tall man, probably six five, but he's uncoordinated and fleshy, not over-powering as a physical presence; his power has more to do with his take-no-prisoners personality. He would probably rather rebuild a car's engine or hack around on his computer than play a round of golf or a set of tennis or paddle tennis, yet he serves as my partner in all these games nearly every weekend of the year. He is stern and driven, traits that show in his hard gray eyes that glare out from beneath heavy, dark brows ("hungry eyes" each of my wives has said). In Bill's world there are only winners and losers, and in every encounter, no matter how polite or friendly, someone comes out on top and someone pays. He likes to tell people that "if you can't make a buck from it or fuck it, it ain't worth your time," and as far as I can tell he has lived by that credo every day of his life. Kern has combined a law degree from Columbia, an MBA from Wharton and his own predatorial instincts to build and manage an empire worth over twenty-five million dollars. And that, he insists, is just a start. He is every bit as bright, and every bit as serious, as Jason Sargent, although, unlike Jason, Kern possesses a sense of humor. He has a quick soaring laugh that responds to cynicism, irony, clever mockery or barbed wit, even that which is aimed at him.

"Send over a double martini, Bombay, extra dry," Kern told the bartender. "I assume this is on you, McWilly."

I had suspected my turn to buy had rotated around again, and while it didn't matter, not yet, each time I faced an expense of any consequence, the projectionist who was now living in my head flashed me a picture of winged currency flying from my wallet.

It was a typical monthly lunch, with the usual empty banter about sports and women and money, until, midway through our meal, in what seemed an off-hand manner but probably was not, Bill Kern suggested that we four ought to "get into a little something on the side."

"Or a little someone," offered Cox, as I tried to ignore the tightening of my guts.

For years now, a source of irritation and disappointment to me has been that Bill Kern has never thought to invite me into one of his schemes, or bothered to carve a place for me in one of his companies. Now here he was, tossing out this suggestion the way he would propose a round of golf.

"A nice little cash cow," Kern added. "Something we could start for, say, a quarter million each? If nothing else, a tax write-off. And a romp."

"My accountant says that's exactly what I need," Jason Sargent told us, conspiratorially. Money matters, to Jason—and probably to most other MDs—were profoundly private. "The last time we spoke he said 'Bring me K1s'. So if you have a project, Bill, don't be shy."

"See that?" said Kern. "Jason's a man who knows his mind and stands ready to back it with his check book. How about you two?" He turned his predator's gaze on me, then on Cox.

"I'm always on the make," Cox said.

"I could go for a little action," I said, but I didn't sound all that convincing, at least to my ears.

"On your wife's checkbook or your own?" asked Cox.

I laughed, and hoped that only I could hear the emptiness in it. "Glady's, of course. Where's a working grunt like me going to come up with two hundred and fifty thousand dollars?"

Especially a working grunt who was no longer working.

"Glady could forget to record a check for that amount and nothing would bounce," said Kern.

"Must be nice," grumbled Cox. "The rest of us had to work for our money, but not McWilly. It took him three shots to get it right, but he finally married the golden goose."

"It is nice," I said, and now I hoped there was nothing in my tone to hint that Glady and I were in trouble. (My life had turned into a war of secrets, with battles fought on many fronts, and the older I became the harder it was to remember what I could and couldn't show in which camp. Once, two years ago, a young woman I was ending an affair with asked what I'd change if I could rewrite my life, and without missing a beat I told her I'd go back before my first lie, then I'd make sure to always tell the truth, regardless of the consequences. She sighed wistfully and asked me why, and so I told her that it was just too cumbersome and complicated to live with a bunch of lies, and of course that made her want me more, which was at least half the intent of my little speech, glib conniving shit that I am.)

"The trouble with someone who's always been rich," I added, "is that get-rich-quick schemes mean absolutely nothing."

"That's *half* the problem," said Cox. "The other half is age." He paused and sadly shook his head. "Even if you scored big tomorrow, McWilly, it wouldn't be quick in anyone's book."

"I'm the same age as you, Cox," I snapped. "In fact, if I'm not mistaken, you're already fifty, while I have almost a month."

"We're talking success here, McWilly. Quality of life. Not accumulated time."

Kern bestowed approval on Cox with one of his soaring laughs. And without letting my expression change, I did a quick study of Cox's eyes, trying to read how much my oldest friend had figured out. Cox's blue eyes sparkled without a hint of intelligent life, and with a relief that almost made me sigh I realized his crack was simply another manly put-down. In this group, the one whose turn it was to buy lunch usually became the focus of a number of barbed remarks; this was simply business-as-usual. Still, the truth of my situation, known outside me or not, burned inside me. And right about here is when I realized how deeply I resented my three best friends.

It came as a shock, and a month later, when suicide began to seem my only reasonable option, I would look back on that moment in the restaurant as one of the events that had pushed me over the edge. I didn't need a shrink to tell me I resented my friends for being everything I was at my worst and everything I pretended to be but was not. Guilty as charged. But beyond all that, my friends grated on me simply because they were so smugly content with their success.

And they all wore beepers. Pagers. Whatever.

Sitting at a table with this trio was like having lunch on a Star Wars set. Every ten minutes or so someone would start to beep like R2D2, and my friends would point at one another as if to say "is that you or me?" Then they'd bend down to check the tiny windows on the black boxes attached to their belts, squinting, because the old eyes weren't what they once were even if the old ego was. Then the guy being beeped would press some buttons and either leave to find a phone— or pull one from his briefcase or inside pocket—or with a dismissing shrug, tune back to our conversation. And of course after having observed this, I became enraged each time I tried to reach one of my friends and wasn't immediately called back.

How random and senseless life was, I thought, and it came as another startling insight. There was no good reason for these three to be the most important people in my life, and yet that is what they were. Chance had seen to it. But if all was random, was there any point? Of course not. No point at all.

So far I'd had three wives and three best friends, and from what I knew after nearly fifty years, all six might as well have been chosen the way we used to pick teams in gym class. "All right, Kiddies! Those who said forty-three million, eight hundred thirty-two thousand, nine hundred and fifty-four, step over there with McWilly."

The ten minute walk back to my cubby took more than two hours because I was so disoriented by the awareness that I hated my best friends and that life was nothing more than a collection of random accidents, starting with the big bang and including the first twitch of an RNA molecule inside a bubble of sea foam. I wandered Central Park, then angled south on a course that eventually brought me to the building on 52nd where I had worked for nearly twenty-seven years. I was past the place before I recognized the tattooed fat man at the newsstand near the corner, then I went back and stood for a few minutes in the busy, echoing lobby, watching the trim young secretaries come and go. For a while I considered dropping in on my old friends who had so far managed to survive the middle-management purge, until I remembered that the small print in the package I'd been given required that I not call or visit for two full years.

What a mess I was, I thought as I walked away. I resented my best friends and everyone else was invisible.

Or was I the invisible one?

The handful of people I've loved—excluding my son and his mother—had long since left my life, and Glady and Ryan were out on the runway now, talking to the tower. I was in free fall and yet, rather than save myself, it was more important to act as if nothing had changed, as if the world and I were on course, as if I still had a purpose.

In the weeks that followed that September lunch, as I endured the endlessly cheerful days of Indian summer, my mind kept reaching into my past as if I thought I might find an answer there to my present situation. My life felt cursed, and so it seemed reasonable that I should be able to locate the decision or the accidental wrong turn or criminal deed that had caused it to go wrong.

From the way I started out, most would have predicted that I'd either be one of life's big winners or dead of unnatural causes before forty. So how could I have ended up such a useless nonentity?

The fault, I have come to suspect, was all my mother's. Who could say what I'd have been had she not moved us out to Bryn Mawr from South Philadelphia when I was sixteen? By now I might be running the Front Street docks or the Philadelphia cops or the Irish Mafia, all of which came to pretty much the same thing. I might have won Olympic gold or become the Great White Hope. I might have turned out to be someone with schemes instead of dreams, a man who eats people for breakfast for the pure fun of it, and in the process makes millions, someone like Bill Kern, instead of this defunct man whose name isn't even a real name:

C, with no period.

Chapter Two

I went to Atlanta to avoid October's lunch with Kern, Cox and Sargent, and while I was there I mourned the fiftieth anniversary of my birth. I had no business in Atlanta, no work to do there, or anywhere else on Earth for that matter, but I stayed for two days and three nights, as planned. I walked the streets, hoping for rain. I wrote endlessly on the unprinted sides of hotel stationery from the desk drawer and masturbated like a sixteen year old to the X-rated flicks they were happy to put on my bill. Then I flew home, but some vital part of me stayed behind.

For twenty-six years, eleven months, one week and three days, I'd worked for the same Fortune 100 corporation, achieving in that time the rank of Manager of Public Information and Senior Assistant to the Assistant Vice President of Domestic Operations. Any creative or literary talents I may have once possessed were squandered, along with most of my intelligence and will, on what I now think of as the opinion control business, at which I was competent enough to have earned the nick names PR McWilly and Dr. Spin.

And as they say, "That and a dime ..."

With me at the helm of the Public Relations Department, my staff and I hunted for or invented facts and deeds and rumors that made our company appear generous, noble, well-managed, successful, patriotic and pure-of-heart. We called this the "Proactive side," and complained bitterly that there were too few hours in the day to pursue it. In truth, we spent the majority of our time and our creativity attempting to conceal, devalue, diminish or put the most positive spin possible on facts and events that made the company seem greedy or evil or indifferent to the public good. So here's the bottom line: for more than a decade, when a CEO or COO or CFO from my firm had to speak out on a sensitive matter, nine chances out of ten it was my words that rolled so glibly off the SOB's tongue.

I was a model employee. Had I been an imprisoned criminal who behaved as well, I'd have been paroled long ago. I arrived early, stayed late and never took my allotment of vacation days. I held my tongue when it was wise and the rest of the time said what was expected. I was steadfast and loyal, and still they set my feet upon this "bridge to early retirement," and banned me from company headquarters as if I might transmit a deadly virus.

Thanks to this bridge on which I now stand, I look the same as always to my friends and to my wife, and for some reason this has become more important to me than anything else in life, although I haven't dared ask why. My alarm rings at the same time as it always has, and I shave, shower and dress as though nothing has changed, rotating my way through the same seven dark suits, white shirts and understated ties. The good people of Metro North deliver me to New York each morning, and each evening they ship me home to Connecticut in the bar car with one, two or sometimes all three of my best friends. Nobody knows that I spend the time between train rides in a seven-by-seven cubby on Manhattan's upper east side, which I rent for $250 a week, just so I can keep on, as the lyrical saying tells us, keeping on. My monthly pay check is the same as always, but even if it changed, which it will in another nine months, my wife won't notice because she has never been particularly concerned with my earnings. (In contrast to the income Glady receives each quarter from her trust, my $6,416.43 monthly take home amounts to little more than lunch money.) Nobody has caught on yet, and while sustaining the illusion has been my single-minded goal, the accomplishment is, perhaps like most, a mixed blessing. The secret, while good for my pride, has become further evidence of my invisibility, and over these months my vanishing has become a source of pain nearly as intense as what the company did to me.

Suicide, until now no more real to me than to anyone else of intelligence and sensitivity, began to be, first, an abstract possibility, then, rapidly—before my plane's wheels touched down at Kennedy after my Atlanta trip—a tangible goal and a source of considerable comfort. Contrary to common sense, my wish to be dead was not a response to feelings of shame or depression or hopelessness or despair; I had survived these for years. And there was no demeaning, demanding voice urging my destruction, as others have reported. The idea of suicide simply hatched in me like an egg whose time had come, and once it was there, my death seemed to have been with me all along, its components kept safely separated until now in different compartments of my brain.

Death became a profoundly comforting and pleasing secret that put a smile on my face and a new briskness in my step. It was a choice now, no longer an inevitable, dreaded destination. This escape hatch, which only I knew about, would deliver me, if anywhere, to a place where the humiliation of having failed at all aspects of life could no longer jab at me, and where I would not have to feel the unrecoverable distance between myself and everyone around me, especially those I loved most. If the blissbabblers turned out to be right, that after death you got another crack at life, well that was okay by me. It wouldn't take much to improve on this go-round. And if the Catholics had it right, if hell, purgatory and heaven were real, well that was just fine with me as well. Same with the notion that I'd be nothing more than worm food. It was the control that mattered, not the destination, and the comfort of having a plan and a tangible goal gave me back the insouciant smile that used to drive people nuts when I was young and brash and handsome, and not yet so entirely civilized.

The other thing I noticed about suicide was that once its components came together, my being dead—although not my actual death, and that seems an important distinction—came to seem more like the good all-embracing mother no one ever had or ever had enough of. It was not, I should add, a thought, or even an idea, but a vision; I saw myself smiling contentedly as I dangled by my neck from the noose end of a rope, the other end of which was attached to a rafter in the attic of the over-sized, over-dressed colonial where I have never been at home and where I am reminded almost daily that it is my wife's inheritance—as happened to my poor father before me—and not my labors, which has kept the sumptuous roof over our heads and the

Mercedes in our garage. (The place is large enough to house four or five times as many people as it does, yet no longer big enough for the three of us who try to live there, and that was yet another good reason to punch my own ticket.) Suicide was a vision, I realized after I had lived with it a few weeks, seen from the point of view of whomever had the misfortune of coming up those attic steps; I hoped it would be Glady—that idea brought a sadistic smile—but the possibility it might be Ryan sobered me and became, for a time, the only thing that kept me alive.

When my friends and I gathered for our November lunch, the vision of my death had already been a comforting presence for weeks. Jason Sargent noticed my enigmatic smile, and told me that whatever I was doing, not only must I keep it up but I should also bottle and market it. At the very least I should share it with my friends.

"Jason, Jason," I said, in a tone that held no hostility whatsoever, "is it because you deal in illness and death every day that you presume to know so much about life?"

"I beg your pardon?" Jason asked, stunned.

We were standing together at the bar, waiting for Cox and Kern. I had no idea what to say now, since I was as shocked as my friend by what had just come from my mouth. It was as if my tongue had become linked directly to my mind, all filters put out of commission by the vision of my death. My tone had been so loving and tender that it should have alarmed Jason even more than my question; indeed, it would have alarmed him had he been a woman.

Fortunately, before I could say anything more, Brian Cox made his grand entrance. He called my name from across the room, making every head in the place turn his way. He stepped to the bar beside me, leaned past me and asked Jason if he had gotten into any good head lately.

"No," said Jason, "but C William here was about to explain what dealing with illness and death has done to my character."

Jason Sargent, brain surgeon and the world's nicest and most boring man, is the only person alive who calls me "C William." He does it to be kind, but sometimes I don't realize he's talking to me. My other friends, Bill Kern and Brian Cox, call me McWilly, and, hearing them, several others at Chamberlain Country Club have taken to doing the same, without the faintest idea why. My second wife Gail called me "Shacks" and my third and current wife calls me "Daddy." ("Daddy," she'll say, "don't you think a six-year-old boy is too young for a sleep over?" The reason for this, incidentally, couldn't be more clear. My role as Ryan's father is, to Glady, my only reason for being, and apparently it is no longer a reason she finds all that compelling.) All my life people have tried to add a period to my C, or to turn me into a "Bill," or even a "William," (although any fool can see my nature is too raw and my self-discipline too casual for that). For some reason though, out of either perverse self-pity or wicked parental mockery, I have identified myself with that solitary consonant. "Hello," I'll say, "I'm C Shackleton." Then I'll stand back and watch the fun. Nicknames are common.

My parents, self-conscious as newly arrived immigrants, were so cowed by this land to which their parents had delivered them, my father as a teen, my mother as a child of seven, that they named me "C William Shackleton" after someone in authority at Philadelphia's Albert Einstein Hospital. They no doubt thought such a dignified-looking name might help their first born succeed in this land of opportunity, and for as long as they lived, I doubt they ever figured out that the man who chose this affectation for the frosted glass of his office door probably had a Cecil or a Caleb or a Cuthburt to back up his C, while mine has stood alone for fifty years, unsupported by hard currency of any sort. (Years ago, my college girl friend, Carol Zeller, for a time in contention to become wife number one, worked for months to make up a sentence using only spelling variations on my first name. The best she could ever do was "Si, Cee-Cee, sea, see?" but she was never able to make one work without a question mark and it might have driven her madder than she already was had I not dumped her in the nick of time. Carol Zeller also began to call me Gregor during the summer between our junior and senior years at Penn State, for reasons she promised one day to explain but never did.) A New Jersey court changed my name to C *Shackleton* McWilly a year or so after college, as part of the bargain that resulted in my first marriage and the birth of my daughter—lost to me twenty six years ago now. Few know about this chapter of my life, and only Brian Cox and Bill Kern remember why I became *McWilly*. Anyhow, the story of my name is the story of my life, which I will return to in due time, but for now, there is Oinkers Unanimous to tell about.

"It isn't just you, Jason," I explained. "We all have blinders on. It's the only way we survive the uncertainty and the meaninglessness."

"Uncertainty and meaninglessness," mocked Cox. "My, my, my."

Bill Kern arrived then and we went to our table, my comments at the bar seemingly forgotten. After our ritualized discussion of sporting events and the stock market, we talked at length about the beautiful young woman one of our newly single friends from Chamberlain Country Club had started to date. She was shapely, with a taste for clingy, lacy, low-cut clothing, which prompted Kern to suggest she was probably spectacular in the sack. Jason admitted he had "not been unmoved" by a recent sighting. Cox said she had given him signals, then he wondered if our acquaintance knew what to do with such a woman. We weren't gossiping; we were being appreciatively lustful, talking dirty, bonding, until I broke the sacred manly pact.

"None of you knows anything about anything that really matters," I heard myself say, and I was as surprised as anyone at the table. My voice was gentle, tender, and my eyes went from one set of eyes to the next, noticing how guarded, and below that, how terrified, my three friends were.

"You know all about power and victory and objects and money, but none of you can really see," I told them. And then, because for the first time it was true, I added, "but I love you three with all my heart."

Kern coughed. "Coming out of the closet, are you?" he said, and drained his martini, including the olive.

Jason Sargent studied me with what seemed like professional interest while Brian Cox looked around for a waiter, rattling his wine spritzer glass.

"We're best friends, right?" I asked, but this question was met with blank looks, each set of eyes, each tightly clenched jaw and awkward smile demanding to know in advance why I was asking such a question. They couldn't even grunt, because that would have been too much ground to give. They had gone into fight-flight mode, and I knew there were three tight scrotums with me at this table; the thought made me chuckle, which probably only irritated my friends that much more. In the past their withering stares would have been enough to make me back off with a wise-crack. But I didn't retreat this time, because when you are as close to death as I was, for whatever reason, you just don't have time to jack around with this macho horseshit. "Beyond family, we're next, right?" I asked, and met each gaze in turn, with a loving, but penetrating, challenge of my own.

"I suppose you could say that," Cox agreed, cautiously.

"Except for Jason, who works strange hours, we see each other almost every day," I prompted. "We ride the train home together most nights. Weekends we play golf or tennis. We go to each other's parties and family celebrations. We meet once a month for lunch. We've been together for years now. Right?"

They said nothing, waiting for the line which they could destroy.

"RIGHT!?"

"Okay, okay," said Kern. "So?"

"And in all that time we've not said one meaningful thing to each other."

"So what's your point?" asked Cox.

"When Kern's daughter was having all that trouble and they were taking her from shrink to shrink and she finally ended up at Hickory Hill, did we ever talk about it? Did we ever let Kern tell us how it felt and what it meant to him? No. We avoided anything like that because we didn't want to know how frightening it must have been to be up against something you couldn't understand or fix. Other than listen to the sketchy headlines, we made sure Kern never had to show us how it felt."

"I told you all I needed you to know," grumbled Kern, although his eyes were a little softer, and his face, usually composed, sometimes hard, had relaxed. It may have been my imagination, but I thought his mouth got a little shaky.

"And when Jason's father died, we all knew how much that rattled him, but did we let on? Did we let him talk about it? No. We distracted him with jokes and intense discussions about sports and the women we'd go after if we had the balls or if we didn't worry it would screw up our marriages or give us crabs or some deadly disease."

"I have a shrink for those kinds of issues," said Jason.

"You have a shrink?" Cox said, feigning shock. "I didn't know that. Why? Are you some sort of fruitcake?"

This was a standard ploy. Pounce on one small admission or

misspoken word or fact out of alignment and send the focus somewhere safe. Thanks to Cox, the whole point I was making was about to be lost.

"Don't you?" I asked Cox, which shut him up.

"Why wallow in shit," asked Kern, "when there's more important things?"

"Important things like what?" I asked, but there was no edge, no challenge in my voice, no tone that implied I thought he had the IQ of a turnip. How changed I was, and all because I'd befriended my death. Clearly they didn't know what to do with me any more than I did.

"Like her," Kern said, nodding to a shapely black-haired woman in an elegant black sheath dress who was walking alone across the far end of the restaurant, heading, purse in hand, for the ladies room.

"Must be her period," said Cox.

"Wouldn't stop me," Kern shot back.

Jason Sargent didn't look at the woman, but the rest of us watched until her shapely backside disappeared through a swinging door that had an equally shapely body painted upon it in glittering kelly green.

"How many of you have actually had an affair?" I asked. The question was put casually, tenderly, although I'm sure there was a challenge in my eyes, and I could feel my smile working, telling them I was not only enjoying this but had someplace mischievous I wanted to take us. My three friends glanced at each other and shifted uncomfortably in their chairs.

"Do one-night stands count?" asked Cox.

"Yes," I said. "And blow jobs."

"And blow jobs!?" said Kern, in mock alarm. This gave us the laugh we needed, and I felt the whole table settle down.

"No, wait," I said. "Let's set some ground rules. Let's put one night stands, quick blow jobs, hand jobs, all that sort of thing, into a separate category. Let's not call it an affair unless your heart got into the act."

"So then there's dick affairs," said Kern. "And heart affairs. Is that it?"

"Right," I said. "Affairs and flings. Take that woman who just went into the ladies room."

"I'll take her," said Cox. "Anywhere, any time. Half time at the Meadowlands. Rush hour on the Cross Bronx. August on Coney—"

"—Of course," I said. "But I doubt you'd get her into bed unless she felt something for you, and it's not likely you could get to know her well enough for that to happen without coming to feel something for her. A woman like that."

"I'd feel anything she wanted me to feel," said Cox, glancing at Kern for approval.

"She knows she's special," I went on. "Everything about her makes that clear. The way she moves. Holds her head. So how do you deal with a woman who won't let you use her? How do you handle the emotional upheaval, the falling in love?"

"Women want a fling now and then just like guys," said Kern. "Even a woman like her. *Especially* a woman like her. Sometimes they get sick of being treated like royalty. Sometimes ladies just want to get laid."

"Sure," I said, even though Kern had just unknowingly touched upon a concept involving the needs and practices of good girls versus bad girls that had only recently stopped giving me trouble, probably because I'd been raised Irish and Catholic by a woman who saw her gender in these narrow terms. "But when you connect with a woman like that one, the kind every man dreams about, something happens inside you. It's got to. Come on. Which of you guys has put your heart where your mouth is?"

"Or your mouth where my dick was," said Kern.

"What about you?" challenged Cox. "What gives you the right to ask all the tough questions?"

"Because you three belong to me," I said, and instantly collected the challenging looks I knew I'd get. "Seriously. You wouldn't be friends if not for me. I connected with each of you, then brought us together. I created you, so I can do anything I want with you."

"Are you feeling okay, C William?" asked Jason. "Any dizziness, ringing in your ears, blackouts, strange smells?"

"Delusions of grandeur?" added Kern.

"Okay," I said. "I'll start. I chase women like her whenever I'm out of town or have to stay over here in town for some reason, but I always end up settling for the other kind, some bimbo with a tit size bigger than her IQ."

"Yum," said Cox.

"I've probably had a dozen one night stands, flings, but in at least half of those I was too drunk to remember what she looked like. I've fallen in love twice, not counting my three wives. Twice I've gone through the hell of being in love with one woman and married to another. The last one almost killed me. In fact, it may have killed me. The votes aren't in yet."

I glanced among my friends and noticed how serious and sober their eyes were, even if their faces remained hard and their mouths poised for mockery. Cox grunted and looked away.

"That's the worst," I continued. "You're on this emotional rollercoaster, with no way to get off that doesn't destroy you. Here you are, this guy who keeps his emotions in check—you wouldn't be where you are in the world if you were a wimp, right?—and yet you find yourself crying in the shower and walking through the world in the deepest gut-wrenching anguish you ever imagined. Just talking with the other woman is better than sex with your wife, and the sex is absafuckingtively out of this world. And after another episode of the best loving you ever had, better than it was the last time you stole some time to be with this new goddess, you're as elated and alive as you ever hoped to be. You want to make it permanent, give up everything, run off with her to hog heaven. But somewhere down deep you don't believe this woman can love you the way she seems to, at least not forever, or you don't believe that you'll go on loving her this powerfully once you both stop trying so hard to be everything the other one wants. You suspect that what you've found can't last, even though you chase it and cling to it as if you believe it will, as if your life depends on it. What you also know, if you face yourself, is that part of what makes this relationship exceptional is its impossibility, that what you really want, when the balance begins to tip too far in any direction, is to keep both women exactly where they are. You'll lie shamelessly to everyone in order to hold on, and you find that you're frighteningly good at deception. You keep your wife in the dark about the other woman and you keep the other woman thinking that the demise of your marriage is only weeks away. You begin to think you missed your calling, that you should have been a master criminal or a politician. You'll do this for as long as the two women allow you to, until you get caught and your marriage erupts or until the other woman gets tired of waiting and crosses some invisible line she sets in her head, a line that can never be recrossed."

"Or until your wife falls in love with the tennis pro," said Kern, an attempt to blow me out of the water with a single shot.

I smiled, amazed by my eloquence and openness and lack of temper or defensiveness. Again I noticed that the eyes of my friends were full of emotions which leaked out beneath looks that said they each thought I had snapped; it was clear that I was touching them, and equally clear that they were starting to hate me for it.

"Anyone here know what I'm talking about?" I asked, but then, suspecting I had pushed my luck, I raised my wine glass and said, "Gentlemen! We are pigs, every last one of us. Swine, to the man. And by the power invested in me as the creator of this quartet, I hereby declare that these monthly luncheon meetings be henceforth considered chapter meetings of a new twelve-step, self-help recovery group called 'Oinkers Anonymous'."

The others chuckled and smiled and touched their glasses to mine, relieved but still resentful.

Cox repeated the name. "Oinkers Anonymous. That's good. That's good. I like that. I like that."

Kern sighed, his chest noticeably rising and falling as he released the tension.

Jason Sargent stared into space.

"But there's already an OA for overeaters," Cox added. "I had a few of those blimps on my show last month."

"So we'll call them and tell them to change their name to Fatties Anonymous," said Kern, "or risk an injunction."

"How about Swine's Anonymous?" suggested Cox. "I've always wanted to be a founding father of something."

"Hello," said Sargent, tuning back in from where ever he'd been. "My name's Jason and I'm an adulterer."

"Hello Jason," I said, in the sing-song way they do at AA.

"I've never fallen in love," said Kern. "You know what I always say. If you can't fuck it or ..."

" ...or make a buck from it," the rest of us joined in, each one almost perfectly imitating Kern's haughty tone, "it just ain't worth your time."

I leaned close to Kern and made three quick pig snorts.

"But you've had one-night stands, right?" asked Jason. "Flings. Isn't that what we decided they were?"

"Does the pope shit in the woods?" offered Cox.

"Too many to count," admitted Kern.

"And you've never once felt love for these women?" I asked.

"At the time, I loved them with all my heart. All twelve inches of it."

"But you never longed to be with one of them again?" I asked. "No one's made you dream of having her with you forever?"

"Sure. In fact, wise-guy, there are a few I look up each time I get into their area. I have, let's see, four women, no, five, who I've seen more-or-less regularly for years now." He leaned forward. "There's this tall blonde in Baltimore, where I go every three months? She's older than I'm used to, maybe forty-five, but what a bod! And God, does she know what to do. Clamp on. Rotate. She's some kind of sexual gymnast."

Once again I snorted like a pig; this time Jason did too.

"I've been in love," said Cox. He looked at his new drink, half gone already, and for a moment it didn't seem as if he'd say anything more. "In fact, I'm going through exactly what you were just describing, McWilly," he added, glancing up at me. "It's like you were reading my mind."

"Cox is in love," teased Kern, his voice high and reedy.

"Why do you think I've lost so much weight? And the most perverse part of it is that when things are going well with Marcy, things get better at home with Lois. But when Marcy gets impatient and pulls away, I'm hell on Lois. Marcy thinks I've filed. Lois thinks the marriage is getting better."

Jason, Kern and I looked at each other, and at precisely the same moment issued a chorus of snorts.

"Guys! Guys!" said Kern. "Beaver shot at three o'clock."

We looked, Cox going first to seven o'clock, then we turned back to each other and all four of us began to oink and laugh so hard that heads turned throughout the restaurant. The woman at three o'clock crossed her legs and smiled. The tall woman came from the bathroom in time to hear our laughter, and to glance, quickly, in our direction. She wore a diamond necklace which caught the light as she moved serenely across the room.

"Do you think she earned those diamonds with what she has above the neck or below?" asked Kern.

"Earned them with her brains," said Cox, pointing toward his crotch.

And once again the four founding fathers of Swine's Anonymous snorted in unison.

Before lunch broke up it was suggested by Jason Sargent, and supported by Brian Cox, that for even more originality we change our name to "Oinkers Unanimous." I readily agreed, and Kern, ready to do battle out in the world again, didn't seem to care one way or the other.

"We are partners in thought crime," said Jason.

Cox didn't tape on Fridays so we spent the rest of the afternoon walking the city, looking at women and oinking.

"It's wonderful," he said, "the way you can just call in and tell them you won't be back. You've really arrived, haven't you, Killer?" (Killer was what he had called me back in high school, and he reverted to it now and then, but only when we were alone.)

"Sure have," I said.

In the bar car that evening, Bill Kern and Jason Sargent greeted us with three raucous pig snorts. All the way out to Connecticut we outdid each other's outrageous comments about every woman we saw, and collected any number of withering looks along the way.

There would be, we decided, an Oink point awarded to the Swine of the Day, and the one with the lowest accumulation of points at the end of each month would buy next month's lunch. Kern became, we unanimously decided by the time we were rolling into Chamberlain station, the recipient of the first Oink point for his story about a girl in Detroit whose former boyfriend had had himself converted into a woman. They had gotten back together and had become lovers again, this time as lesbians, and when she was with Kern she kept talking about how nice her old boyfriend's new snatch turned out and how she dreamed of getting all three of them into bed. So Kern, never one to turn down a carnal adventure, had gone to bed with this girl and her former boyfriend, with his nice new snatch, and the only thing he would say about the experience was that the guy wasn't half the man he used to be.

Those hours between the creation of OU at lunch until the train delivered us home that evening constituted the longest span in weeks that I had gone without envisioning myself hanging dead in the attic. But of course it was only a postponement.

Chapter Three

The first one at home to notice the changes in me brought on by the prospect of being dead was six-year-old Ryan, or at least my boy was the first to say anything about it. We were finishing yet another bedtime search for Waldo when Ryan gave up trying to locate that candy-cane-shirted geek and began to search instead in my eyes.

"What?" I asked him, self-conscious under the intense green-eyed inspection.

"Something's different," he said. There were more seconds of scrutiny before he added, "I think maybe you love me more."

I laughed, relieved. "And what makes you think so?"

"I don't know. You have softer eyes."

"I've got news for you, kiddo," I said, and squeezed him in a head-lock. "I couldn't love you more than ..."

I looked away because I felt my eyes fill as my mind clogged with the terrible vision of this innocent boy climbing the attic stairs to encounter his father swinging from the rafters.

"It's okay, Daddy," Ryan said. "Mom says that after a few weeks you won't remember you have a son and after a few months she'll find me another father."

"Is that what she says?"

I had suspected there was another man in the wings, and this pretty much confirmed it.

"Uh huh." He popped out of bed, leaving me stranded there, and rummaged in his closet until he found his Masters of the Universe sword and his pirate's eye patch.

"And do you believe her?"

"I don't know," he said, absently. "I mean, Mom never lies. But then, well ..." He poked the sword into the belly of an imaginary enemy. He lopped off a head. He stuck the point under my chin. "We'll see just how tough you are after we keel haul ya and make you walk the plank in shark-infested waters."

I knew that what Ryan had seen in my eyes was there, that my love for everyone, even Glady, had expanded in me to the point that it now spilled over almost all the time. But where Ryan was concerned, the love I felt was overwhelming, deeper and more profound than anything I'd ever known. It was also a love full of worry. Ryan was a male child. A white male child. And it seemed likely that for decades to come, white males were going to catch several generation's worth of shit; what happened to me, I thought as I sat in my cubical the next morning, was probably just the beginning. Ryan would come of age empty-handed, his sense of purpose even murkier than mine, his power and his entitlements as constricted as his father's emotions. Meanwhile, women and people of color would be soaring past him on the strength of their righteous liberation. I would have given all the life I had left, little as that was, for an instant of brilliance that might have illuminated for my boy a different way of being male in this world. But I was among the worst examples of what the old ways had produced, so there was nothing I could do, except to get out of Ryan's way. All my striving and wishing hadn't mattered one wit when it came to anything or anyone I'd ever cared about. And wasn't that precisely the problem? The circle of love and concern kept bringing me up short, and I understood now that my short fall, my defeat, my entire life, mocked the high-minded desires I felt on Ryan's behalf. Better, I told myself, to be gone, to be wiped clean like a spot of mold on shower tile, before my natural urge to corrupt all that I touched had more time to take over.

I thought these thoughts and doodled at my desk, drawing interlocking circles, monster faces, a ship, a treasure trunk.

All the men I knew—Kern, Cox, Jason Sargent, the rest of the guys at work, when I had work, and out at the country club—were either predators who ran on the heady fuel of power and control, or they were wimps enervated by their own emotions and full of this New

Age blissbabble about the savage within, the wild man and inner child. Few men dared face, beyond those brief, solitary glimpses at three-thirty-three in the morning—which they rarely mentioned to anyone—whatever it is that lurks inside them, below the layers of concrete. What, I wondered, could possibly be down there that was more frightening than it is to live all walled up like this? Was it a gut full of unspeakable urges, too primitive to be allowed out? Or was it the knowledge that there is no winning this fight, and yet nothing to do but keep on fighting, since fighting is what we were bred for? After all, what, exactly, is one to do when one runs out of woolly mammoths to kill or fuck?

But no. It wasn't a woolly mammoth who terrorized my depths. Whatever was down there felt more like the silent shrieking dread of the little boy who knows, KNOWS, there's something nasty under his bed, but he is now too big, too brave and proud, to call for his mommy. No wonder we men are so consumed by sports and sex, I thought, and smiled at some of the recent bar car snorting escapades of Oinkers Unanimous. Sport celebrates manly aggression, and television lets us participate without risking either our bodies or our civilization. And sex is the only thing left that carries the zap of conquest and real emotion.

Odd, I thought, but these two—sports and sex—were among the few places where Nature seemed to support man's nature. Everywhere else Mother Nature was aligned with women. Sports and sex. And of course, death. All else, I decided, was civilized suppression.

I found myself thinking these thoughts at the bow rail of my schooner, and this commingling of worlds made my mind go TILT. The air was charged with salt spray, rain and lightening, and the sea was rolling under and over me. There was a storm building. The sky was the same angry gray as the ocean, which rose up around me with a fury that treated the two-hundred-foot ship like a bath tub toy. Wind shredded the canvas behind me. Waves built and crested and the bow crashed into the troughs with a jarring thud that made the wood joints and ribs groan and the great masts shudder. And I stood at the bow thinking about man and nature and the treachery of civilization, and worrying almost to tears about the future in store for my six-year-old son.

And so another day was wasted.

By tradition and design, December was the one month my friends and I did not meet for lunch, and that was probably for the best, too, because had we gotten together I might have tried to express some of my thoughts about what makes most men such assholes. And had I, I no doubt would have been disappointed by the reactions of my fellow oinkers, or perhaps even drummed out of the club I'd fathered. Meanwhile, each evening in the bar car, we three behaved like perfect swine and snorted our way home to Connecticut, keeping score. And the odd thing about this is that we in no way stood out from the rest of the commuters.

It wasn't that I had any hope Oinkers Unanimous would actually change me or my friends; all four of us were so well-practiced in the arts of superficial manliness that to become open with one another now, or to in any other way change our snouts, was out of the question. Still, to have this safe humor under which to approach the dark side of my masculinity postponed my suicide for a time, although my attic vision remained powerfully with me, and sometimes in the sleepless mornings, the urge to leave my bed and hang myself was nearly irresistible.

My love for Ryan, and my emerging tenderness toward my fellow man, helped me escape, for the first time in my adult life, my annual bout with the pre-Christmas funk. Indeed, we were well into Christmas week before it even dawned on me that in years past I would have by now logged three or four weeks of nagging depression. I asked Glady to buy me a good strong rope for Christmas so I might do some tree work in the spring with the chainsaw she gave me two Christmases before, which I had yet to fire up. She put the rope in a suit box from Brooks Brothers left over from some other Christmas or birthday, and wrapped it in embossed, metallic gold paper that probably cost more than the rope. She put a huge red bow on it, with spit-curls. She also bought me a CD player for my Jeep and a first class airline ticket to Phoenix, along with a reservation for a solo week of golf at The Boulders, date to be determined. (It turned out that the other three wives had done the same for Kern, Sargent and Cox.) I gave Glady earrings with emeralds, which I had ordered in November from a flyer that came with my Diner's Club bill; I would pay $36.95 each month for the next three years, and of course the arrangement made me wonder what the fine print in my credit card contract had to say about debts left behind by those who hang themselves in their attic with a rope provided by the recipient of the merchandise in question. Would Glady, irrefutably responsible for said untimely demise, perhaps be held accountable for the unsettled debt? I could always hope.

On New Year's Eve and the following day there would be one party after another, beginning, as the ritual did each year, with a meal of ersatz French design at Bill and Sherri Kern's house, served by their daughters, including the younger one who wasn't quite right in the head, followed by dessert and champagne and midnight kisses all around at Jason and Bonnie Sargent's obsessively contemporary two-million-dollar experiment in modern living; the next day it would be brunch as usual at our place—catered, of course—and then for the rest of the day a marathon of college bowl games on Brian Cox's large screen television for the "boys" while the "girls" played bridge and gossiped out in princess Lois' airplane hanger of a kitchen.

Ryan would go to his grandparents' mansion down on the Sound in Greenwich on New Year's Eve morning, and return when Glady went to retrieve him sometime on the second day of the year, after hangovers and resolutions had been gotten over, all of which meant, I decided as I fingered the hairy texture of my new rope on Christmas morning, that the last day of the year would be a good day to die.

The day after Christmas I took my son bowling, and as we were leaving, Glady held me back and, whispering in my ear, suggested I might want to talk with Ryan about separation and divorce.

"Has it come to that?" I asked, surprised, but not really.

"I think so. In any case, it's better not to take him by surprise. He's heard it from me. Now he should hear it from his father, which is you."

"If we're splitting up, why all the wonderful presents?"

She shrugged. "It's all the same to me," she said, as if I'd been a fool to ask.

At the bowling alley, if you ask them and they aren't too busy, they'll put big plastic tubes in the gutters so it's impossible to miss the pins, even though one can need a new haircut in the time it takes a six-year-old's ball to tack all the way to the place where the pins are waiting. After bowling, it was on to McDonald's for Happy Meals.

Ryan's food came in a box decorated with games he was too young to play. There was also, almost as an afterthought, a burger which was mostly bun, a bag of fries—his favorite thing in "this whole live world"—and a miniature Frisbee, about the size of a compact disc, imprinted with such indifference to detail that it was impossible to see if Ronald McDonald wore a smile or a grimace. I had a Big Mac, large Fries and a Chocolate Shake; where I was headed, a few extra calories today weren't going to matter.

"Mom says you got one foot on a bar of soap and the other on a banana peel," Ryan commented, his mouth full of mushed fries.

I had been unable to begin the conversation, and now, innocent that he was, Ryan had shown the way.

"Mom says that?" I asked, casually.

"Yup." Ryan chewed, swallowed.

"What do you think she means?"

"She means, this month it's the guest room; soon it's out the door with you."

It caused explosions of brain cells each time I heard my wife's harsh words in my son's sweet voice. By speaking so unguardedly—"I'm simply telling the boy the truth,"—Glady was slowly poisoning Ryan's mind against his father, in the process making me dispensable, which was no doubt her intent. Glady, I'd learned over these years, could do more damage with honesty than most people could do with a flame-thrower. I took a deep breath, in preparation for plunging to the heart of the matter, something that has never come easily. How ironic, I thought. This time two years ago, as my second love affair was gaining critical mass, I struggled every hour with the urge to leave Glady and the equally powerful urge not to inflict loss on Ryan. Now, having given up on love for the sake of family, I found myself faced with a wife who had lost all interest in me and was trying, quite successfully it seemed, to make me vanish.

"So, Ryan," I began, sounding as casual as I could, "how do you think it'll be if I live somewhere else?"

"Won't be any different," Ryan said, absently. "I hardly see you now anyhow. And after a while you'll just forget me."

"Did Mom say that?" I blurted.

He shrugged and nodded. "It's no big deal," he added.

It was true we didn't spend much time together, but mostly that was because Glady kept Ryan hopping from soccer to swimming to karate to Cub Scouts to gymnastics to French lessons.

"And do you think it's true?"

Ryan chewed a mouthful of burger that was nearly too much for him. His small shoulders rose and fell. "How should I know what's true and what's not true? I'm only six years old."

"Well it's not true," I said, knowing that by fighting Glady's words I was putting our son in a terrible bind. Still, I had to give him an alternative to her poison.

After we were divorced, it would be only a matter of months until she and her lawyer found some reason to keep me from my son, and wasn't that just one more reason not to hang (ha!) around? If my life ever had a purpose, it had been served. I was now a throw-away man, dispensable in my marriage, dispensable in my work.

"Look," said Ryan. "It's raining harder. I thought you were going to start your diet."

"I was," I said, speaking around the straw through which I was drawing into myself several hundred calories of chocolate shake. "Maybe tomorrow."

"Sure," my boy responded, although I couldn't tell if the derision in his tone was intended; I've never trusted myself when it comes to Ryan's precociousness.

"I was skinny once," I told him.

"I know. Back when you were a boxer. Then you fell in love."

Ryan dunked a bouquet of long golden-brown French fries into the puddle of catsup I had made for him on the upturned plastic top of his soda. He pushed the fries into his mouth as if feeding tree branches to a chipper. The process left a smudge of red on his chin, and with the next fist full of fries he inadvertently wiped it away, then transferred it to his shirt.

"I guess I've told you about that time."

He nodded. "Several hundred times. But you can tell me again." He paused to swallow a wad of potatoes just about the size of his throat. "I like to hear about Uncle Brian and you when you were kids and the time you saved him from that motorcycle gang and the State Championship and how you went to college but couldn't eat because the animals stole your food."

It was odd to have Ryan summarize my adolescence this way, since for months now I had been looking for something in my boyhood to blame for what had become of me as a man. For most of my first sixteen years I was as tough as a shipyard welder. I could see a punch coming before the other guy knew he was going to throw it, and usually managed to lay him out before he'd cocked his fist. Then my mother—the butcher's heiress—moved us from South Philadelphia out to Bryn Mawr, and the Main Line set my feet on a much safer path through life, one that would turn me first into a handsome, glib, vacuous college frat boy, and then, in a mindless blink, into a company man for whom truth was a product to be manufactured and words were tools with which to paint pretty pictures. And the corporation, having availed itself of my vitality and any talents I may have possessed, handed me a package the year before I hit the big Five-Zero, and in so doing made me one of life's quiet losers.

Back when I was sixteen, in my first week at my new school, a Bryn Mawr coach watched me rough up a couple of tough varsity football players in the parking lot, and from that moment on, until I graduated, he dedicated his life to shaping me into what he kept calling "a-once-in-a-lifetime world class competitor." Who would not respond to such powerful, almost paternal attention? Meanwhile, to complete the metamorphosis, the Bryn Mawr girls let me know that if I ever wanted to touch another breast I had better lose my crude street ways. I fought them all at first, the girls and the coach, because I was homesick for South Philadelphia and the docks and the streets and girls who were mine because I was tough enough to keep them safe. I missed the thrill of turf protection and the sense that survival was an achievement. I missed more than anything the trust that develops among warriors who are lucky enough to know their enemies. I missed Tonya Angione, a piece-of-ass in the making who'd been my girl until she moved away to New Hampshire. I missed the way nights felt when dark settles on concrete and brick, all alive and dangerous. In my new world of big lawns and keg parties and labeled clothing and trips to Long Beach Island on the Jersey shore, everything was smooth and easy, and no one said or did anything to stir things up. Nobody got into anybody's face and viciousness and cunning, a nasty tongue and fast fists, were liabilities now, not assets. But I was, if nothing else, a quick study. And being a Mick full of blarney and charm, by the time I graduated from high school I had turned myself into a golden-tongued, Ivy League all-American boy capable of talking the Virgin Mary out of her panties. I was Vice President of my senior class (my friend Brian Cox was President), and the school's most beautiful girl belonged to me.

As I watched my son feed fries into his mouth, I saw, in rapid montage, a beautiful, soft, yielding long-limbed young woman spread naked before me on a blanket among rolling sand dunes, a sea-side inn on the Jersey shore that had once been called The Mooncusser, silver gulls circling on invisible strings and a Puerto Rican Justice of the Peace who lived just over the Delaware line and whose command of English was limited to the nuts and bolts of the marriage ceremony and the basics of U.S. currency. It seemed as if one day not that long ago I wasn't quite twenty years old, an athlete with the world spread before me and a girl who loved me. Then, somehow the years rolled away and all at once I was soft around the middle, twice divorced, out of work, a half-century old and planning to die. I had run out of hope that my life would reach a destination of any worth, and thanks to Glady, I would soon have nothing to live for at home, and no home to live in, for that matter. And while I was ashamed of myself for being so sentimental and self-pitying, I didn't seem able to pull myself out of this funk. All that golden potential, gone, gone, gone. (This, to Righteous Brothers tones.)

When I arrived in Bryn Mawr, Brian Cox, and a tall red-head named Erin Henry were the king and queen of the sophomore class, the blue ribbon best of the best. And I was a street mutt set loose among these Main Line pedigrees. Everyone was afraid of me, a reaction I exploited because of my own uncertainties. But Brian Cox, a football and track star with a state record already on the books, pretended not to be afraid, and after a few weeks he started to enjoy watching his sophisticated friends cut themselves on my sharp edges. His girl, even more of a blue blood than Brian, found my dangerousness exciting and seemed to like Brian better when he was with me. I carried a flask, sold joints and ran shell games and three-card monte under the bleachers during football games and in the men's room at dances. And several times I scared off Brian's enemies, usually without having to throw a punch, although that wasn't the case with the fat motorcycle hood he somehow antagonized while driving his T-Bird home from Philadelphia one night, with Erin in the bucket seat beside him.

Chased by a posse of would-be Hell's Angels, Brian drove straight to my house, pulled into the drive and leaned on his horn. Four greasers on noisy hogs were circling his locked car when I came out. Cox was pale with fear and Erin was red with fury. I had to hurt two of the hoods pretty badly before they decided to retreat, cursing and promising to come back. The story went around school the next week that Brian and I had wiped out a whole gang of Hell's Angels, and I said nothing to contradict that rumor, even though Brian Cox had never left the safety of his car.

A year later, as a junior, I was in the running for the State Wrestling Championship, which I lost to the reigning champ, but not by much. I took the city and the regional Golden Gloves titles with ease, but was in bed with pneumonia when the state tournament was held. After these achievements I was suddenly everyone's good buddy, the school's token street punk and its main claim to fame.

That summer Erin and I became lovers. It was a first for us both, or so we each claimed; I was lying, and so was she, if Brian Cox was to be believed. We were staying at an inn on Long Beach Island called Ireland by the Sea, where we worked for Erin's nutty Aunt Dot during the day and each evening made love out among the dunes. Brian was a counselor at a camp in Maine, and we felt guilty about him, but not guilty enough to keep our hands off each other.

When our senior year began, Erin and I confined our relationship to secret looks in the halls and an occasional late night phone call. But by the Halloween Dance, unable to stand the subterfuge any longer, Erin broke off with Brian, who took it pretty hard for a few weeks, until he found himself a minx named Dawn who really did put out. From early November through the holidays Erin and I dated on the sly, because neither of us wanted to hurt Brian's feelings, but her parents caught on and, knowing my background because of all the publicity that went with my wrestling and boxing achievements, demanded that Erin stop seeing me. She tried, but their injunctions convinced her I was the only man in the world who could make her happy.

Just after the New Year began, I told Brian the truth about Erin and me, and of course he pretended not to care. He and Erin got back together again that winter, as far as everyone else in the world was concerned, and I began to go steady with Dawn, who could give a guy a hard-on with just the look in her eyes and the way she moved her mouth when she spoke or chewed on her lips when she listened to you, as if she was considering something wild and nasty. I wore my senior class ring for an hour or so after it arrived, then it took up permanent residence on Erin's left hand, held in place with a three quarter inch wad of adhesive tape painted with pink nail polish. It had "CWS" engraved inside its gold band, not "BLC," although Erin's parents never tumbled to that one. They remained proudly convinced that Erin had landed Eugene and Alice Cox's eldest son, and now that Brian's a TV star they probably still crow about it, even though they probably haven't spoken to their daughter in three decades.

Erin and Brian were photographed on either side of me, hugging my sweaty body, after I finally won the state wrestling championship. And they, along with Dawn, were in my corner after I successfully defended my Golden Gloves title down in the city. (I went on to lose the state title to a muscular and seemingly impervious black kid from Pittsburgh in a brawl that left me with a broken nose, two cracked ribs, a dislocated jaw and a full ride to State.)

We three ordered special-colored, non-glare portraits of our senior pictures, air-brushed to take care of any imperfections our dermatologists had missed, and we made a solemn ritual of the exchange. In the Spring, Dawn and I were voted "cutest couple." Brian Cox was voted "most likely to succeed." Erin was voted "Miss Lifeboat," the woman with whom the men would most like to be stranded.

Brian went off to Maine again after graduation, even though Erin and I tried to talk him into coming with us to Aunt Dot's place on the shore. He had worked too hard, he said, and for too many years, to pass up the Chief Counselor job now that his turn for total authority had finally arrived.

After another summer of making love in the open evening air, with waves crashing nearby and dune grass tickling our asses, Erin and about nine steamer trunks of clothing headed off for Princeton, while I started at Penn State on a boxing scholarship. Brian was up at Holy Cross playing football, and I found that I missed them both more than I could stand. I was still tough as nails, and I never lost a bout that first year, but a pussy-whipped wimp was staging a coup inside me and there wasn't much I could do about it.

"And you couldn't eat," my boy prompted, after hearing yet again about the way I had run the bleachers to strengthen my knees and about the rough workout sessions with the free weights and the speed bag and the heavy bag and the jump rope and how they never did manage to find an opponent who could last with me more than three rounds, even when we went into the prisons for our sparring matches.

"No. I couldn't eat," I acknowledged, and remembered, but did not mention, all the lonely letters and phone calls and the yearning and, finally, the enervating heart break when Erin told me about the wonderful new friend from Newark she had made. "I'd get a tray," I explained, "bigger than this one here, and heap it high with food because when I went through the cafeteria line I'd be starved, but the minute I sat down I'd feel all filled up and I'd push the tray away after only a taste or two. And of course the moment I did that the animals at the training table would attack my food like sharks. Lost so much weight I fell out of my class. Then I got so weak nothing happened when I gave someone one of my best shots. Didn't make varsity the next year. Didn't make the Olympic squad. Lost my scholarship."

"All because your eyes were bigger than your stomach," Ryan said. "That's what Mom says when I do that with my dinner." Ryan looked at my unfinished fries, no longer golden-brown because the fat had coagulated. "Could we go see the sharks like last time?" he asked.

"Sure. Finish up. You want the rest of these?"

"Naw. Once they get all shiny you may as well toss 'em."

We dumped our trash into the bin with the red swinging door, except for the box Ryan's food had come in, which had games and puzzles printed on it that he said he'd one day learn to play.

The windows were steamy, and the downpour turned the passing cars into a blur. We waited under the overhang where the drive-up window was and traded karate chops as we looked for a break in the rain. I used to have this vague need to hurt Ryan a little by using more force than I should when we played like this, and I was glad to find that the urge was no longer there. Ryan seemed to notice too.

"Come on!" he said, and gave my thigh a hard roundhouse kick.

"You're not trying."

We ran out through the rain and climbed into Glady's Mercedes; as always Ryan messed the leather seats with his shoes; as always I warned him not to after it was too late. We set out for the Maritime Center in South Norwalk, but because of the heat and the hypnotic slap of the wipers and the Happy Meal bloating his stomach, Ryan fell asleep before we had gone a mile. So I put my arm around my boy and drove aimlessly through the rain while my muscles stiffened from the bowling and my mind got lost again somewhere in a span of years it hurt too much to tally or remember.

Chapter Four

Fate would have been kinder had it not granted my callow wish that Erin Henry and I one day get back together. But that is hindsight. We met again, nine months after our respective graduations, our reunion made possible by Brian Cox. Eventually we married and had a daughter. But that was later.

During my senior year, friends began to get engaged and accepted jobs or made plans for graduate school, and eventually I realized it might be a good idea to give my own adult future some thought. Graduation felt like a death sentence, and I suppose for a time, as I counted down the weeks, I was suicidal in the way I drank and drove my car. How else to explain why, when everyone around me was devising elaborate schemes to be declared 4F—unfit for military service—or to prolong their student deferment, I was attending interviews at recruiting offices that brought me to within the roll of a ball point from enlisting. But that was later, too.

I had a girl friend, a genuine Pennsylvania Dutch girl from Penn's Woods who said things like 'ferhoodled' or 'oofgabollixed' and called her mother "Memmy Zeller," which seemed foreign and charming to me at first, but later got on my nerves. In our junior year, after we'd dated six months and had been sleeping together for five, Carol took me home for Easter. I made lame excuses, but she insisted it was time, and while I expected to encounter severe people in black who lived without cars or electricity, the Zellers, apart from all their German clap-trap, and a certain spooky other-worldliness, were no different from any other family. On our way back to campus, Carol explained that the Germans of Eastern Pennsylvania had come to be called "Dutch" because the people around them couldn't pronounce the word "Deutch."

"I know nothing of tulips or wooden shoes," she told me.

"Yeah," I said, "but what's with your mother?"

"Oh, well Memmy, she's got the Moses magic," Carol told me, as if I shouldn't have had to ask. "She saw right through you."

"So she knows about us?" I asked, referring to our fairly exuberant sex life.

"Of course. She knew five months ago."

"Because you told her?"

Carol shook her head. "She just knows. And when she knows, and lets it continue, you can be sure it was meant to be. That's how come I knew it was safe to bring you home."

"Then she approves?"

"I didn't say that. Memmy doesn't always like reality, but she knows what's meant to be and what is not meant to be. And you and I are meant to be."

"You make it sound like death and taxes."

"I know," Carol laughed, and shook her head, hard, making her short blond hair fly about. It was strangely mechanical, designed, it seemed, to drive something out of her mind.

"What?" I asked.

"Memmy said our road would be bumpy because we weren't in harmony with our time and place."

"What does she know?" I said, trying to make light.

"Believe me. She knows."

Carol's mother, I learned that day, was something called a "Powwow Doctor," and whatever that was, Carol hoped one day to be one, too. She said she wanted to be her mother's Designate, although her older sister, she told me, with ill-concealed bitterness, had the inside track on that prize, simply due to the accident of birth. For as long as anyone could recall, Carol's people had believed that Moses was as much magician as prophet, demonstrated by the way he parted the sea and sent plagues of hail or gnats or locusts or frogs to torment and distract his enemies. And Memmy Zeller, Carol claimed, possessed the secrets of Moses, which her ancestors had blended a couple of centuries or so ago with the mystical teachings and healing mysteries of the local Indians.

"She put a spell on you at dinner," Carol told me, and after that, no matter how I begged or pressured, she would not reveal what her mother's spell was designed to accomplish, other than to say that "it would be good if I was."

A month after our visit, Memmy Zeller showed up in Carol's dorm to hand-deliver a ragged, leather-bound book in an old, blue suede sack decorated with gold alchemist symbols. She instructed Carol to sleep for two nights with the sack under her pillow, and then to open it on the third night, sitting alone under a tree, under a full moon.

On the appointed night, thinking this was all very strange and silly, I waited on the library steps while Carol performed her ritual, and even from a distance I could see her chest heave and her shoulders shake as she burst into tears. The book, by Johann Georg Hohmann, was her mother's most precious possession, she told me later. *Lang Verborgener Freund*, was its title, which meant, Carol was eventually able to explain, "Long Hidden Friend." It also meant that she, and not her sister, was to be her mother's Designate. From that day on, the Hohmann book, heavy as it was, occupied the space in Carol's book bag that had once belonged to Kafka, and the one time I made the mistake of touching it I got my hand slapped and triggered a six day cleansing ritual that required me to donate an eye-brow hair and a gob of spit.

To her credit, Carol Zeller, at least when she was with me, approached her mother's mysticism, and so her own, with a certain worldly humor that saved her, at least at first, from seeming entirely bonkers. Irreverent and cocky young fool that I was, I mocked the ancient book, starting with its verbose subtitle, which was this:

Wonderful and Well-Tried Remedies and Magic Arts, as Well for Man as Beast, with Many Proofs Shown in This Book, of Which Most Are As Yet Little Known, and Appearing Now for the First Time in America.

Carol took my teasing well, and after a few weeks there developed from that sentence a private joke which made us feel very clever and superior.

"Appearing now for the first time in America," one of us would say, with fully-intended irony, in response to some surprising act of kindness or love or honesty. An example of sane authority or an honest politician could trigger the line, as could a male who for a moment didn't act like a sex-crazed ego-maniac or a woman who wasn't a cunning conniver. And the other would dutifully laugh like hell.

From September until June of our Senior year, Carol had to struggle to maintain her four-point average in the School of Education, where she was preparing herself for a career as an elementary school teacher. Her distractions were many and at the top of the list, tied with her studies in her *Long Hidden Friend*, was her almost insatiable desire to be in bed with me and what we now called my "long, hidden friend." She was the first woman I knew who adored semen, and if it was an act put on to please me, it was a good one. She relished everything about sex, especially "that delicious stuff you men manufacture," and I found this incredibly liberating.

Carol saw sexual acts and sexual body parts everywhere: in the clouds, in the patterns on the bark or among the leaves of trees, everywhere; if there was a double meaning to be found in a sentence, Carol was sure to find it. She made each meal, each walk in the woods, a sensual experience, and she was wildly inventive with our love-making. Strangely enough, at least to a boy with Irish Catholic roots, there was a profoundly spiritual aspect to all of Carol's lustiness. For instance, what to me had always been sticky evidence of my bottomless depravity was to Carol a sacrament, a magical salve, a life-giving gift. (I was so enamored by this that I never bothered to wonder if I was in love. I still thought about Erin Henry several times each day, but I dismissed my obsession as a touch of insanity picked up from my Irish ancestors. I even took Carol to Long Beach Island before we started our senior year, thinking it might exorcise Erin if Carol and I made love among the dunes just to the north of Ireland by the Sea. But it did no good. Incidentally, it was during that long weekend at the shore, as we stood looking at Ireland by the Sea, our backs to the pounding surf, that Carol started to call me "Gregor," for reasons she would never explain.)

Also high on Carol's list of distractions that year were the bride magazines that arrived almost daily at the Theta house, and by the time the subject of marriage came up between us, she had our wedding planned to the last tiny detail. And it was all done for my sake. Carol's idea of a way for me to avoid getting killed in Vietnam involved a quick trip to the alter and, the moment nature allowed, the making of a baby, and while I agreed with this strategy, in principle, I see now that I agreed with all the verve of an ox yoked to the village pump. Each time our future was discussed, which was nearly every time Carol and I got together that last semester, and always during afterglow, I felt good about our plans and my enthusiasm, as far as I knew, was sincere. It did seem strange, though, that an hour or two later I'd find myself guzzling beers and talking seriously about becoming an officer in either the Air Force or the Navy. My options, marry and make a baby to avoid the draft or sign up with the military to avoid marriage, were equally attractive and frightening, and each evening, after eight or nine beers, they canceled each other. And all the while Erin was there, above, beyond, like a face in the clouds.

The day before I was to sign on the dotted line or give up my place in the next Officers Training class, I happened to read a notice from the placement bureau about a public relations job with General Motors. It involved travel and public speaking, and, best of all, it required only a three month commitment. "Recommend single men only apply," the small print on the bottom said, and that was enough for me. I signed up immediately and put everything else on hold.

The Fisher Body Craftsman's Guild representative turned out to be a pleasant but uninspiring fellow in his early twenties named Ron, who moved and spoke like a robot and looked like Manners the Butler. He put me off at first, but he left me thinking that if he could do the job for which he was recruiting, then certainly I could, being the smooth, glib, charming son-of-a-bitch I'd become since I was transplanted from the streets of South Philadelphia. I expressed my sincerest interest in a letter that probably beat Ron back to Detroit.

The next interview took place at the General Motors Tech Center, in Warren, Michigan, and turned out to be, in hindsight, the closest a male in our culture ever gets to an initiation ritual designed to test his readiness for manhood. I was greeted by a bland, handsome man, not more than a year older than me, whose name was Stan and who led me through what seemed an endless maze of corridors, and finally down a stairwell, talking all the while in a friendly manner about things too trivial to recall. We went through a basement mail room where duplicating, collating, stamping and bundling machines chugged away, and then into a windowless chamber which we entered through what seemed an air-tight metal door at the end of a corridor formed by rows of dark green metal racks.

The air was stale and smelled of oil and grease. The walls of this cave were lined with shelves where a dozen movie projectors stood in a row, along with various tools and mechanical devices whose purpose I couldn't guess. Had there been crude drawings of woolly mammoths on the walls I would not have been surprised. I was ordered to sit alone at the end of a conference table, where I found a strange assortment of objects: three balls, each a different color; a round red fire extinguisher; a pencil. Four men, five now that Stan had joined them, sat at the table's opposite end, miles away from me it seemed. The guy I'd met on campus, Ron the robot butler, was among them. There was nothing to do but say, "Oh-oh" inside myself while I smiled as if I found the circumstances as comfortable as the front seat of my car.

My smile got no response that I could see from this distance, and for a few awkward moments the five stared at me as if they expected me to begin the interview. Four of them, including Stan and Ron, were at most a year or two older than I was, while the fifth man, who sat facing me, was in his mid-forties, large (soft but not fat) and bald, except for a nearly invisible fringe of hair that ran along the sides of his great round head. I fought the urge to run. I fought the urge to smile or glare. And although I wanted desperately to fill the silence with babble, I did not let myself speak. Somehow I kept all this from showing in my eyes or on my face, an accomplishment which, more than any of my answers to the questions that would come, probably won me my first real job.

Whatever else it may have accomplished, that Fisher Body stress interview solidly united the eight of us who survived it. Magically transformed from college kids into young executives, we came together in Warren, Michigan, on a Sunday night in early August, set to report to work the following morning. We were housed across the street from the building where our interviews had taken place, at the Executive Inn, where we each arrived in a brand new suit, and filled our closets and bureau drawers with shirts and underwear and ties and socks still adorned with tags and sticky paper strips. And then, over pitchers of draft in the motel bar, three of us, then four, then six, then eight, broke the ice by laughing off the interview we had each endured. Like victims of a natural disaster, we had a powerful need to tell the story of our trial by fire, even though one story was not substantively different from the rest, and all eight of us probably lied. We acted blasé and implied that we had seen through the set up. And as we drank we imitated the cold looks we had faced and tossed at one another the questions that had been asked of us down in that terrible cave.

"Tell us why you'd be good for this job."

"Take a few minutes to look over that fire extinguisher then stand up and sell it to us."

"Examine those three rubber balls then stand up and, using them as a visual aid, give a speech concerning something you feel strongly about."

"Tell us the difference between 'imply' and 'infer'."

"Give a one minute talk about how a pencil is made and how it works and its significance in history."

"Tell us something you'd have to overcome in order to excel at this job."

We all claimed, of course, to have met each challenge fearlessly and brilliantly, although most of us were honest enough that first night to acknowledge that we had driven away from our interview thinking we'd blown it.

Training was intense. It involved a simultaneous mastery of public speaking skills and the development of a forty-five minute pitch featuring industrial technology as the truth, the light and the way into an ever-brightening future. We would soon go out on the road as missionary preachers: our religion, America Incorporated, our sect, Automotive, our church, the Fisher Body Division of GM, and our God, competitive democratic Capitalism. The material we were given to work with was a bunch of "Oh, Wow!" gadgetry, most of it technology under development for automotive application. During our training weeks we built our sermons around these "demos," half of which would work onstage almost half the time, and little of which ever showed up on any car I ever heard about in the nearly three decades that have elapsed since my days at "The Fish."

In early September, hard to believe at first, we were to be assigned in pairs to one of the four Regional Supervisors, each Supervisor, or

"Sup" (Pronounced "Soup") representing a point of the compass. Arranged in trios, we would go forth to deliver our sermons twice a day for the next three months to audiences of junior and senior high school kids across the entire country. We had no idea how the final assignments were to be made, but it wasn't long before our training became an intense scramble for affiliation. Everyone wanted to travel with Stan, the Sup of the West, because he was a nice guy who was anxious to be liked and had the best territory. Just as powerfully, everyone dreaded the idea of being assigned to the Sup of the East, a guy we called "The Thing in the Basement," although not to his face. His real name was Bill Kern. Our chances, of course, were one in four; one in four we'd go to heaven in the west; one in four we'd go to hell in the east. And fifty-fifty we'd fall somewhere between.

While the other three Sups gradually shaped us into polished public speakers, Bill Kern worked alone in the same windowless basement room where our hiring inquisition had taken place, tinkering with the demos we would soon have to truck from town-to-town and use in our assembly programs. All those weeks away from sunlight and his fellow man, we reasoned, had done a number on poor Bill. He was pale. He never smiled. His face was long and grim. Under scowling brows, his eyes seemed to contain a paranoid hostility that told you this was a good person to avoid.

Every day we'd be sent down to the basement to have Kern train us in the use and maintenance of another piece of "his" equipment, usually as the clock ticked beyond quittin' time. With his stern delivery, Kern somehow managed to imply, or at least we inferred, that he would see to it horrible things befell the man who abused his square of sun-sensitive windshield glass or his heat-deflecting carbon-cloth or his cadmium sulfide light-sensitive gizmo or the six-foot-long plank of flexiglass—which, if it broke, miraculously became a handful of gems with no cutting edges—or the hypnotic wheel used to demonstrate the lubricating power of air, which when spun, more often than not quickly ground to a halt with a horrid shriek of metal torturing metal.

Kern's threatening manner and aloof disdain had, it turned out, a higher purpose. It allowed him to watch the Reps and Sups maneuver for affiliation without getting caught in these games. And, since Kern's fellow Sups were nearly as intimidated by him as we Reps, it pretty much assured him of getting his choice from among the eight of us.

Employing what he called his "built-in asshole detector" to eliminate six of the Reps, he silently zeroed in, mostly by default, on a grinning, high-living poet named Wes Phillips, and me.

On a Friday afternoon in mid-September, I signed out a new yellow Chevy wagon with the Fisher Body crest on its front doors, loaded it with Craftsman's Guild equipment and my luggage, and set out for twelve straight weeks on the road. Kern had scheduled an equipment drill in his motel room in Erie, Pennsylvania, for eight o'clock Sunday night, and so, with time to kill, I stopped Friday to see a friend from college who had taken a job in Cleveland. Carol flew in from New York, and the way we consumed each other that weekend, you'd have thought I was on my way to Viet Nam.

The week before this reunion, Carol had begun an entry level job at a Manhattan ad agency, having discovered during her stint as a student teacher that education wasn't "her bag." She was still hard at work with her "Long Hidden Friend" in order to be worthy of becoming the next generation's Pow Wow Doctor, a designation I suggested would come in handy as she struggled to find new ways to sell Tide and Coke. During the weeks I had been learning to give speeches to school children on the wonders of industry and the promises of technology, she was studying what she called "esoteric healing and elementary curses." She had also turned herself into a *Witakultruntufe*.

"God bless," I said.

We were lying together naked in my friend's bed in Cleveland, smoking and catching up.

"It means," she told me, "*She who carries the drum.*"

"Appearing now for the first time in America," I announced, "a mild-mannered, sexy Account Executive who is also a closet Witakultruntufe. Great in the sack and a hell of a drummer."

Carol had recently learned to sing something called "The Tayil," an obnoxious-sounding song designed, she said, to "Pull Ancestors." When she sang—and that was her word for what she did, not mine—she forced air through her clenched teeth, which she used, she said, to cut through time and hold back evils of our age that might contaminate the pure beginnings of all things. "And that's what life's about," she told me, brimming with tears of innocent fervor. "Time. It's all about time, Gregor."

"I wish you'd tell me why you call me that."

"Someday I won't have to tell you," she said. "And then I will."

"I'm starting not to like it when you get this way."

"Time is everything and nothing, Gregor. You'll know that one day, although I'm fearful it may take years and years and years and years. It's so hard to get it all just right, the mix of time, place and person. And two out of three won't do. But I'll wait. No matter what, I'll wait."

Carol performed a Tayil over me that night, and when she was finished she said she had called forth an ancestor of mine named Fat Duncan, who would see to it I didn't have to go fight in Viet Nam. In his time, Fat Duncan had fought and killed and died enough for me not to have to, Carol told me. And to further protect me, she presented me with an amulet that her mother had forged and blessed. It was about the size and thickness of a Life Saver candy, but heavier, being made of solid gold. A wolf claw was embossed on one side and a balance scale on the other.

"It holds inside it the same spark that started life eons ago," she said. "Anything you wish for when you hold the Libra Wolf will come true, as long as it is in harmony with all that is meant to be. And any harm wished upon you by an enemy will befall them instead."

"Cool," I said.

I really never knew how to respond to Carol at moments like these, and starting that weekend in Cleveland, her mysticism began to get on my nerves. The hippie movement had begun to spread east from San Francisco, so Carol's strange ways didn't set her apart as much as they had the year before. Still, to me she seemed more and more like a candidate for the loony bin, and eventually this would make me wonder if I really wanted us to become attached forever. (I know now that when she gave me Fat Duncan and the Libra Wolf, it was her way of making sure we didn't marry for the wrong reasons, although I wouldn't see that until I had married someone else. I'm sure she never intended that I would wish on the Libra Wolf to have Erin back, but that is what I did, swine that I am.)

Carol and I looked forward to November and December when my tour would be close enough to Manhattan for weekend visits. And we dreamed aloud of how it would be to live together in New York after I finished my three-month stint with The Fish. I knew Carol expected a diamond ring in her stocking, and I think I even intended to shop for one here and there as I traveled with Wes Phillips and Bill Kern, although I somehow never got around to that chore, which should have been another clue, but was not.

Carol's flight back to New York from Cleveland was delayed by two hours, and since I didn't have the heart to leave her alone at the airport, I was an hour late for Kern's equipment drill in Erie. He blistered me with a lecture that seemed to place the future of General Motors and the well-being of all its stockholders on my promptness, and while his reasoning seemed spurious, and his sense of our importance a touch grandiose, there was nothing to say in the face of his righteous ire.

The first few assembly programs I did for The Fisher Body Craftsman's Guild were frightening experiences, but I soon became comfortable enough to add spontaneous touches of humor, including references to local rivalries, and these made me a hit with my young audiences. After that, the only nerve-racking aspect of my first grown-up job was navigating my way to the right school in a new city, often during the morning rush hour. Somehow, no matter how early I left my motel room, I never seemed to give myself time enough to charm the principal the way Bill Kern wanted me to, unload and properly set up my equipment, train the ushers from the AV Club, identify the most attractive unattached females on the faculty, glean some insider information to spice up my program, then find a place to tuck in my shirt, comb my hair and focus myself before "GOING ON."

My glib stage persona, my ability to read and connect with audiences, and my spontaneity were, almost from the start, beyond anything Bill Kern could accomplish when he performed his programs, and he was honest enough to acknowledge this, even as he minimized the importance of my skills. He was, he insisted, more prompt and, being more technically proficient, he was also more consistent, while I, although capable of putting on a superior performance, was also capable of giving offense by arriving late and being occasionally "off", and therefore doing a "prog" far inferior to any he had ever done. "And one bad prog," he liked to point out, "can't be made up for by a hundred brilliant progs because the audience you cheated never gets to see one of the better progs and three or four hundred human beings go through life with a bad impression of General Motors and Fisher Body." And each of these people, he reasoned, would influence at least a dozen more, all of whom would probably buy a dozen cars in their lifetimes, and so each time I was "off", I cost General Motors between sixty and eighty thousand dollars. Worse than that, each time I arrived late to a school I gave the Craftsman's Guild a black eye, which meant we probably wouldn't be able to schedule that school again, which in turn meant several thousand more lost car sales for GM.

It was difficult to take Kern's passion for GM's bottom line all that seriously, but any hint of inattention or cynicism was punished by an extended harangue, delivered with increased volume and zeal. Like most young men thrust too soon into positions of authority, Kern failed to recognize the impact he had. He was far better at dishing out criticism and issuing corrective orders than he was at offering compliments and letting things unfold at their own pace. He rode me unmercifully about the casual way I dressed and how I was always a minute or two late, and it drove him crazy that I didn't take what he had to say seriously enough to change my ways. But unfortunately for him—fortunately for me—I wasn't his biggest problem. The other rep, Wes, though intelligent and always eloquent, seemed incapable of making his stage look any more orderly than an adolescent's bedroom, and so Kern's most withering blasts were aimed at him. And for a time Wes endured Kern without complaint.

Wes and I were soon good friends, unified by an unspoken but gathering resentment we each felt for our boss, and by a brotherly connection neither of us bothered to put into words.

"You know that interview," Wes said to me one night. I forget where we were, in which of the thirty motels, but it hardly mattered.

"I bet you're the only one who knew the difference between 'imply' and 'infer,'" I said. I had only hit upon it in the car on my way home, and told him so.

"That's okay," said Wes. "That guy Bob, my roommate back in training, still insists there is no difference. So what did you do with the balls, that's what I want to know?"

"Oh God! I was so lame," I said. "I discovered that they bounced different—you know, that one of them didn't bounce at all, one was about what you'd expect and the other went sky high even if you didn't drop it very far—so I used them in a speech against professional boxing. You know, here's your bounce-back before you've been hit a few dozen times, after you've been hit a few dozen times, and after you've been hit too many times to remember."

"Whata ya got against boxing?" Wes asked, sounding like Brando saying "I coulda been a contendah."

"Nothing," I said. "I used to be a boxer. I just needed something to say. What'd you come up with?"

"I forget."

"You know," I said, "I doubt our answers mattered for shit."

"Of course not," he said. "You'll find, son, as you go through life, that that is, more often than not, the case."

He had figured out long ago, he told me, that the interview was designed to test our composure under pressure.

"You know what else that interview did," I said. "After that ordeal, could you have turned down this job?"

"No way."

"Me neither."

"I wonder if anyone ever turns them down," said Wes.

"And I wonder where people end up who start here."

"Ahhh," he said. "Now THAT'S the real question."

For Wes, the answer would be provided by Uncle Sam; for me, by Erin Henry. Wes would be fragged a year later in Viet Nam, shot dead from behind by one of his own men. And a year later I'd be married and about to become someone's father.

Chapter Five

My friend Wes traveled well. He was all amazement and play on the surface, but inside he was full of poetic passion, which showed in the way he consumed each city and town we visited. He lived in the moment—before all this New Age blissbabble made it fashionable—and seemingly gave little thought to his future, which was just as well since fate didn't have much of a future planned for him.

I was a crew cut, button-down All American boy, one of those obnoxious young men adults always admire so and wish their children were more like. I was glib, self-assured, charming and too shallow to know it was all a show. This was, I now see, the civilized costume chosen for me by my mother to help me succeed in life, or at least to survive; nowhere in evidence was the street punk I'd once been, and sometimes, when the taste of my own niceness sickened me, I missed him.

I had no thought as to what I wanted to do with my life that didn't begin as someone else's idea. So instead of following some dream of my own, I existed behind pleasing surfaces. And by acting the part, I fooled myself into thinking I knew where I was going. In that way, although I wouldn't know it for almost thirty years, I squandered my life.

One night in Manchester, New Hampshire, having struck out in the bars and having returned, defeated, to our rooms, I went searching in my address book for someone to call. I'd already spent an hour on the phone with Carol, who had sung me another of those weird songs and had called me Gregor three times. And I logged fifteen minutes with Brian Cox, who was flunking out of law school at NYU and working as a page at NBC. I ended up dialing a number in New Hampshire's White Mountains, the last listing I had for a girl named Tonya Angione.

In my South Philadelphia days, Tonya had been my playmate, my buddy, my partner in crime, and then my first sex object. We had crossed a few frontiers together, but we had moved away from the Front Street docks a few months too soon, Tonya to New Hampshire, me to the Main Line. Tonya was the owner of the first breast I touched after infancy, the first hand to get me off that wasn't attached to me, and the first vagina I fingered—who knew about clits in those days? She was the first girl to whisper "I love you," while we panted and groped, and the first to make me break my promise that I'd be hers forever.

I dialed with no real hope of making contact; it was just something to do with another endless motel room night. I'd either get an operator telling me the number was no longer in service, I thought, or I'd get someone who had never heard of Tonya Angione. But after six rings, as I was about to hang up, Tonya's mother answered. It was odd, but I recognized her voice at once from long ago, when using the phone was something of a challenge. I remembered Mrs. Angione as a gaunt but pretty woman who always seemed to show lots of chest. On her end, she seemed to recognize my name the moment I said it.

"Your dad still have his meat shop?" she asked.

"No. He's retired."

"But he's doing okay?"

"Yeah, he's fine."

She took my number, promising to pass it on to her daughter the next time they talked, and after we said goodbye, something strange was left hanging. I wondered about it for a few seconds while I flipped through the channels, looking for *I Spy*.

Tonya and I had corresponded for a few months after South Philadelphia, until I fell in love with Erin Henry. She wrote about the beautiful mountains and the quiet of snow and how she missed the noise and gritty excitement of the city. She wrote that the kids she met all seemed afraid of her. They put her down, she said, and called her a slut because of the way she dressed and the way she made friends with boys. I wrote back to say it was too bad she hadn't let me teach her how to box because when everyone knew you could kick their ass they weren't half as unkind. I told her how my father took the train each day into the city with the other executives, except that he was probably the only one to put on a bloody butcher's apron at the other end of his commute. I told her in my letters about the snobs who were afraid of me and how I used some of the old street games to con them out of their allowance. Then Erin and I became lovers that summer on the Jersey shore and my correspondence with Tonya abruptly stopped.

The next thing I knew, Tonya and I were on the phone, catching up, reminiscing about the 7th grade. We spoke for almost two hours, then made arrangements for her to visit me in Manchester, which she said would be better than my driving up to where she lived.

Late the next afternoon, we met at a restaurant a few miles from my motel.

"You look great," she said. "So tall and handsome."

"So do you," I told her. But it was a lie. She looked gaunt, almost skeletal. What a shame, I kept thinking, and she probably read it in my eyes.

She'd already had two kids, including the one who had caused her to marry at nineteen. Her husband, Billy, was an auto body repairman and a mean drunk.

"He hits me sometimes," she added, as if it was expected.

Feeling like a boy who had yet to step into the real world, I told her about my job and about boxing in college. I told her about the heartbreak of Erin, but for some reason I did not tell her about Carol Zeller.

I bought her dinner, and over coffee, she took my hand and told me she believed in Karma. I restrained myself.

She told me her life wasn't turning out and she cried.

I sympathized and patted her hand. After a few more hours of this, to my great relief, she went away.

Carol laughed when I told her about my dinner with Tonya Angione. If she wondered why I had dialed Tonya's number, she didn't bother to ask, and if it made her jealous, she hid it. (She was, in hindsight, the least possessive woman I ever knew.) And Brian Cox, the only other person I told, said it was a pretty sorry state of affairs when a guy had to reach back to the 7th grade to get laid.

Three days deeper into our itinerary, in some nameless burg north of Boston, as I was pulling my suitcase and wardrobe bag out of my Fish Wagon, a taxi pulled to a stop nearby and out climbed Tonya, followed by three suitcases, one toddler and, finally, an infant, whom she held under her right arm like a football. When she spotted me, she began to gesture frantically.

"Get us inside," she said, and handed me the baby.

The moment I unlocked my motel room door she marched the other child, a little girl, into my bathroom. As her kid peed, she told me all about their bus ride and the cab driver who had brought her here and how her husband was probably just now discovering she'd left him.

"I doubt he can trace me," she said, "unless I was spotted getting on the bus by someone we know. You look stunned. Aren't you glad to see me? If we're too much trouble, I can just ..."

"No, listen, it's just that ..."

"Well, good. Now this big girl here is Justine," she said, taking hold of the shoulders of the toddler who had just emerged from the bathroom and was awkwardly rubbing her pudgy wet hands together. "I named her after my baby sister. OUR sister, I should say." She winked, knowingly. "And this itty bitty witty whittle girl is Heather. You have room for us in your company car, don't you?"

"Well, the company policy doesn't ..."

"And look at this room. Two big beds for just one person. Are all the rooms so huge like this?"

"Most of them, but ..."

"And where are we going next? Didn't you say something about Boston and New York?"

I nodded, dumbfounded. At all costs, be nice.

"Oh, I know I'll just love Boston. Of course it'd be better in the Spring; can we come back to Boston in the Spring?"

She said she'd be good for me. She said she'd show me how good love could be. I decided it was time to tell her about Carol, but she blew that off with a snort.

"If you were really in love, you'd have told me about this Carol straight away."

She reminded me that she had given me my first hand job, and that there was more good stuff where that had come from. She had only been a raw beginner back then, she said. But if I didn't want her, I should say so now, before we got too involved and she and her kids became dependent on me.

"I don't know what to say," I said. "I can't really have you traveling with me."

"Could if you wanted," Tonya said.

Had she been a man, I'd have told her to get lost, but women, starting with my mother, have always cut through my toughness. I have never been able to take one on, directly. Ever. And it has cost me dearly. I fed her and let her spend the night, but I made it clear it was just this once. She offered to sleep in my bed but I said I didn't think that was a good idea, the children being so close. Of course she took my prudishness as a sign of true love.

"I've never really been in love with anyone else," she told me, and tossed aside her bra. Then she laughed at me for averting my eyes as she slipped a long T-shirt over her head and climbed into bed.

She and her children slept together, and as I lay awake I promised myself I'd get rid of them in the morning, although I wasn't sure how. The children woke up before the sun. Tonya asked me for money to get food.

"On the bureau," I said.

"Aren't you coming?"

"No. You go ahead."

"Then can I have the car keys?"

"Nobody else can drive my car."

"Oh, fiddle sticks. A car's a car. Are these them?" She held up my keys.

"I could get fired," I said, sitting up.

"Then come with us."

I told her there was a restaurant in the motel. She told me the food in motel restaurants wasn't fit to eat. She knew, she said, because she had worked as a waitress in several motel restaurants. Besides, her kids wouldn't eat anything but McDonald's. I got up and dressed.

"You know," she said, watching my face, "you don't seem too happy this morning. Don't you like having us here? Some men would think they'd died and gone to heaven."

I told her again that I was committed to my college girlfriend, but even I could hear how lame it sounded. "Besides," I added, "it's against company policy for me to ..."

"Right! Right! I heard all that. General Motors may own the world, but it don't own me. I can tell you feel the same, but just don't know it yet. Sometimes men need time before their heads catch up with their hearts. It's karma, that's what this is, and if you'd relax you'd realize it."

"I think you're fooling yourself," I said. "I don't know you anymore. And I don't want you with me."

It felt as if I had slugged her in the mouth when I said that. She stared at me hard for a few seconds, then her lips began to twitch and she turned away.

"Kids," she said, "I guess we know when we're not wanted. Nobody has to hit me with a sledge hammer."

She packed her bags and called a cab, and I felt terrible as I waited with her, although not terrible enough to say anything that might have made her stay.

Bill Kern and Wes wanted to know if I'd gotten laid, and I said enough to leave them thinking I had. And of course this time I didn't mention anything about Tonya when I spoke next with Carol or Brian in New York.

By now the glimmer had worn off our tour and the constant travel had turned tedious. If a town had as many fine restaurants as we had evenings to kill, we considered ourselves blessed. And if one of us met a teacher, a waitress, a girl in a bar, it was like winning Olympic gold; the other two gave him room to operate, in return for an introduction to her friends or, failing that, a full report on the conquest.

Bill Kern didn't let himself get too close to either Wes or me during these adventures, needing to retain some of his aloof, authoritative sternness, probably to protect himself against regressing to the fuck-up he'd been two years earlier at college.

In contrast, Wes and I were easy with one another, at least when Bill wasn't around, and although I never told him about the problem that had chased me down from New Hampshire, we had become good friends by the time we reached Boston. That may have been one reason why I didn't intervene the night at Durgin Park when Wes invited Kern to step outside; I knew how badly Wes wanted a piece of Bill, and I didn't dare take a piece of Kern for myself because I knew I might do serious damage. (While they were gone I ate their cherrystones.) No blows were exchanged and they returned with some sort of tense pact established between them, although neither one would tell me what had been said out in the alley.

My stay in Boston was not five days old when I returned from my last school, unlocked the door to my hotel room and found it occupied. "Excuse me," I said, and started to shut the door; somehow, I'd entered the wrong room, I thought, until I realized I had been rejoined by Tonya and her kids.

When I opened the door again, Tonya rushed to me as if I were hubby-home-from-work. She kissed my lips, my nose, my eyes. She held my face in both her hands. She squeezed my cheeks and squealed as if she could barely control her delight. The toddler, Justine, was watching TV and playing with a doll. The infant, Heather, was having her diaper changed on my bed. She was fingering herself. Her genitalia seemed huge.

"You didn't mean it," Tonya said, still holding my face and looking into my eyes. Then she let go and went to her baby. "I could tell by the sadness in your eyes as we were pulling away that you didn't mean it, so I just gave you time enough to think over your mistake."

I closed my eyes and shook my head. "How did you find me?"

"With this." She took from her bag of baby supplies a copy of my itinerary which she must have stolen from my briefcase.

I felt something clamp tight under my jawbone, right where a hangman's noose would do its damage.

"Tonya," I said, forcefully. "Really. I'm sorry but I can't have you here."

"Of course you can. You'll like having me, once you relax and accept the idea. Why do you insist on wasting more time?"

"I don't want you with me," I said, and in my mind I was imagining how Bill Kern would have handled this; no woman, I told myself, would have walked all over him this way. He knew how to harden his heart when it was necessary.

"So what did you want from me then?" she asked. "I mean, how come you phoned? You were like an answered prayer."

"I don't know. Just to see how you were doing, I guess."

"And so? I'm doing pretty shitty, don't you think? I mean, look at me."

"I guess. But is that my problem?"

"Did you think we might screw?"

"No. That wasn't on my mind."

"Not even a little?" She was smiling at me coyly, enjoying this game, delighting in my discomfort.

"No."

"No? Then you musta wanted another one of my special hand jobs?"

"No. Swear to God."

"Not even one?"

Her little girl watched us without expression.

Tonya held my eyes for a few seconds, knowing the truth, then went back to work on the infant, clearing away shit with one of the hotel wash cloths. When she was finished she stood, a used diaper in hand, and said, "I think we should fuck. Don't you? We never got around to that back in the 7th grade. What's wrong with right now?"

"I'm not sure it's a ..."

"Or are you some kinda queer?"

I shook my head in a mix of denial and wonder at the balls on her.

"Or one of those guys who needs a female around to tell him all the time how great he is, but hasn't got clue one what to do with her?"

I shrugged, not knowing how to respond but knowing that with this last volley she had scored. Women were, I'd known since my freshman year of college, my Achilles heel.

She glared at me, her chin jutting out, and for a second it seemed she was inviting me to hit her. I sat down beside the infant to keep her from rolling off the bed. Heather cooed at me and fingered herself.

Finally Tonya turned away, perhaps to hide tears, and went into the bathroom. I heard her flush as I put a new diaper on her baby. I'd never done it before, and it went badly.

"I can't have you traveling with me," I said, softly.

"You can't stop me." She called.

She peed with the door open, flushed, then came from the bathroom and picked up the baby, who seemed happy enough on the bed. Heather's diaper hung from her body. It would do her no good at all. Tonya bounced Heather as if to stop her crying.

"What if I just show up?" she asked. "Let's see. Worcester is next, right? Then Hartford, New Haven, Greenwich, New York. It's a free country. I can go to those places if I want."

"True," I said, shouting to be heard over the baby, who had now started to wail. "But I don't have to drive you."

"You mean you won't even give us a ride if we happen to be going to the same place as you? You won't even help an old friend get away from her bastard of a husband?"

I shook my head, holding to the image of Kern's face.

"You'd just toss a mother and her two helpless kids out into the cold? Is that what you're telling me?"

I knew if I didn't handle this right, and right now, I might as well marry this crazy lady and adopt her kids; even so, the urge to be a nice guy almost conquered common sense. "Yup," I said. "That's the kind of guy I am."

"I don't believe you."

"You'd better believe it."

"You owe me."

"I owe you? What for?"

"For teaching you about sex."

"Oh, horse shit. If it wasn't you it would have been someone else."

"Then what about karma?"

I just stared at her, hoping I looked solid and stern, while inside I felt myself weakening. There was part of me that did love this woman, or at least the South Philadelphia toughness she radiated, and part of me felt sorry for her, too, and wanted to rescue her from her husband or from the life fate had carved out for her. But I kept all that hidden.

"Shit," she said, gathering her things. "Billy's looking better by the minute. At least he'll do me now and then."

"Go back to him then. Make a life."

"You know you owe me. You know why this is karma."

I just glared, pretending to be Bill Kern.

"You owe me because of Justine," she said. "That's why."

"Your daughter? What's she got to do with me?"

"No. Not this Justine. Our sister."

"You mean your baby sister? That Justine?"

"Right. But she's *our* baby sister. Didn't you know you and I have a half-sister in common?"

"What the hell are you talking about?"

"You heard me. Justine is as much your sister as mine."

"I heard you, but ..."

"What I mean, stupid, is that your father and my mother made a baby. She was six when we moved away."

"Bull."

"It's the truth."

I wanted to argue, but something stopped me. Knowing Dad, it probably was the truth. "Okay," I said. "So what? What's that got to do with you and me?"

"Don't you know anything? Don't you know about the sins of the fathers visiting their sons? Well I'm your curse, buddy boy. And don't you forget it."

Something recoiled inside me, and she must have seen the change in my eyes.

"Okay, okay," she said, backing away, holding up her hand. She winced and ducked as if I'd started to swing at her. "I'm going."

For the rest of my tour with The Fish, (and maybe for the rest of my life), I would never enter a motel room without expecting to find Tonya Angione waiting for me. And I thought almost constantly about Tonya's mother and my father. I knew in my bones that what Tonya said was true, even while I told myself repeatedly that she'd lied just to hurt me. Finally I called Tonya's mother and asked her if she and my father had had a child together. She answered by telling me she'd always been in love with my old man, but that he'd only taken her to bed twice before guilt drove him back to his wife. She was obviously drunk, which meant she probably blurted out the truth.

"But what about the baby?" I asked.

"What baby?" she said.

"Your youngest daughter. Justine."

"Oh, her. Well, who can say where a baby comes from?"

All this rattled me in ways I didn't understand and caused me to withdraw entirely from the great pussy hunt in which Bill Kern and Wes Phillips were endlessly engaged. Besides, we were moving steadily closer to New York now, which meant I could visit Carol on weekends. Bill and Wes talked more than they scored, I'm sure, while I came back each weekend smiling and silent. (To this day I tease Bill Kern about his lame attempts to get laid, and he reminds me that our time of living high off the Fish took place in another era, when pussy was nowhere near as plentiful a species out there in the jungle as it is in this day of the liberated female libido.)

Although still shell-shocked by Tonya, I was happy during that phase of our tour, but I could tell that Carol wasn't getting from me what she wanted, and as Christmas approached, she seemed to realize that it was her commitment alone that was moving us toward marriage. Each weekend visit, each evening's call, eventually became tense with silence as she waited for me to deliver what simply wasn't in me. By the time the tour arrived in Manhattan for our two week stay, each of my visits with Carol, no matter how brief, left her fighting back tears. Had she been even slightly conniving she'd have landed me without a fight, but she left me free to be as close or as distant as I needed to be, and I failed entirely to appreciate what a gift that was. I thought she did it because she was caught up in becoming a pow-wow doctor, or, as I teased, a witch, but that wasn't it.

Carol told me during one weekend visit that she had learned to enter other people's dreams and did so now at will. She had already entered my dreams, twice, and had been tempted, she told me, to cause me to start dreaming of a life of marital bliss. But she didn't want me, she said, if she had to use magic to get me.

She claimed to be able now to ward off the evil eye and cast spells, so if I was wise, she joked, I wouldn't mess with her emotions much longer. The conversation, playful as it was, left me wanting to get as far away from her as possible. I started making business excuses to avoid her, and spent time with my friend Brian Cox, who was struggling to stay in law school while balancing a half-dozen NBC secretaries and pages and hanging out around the TV studios. One night I met Brian for a drink because he said he had a surprise for me, and when I arrived at his place, Erin Henry stepped from his closet. She was even more beautiful than in my memory, and I knew in that moment I had never stopped loving her.

Erin's last name was now McClinch, and so I assumed, incorrectly, that she had gotten married. In a way that was a relief, because my first impression was that she and Brian were together. And that, it turned out, was true, although I wouldn't find out until later.

I had a pleasant evening with my two old Bryn Mawr friends, then

I went on with my tour as if nothing had happened, still pretending I was in love with Carol Zeller and still on the lookout for another visit from Tonya Angione and her children. Why I had to play it so cool with Erin I have no idea, but it probably had something to do with pride. If Erin was married, then in a way she was as good as dead. And if she was with Brian Cox, that posed problems I didn't even want to think about.

The tour stopped in lovely Elizabeth, New Jersey, then Trenton, and a week later I turned in my equipment and my Fish wagon, collected my last check, went for a ride in Kern's cherry antique Corvette, had a last drink with Wes Phillips, then drove back over the Pennsylvania Turnpike to spend Christmas with my folks. After that, simply because it was our plan, I moved in with Carol in New York, where I spent my days looking for work and my nights listening to Carol's mumbo-jumbo and sneaking up on the conclusion that if I didn't break this relationship off soon I'd be saddled for life with a total nut case.

I spent more and more of my time out drinking with Brian Cox, and it was in some East Side bar, smashed out of my mind, that I fingered the Libra Wolf Memmy Zeller had blessed and behind closed eyes, while the world threatened to spin out from under me, wished Erin back into my life. I thought about Erin constantly and tuned in whenever Brian mentioned her, but I never let myself seem very interested and I never asked about her. It was from Brian that I learned the truth about Erin's name change. I also learned that my two old friends were involved, but that he was cheating on her with several different women, several times each week, and suspected she was doing the same.

Carol was hurt because she hadn't gotten a diamond ring for Christmas, but all her training had paid off because she claimed not to have been surprised. She also knew, she said, from having entered more of my dreams, that Erin was back.

As the weeks of the new year accumulated, the disappointment enlarged inside Carol, and as it did, my yearning for Erin grew more compelling, especially after I learned she wasn't married. I finally worked up courage enough to end things with Carol, but before I could act, Carol—always a step ahead of me—finally had enough despair to end things with me. She was, she suddenly announced, going home to study with her mother full time, but she had one last thing to say to me and she hoped I would take it as the gift she intended it to be.

"Of course," I said generously.

"Your life will enlighten you if you let it," she told me, "or at least it will make you human. But not if you never discover what love is, or which dreams are worth chasing."

"Right," I said, and thought about Erin.

"Of course there's no hurry," she added, as if to comfort me, "because time is just one way of thinking about things. Time's an illusion. But the illusion can't last forever, Gregor. And it may be possible for one to throw away his destiny."

"I understand," I said, lying. I had no idea what she was talking about, and I'm sure she knew it.

"And since I am committed to wait for you through eternity, for both our sakes I hope you catch on sooner rather than later."

I think I said something lame at this point like, "I'll try." Then I offered to give her back the Libra Wolf.

She held up her hand and shrank away.

"Just go," she said.

There were tears from both of us, but the relief I felt was confirmation enough that I was finally moving in the right direction.

"Don't wait," I told her, after I had kissed her for the last time.

"What I mean by waiting and what you mean by waiting are two different things. My soul will wait, but my body will be otherwise occupied."

Within an hour of leaving Carol's, I was at Brian's place, where I would live just long enough to steal Erin away from him again, as I had when we were in high school.

Chapter Six

Erin and I came together again in a rush of passion and a flood of promises. We were meant to be, we whispered to one another.

"WE ARE MEANT TO BE," we shouted one evening from Lady Liberty's torch.

Neither of us was gainfully employed, so we abandoned New York in late March and moved to the Jersey shore, where Erin's crazy Aunt Dotty still had her inn, the one where we had worked summers during high school and where we had first fallen in love.

Ireland By the Sea was a big, weather-beaten place that displayed its name on a twelve-foot plank that had washed up on the beach some fifty years ago, after a storm that destroyed several of the island's other hotels. The plank, with its crude woodburned lettering, was nailed in place just above the sagging roof of the verandah, where a line of white wicker armchairs offered guests a view as far across the ocean as their eyes could see, which was probably not all that far since there was rarely a guest in those days younger than sixty-five.

Erin had been disowned by her parents for, in descending order of offense, dropping out of Princeton, getting impregnated by a scholarship student from Newark—the boyfriend she'd had after me—and having an abortion. Aunt Dot had taken Erin in and now seemed to regard her as a daughter, which meant she was suspicious of me and did everything possible to keep us apart.

Dot's mission in life, other than protecting Erin from me, was to make a home for the strays and misfits of the world, which seemed more important to her by far than running a successful inn. Her one demand on those she adopted was that they change their last names to something starting with the prefix "Mc" or "O" or "Fitz." (It was for Dot's benefit that Erin's last name had evolved from Henry to McClinch, a name Erin had spotted on the side of a construction truck while walking down an Upper East Side Manhattan sidewalk.) Unlike Erin, most of the other "Micks" at Ireland By the Sea that winter simply added Dotty's preferred prefix to the names they'd had all along, so in residence back then was a McObermyer and a Fitzkurtsberg. And they told me a guy named O'Kinelsky had just moved out of the room I was in. To suck up to the old gal, I became McWilly.

Erin and I worked at the inn, as we had when we were kids, she in the kitchen, me anywhere I was needed, and, as before, we made love at night among the dunes, impervious to the weather. We were out there consuming each other on cold March evenings and on summer nights so hot the mosquitoes could hardly move. Dot wouldn't allow us inside each other's rooms; she housed us in separate wings, on separate floors, and came around once or twice a night to make bed checks. "You can be together in the same bedroom once you're properly married," she'd say when one of us protested, and Erin would make sounds as if marriage was the furthest thought from her mind.

We became engaged that summer, but we had no money for a ring, so I gave Erin the gold charm Carol Zeller's mother had blessed for me, the one with the claw on one side and the balance scale on the other. Erin wore the Libra Wolf proudly around her neck, but refused to tell anyone it signified our intent to marry, and that should have been an omen to me, although I was too in love to see it. Alone among the dunes, marriage was all we spoke of, and by the time summer ended we were full of dreams for the future, a good job for me back in Manhattan, children, eventually a home in the Jersey or Connecticut suburbs.

Life seemed to fall nicely into place, and with our summer earnings, and promises to Dot that we'd marry on her verandah the following spring, if all went well over the winter, we moved back to New York. I took the first job offer that came to me and, lying to Dot, we moved in together. Erin dedicated herself to becoming a flower child in Greenwich Village while I worked even harder to make myself indispensable at the Fortune 100 company to which I had arbitrarily elected to devote my life. We shared a shabby three-room walk-up on East 33rd, opposite Kipp's Bay, but after less than three months of blissful cohabitation, we discovered that, beyond lust, we had little in common and almost nothing to talk about. (Toward the end, through April and early May, we talked incessantly about the baby growing in Erin's womb, but that didn't really count.) She was nights, and now that I was a young executive who had to be in the office each morning at eight ready to do battle, I had become days. We rarely saw one another anymore.

Twice that spring I tried to break us up, but Dotty McConkle intervened, finally promising to leave her inn to me if I would marry her niece before she delivered. (Dot wasn't worried about Erin so much, she later said, but she hated to see a baby arrive in this world knowing it wasn't wanted.) All I had to do was see a lawyer and have my name changed officially to something that started with a big M small c, or with an O and an apostrophe or with the letters "F-i-t-z." McWilly, Dot suggested, seemed an appropriate enough choice. So I became Mr. McWilly and Erin and I married, although neither of us felt particularly good about it. We were married twice, first in July by a Delaware JP, then, in August, by Dot's brother Patrick, a gawkish priest over on a visit from the old sod, and a man on a perpetual bender. The second ceremony took place on the verandah of Ireland by the Sea, attended by Greenwich Village folk singers and girls in their grandmothers' dresses. Bill Kern, now at the Wharton School of Business, was an usher, and Brian Cox was my best man.

That evening, after the brief ceremony, I sat on the verandah with my two buddies while Erin was inside getting drunk with her friends as she packed for our honeymoon. Bill Kern, Brian Cox and I each had our own bottle of cheap champagne, which we pulled on as we gazed at the ocean and spoke of deep things. And somewhere along the line my name was changed once again; this time McWilly became not only my last name but my only name. We were talking, naturally enough, about how daffy my wife's aunt was, with her need to turn everything and everyone Irish, when suddenly Brian Cox stood and ordered me to kneel. He pretended to tap my shoulder with a sword and made the sign of the cross on my forehead with champagne. "McC

McShackleton McWilly," he said, "for as long as I've known you, you've been in need of a first name. And so now, by the power invested in me by the spirits in this bottle, I hereby dub you, firstly, middlely and lastly, McWilly."

"So be it!" shouted Bill Kern. "Long live McWilly."

All three of us fell asleep out there, with the ocean crashing nearby in the dark and while my new wife and unborn child, both also inebriated into unconsciousness, slept alone in the room Dot had given us.

Our daughter, Dorothy McWilly, whom from the start we called "Little Dot," was born in early November, in time to celebrate both Thanksgiving and Christmas at Ireland by the Sea. And seven months into the new year, on the anniversary of our first wedding, mother and daughter vanished into a steamy July night while I slept off a snoot full of single malt out on the verandah of the inn I hoped one day to own. I think Brian Cox was there for that event, too, but he doesn't remember.

My marriage was dissolved with unintended poetic symmetry by two divorces, and it would be nearly three years before I'd let myself think about love again. As part of my recovery, I became a dedicated womanizer, which can be quite therapeutic, especially if you love love but fear intimacy. I had a keen sixth sense that zeroed me in on females who wanted only a few months of uncomplicated fun-fucking; if there was one such woman in attendance at, say, Madison Square Garden or Lincoln Center, I would find her. So while everyone else my age was protesting our country's involvement in Southeast Asia, mourning the violent losses of first King, then Robert Kennedy, and learning how to play with recreational drugs, I was sport fucking. Dot kept in touch and urged me to hang on, using all her Irish wit and wisdom to keep my hopes alive, and reaffirming her pledge to will me her inn no matter how this all turned out. "Give her air to stretch her wings and she'll fly back to you," Dot would tell me once or twice a month. "Give her time. Give her time." And what if she never comes back, I'd ask. "I still want you here," Dot said, warming my heart. "You bring a spark to Ireland that has been missing since my husband died."

It was clear to me, though, in spite of Dot, that Erin McWilly, or whomever she happened to be by now, had no intention of coming back, and on the other side of the equation, it was unclear to me why

I would wish her back. (Had I still possessed the Libra Wolf, I doubt I'd have used its power, which I didn't really believe in, anyhow.) I had come to enjoy the life of the serious womanizer, although now and then, at three-thirty-three in the morning, I'd wonder how my daughter was doing, and I'd let myself miss her. And now and then I'd regret the loss of Carol Zeller, although not enough to try to win her back.

I only heard from Erin once, in a letter designed to hurt me and maybe to purge me from her mind. She was back to calling herself Erin Henry, at least for the purpose of writing to informed me that I was "a big nothing, a total shit with all the feelings of a cinder block."

"Be certain of this if nothing else," she told me, in her second sentence, "all the women you have ever loved agree with me."

She had changed our daughter's name and her own name so that I could never find them again, she said.

"I hate you, loath you and despise you for the way you used me and tried to change me and suppress me and prevent me from becoming what I was destined to be and also how you took away my youth and my potential and my heritage. I never want to see or hear from you or even think about you ever again."

That was how the first paragraph ended. The next paragraph began: "So, how's life been treating you?"

She'd taken the trouble, she informed me, to look up Carol Zeller in Penn's Woods, and then to travel to New Hampshire where she had tracked down Tonya Angione. She had always loved the story of Tonya's pursuit of me during my Fish days and had made me tell it several dozen times, often in embarrassing circumstances. Of course I had withheld the part about my father and Tonya's mother, so when Erin made reference to that sordid bit of business later in her letter, I knew she was telling the truth. Carol Zeller was still living with her mother, "who's some sort of doctor. They make weird sounds and cast spells. I told her you gave me her wolf charm instead of an engagement ring, and she said she wishes she never gave you Fat Duncan(???) because after I tossed the Libra Wolf off the verandah of Ireland into the sand, Fat Duncan was the only thing keeping her from zapping you. She and her mother, who both call you Gregor(???), have put a spell on you, I thought you'd like to know. They have asked fate to bring to you during this lifetime all that you deserve. Isn't that nice? You really should have stuck with her."

And Tonya Angione, Erin wrote, was "very, very, very happily married to a beautiful, gentle, sincere lawyer." (Was there a contradiction here somewhere?) She had three kids, the youngest, a boy named Billy, being only two months older than our Little Dot. "We have so much in common," Erin wrote. "The best thing to happen to both of us so far in life was getting rid of you. Tonya and I and all the kids sat around at night and talked about how much we hate you. Sometimes your half-sister, who is only eighteen, joins us and we really get the hate going."

I'd have shredded the letter then and there, or burned it, had it not been for Erin's closing paragraph.

"About now," she wrote, "you're probably saying to yourself, in wounded innocence, 'what in the world does this crazy lady think I did to her?' Well, I'll tell you. You fooled me. That's what you did. You made me think you were strong enough to take on life and that you also had feelings. You made me think you were kind and tough. You made me think you could see me. Then you turned out to be another selfish tit-sucking male beast."

She signed off: "Your X, Erin Henry."

Then came a "PS" followed by a "PS, PS."

The first PS said: "That's the last time I'll use that name."

The second PS said: "I hope you enjoy the inn when you get it. I hope the place falls down around your ears and kills you."

I smiled at the thought of Erin running around informing all the women who ever liked me that I had conned them. It hurt, of course, but it also let me know that in her own sick way she was still hooked on me, and had she provided a return address I'd have sent her twenty more names from my womanizing phase.

Anyhow, a year and a half after I was abandoned by my first wife, I consulted a New Jersey lawyer and initiated the complicated process of divorcing someone *in absentia*, whose name I no longer knew. That was divorce number one. And a year later Erin did the same, even though, unlike me, she could have easily tracked me down through her aunt, the way she had when she sent me her hateful letter.

In the months following Erin's letter, without thinking it had anything to do with my decisions, I stopped my womanizing and left the city. I moved alone up to Connecticut, to a rental on the beach in Westport, and I didn't see anyone for nearly a year, which gave me a wonderful new perspective on life and finally allowed me to fall in love again, this time with a degree of sanity. My second wife was "a country gal"—her phrase, not mine—from Virginia, uncomplicated by magic and almost entirely without guile. During our first five years together she conceived twice, but lost both babies in the first trimester, miscarrying in each case the day we learned our child's gender: both girls. After that, an operation necessary to save Gail's life made future pregnancies impossible and birth control unnecessary. That marriage lasted nearly 15 years, until a seductress named Glady stole me away. And by then Gail was just as glad to see me go because she had fallen in love with our tennis pro but lacked the cunning required to hide it or the selfishness necessary to act on it.

As New Year's Eve and my scheduled departure approached, it seemed proper that I say my good-byes to the important people I'd be leaving, and unlike Erin, Gail was reachable by phone since she and her tennis pro were living in my old house. So I dialed my old phone number, wondering what crimes poor sweet innocent Gail had committed in her last life to have deserved me in this one. Unfortunately, or perhaps not, I got an answering machine and after the long beep I left a message. I told Gail that she was the finest woman I'd ever known, then I hung up and decided I needed to tell Carol Zeller the same thing. I picked up my phone again, asked for an outside line and dialed information in Penn's Woods, PA. But no Zeller was listed there. And nobody named Angione had a listed phone in North Conway, New Hampshire, either.

I was not really surprised. It had been twenty six years, and, in spite of appearances, life did move on.

I dialed 1-609-IRELAND, and after some mechanical switching way off in the electronic void, the phone rang seven times. I could see it, one of those cumbersome black rotary models from yesteryear, squatting on the table in the lobby near the front desk, beside a Victorian love seat, and the other, on the sill of the big bay window in Dot's sitting room, with seven silver sea gulls suspended above it on invisible threads. The last time I'd called—what was it, five years ago now, ten?—Aunt Dot hadn't a clue as to what had become of Erin and my daughter, so odds were that nothing had changed. I reminded myself not to ask how she was, because for twenty years now, when asked that question, Dot always replied "Nearly dead."

A man, quite elderly from the sound of his voice, said "Ireland by the Sea," and those words, spoken in a slight brogue, transported me more than a quarter century into the past. I relived it all, and emerged from the reverie dazed and depressed.

"Hello. Hello," said the man on the phone. "Is anyone there?"

"Hello," I said, my voice shaky. "Is Dot McConkle available?"

"Ahhh, well, no. Not really. Who's this calling?"

"Tell her McWilly's on the phone."

"Oh, Mr. McWilly. Well, yes. That makes a difference, I suppose." He sighed. "There's a heap of bad news waiting here for you, Mr. McWilly. Hold on and I'll get someone."

There was a series of sharp thumps and the sound of footsteps on a bare wood floor. Maybe five minutes later a woman came on the line.

"Mr. McWilly?" she asked.

"Yes."

"Can I help you?"

"Well, I'd hoped to speak with Dot. I'm trying to find my ex-wife and my daughter."

"I see. Well ..."

"Is something wrong there?"

"Mr. McWilly, I'm afraid you'll have to wait and go through proper channels."

"Proper channels? I don't understand. Who is this?"

"I'm sorry," the woman said, and hung up.

I sat for an hour and looked at the wall of my cubby, on which the rent was paid for only another day, until the end of the year. Then I called Bill Kern to say goodbye, because I remembered that he wouldn't be on the train home tonight.

"How's it going?" he asked, distracted.

"Great. Remember the Fish?"

"Of course," he said. "Best damn years of my life. Listen, I got two calls on hold, one from someone who wants to sue me for five million and one from a guy who wants to settle a suit I've got going

against him for about the same."
"Patch them together and tell them to work it out," I said.
"Great idea. So, I guess I'll see you tomorrow night?"
"Goodbye, Bill."
"AMF, baby," he said, and hung up.

Adios Motherfucker to you, too, I said to myself, smiling vaguely. I stared at my phone for another half hour, without a single conscious thought passing through my brain.

What a life, I said to myself as I walked down Park Avenue toward Grand Central. From three different Connecticut houses, each more wonderful than the last, from two wives—Gail and Glady, as different as human beings of the same gender can be, but a bad trade in the end—and in a succession of ever more sorrowful "station" cars, I had spent my life commuting in and out of New York City to a job that had accomplished nothing. And now, with no fanfare, I was about to take my last train ride. I had worked for the same company for nearly twenty seven years, and for the best part of a quarter century I had commuted, on average, 234 days a year, for an estimated total of 15,600 hours on the choo choo, all to earn a living that I never got around to living. Why was it I had to go crazy before I could see how crazy that was?

With that question nagging at me, I snorted my way home with Jason and Cox.

Chapter Seven

My son's departure on the year's last day was an odd affair, since only I realized what a significant parting it was. The boy, eager to see his Gramps down in Greenwich, could hardly be bothered with my intense hugs and kisses.

"Goodbye, Ryan," I said, setting the boy on the ground.

"Let's get going, Mom," Ryan called, as he pulled at his mother's mink sleeve. "See ya, Dad."

"Happy New Year, Son," I said, my eyes filling.

Glady looked at me strangely as I turned away. It was nothing, really. She'd been looking at me that way several times a day for months now.

"Oh yeah. Happy New Year, Dad. Don't drink too much."

They drove off. I went to get my rope.

It wasn't in its Christmas box under the tree, where I'd left it, and it wasn't out in the garage with my chainsaw—a logical place to look, since Glady is compulsive about giving all things their proper home. ("The screwdriver and flashlight live in the far right hand drawer beyond the sink. The corkscrew and flipper live over nearer the stove.") I finally found my rope down in the playroom, where Ryan had used it to make a corral. It took me twenty minutes to untie the various chairs and table legs, and as I worked I found myself thinking again about Erin Henry, and then about the first job I'd had after college at The Fish, where I'd met Bill Kern.

I was moving in a trance, mechanically following the plan that had formed in my brain since October, because it was the one solid thing in my life. I didn't write a note. What I was doing was beyond reason, and I hadn't managed yet to explain myself, even after all the words I put on paper since my trip to Atlanta last October. The writing I brought home from Atlanta, and the pages I'd written in my cubby, were filed away among the business papers in my briefcase, and if one day anyone bothered to read what I'd written, then perhaps some sense might be made of my passing. At least this was what I told myself.

The attic was chilly and crowded with boxes of books and clothing and tables and chairs and chests and strange shapes under blankets and sheets and out-dated lamps and love-stained mattresses and outgrown toys and the equipment of Ryan's well-stocked infancy. It was a vast space under a high-peeked roof, only partially-floored with a five-foot-wide strip of boards running up the center and lit by three bare bulbs that hung from beams every twenty feet or so. I hadn't been up here since the end of the last holiday season, when I lugged the great boxes of ornaments and wreaths and twinkle lights and mangers and plastic holly back to their home under the rafters, and as I looked around for a suitable beam, high enough and situated so as to leave me visible from the stairs, I wondered, vaguely, who had lugged all that Christmas cheer down from here this year. It hadn't been me, that much I knew, and it didn't seem likely it would have been Glady. (I had come home one evening to find the place fully decorated, and while I had given it no thought at the time, now I wondered if perhaps Glady had paid someone. Or had she discovered, like Gail before her, the charms of our tennis pro. No, I thought. The golf pro was more Glady's type.)

I found a small stool decorated with moons and cows, with a hole in its center to aid in potty training, and, standing upon this flimsy piece of furniture, I tied the straight end of my rope over a thick structural beam that linked the front rafters to those in the rear of the house. I wasn't thinking anymore. I certainly wasn't letting myself think about Ryan, even though I was standing on the stool that taught him how to take a civilized shit. I slipped the noose around my neck, tightened it, and then, closing my eyes against the pain, as well as whatever horrors the hereafter might hold, but otherwise hesitating not one second, I stepped off into unsupported and, I hoped, quick oblivion. To insure I wouldn't change my mind, I kicked the stool away.

There before my eyes was a red and white '55 Corvette.

I didn't recognize it at first, and of course I couldn't begin to imagine why it was waiting for me on the other side. Then I realized that this was the car that had belonged to Bill Kern back in Michigan, which I'd first seen when we returned from our Fish tour. The car didn't move. It just sat there looking at me with its headlights. It was, I realized, watching me die. And here I'd been prepared to have my life flash before me.

In the first instant of my dying, after the Vet, I saw a shower of shooting colored lights that were at first large and slow but quickly became smaller and faster as the burning in my throat roared up through, under and around my ears and finally exploded in my brain. Vaguely, far away through the noise, I felt my legs start to kick as my feet reached involuntarily for something solid, and as hands, my own I suspected, clawed at the rope that slowly choked the life out of me. My throat was on fire. My head was roaring and pounding and brilliant colored lights were swarming like fire flies behind my eyelids, swimming against a pulsating maroon screen. And still the highlights of my life hadn't begun to flash. Or maybe I'd already done the highlights. Maybe that was what all my recent mooning about Carol and Erin and Gail and my days with The Fish had been about.

Tiny lights sparked across a darkening screen. My brain and lungs were trying to explode. I felt violent spasms move me and then I saw myself from a place beyond my body. I was a big brass pendulum. I was a rustler swinging from an old oak tree. I was a ghost balloon suspended from a bush in late October, thrashing and bobbing in the wind. I began to turn away from myself, but then, suddenly, I was back in my body, and beyond the roaring in my ears, beyond my burning need for air, beyond my exploding temples, I heard a cracking, splintering sound, which I took to be my neck breaking. The pain in my throat and lungs vanished. Air rushed in, only to be blasted out of me again. I seemed to be breathing, but it felt strange, like the way you breathe underwater in a dream. The fire flies were dispersing, and as they did, I became aware of a softness beneath me. Then after one last thought, there was nothing. My last thought was this:

Being dead feels a lot like going to sleep.

What a sight my wife found waiting for her when she returned from delivering Ryan to her parents house in Greenwich. In my imagination, I see her walk absently into the vast master bedroom, where I had not set foot, even as a visitor, for more than two months, to find me asleep on her king-sized bed, covered in plaster dust and surrounded by great chunks of ceiling. My Christmas rope, fastened around my throat, trails over the comforter and down onto the floor, still showing the twists and bends of the knot that failed to hold. No matter how you construct this picture, there can be little doubt about what has nearly happened, and yet the real horror and total selfishness of the event was not acknowledged between us, then or ever. I see this scene from Glady's point of view again and again, and even if my first response is to cringe with shame, it never fails to make me smile. At the time, though, I was only dimly conscious of my wife's startled intake of breath and then her absurd question:

"And just what is it you think you're doing?"

I opened my eyes and found her glaring down at me.

Her face was still red from the cold. In her left hand was an envelope, so I knew she had stopped at the mailbox. My third thought, after realizing I wasn't dead and that I had fallen through the attic floor, was to wonder if there was any mail for me. As if she read my mind, Glady tossed the envelope she was holding upon the bed.

"Here," she said. "I hope you don't think I'm going to clean up this mess."

"I'll do it," I said, sitting up and loosening the hangman's noose at my throat as I studied the envelope's imprinted return address. It was from the law firm of Asp, Brinkhoff and Bernbaum, of Ship Bottom, New Jersey.

"According to wishes made in her last will and testament," the letter began, "the late Dotty McConkle has bequeathed to you title to real properties described in deed 20576969 filed in the town of Harvey Cedars, County of Mammoth, State of New Jersey, and shown on plot map A426, including the structure presently known as "Ireland by the Sea," built on said property, as well as all furnishings and assets contained therein, possession to transfer to you on or after the first Saint Patrick's day subsequent to Ms. McConkle's demise."

It took a full minute for me to realize what the letter was telling me. And then all I could think to say was "I'll be damned," which I must have said a dozen times.

The plan that would lead to my salvation formed as I cleaned up after my fall through the ceiling, and with the instrument of my aborted death still dangling from my neck, I grabbed the bedside princess phone and punched out Bill Kern's number.

"Bill," I said, the moment I heard his voice. "I think I have an interesting proposition for you."

He must have heard something solid and serious in my voice because he didn't make a quip about the word "proposition," as normally he would have. "Oh?" he said. Just that, and he said it with serious interest, too.

Already things were different, I told myself. I was being taken seriously. And it felt great.

"Yeah. Listen. Did you mean it when you suggested the four of us should get into a little deal together, or were you just shooting off your mouth?"

"When it comes to deals, I never shoot off my mouth."

"Okay. Let me crunch some numbers and get some papers together. I want to start with you. If we hammer out the details, and if it still looks good, then we'll present my plan to Jason and Cox as a done deal."

"That's the only way to fly," he said. "So what is it?"

"I'm not going to tell you yet. But if it's what I think it is, it'll amount to a risk-free deal, at least for you three."

"Nothing's risk free. I learned that the hard way a bunch of times."

"Well, of course. But when you do a leveraged buy-out, don't you go in knowing the inventory and real estate can pretty much cover you?"

"In the best of all possible worlds," he said. "But those sweet deals are rare. In the good old days, you could pull off something like that, but not anymore."

"What I have is the next best thing. At least I think it is. We'll see. Let me do my homework and get back to you."

"Sounds good," he said. "See you tonight."

"Oh?" I asked. "What's tonight?"

He laughed. "Right!" he said. "What a joker." Then he hung up.

I went downstairs, whistling. I came up behind Glady and hugged her and kissed her neck. She pulled away, startled, and looked at me as if I'd gone mad.

"What are we doing tonight?" I asked, rummaging in the refrigerator for something cold to soothe my throat.

"Same as every year," she said, and turned back to the Yellow Pages.

"I may drive down to New Jersey."

"When?"

"Right now. Want to come?"

"It's New Year's Eve. We'll be going out in less than two hours. And you're not leaving this house until that mess in my room is cleaned up. I've been calling plasterers, but none of them will come out until next week."

"That's okay," I said. "I'll do it."

"You'll fix the ceiling?"

"Of course. Piece of cake."

"What's gotten into you today?"

"I don't know. I just love New Year's."

"Was there something interesting in your letter?"

"Not really," I said. "Just maybe my whole life."

The most complicated aspect of having survived my own death was talking my way back into my Manhattan rental space after the long New Year's weekend. The landlord had taken a deposit on my cubby from some other poor jerk who had lost his job but needed to keep up appearances. And of course my phone number had already been reassigned. It took a half hour of pleading and negotiating, and a hundred dollar bill, before the landlord let me have a table out in the hall. I wrangled with the phone company for the rest of the week, and finally managed to get my old number back.

Now I was ready to get to work, although of course I had no idea where to begin. People went to school for years to study Hotel and Restaurant management, and I was plunging into that risky world without even taking a book out of the library. I sat at my desk in the hall, people moving past behind me every few minutes, and I made lists, in no particular order, of things I'd need to do.

As the second week of my second life began, a woman I'd never seen before stepped up behind me and tapped my shoulder. She was tall, with dark hair, blue eyes, a freckled nose and a full mouth. And she seemed angry.

"Do you think you're better than everyone else in the world?" she asked, her voice trembling. Confrontation did not come easily, I could see. She was forcing herself to do this. And wasn't she going to feel like a fool, I thought, when she found out she had the wrong guy?

Her face was red and she looked as if she might cry. She was young, not far into her thirties, and she was conservatively dressed, a blazer worn over a blouse buttoned to her throat and a pleated skirt of modest length. Even so, there was a powerful sensuality here, probably radiating from the slightly musky aroma of her. And her figure was spectacular: long legs, full breasts, long neck. Clearly this was someone I should know.

"How would anyone sitting in a shit-hole like this be so self-deluded as to think he was better than everyone else?" I asked her pleasantly.

"Then who do you think you are?" Her words slashed at me, a powerful whisper formed in her upper throat. It must have hurt, too, judging from the way it made her eyes water.

What had I done to this woman? I wondered, suspecting suddenly that she might be someone I should remember.

"Actually," I told her, "now and then I think I'm a passenger on a big schooner that is mid-way through a stormy winter crossing of the North Atlantic. Other than that, I really haven't the slightest idea. Why do you ask?"

"Because for almost four months now I've done everything I could to get your attention, short of ripping off my clothes and flopping on your desk."

"You have?"

"Yes. I have. And you act as if I'm invisible. Do you have any idea how many men I turn down each week, just walking around Manhattan? Do you?"

"Quite a few, I'd imagine." She was gorgeous. How in the world had I missed her?

"Are you gay?"

"No."

"Happily married?"

"No. About to become unmarried, in fact." I told her, briefly, about Glady, including the fact that we've been in separate bedrooms for a couple of months, since that seemed immediately in my best interest. In response, she told me her name, which was Jill Rouse, and that this happened to be her last day of work. Otherwise, she said, she would never have found nerve enough to say anything to me. She'd taken a new job, she explained, without bothering to tell me what her old job had been; clearly she assumed I knew.

"Actually," she said, "I'll be working for peanuts for one of the premier marketing consultants in the travel and leisure industry. And when she gets through with me I'll be able to write my own ticket. I can't tell you how it turns me on. I thought I wanted to help people, you know, by becoming a therapist. So I worked the switchboard here and went to school nights. But I don't want to help people. I want to move people. I want to move great crowds of people with great credit lines on their Visa cards. I want to move them to enjoy themselves. I want to spend their money."

"Young lady," I said, standing and offering my hand, "you have just landed your first client. Why don't I buy you a drink and tell you about this little project I'm working on?"

Chapter Eight

Jill and I went by cab to a quiet pub in SoHo, where we ate spicy ribs and drank sangria by the pitcher. I told her all about the inn on the Jersey Shore I'd inherited and what I intended to do with it if I could persuade my three best friends to put up the funds. She warmed to the project from the start, and all the way up town to her apartment she spouted ideas designed to make Ireland irresistible to the affluent swinging singles of Manhattan and Philadelphia. She only stopped babbling when I kissed her.

"What's this?" she asked, gently fingering the red mark around my throat left by the rope Glady had given me for Christmas. I'd kept it covered since the last day of last year by wearing turtlenecks instead of ties, but Jill wasn't about to let me keep my turtleneck on while we made love.

"I had a near-death experience," I told her. "And do you know, I never once saw a wonderful golden light or a shimmering tunnel or anything like that. And the highlights of my life were never flashed before my eyes. I think I was cheated, don't you?"

"Was it an accident?"

"Not really. More like self-criticism."

"A suicide attempt?"

"You might call it that."

"Then why aren't you in a hospital?"

"Because I wasn't hurt," I said, pretending not to know what she meant. She began to cry. I'm not sure I ever had anyone cry over me like that before. At least not in my presence. So of course I asked her to marry me.

"Oh," she said. "I can't. Not this week."

"I can't either," I said. "Technically, I'm still married."

We both laughed, and then, through her tears, she told me that she really did have a boyfriend.

"It's in the process of ending," she said. "I told him I had these feelings for this guy I'd never spoken to and I couldn't give myself to him until I understood what they meant."

"So what do they mean?"

"I don't know yet. I need more research."

"Some things take longer than you think," I said.

Of the next five nights, including the weekend, I spent three with Jill and only twice made it home to Glady's guest room. If my wife knew, she was well beyond caring; I was entirely invisible to her now, and had been since long before I almost hanged myself. I held nothing back from Jill as she did her research—complete with one of those tiny tape recorders—and it felt wonderful. Without spin, without a secret agenda, I gave her the story of my life, from my South Philadelphia boyhood to the plunge through Glady's ceiling. She asked about my parents, my grandparents, my aunts and uncles and siblings, my first sexual experiences, my best sexual experiences. Within days she knew me better than anyone on earth.

"What a dreary bunch the Shackletons were," I found myself saying to her one night, as we lay sprawled naked on her bed, her thermostat cranked up all the way. "In spite of their laughter and blustery confidence they were really a bunch of sad sacks."

"Depressed?" she asked. "That runs in families."

"More like *disappointed*," I said, then explained how my parents, grandparents, aunts, uncles, and cousins had all aspired to membership in the American middle class, yet those who attained their goal, including my parents, treated their new status as a shameful affliction, or perhaps even some sort of banishment. Something in the past, some spore clinging to them from the old sod, I told her, seemed to turn success into forbidden fruit.

When my family established its foothold in this country, the century was still young enough for the ways to power to be uncluttered by laws and racial quotas and union regulations, and so my paternal grandfather, and then my father, became cops. "They weren't corrupt," I told Jill, "at least by the standards of their day, although now they'd be facing serious time for graft. But they were tough and they brought their physical authority home with them, where they ruled with their mean boozy tempers, their whipping belts and sometimes their fists."

"Tell me," she said, and touched my face in a way that made me want to cry.

The clan, I explained, settled near the Front Street docks, where they lived and bred in good-humored, well-concealed mistrust of the Germans, Swedes, Italians, and Afro-Americans who were drawn to the area in successive decades. And had it not been for marriage, my father would never have left South Philadelphia.

"Tell me," Jill said.

"My mother's father was a butcher who made it big and left my parents his shop. It was his money that paid for our move to Bryn Mawr, and that ruined my life and killed my father. He drank himself to death over the next fifteen years. Nobody ever called it suicide, but that is what it was. And with no children or husband left to care for, Mom shuffled off a few years later. And they both died without forgiving me or reclaiming me."

"For what?"

"For my betrayal of THE CHURCH, they would have said."

"The Church," snorted Jill, "is one of the most corrupt forces on earth. If I was the devil and I was going to pick a place to conceal myself and do my dirty work, I'd go for the Catholic Church, hands down."

"But religion was only the superficial reason," I said.

I had realized a few years after my parents were gone that their disdain had been only superficially related to the Pope's stand on divorce. Its deeper roots, never acknowledged, were embedded in my apparent success. And if I was right about this, then from their heavenly home my mother and father must certainly be proud of their blue-eyed boy these days.

Opening myself to Jill, being loved by her, listening to her, I began to think that I might be something more than a dick looking for a soft moist place to hide for a few minutes at a time. Each day I could feel myself come back to life a little, and I began to think I might pull off this new dream of mine.

The key to my dream for Ireland by the Sea was Bill Kern; once I had him committed, he and I would have no trouble bringing my other two friends on board. But Bill was nobody's fool. I'd have to have, as Jill put it, all my I's crossed and T's dotted before I dealt with him.

January's lunch with Kern, Cox and Sargent was so tense we decided that next year we'd skip both the last and first months. Cox was edgy because his contract was being renegotiated. Jason was depressed because the widow of a man who died on his table last fall was threatening a malpractice suit. Kern was preoccupied by some deal he had going on Shelter Island. And I was on edge because my future depended on these three distracted men. I wasn't ready to discuss my plans yet, because there were questions I wasn't prepared to answer, but I expected Bill Kern to press me at lunch in response to my New Year's Eve phone call and I wasn't sure how I'd both hold him off and sustain his interest. But there was no need to worry. We talked about the Hillary Clinton presidency and we tried to get piggy, but it was stale and we broke up without ordering coffee.

Getting Jill's ideas on marketing and advertising down on paper was, it turned out, frosting on the cake. The rest of what I needed arrived by mail as the last week of January began. The manila envelope was waiting for me at home in the same pile as the letter from my lawyer telling me that divorce papers had been served. Glady had instructed her attorney to have the documents served on my attorney, which was kind of her. In return, I had instructed my attorney to accept any settlement the other side offered. And in other news, the New Jersey appraiser I'd hired reported that a conservative estimate of Ireland's worth was two million dollars, a figure arrived at by placing as little value as possible on the building.

I was ready for Kern.

I called him the next day, and it took ten minutes for his secretary to track him down and patch us together. He was on Shelter Island again. I prided myself on my ability to reach Kern. He was, after all, a most important man. He bought and sold companies and pieces of real estate worth millions, a few dozen a year; on any given day, he might have three or four, or sometimes as many as eight, once-in-a-life-time deals going. I had no idea what he was doing out on Shelter Island, but I knew it had to be big for him to devote so much time to it.

"Bill," I said, when he came on. "McWilly."

"Hey, how's it going?"

"Do you remember your Fifty-five Vet?"

"Of course," he said, a little impatiently. "That's like asking do I remember my dick."

"So you do?"

That was a joke, but he didn't catch it.

"Of course I do. Why?"

"No reason," I said. "I was just thinking about it."

"Is that why you called?" More irritation.

"It was such a great car. What would a car like that be worth today, all fixed up?"

"Why in the world are you asking about my Vet?"

Before this, I'd had no idea how to begin. Certainly I had not intended to mention the car he had owned when I first met him. Now what was I going to say? *Well, see, I tried to hang myself a few weeks back and the first thing I saw when the rope squeezed off the blood supply to my brain was your Vet.*

"You bought that baby before you had a pot to piss in, and if you'd kept it, just think."

"That's true," he said, humoring me. "But of course now I could buy a fleet of them, all reconditioned and cherry."

"You probably could," I said. "Anyhow, listen, I've got the plans worked out for our little deal. When can we get together?"

"Any time, I guess. What little deal?"

That wasn't a good omen.

"Remember the idea I mentioned to you on New Year's Eve?"

"Oh, yeah. Of course. Well, vaguely."

"Great, well ..."

"Actually, no, I don't. I may have been in the bag. What was it again?"

"I didn't tell you."

"Then how the fuck was I supposed to remember it, McWilly? Jeeze. You sure have been acting weird lately. Are you going through the change, or what?"

I laughed. "All I told you was that I had an idea and that if it worked out at all, it'd be risk free."

"Right. Right. I remember that part. So what is it? I have people waiting."

"A resort spa on the Jersey shore."

"A spa?" He sounded dubious.

"Right."

"On the Jersey shore?" Dubiousness redoubled.

"For the affluent, sexy, youthful men and women of Philadelphia and the Big Apple."

"Lots of tricky questions with a deal like that," he said. "Where on the shore are we talking?"

"Weekending distance from Manhattan."

"Hmmm," he said. His interest had gone up, but not by much; he was a long way from reaching for his checkbook.

"And close enough to Atlantic City to make that one of the attractions. Particularly if we run boat tours down there."

"That's not a bad idea." It was the kind of thing you say when you don't have anything else positive to tell someone.

"I got appraisals. I got a marketing plan."

"Okay," he said, still not convinced. "I'll be glad to take a look." His voice had a weary, guarded quality, as if inside he was saying: Oh, shit. I hate it when friends try to hit you up with their stupid schemes.

"And I already own the place."

I tossed this last piece in casually, but I knew it was my second best clincher.

"Ahhh!" he said. "Now you're playing my tune. Tell me where I can get you later. Say, in an hour or two."

I gave him Jill's number, then went directly up to her place and let myself in with the key she'd given me. Bill called an hour after I got there.

"Can you get free tonight?" he asked, without bothering with pleasantries.

"Probably. Why?"

"Get over to the East Side Heliport by six. I'll have you picked up there. On your way, stop by a men's store and grab a change of clothes. Shit kicking stuff. Get a warm jacket. It's cold out here. And toiletries. I'll get you back for work in the morning, although you'll be late."

"Where am I going?"

"Into the 17th Century. See you in a few hours."

Jill went with me to buy a toothbrush and a disposable shaving set-up. At a men's store on Third we picked out a rust-colored cable-knit sweater, a down jacket, hiking boots and a pair of Levis, the first pair I'd owned in years.

After our shopping spree, we stopped for a drink, and over red wine Jill told me her boyfriend had found someone new and wanted to explore his feelings for this lady before he decided what to do about their relationship. It was the first time he'd come up in weeks.

"So what happened?" I asked her, wondering if this was good news or bad.

"I was surprised how jealous I was."

She seemed to be watching me for a reaction, but there was none, which surprised me and probably disappointed her.

"He's looking for his soulmate. I'm looking for my soul mate. He knows it's not me. I know it's not him. But we're great together and we both sometimes suspect that there's no such thing as soulmates anyhow."

"Tricky stuff," I said.

"How's anyone to know about anyone else?" she asked, but the question was aimed at the ceiling and at the world beyond, not at me. "Life's such a crap shoot."

"Isn't it," I said, feeling closer to her than I had to another human being (other than Ryan) in a long time.

After our drinks, we walked the rest of the way out to the river. Jill took my arm.

"So I guess now I just have to do my time in the pits," she said, "and wait to see what happens on my insides."

"I suppose that's right," I said.

"What about you?" she asked. "Are you okay?"

"Never better. Got my deal cooking. Feeling okay about my divorce, except for the boy."

"I mean about this. About us. About what I'm saying."

"Feeling okay? I'm sorry you're confused. Or upset."

"Sorry because of us? Because it changes things."

"I'm on my way somewhere else, Jill. I don't have anything solid to offer anyone, not even my own son. Maybe in another year, but not now."

"How long can you live at your house?"

"As long as I need to, I guess."

We were quiet while we waited with a half dozen others in the small heliport terminal. There was a noisy group of four men, three of them smokers, and two solitary men. Jill drew a lot of attention. She squeezed tight against me as we looked out across the landing pads to the water. After a few minutes she turned around so that we were face-to-face. She said she thought we were surrounded by the FBI. "Those are standard issue trench coats if I ever saw one," she whispered.

"It's you they're after," I told her.

"Not me, baby face. You're the dirty double-crossing traitor."

Her whisper was loud enough for everyone to hear, although if anyone did, he didn't let it show.

"Just think what we can do with the money," I said.

"What good is money if you're dead, which is what you'll be when Ivan finds out you double-crossed him. You'll be in hot borscht, I promise you."

I laughed, but she kept a straight face.

"Does this mean you won't be taking the helicopter with me?"

"And have you push me out over the ocean?"

Not a single expression changed, and not one pair of eyes darted our way. The intense conversation among the four in their cloud of smoke shifted focus from the Mets to the Giants.

A large helicopter arrived, the shuttle to Kennedy, and all but one of the men went outside and climbed aboard. Once the shuttle was gone, a man in a blue uniform asked the other man if he was Mr. McWilly. I identified myself, and the uniformed man said my helicopter was coming in now.

It looked like a tiny dragon fly after the helicopter we'd just seen.

"You sure you won't change your mind?" I asked, still role-playing, or at least so I thought.

"Go on," she said. "Just fly away. Fly away. Bye, bye."

"It's your last chance."

"If I'm not worth fighting for, and if money's more important to you than love, then I don't want you anyhow."

I shrugged. "Okay," I said, realizing, too late, that somewhere along the line we had stopped play acting.

There was no audience left, except for the man over at the counter, who was trying to trade in the ticket he had for one on the next shuttle to LaGuardia.

Jill hugged me and kissed me.

"Give me a week or two to get my head straight, okay?"

"Sure," I said.

"I have no idea what I'm doing anymore and it scares me to be so out of control."

"You got it," I said. "I'll call you before I leave for the shore."

"And be careful. Your friend Kern sounds like a rat."

"He is," I said, holding her. "But he's my rat."

Chapter Nine

The evening helicopter flight out of the city was a thrill. We lifted off slowly, the lighted cityscape becoming miniature. This was something I'd never done before, although I'd implied to my friends that commuting by helicopter was as commonplace an experience for me as it was for them. We went northeast, over the river and the lighted bridges, and soon we were speeding along the north shore of Long Island, the lights of Connecticut off to my left across the dark water of the Sound.

We landed on a large lawn surrounded by hedges, where I was met by a pretty young woman with a blond pony tail hanging out from above the adjustable strap of a red baseball cap. She wore a puffy, down jacket and jeans, and she looked to be Jill's age, maybe a year or two younger, which put her in her late twenties. She eyed the briefcase and the plastic shopping bag that was my luggage, smiled at the handsome young pilot, and led me over a frozen lawn to a red Jeep, which was a newer version of my station car, by a good ten years. She made me buckle myself in, and as we bounced over the lawn, she asked if I was a business associate of Mr. Kern's.

"Just an old friend," I said.

"It's best to be friends with a guy like that," she said. "That is, if you have to know him at all."

In less than a minute we turned from the lawn onto a narrow paved road, and after traveling only seconds more, we turned between twelve-foot high pillars toward a sprawling gray stone castle. All along the drive, lights shone down through the bare branches of evenly-spaced maple trees.

"Follow me," the young woman said, as in one motion she set the break and climbed from the Jeep. She took the stairs two at a time and threw open the great double front doors as if she owned the place.

She led me across a sumptuous, marble foyer to a richly paneled room where Bill Kern sat drinking brandy and smoking a big cigar with three other men. All four were dressed like campers. The young woman nodded as she held the door for me, smiled warmly at one of the men, then closed the door as Bill ticked off names that didn't stick in my brain.

"We'll wrap this up in a few more minutes," he said, and told me to make myself a drink.

I made a martini, then sat in a wing-back chair beside a floor-to-ceiling window. Through the lighted trees and the darkness beyond, I sensed the presence of the ocean. I liked that and I let myself dream a little about Ireland by the Sea.

There were land maps spread out on the coffee table in the center of the room, and every once in a while one of the men would lean and point to one of these maps to support something he was saying. They mentioned abutting property lines and easements, deeds and Royal Charters, friendly take-overs and hostile take-overs, leveraged buy-outs, bank officers who could be put into your pocket. Kern tossed out questions and acted as if the answers he was getting were inadequate. Even in my boredom I admired his approach, and promised myself that if I was able to launch this last dream of mine, I'd be more like Bill and less like me.

Kern was attentive to everything, leaving nothing to chance. For as long as I had known him, he had diligently controlled all that could be controlled, igniting into a blistering rage if the world, fate, or some hapless soul defied him. In contrast, I have watched life unfold around me and have made almost no attempt to be influential—yet somehow I always took it personally each time life let me down. In his stern way, Kern demanded and usually got the best from people, while I, at least since I was removed from the streets of my beloved Philadelphia, demanded little and usually ended up disappointed. Of course, the boy I once was could have eaten seven Bill Kerns for breakfast, even if the man I became had teeth only for smiling. Once I had been as dangerous and tough as an old barracuda, I thought, looking for the ocean, but a barracuda in Bryn Mawr was still just a fish out of water.

When the meeting broke up, Kern suggested we go out for dinner. We put on heavy jackets and took the Jeep that had brought me here. I asked Kern about the blonde. He said she was the daughter of one of the three men we had just left, the one who owned this Jeep and until last week the house we were now driving away from. They had been land poor, he explained, and he was allowing them to rent their home from him until they were able to find something else. In return, the girl's father was helping him with what he called his assault on Shelter Island.

Anxious as I was to make my presentation, I decided to wait until Bill gave me some sign. Over dinner we talked about women, of course. He'd just had a one-nighter with a gynecologist he was helping to buy a building in Manhattan where she could house her practice, her psychiatrist husband, his practice, their nanny and their two gifted children. He and this lady had been standing in an unfurnished room with a wall of windows facing the Hudson when she told him, flirtatiously, that she wasn't sure she should trust a man with such hungry eyes and such a silver tongue. "No woman's ever registered a complaint about my tongue before," Kern told me he had told her, a line which, according to him, had them frantically going down on each other right there on the bare hardwood.

I considered telling him about Jill, but realized in time that the story might have revealed my current employment status, or lack thereof. So I made up a relatively uninspired tale about meeting a black-haired, brown-eyed minx on my last business trip to Atlanta who was on the road selling group health insurance packages, and fucking her all night at the hotel where we both happened to be staying. It seemed to satisfy.

"So what's this big deal you wanted to talk about?" Kern asked, as we were heading back to the mansion.

"Oh, it's just a little idea I had. I'll tell you about it in the morning." Meaning, when we were both sober.

"What's wrong with now? We got nothing but time. Besides, in the morning I want to show you what I got going here."

"Well, it involves an investment of cash from you and Cox and

Jason, maybe a quarter of a million each, but ..."

"And not you?"

"No. I'm putting up my inn, which is appraised at two million, based mostly on the value of the land."

"Okay." He raced around the circular drive and stopped beside the steps. "Let's hear the rest over brandy."

We walked inside, and as Bill poured, I remembered that he had been to Ireland by the Sea years ago for my second wedding to Erin, so after we sat down beside the hearth, where someone had built a fire, I reminded him of that.

"Ah," he said. "That old place. So the old bird who made you change your name finally croaked, is that it?"

"Right. And fixed up cosmetically," I said, "the inn could be worth three million, easy. So your investment is a hundred percent backed up by real estate."

"Tell me how the deal's structured, how it pays out?"

"I'm open to any structure," I said, "but I thought we should start a company with assets of two million. I keep forty percent of the stock. You, Cox and Jason each get twenty percent of the stock for your quarter million. I turn Ireland by the Sea into a sort of Club Med of the North Atlantic. We use Cox in an ad campaign that draws from Philadelphia, Washington-Baltimore and New York. We offer boat shuttle service to Atlantic City, which I'm pretty sure we can get funding for from the casino owners, and on site we do all that swinging-singles, sports-rec-fitness stuff they do in the tropics. Only it's all just a couple of hours away, an easy weekend shot."

"Not bad," said Kern. He puffed on his cigar and watched the fire. "I like it. Especially since it's fully collateralized. Let's go over the numbers when we're sober."

"My thought exactly," I said, grinning inside at having so easily passed the first, and, as I thought then, highest hurdle.

Kern showed me to my room, which was next to his, and I heard him snoring before I had time to undress. Some time later he awakened me by crying out in his sleep. He yelped twice, in a voice that didn't sound like his, then he said something about a Lion. "Watch out for the lion," is what it sounded like, but the words were spit out so bitterly and rapidly I couldn't be sure. A moment later he muttered,

"Oh, man," and then something garbled. Whatever it was, he said the same thing three times, then he was quiet, breathing steadily and deeply, not quite snoring. I was almost back to sleep again when he very forcefully and clearly told someone to take his "big black fucking dog and stuff him."

Bill and I were out early the next morning, me a little hungover, Kern somehow fully energized and eager. We took covered mugs of coffee with us in the Jeep. The ocean came into view when we rounded a curve and after driving a little further, Bill stopped on the crest of a hill.

"Soon," he told me, "I'll own just about everything you can see from here. There are only a half-dozen hold-outs, and I've got leverage on four of them."

I was looking at perhaps twenty homes, most fairly large, some qualifying in anyone's book as mansions. I asked what he intended to do here, but he only smirked.

"Will it be a resort?" I asked.

"Nope. It'll all be for me. But I've already lost my hard-on for this deal. Look out there." He pointed across the water at a blob of land that was barely visible in the haze. "That's Gardiner's Bay," he told me. "And way off in the distance is Gardiner's Island, which looks almost exactly the way it did when the Indians owned it. It's been in the same family since sixteen thirty-nine."

"That's pretty amazing," I said, just for something to say.

"That's my new dream," Kern said. "I've got to find some way to get my hands on Gardiner's Island."

"Is it for sale?"

"Don't be a jerk. If it was for sale I'd either have bought it or I'd have decided I didn't want it. It's tied up in court at the moment. Descendants of the man who cheated the Indians to get the island are fighting over it. I'd give anything to get my hands on it. Everything. But it may not be possible."

Which was, I thought, precisely why he wanted it so badly.

Over the years, as a result of shrewd investing, leveraged buy-outs and divestitures performed with uncanny timing, Bill Kern had amassed a fortune. He controlled, the last I heard, nine companies, and his ever-expanding empire now included a cable network, a fledgling bio-genetic pharmaceutical company and what he referred to as a space-age refuse operation. He also owned an impressive chunk of Manhattan real estate, and he had holdings in Colorado, New Hampshire, and the U.S. Virgin Islands, where he was building a condominium complex. It seemed impossible that there was anything on earth he could still desire, and even more impossible that something he wanted was beyond his reach. But acquisition was his passion and the older and wealthier he became, the harder it was to find impossible goals.

As we drove back to the helicopter, I asked what he'd do with Gardiner's Island if he got his hands on it. He shrugged, as if he hadn't given the question any thought yet, which I knew wasn't true. We flew over and around Gardiner's Island for almost an hour. There were great stands of trees—oak five centuries old, according to Kern—open meadows, sandy beaches, limestone cliffs, what looked to be a dirt road winding and circling about, an old windmill, a mansion. Kern looked down like a child looking through the window of a pet store.

When we were back in the mansion on Shelter Island, in what Kern called his "war room," he told me he would do "everything and anything I can to get my hands on Gardiner's Island."

The girl who had driven me from the helicopter served us coffee. Bill laced his with brandy but I waved away the bottle.

"So," Kern said, when she was gone, "do you have paperwork on your Jersey deal?"

I went into my briefcase, then offered him the file folder I'd carefully prepared, but he waved it aside.

"Present it to me," he said, then lit a cigar.

Knowing he'd like the hard data first, I started with the appraiser's report, which included a sampling of what similar structures, similarly placed, had sold for over the last six months. I read him my projected costs of materials and labor necessary for the face-lift the inn would need; old pro that he was, he could tell that when in doubt I had estimated high, and he seemed to like that. I read him Jill's market analysis and earnings projections. I read him her marketing plan, or at least the summary I'd had her prepare, and the outline of the advertising campaign she'd suggested. I had worked out the Inn's staffing needs, and I saved this for last. Staffing, I told him, would include at least a half dozen women whose qualifications were the same as those required by Heffner for his now defunct hutches.

Kern, who held my fate in his hands but didn't know it, asked a question here and there, but only for clarification, and when I was through, he sat in silence for at least five minutes, looking at the ashes in the hearth and thoughtfully puffing on his cigar or sipping at his laced coffee. Then he got out his notebook computer, took my file folder, and began punching keys, his eyes scanning my sentences and columns like an eagle looking for his next rodent. Now and then he'd say, "Ahhh" or "Hmmm," but he came to no conclusions, other than to say I'd obviously done my homework.

The girl drove us out to the helicopter and Bill kissed her goodbye in a possessive way. The helicopter's engine was running. We crouched and ran to the door.

"So you really believe in this plan of yours?" Kern asked me, after we were airborne.

"Sure do," I said, ready to play my trump card. I knew the numbers had been persuasive. I also knew what Kern's one real objection would be. "I believe in this so much," I told him, "that if I can't get you guys to go in on it with me, I'll do it on my own, through a bank."

"You mean you'd mortgage the place?"

"Right. I'll do whatever it takes."

"That could be expensive."

"I know. And I'd rather do it with friends. I think it's a great opportunity for all of us, but if you don't think so, then I'll get the funds and do the project on my own."

"Uh huh," he said.

"And when I do get funded, I'll quit my job and go down there and make it happen."

"Quit your job? Is that what you said?"

"You heard me."

"You'd resign?"

"Someone's got to be on sight to run things. No way you can trust a deal like this to a hired hand."

"But quit your job. I mean, that's pretty amazing, McWilly. Are you really prepared to walk away from twenty seven years?"

"That's how confident I am," I said.

"Well, goddamn!"

After the helicopter deposited us back in Manhattan, as Kern was about to step into his limo, we shook hands in what seemed a more meaningful way than usual.

"I'll be in touch," Kern said.

I wandered west along 62nd for five blocks before I even considered a destination. I couldn't go to Jill's because she'd made it clear she needed some space for a couple of weeks. So I walked south for twenty blocks to Grand Central Station, where I had to wait for forty minutes for a milk run. The train got me home just after Ryan's school bus let him off.

"Hey, bud," I said.

"Hi Dad." He had lost his two upper front teeth and when he smiled he looked like a baby Dracula. "I'm not used to seeing you in daylight," he said, and laughed.

"Why? You see me on weekends."

"Not much. It's usually just getting light when you kiss me goodbye in the mornings and already dark when you sneak in at night. Mom says you'll be gone soon. Is that true?"

"Yes. We went over all that business about the divorce the other day, didn't we?"

"I know. I know. You both still love me and you're still going to be my parents. You just aren't going to be married together anymore. I got that part. I just don't know where you're going to be or whose going to take care of you."

"Ah, then have I got news for you. I'm going to live in a huge place right on the ocean, and when you come visit I'm going to teach you how to body surf and belly board. I'm going to fix the place up and it'll be like a hotel, only better."

"Mom told me about this. She said you were dreaming about the pipes again."

We talked a little more about the inn on the shore where I'd soon be moving, and it seemed to ease his mind that I'd be hiring a staff to cook for me. Then the mother of one of his buddies came to pick him up for a Cub Scout meeting. Glady was no where to be found; if I hadn't been home he'd have waited for his ride all alone.

Oddly enough, I found out through Glady that Bill Kern had decided to back me.

"I understand you and Bill have a little deal going," she said late that night, coming to the door of the guest room.

"Where did you hear that?"

"I was playing paddle with Nancy late this afternoon. She said you were going to start a company called OU Inc. What does OU stand for? And why do you look so surprised?"

"Because it's amazing how things happen."

Cox and Jason came in without any hesitation, Brian writing a check from his Shearson Money Management account at the lunch table, Jason bringing a bank check over to Kern's office after talking the deal over with his wife. And a week after my trip to Shelter Island, Kern presented me with two bound documents, one a partnership agreement and the other a document that gave life to our new corporation. We were in the bar at Chamberlain Country Club, having just finished a ladder paddle tennis match.

Skimming what Bill had prepared, I saw a few clauses I didn't like that pertained to the process by which voting partners could decide to liquidate company holdings, but Kern talked circles around my objections and ended up changing only a word or two. There was also a strange clause which said, in essence, that if a partner wanted to sell his shares, he had to be prepared to buy as many shares as he had to sell, and at the price he had asked. Only if that process resulted in a stalemate could he make an offering outside the company, and for a price set by an eighty one percent majority vote, which, when I looked, was how a majority was defined throughout.

"Doesn't this give leverage to the guy with the most cash?" I said.

"Exactly." He smiled and I saw shark teeth.

"And it seems to nullify any advantage my larger stock position gives me."

"Ah, well, I suppose, in a way it does, but ..."

"But nothing, Bill," I said, whispering so as not to make a scene. "This sucks! Don't try to fuck me like this, right out of the starting gate."

"It's business," Kern said. "Friendship ends with a business agreement. Sort of like marriage."

I gave myself a minute to think. Was this a hill to die on? "Make it sixty percent," I said.

"No deal."

"Then you're right. It's no deal. I'll go to a bank."

"You're crazy. After all I've done?"

"What you've done, you bastard, is use these documents to put yourself in the catbird seat. Drop it back to sixty percent or give Jason and Cox their money back."

"Sixty one percent."

"You just can't do this on level ground, can you? You'd go for the throat of your own grandmother."

"And have. What's wrong with sixty one percent? I mean, shit, I drop back twenty whole points, and you can't budge one single point."

"You are a total fuck, Bill. Tell you what. I'll make this happen with Jason and Cox and go to the bank for the rest. Get lost, okay?" I stood. Some members were glancing at me. This was not appropriate country club behavior.

"You'd drop me over one measly point?" Kern asked, spreading his arms, palms open, in injured innocence.

"Who do you think you're dealing with, Bill?" I leaned on the table and put my face in his. "You must think I'm one of the Indians who sold Manhattan Island to the Dutch." For some reason that seemed to make him wince. "At sixty percent, if I want to act I have to get one other vote, and that seems reasonable. But from sixty one percent up to eighty percent, I need two other votes. And at eighty one percent, I need a unanimous vote, which means you end up in control."

"Or Cox. Or Jason."

"But it's you. It would never be one of them."

He looked at me hard for maybe twenty seconds. Then he smiled.

"Good on you," he said. "I think this fucker may just fly." He leaned forward, slashed out the eighty one percent and wrote in sixty percent.

"That looks better," I said.

"I'll get these corrected and duplicated and we'll have ourselves a signing ceremony. One bottle of Dom each. I only wish my other deals would fall together as easy."

Book II
McSea

Chapter Ten

Barnegat Bay was choppy and a darker shade of gray than the sky. The causeway had been reduced by Jersey barriers to one narrow lane in either direction, and as I started over, Long Beach Island was only a dark presence ahead in the gray. Even so, this silhouette told me how much the island had changed since I was last here, back in 1968.

Ship Bottom's main intersection, where I turned north for Harvey Cedars, reminded me of a scene from some low-budget post-Apocalypse movie. The traffic lights had been turned off, the shops, motels, condos and cottages were closed and dark. And what few cars I saw were parked in driveways or by the road and gave the impression they might never move again. I passed a lifeless restaurant on the bay side, which was to my left, with a sign that claimed the place was "Open All Year 'Round." A bookstore's heavy wood marquee, in the shape of an open book, hung tilted over the sidewalk by one chain and clattered against the building in the wind. After a mile or so, a car turned onto the Boulevard perhaps ten blocks ahead and went north, toward Loveladies; I had to fight down the urge to catch up so we two wouldn't be so alone in this nuclear winter.

Starting in Harvey Cedars, Long Beach Island narrows to the north, and the houses there, especially on the ocean side, were bigger and stood only three or four deep between the beach and the Boulevard. Some of the older mansions and a few newer contemporary creations occupied entire beach-to-boulevard plots, their backs to the road, and since Ireland By The Sea was one of these, I had no trouble picking her out.

Alone among LBI's big hotels, Ireland had come through the storms of 1944 and 1962 entirely unharmed, and so people claimed the place was charmed—those who didn't believe it to be haunted or cursed—and often suggested the charm had something to do with the name bestowed upon the inn back in 1941 by the forever homesick Dotty McConkle. Built long before the town was a town, its seniority over its neighbors was apparent; it looked, I realized as I pulled into the large, gravel lot, exactly as it had more than a quarter century ago, which wasn't entirely good news.

A turret in the far front corner, which I could hardly see from this angle, a widow's walk in the center of the front or ocean wing, numerous bay and bow windows, and eight gables along both the front and back roofs, gave Ireland a vaguely Victorian look, but in truth the building was of more humble stock. She was constructed of two rectangular boxes, one set against the other to form a backward L, if looked at from above, the foot of which—the sole of the foot of which—faced the ocean.

Leaving my suitcases and duffel bags in my Jeep, I went up an alley of sand on the south side of the inn, between weathered red snow fences. The sand was soft and my heavy wing-tips seemed to sink a foot with each stride. As I went down over the crest of the beach toward the ocean—a beach that was narrower than I remembered—gusts of wind threw an icy salt spray in my face. To the south I saw a curve of cottages and to the north, larger beach homes, most with slabs of plywood blinding their easterly windows.

It was the first Saint Patty's day after the passing of Dotty McConkle, and in keeping with the letter of her will, I had come to Long Beach Island to take possession of Ireland—I loved saying it that way in my head. I had yet to go to the office of Asp, Brinkhoff and Bernbaum because the lawyers were off on their annual golfing excursion to Florida, which meant the place was not yet officially mine, which in turn meant it wasn't too late to drive away; I took some comfort in that.

My face burned with the cold as I pivoted to take my first good look at Ireland by the Sea. I saw the wide verandah on which I had married Erin Henry for a second time back in 1967. Above the verandah's sagging roof was a huge plank that had the inn's name woodburned on it, then a row of windows, all dark except for the one in the turret, then the steep roof of the front wing, with four gabled windows facing the sea. The turret was to my right, on the building's north front corner. The widow's walk in the center was a railed platform flanked by stone chimneys. I could not see the rear wing from where I stood, although I saw the tops of its two chimneys, which were made of red brick. On the ground floor, under the verandah roof, huge bay windows flanked the front door, both of them full of light.

The building was weather-beaten and time-worn, but she had been that way forever. Time, it seemed, had long ago done all the damage it could to Ireland by the Sea. Sandblasted and shabby as she was, though, a festive warmth radiated from the inn's glowing windows and a friendliness was broadcast by smoke whipping about her chimneys. On a blustery day like this, she was a glad sign of life along this beach.

"The old gal's lit like a Christmas tree," I said, feeling good about it until I remembered who was paying the bills. "Like a goddamn lighthouse." But the largeness, the stolid shabbiness of her! It would be less of a challenge, I thought, to tame the nation that shared this old inn's name.

Three fat gulls rode the wind directly above me, tilting their boomerang wings as if they were suspended there, like the silver-plated plastic birds on the mobile that used to hang in Dotty McConkle's bay window. Expecting the worst, I glanced up at the gulls, then out at the storm clouds on the horizon. I held my alpaca coat closed at the throat with my gloved left hand as wind-driven sand swirled around me in ghostly shadows. Razor sharp grains stung my face, already raw from the cold. The gulls cried down in mocking tones. The ocean hissed and boiled at my back, and all the while the lights of Ireland drank my blood. Good Christ on the cross, I thought, setting off. It'll take five million to give her the face-lift she needs. My heart felt as leaden as the sky as I trudged back toward Ireland, helped along this time by the wind. Five rotting wood steps took me onto Ireland's verandah.

"*Rebuild entire porch*," I said to myself, making a mental note to make a real note as soon as I unpacked. In four places there were holes where guests had probably stepped through the planks. "*Explore liability coverage.*"

Once again I turned to face the sea, standing in what may have been the very spot I had occupied when a drunken priest from Ireland—the only one present who didn't know Erin and I had eloped—

decreed that we were "ash one." My imagination wasn't good enough, sour as I was, to color the beach with sunshine, or people it with glad children and shapely women wearing almost nothing. An armada of clouds, gun-ship gray and, from the look of them, every bit as solid, was massing on the horizon, and, closer, the ocean frothed and fumed as if enraged by my presence.

Had I really been foolish enough to think I could waltz down here and in three months have Ireland spruced up and ready to entertain herds of affluent singles from Manhattan and Philadelphia and points between? Yes. In fact I had believed it so strongly I had talked my three best friends into the deal, to the tune of a quarter of a million each—pocket money for all, but still ... Unless I worked a miracle, those moneyed singles would take one look at Ireland and turn their BMWs for home, I told myself, giving my leg one last hard slap. It seemed hopelessly laughable now, this dream I had financed with my soul, as if that hadn't been mortgaged to the hilt long ago. "Spend the weekend in Ireland," I muttered, my voice lost in the hefty tumble of a wave. It was the slug line of an ad campaign scheduled to be launched in Manhattan in May, which my old friend Brian Cox would fly off to film next week on the island of Saint John. "SPEND THE WEEKEND IN IRELAND," I shouted, my voice small in the wind.

It may have been sadness, or it may have been fear—I would have sworn it was the chill wind—but tears began to roll; Sweet Jesus and Joseph, I thought, here I go again, drowning in my own salt.

"You must be Mr. McWilly," said someone behind me, and I glanced back to see an old man holding open the front door, head cocked as if trying to hear something in the wind. "I'm Jimmy McCaffery," he added, probably in response to my surprised look. "Welcome home, Sir."

I turned my face back to the ocean and knuckled away my tears. I coughed into my glove. "Good to know you, Jimmy," I mumbled, then abruptly walked past the old fellow and into the warm lobby of my inn.

"You must be frozen solid," Jimmy said.

"My luggage is in my car," I told him, and gestured with my left hand in the general direction of Ireland's lot. "It's the red Jeep. Bring it to my room right away, will you? And I'll take a whisky when you can."

McCaffery didn't say a word, but looked at me quizzically. Then he smiled. "Anything to help," he said, and set off, wheezing with the effort of each step as he shuffled across the lobby, down a half-flight of steps and then out the rear door, which banged shut in his wake.

The lobby looked the same. Hanging from the eighteen-foot ceiling was a huge dusty chandelier. It was round, with what seemed a thousand eggs of cut glass, each with dozens of facets to reflect the lights, had any of the bulbs worked, which they hadn't for years already, even when I was last here.

"Clean chandelier and replace bulbs. Rewire if necessary. If necessary, rewire entire inn."

Against the side wall to my left was the door to Dotty's suite and then the front desk, with its alcove of numbered mail boxes. To one side of the desk was a three-foot urn sprouting a plastic fern that had already accumulated several years of dust when I was last here, over a quarter of a century ago. Beyond that stood a love seat that looked as if it may have been recovered in velvet since I last saw it. The small velvet sofa, no doubt once purple but now simply pale, was flanked by tall wood end tables that were covered with magazines. The table on the right of the sofa, the one furthest from where I stood, held the inn's guest or "house" phone, a black rotary model. Directly in front of me, at the rear of the lobby, was a wide staircase that went to a landing with curtained windows, then broke left and right to the second floor. A closet and bathroom were located off the lobby, in the alcove to the left of the stairs, and tucked in to the right was a short hall that led to the rear wing and, before that, to four steps down to the rear exit and the gravel parking lot, with another stairwell heading from there into the basement. Closer to the front door, immediately to my right, there was an arch that opened into the parlor, furnished, with one notable exception, exactly as it was when I was here last. This was a front corner room, with a huge bay window that matched the one in Dotty's sitting room and offered a spectacular view of the ocean. The only thing new in there was a large screen projection television, which seemed like a visitor from outer space the way it faced off against a row of ancient white wicker chairs and love seats that had fat, floral print cushions on them. Further back along the right wall of the lobby, there was a blue door, then a door marked "staff only," which I knew led to the kitchen, then, set on an angle, the closed and curtained French doors of the dining room.

After a few minutes I heard McCaffery thudding up the back steps. "I'll be in the front suite," I called to him, then crossed to Dotty's door.

How many hundreds of hours had I spent in Dotty's sitting room, half listening to the old gal's stories about her people's struggle against "those bloody invading British bastards," while the rest of my mind plotted to get Erin naked out among the dunes. A song ran through my mind then, poorly recalled but nonetheless haunting. "*Oh, feather beds are soft, and painted rooms are bonnie, but I would trade them all, for my handsome, winsome . . .*"

Behind me, McCaffery stumbled into the lobby, dragging my two huge leather suitcases along the wood floor, sweeping away an ancient Persian runner then tripping over its accumulated folds.

"Careful there," I said, and pushed open the sitting room door. Surely I could get better help!

Jimmy McCaffery struggled past me, dropped the bags on the floor, then rested, hands on knees. His cheeks, ruddy with tiny veins, puffed like bellows.

"I'd be happy to help with the rest," he gasped, "but I'm afraid my carting and carrying days are done. I'll go pour us a whiskey."

"And maybe fetch some logs for this hearth," I suggested.

McCaffery, already a step into the lobby, stopped and spoke without turning. "Begging your pardon, Mr. McWilly," he said, "but would you be thinking I work for you?"

"Of course," I said. "What else would you be doing here?"

"Well, you see, Sir," he said, "Ireland is my home."

A stiletto-sharp instrument near my stomach, keenly attuned to signs of impending disaster, offered a tentative poke—nothing lethal, not yet—but the sharp point remained in place, poised for a killing thrust.

"Your home," I echoed, with little inflection. It wasn't a question or an exclamation. Who knows what it was? A moan, perhaps.

Having been twice divorced—and nearly thrice—and nearly murdered by my own hand, I didn't think life could do anything more to hurt me or even take me by surprise, since I expected my dreams to fall short or shatter. So this warning pain, this feeling that my stomach might be pinned to my spine any second now, confirmed a reality somehow deeper than dreams, and the confirmation lent a certain comforting smugness to my gathering concerns. "See," it said. "I was right."

"My room is right across the lobby there." McCaffery said, pointing to the blue door between the Staff Only door to the kitchen and the arched opening to the front parlor.

"So you rent, is that it? You have a lease."

"Not exactly. What I pay comes to sixty a week, plus a little something for the kitchen crew. Thanks be to Jesus, Joseph and Mary for Dotty McConkle, rest her generous soul. I say that every day, first thing upon opening my eyes. 'Thanks be to Jesus, Joseph and Mary,' is what I say, although lately I've been mentioning Dotty second, right after I thank the saints to be opening my eyes at all. 'Thanks be to Jesus, Joseph and Mary for Dotty McConkle,' I say, first or second thing. I say it looking up at the ceiling, where the cracks, by the way, are beginning to shape themselves into a map of County Cork."

"Ahhh," I said, as if that meant something to me.

"I used to be up on the third floor, in the back, where Shannon is now. Then I moved up front into the turret room on Three, before it became part of a larger suite, so Shannon could be next to Heather. That's as fine a room as Ireland has to offer, that one is, but once I hit seventy Dotty insisted I come down here so I wouldn't have to do the stairs. Sometimes I say it two, three times a day, and sometimes I say 'Thanks be to Jesus, Joseph, Mary and Saint Dot,' but I know she'd call that blasphemy. You must have known her very well, Mr. McWilly, to be left this place in her will, so you know what I mean when I talk about her generosity and all. But I don't think it's blasphemy, especially if I ..."

"Yes," I said, grasping this opportunity to interrupt the old man's sudden effulgence. "I knew Dotty well. But a long time ago."

"She was a pip. Why, she would—"

"—I know. I know. Now listen, Mr ..."

"McCaffery. Jimmy McCaffery."

"Mr. McCaffery. Do you have a place you could go? I mean, is there any place you could ..."

I let my voice trail off. Damn! I was doing it. I was softening what I really meant to say, which was precisely what I promised myself I wouldn't do this time. No more Mr. Nice Guy, I had pledged. I cleared my throat, as if my charm, in this case my false concern, could be dealt with like so much phlegm. "Mr. McCaffery," I said, "I expect you out of my inn by the end of the week, is that clear?"

"I expect you do," the old man said evenly, and shuffled off to his room.

I watched until the blue door closed behind him, then I softly shut Dot's door and crossed the sitting room to the bay window. McCaffery had not been exactly bowled over by my assertiveness, I thought, and warned myself not to expect an easy time evicting him.

See New Jersey lawyer who can handle eviction.

An antique ship's lantern, two feet wide and four feet high, its glass as thick as a myopic's lenses, hung in the center of the window. Dotty had called it the Wrecker's Lamp, and usually let it burn all night if any of her "clan" was not "safely ahome." How many nights, or early mornings, had Erin and I followed that lantern beam back to the inn, after falling asleep in the dunes? We were, we had joked, the Mooncussers of our day.

Beside the Wrecker's Lamp, the same old seven gulls hung at staggered altitudes on strings that were nearly invisible. They moved in spasms of flight, driven by gusts of cold wind that found their way through the uncaulked window lights. I looked at the ocean and before long I was thinking of Erin and marveling, as I brought her face to mind, at what my mother had called "the tenacity of the broken Irish heart."

For years now I had been haunted by regret, I realized as I stood there. Regret for the loss of her and for the loss of the time I'd wasted on her; regret that it had been my fate to have known her at all. Regret and accumulated failure, I thought. These were the measures of my life, and they had left me with the cynicism of a man with half again my years.

In a way it was funny, or at least it had its humorous side, humorous at least when I was in the right frame of mind, which from now on would probably be seldom to never. Lately, when I saw young lovers looking happy with whatever they were telling each other about the future, I had the urge to grab them and shake them and, like the embittered curmudgeon I was becoming, warn them of their folly; once I had lost the fight enough to mutter a few warning remarks in the general direction of a couple necking across from me on the train, and so I already knew, even at the tender age of fifty, the shame and humiliation of the ancient madman whose truth has gotten lost in the telling. Of course I was too young to be so bitter, but was that my fault? In reality, I had lived with my pain over Erin and my daughter longer than I had been alive when these wounds were inflicted. And I was beginning to understand now that my other women, rather than heal me, had only kept my wounds festering. So was I clinging to my pain? I supposed I was, yes. After all, it was all I had left of Erin. And what was an Irishman without his sadness and his whiskey to keep him warm?

How odd, though, to be here where my best memories of Erin were created. How odd and pitiful and empty and meaningless. Erin was gone! Gone and presumed remarried. Even Dotty had lost track of her and the child. Little Dot was what we had called my daughter, which was perhaps the main reason I had turned out to be Dotty McConkle's chief heir. That and the promise she'd made when I agreed to marry her niece.

"Excuse me," Jimmy McCaffery said, shuffling back through the door, which he opened without knocking. "You may have some interest in this document."

McCaffery handed over a folded piece of parchment which felt as if it might crumble to dust as I opened it. There was a blue filigree border, as on a stock certificate, and an official gold seal, officially stamped. I recognized it at once as a deed and, as my eyes took in what it said, I realized that this fragile piece of paper was a far greater threat to my dream than Ireland's sorry condition.

For the sum of one dollar, Dotty McConkle had sold "to one Jimmy McCaffery, for life, the room with the blueberry blue door on the north side of the lobby of the inn known as Ireland by the Sea." McCaffery was required to pay "reasonable" common charges, "to be set by management," and "reasonable fees for services and what meals he takes in the common room." Other than that, the room with the blueberry blue door was his, free and clear, until he died. The only bright spot was that once McCaffery shuffled off, ownership of the room reverted to the owner of Ireland, and was not to be part of McCaffery's estate.

"Of course I'll want my lawyers to go over this," I said, without emotion. "Do you mind if I hold onto it?"

"No offense, Sir, but yes, I do. Mind, that is." McCaffery's cheeks and forehead turned red as he spoke. "But I'll get to the mainland one of these days and have a copy made for you and your lawyers. Most folks only need one. Lawyer that is. You must be a very important fellow. So will you be needing more than one copy of my deed?"

"One copy will be fine. I'll drive you over tomorrow." Seemingly unruffled, I handed back the deed. "There you are, neighbor."

"I may as well tell you, since you'll find out soon enough," McCaffery said, "and getting bad news all at once is better than having it parceled out, I always say. Unless you disagree, in which case I'll hold my water until—"

"—Tell me what?" I closed my eyes, as if not being able to see the old man might make his incessant ramble more tolerable.

"I'm not the only one," McCaffery blurted.

"Not the only one what?" I did not want to believe what I knew was coming.

"There are other deeds like mine." He rattled the paper.

"Oh, God," I said, and turned away. Even for an old poker player, this was too much to take with a straight face. "How many?"

"At least six. Maybe seven or eight. Depending who you count and what was done official and what wasn't."

"Eight rooms out of, what is it, twenty-seven? Thirty-two? Is that what you're telling me? Dotty gave away eight rooms?"

"I think it's more like seven rooms, but yes, Sir, that's the long and the short of it."

"Why would she do something like that?"

"Who's to fathom the doings of a saint, Sir? I always ..."

"Who?" I asked, paying no attention to McCaffery.

"Not me, that's certain. I hardly understand my own comings and goings, let alone one so—"

"—No, no, you ..." I was going to call him a twit, a name I never used, but one Dotty McConkle had applied generously to everyone around her. I stopped myself in time. "Who owns the other rooms?" I asked, evenly.

"Oh. Well, let me see now. One small room under the eves up on Three belongs to Heather and Marty McMittleman. Then next to them is their adopted daughter Shannon McGideon, but I don't know if she has her own deed or not. Now Shannon, she's ..."

He went on, but I was hearing his voice through a swarm of buzzing flecks and so most of his words were lost. I felt my knees go rubbery. But if any of this showed, it didn't register on McCaffery, who kept right on talking.

"...they spread out a bit up there on Three I suppose when the inn is vacant. Heather and Shannon work the kitchen and the dining room to pay their keep, and Shannon, she's a pretty thing, goes to high school over the bridge—made the cheerleader's squad this year—but has trouble with her studies. I help her with her literature and history lessons when I can, but I'm afraid the sciences and mathematics have gotten beyond me. She's not at all like the rest of the young ones these days, although she's no wilting flower, either, if you take my meaning—why she can—"

"—Who else?" I managed, and found myself sitting on a ladder-back chair whose ragged caning poked at me.

The old fellow coughed into his hand. "Another room, a suite to be precise, south front corner of Two, belongs now to Bernie and Francine McCohen's son Cyrus, who is some kind of doctor or marriage counselor up in Trenton, and only uses his suite weekends in season." McCaffery startled me with a lecherous wink, but said no more about Cyrus McCohen. "Then there's the two-room suite in back here on One that belongs to Irma McCreedy, the famous lesbian trance-channeler, but she's no bother since she's always away on speaking tours or off promoting the most recent book her ghost writer has dashed off, if you'll pardon the pun. Although having no sooner said that, I have to call myself a liar, because don't you know Irma arrived here last week in a long white limo, with Justine, her secretary, who's also her ghost writer and companion and whose name when in residence is "McJustice." That was Dotty's idea. And they arrived looking like they intended to stay a while, too, and that generally means trouble for someone, if the past tells the future. There's a rumor McJustice was deeded a room of her own a long time ago, back in the late Sixties, although nobody knows that for sure. Then there's Miss McX up in the tower room on Two, although nobody's set eyes on her, as far as I know. I never have, and I've been here as long as anyone, except McJustice, if the rumors about her original deed are true. McX has the north front corner room directly under my old room, but I never heard so much as a thump or a creak out of her. And did I mention Bernie McCohen in the basement? He's a real go-getter, that one. A Harvard professor of something or another, until he got crazy obsessed with pollution and nuclear mass destruction and they let him go. He and his wife used to be up in the second-floor suite which now belongs to their son, but then inspiration hit him one afternoon when he was taking a walk with Irma, and he started his business and moved down to the basement so he could spread himself out without intruding on anyone. Turns out Bernie has the touch of Midas. His money arrives here by the sack full."

Famous lesbian. Harvard professor with the Midas touch. Trance-channeller. Miss McX, who I just knew was Erin, my long lost wife. (If so, that meant Little Dot was probably around here somewhere, too, living under some other name. Maybe she was Shannon the cheer-leader. My head spun as I felt excitement surge up from my stomach. The projectionist in my brain sent a picture of Dotty laughing like mad up among the clouds.)

"And you're sure these people all have deeds?"

"Of course I've never actually seen them," McCaffery admitted, "but I've always just assumed ... You look pale, Mr. McWilly. I'd best fetch us that whiskey now."

"Do that," I said, standing, turning back to the window, steadying myself on the frayed top of Dotty's favorite wing-back.

It was hopeless. I was stopped before I had begun. I saw an Olympic runner shot in the head by the starter's gun. If I challenged the deeds, Ireland would be tangled in court for years, which wouldn't do me any good. Maybe I could buy back the rooms, although that would cut into the money available to turn Ireland into the kind of place where people from civilization would want to spend their vacation. I was stuck. And it sounded as if Dotty had deeded away some of the best rooms in the Inn, too. An overwhelming urge to give up took hold of my body as I ducked under Dotty's flock of silver gulls. I had never felt anything like it in all my previous defeats. Even with the loss of my job, the loss of Erin and little Dot, even through all those dreary months of commuting with no place to go at the southern end of my train ride, except to my rented cubby, even when I had taken comfort in the idea of being dead, I never once felt this kind of enervating pain. It started in my legs, which suddenly felt too heavy for movement and too weak to support my body, then spread upward through my crotch, where my genitals instantly atrophied and turned numb, and into my guts, which became all at once hungry and sick. It was precisely how you feel when you've taken a knock-out punch, seconds before you wake up to find yourself being counted out by four or five refs, although I know that's not an example many people can relate to. In the next instant the feeling reached my heart and head, rendering both too leaden for feeling or thought. It took me far beyond tears, far beyond moaning. I saw my face in the window, and recognized the lifeless stare from somewhere; it was my father looking at me moments before he died, and it made me jump back a step.

Wind spattered the glass with a mist too gritty to be rain. Heavy clouds scudded past, wisps of gray breaking off to curl and melt upon the sand. The dune grass leaned away from the sea, hardly wavering under the wind's relentless force. Shutters rattled, and from all around came a harmony of groans, which I supposed was the wind, with its cargo of sand and sea, working its way inside Ireland through a thousand fissures. In the groans there were voices that pulled at my mind, which just then and perhaps from now on was pretty much up for grabs.

Jimmy McCaffery had the good sense, and the grace, to deliver my drink without a word, and then vanish across the hall to the room with the blueberry blue door. I stood beside the window, sipping Irish whiskey, neat—something I never do—while dusk claimed the beach; it wasn't until I was looking through the bottom of the cut crystal glass that I remembered the promise I'd made myself not to touch booze until Ireland was a success. The fact was, I realized, that I'd drunk very little since the day I hanged myself. Nothing like a touch of death to put some glue into a New Year's resolution.

"Tomorrow," I promised, then stretched out on Dotty's horsehair sofa and let my shoes thud upon the floor.

I heard a bell, probably calling people to dinner, but although I was hungry, I was too sleepy to move. Later I heard voices, and laughter. It sounded as if a television was playing, so I imagined that there were people gathered across the lobby in the parlor. I didn't really sleep but I didn't fully awaken either. Finally the inn settled down around me. I dreamed about being in a peanut-catching contest with a woman who looked like Jill, and also like Erin, (and of course Jill and Erin didn't look at all alike) and who could somehow toss a nut into the air and nab it with her mouth while hanging upside-down from the ceiling.

Chapter Eleven

I stood in my socks at the water's edge, squinting and trying to block the sun with my hand. The ocean was calm. There was no wind. The beach was empty. The world seemed oddly pure, renewed. The sun was a half-orb being pulled from the horizon like a tea bag. It was morning, I realized. Now if I could only remember how I came to be here. I was in my suit, my tie askew. I balanced on one foot, then the other, to peel off my socks.

The sun warmed my left cheek as I walked. Small waves rolled gently over the sand, leaving lines of foam. The air, I realized, was cold. The sand beneath my feet was colder still. Sandpipers searched in the seaweed and among pebbles and shells that rattled like bones as each wave withdrew.

Ever since Erin Henry brought me to this shore from Bryn Mawr, when I was not quite seventeen, I have believed I was a man of the sea, but other than walk beside it on occasion, feeling like a poet who has lost his way with words, I have never had much to do with oceans. I don't sail or wind-surf or fish or scuba dive. I don't collect shells or sun bathe. And I don't swim in oceans if there's much of a surf. Athletic and tough as I am, I become terrified in large breaking waves. Surfing, belly-boarding and body-surfing all look inviting as I walk and watch, but the few times I've screwed up courage enough to try, I've felt a panic that seemed powerful enough to drown me. Still, I truly loved the ocean and could walk beside it for hours, even on a chilly March morning like this. Regardless of how devastated I am, water that reaches the horizon always gives me hope.

My plans needed revision, I kept telling myself, trying to prime the creative process. To make Ireland the inn of my vision, I'd have to start with a bulldozer, and I had neither time or funds for that. I'd have to stick with the basic structure and the rustic look, which wasn't that bad. What did people expect when they came to the shore? Disney World? Rustic would have to do.

Better, I reminded myself, was the sworn enemy of *good enough*. I'd fix the cracks and the broken boards. I'd stain the wood and paint the trim and make the place look clean and well cared-for. I'd polish and rewire the chandelier, and replace its bulbs. I'd paint and paper and refurnish the rooms. New beds. Queens and kings. And new bureaus all around. I'd put in modern bathroom fixtures, too, and retile, because bathrooms were the measure of a place, at least to a woman, and it was women, not men, who determined if there'd be a return visit. Once the cosmetics were taken care of, I'd gut the basement and put in the work-out equipment and the spa and ...

I needed a list. Things were slipping through my mind and I couldn't afford to let any of them get away. But what about the deedholders? Or had that been a bad dream? What was that old guy's name? McCaffery. And something about a cheerleader and a lesbian trance-channeler and a guy from Harvard living in my basement.

Buy them out, I told myself. Give them enough to afford condos. Paint the blue door red. Or bump them off one by one. Seven little Indians, plus anyone McCaffery forgot to mention. Make the common charges so steep they beg to be bought out, dirt cheap. That had possibilities, especially if each deed was written the way McCaffery's was.

That's the spirit, I told myself, realizing that Bill Kern would have been proud of my thinking. I had a fight on my hands, and I had to handle it the way Bill would. Wasn't that what a man was built for? If there was nothing to overcome or vanquish or bag for the fire or pot, what good was he? Left with nothing to hunt or explore or fight for, his sole purpose became the manufacture and provision of sperm, and while that was nice work if you could get it, it was nothing to build your life around.

I let the sun warm my right side now, heading back.

Maybe I'd call a partners' meeting. Maybe I'd call off the filming of our ad. Or might that cause panic among my partners? I'd have to think carefully about each move I made. Meanwhile, today and over the weekend, I would explore the building and rough out my renovations, then begin to wheel and deal with these local yokel contractors while I waged war on the deedholders.

The inn was silent as I crossed the lobby. The gulls caught me and I stood for a time in the bay window, unaware of the rising sun or the sounds of people beginning to stir around me. The gulls circled slowly, banking their sharp-tipped wings, making the sun twinkle in my eyes. As before, there were groans all around me that seemed to conceal voices, but I was not conscious of human movement, and I would have sworn that I stood mesmerized by the gulls the whole time. But when I tuned in again, my bags, including those that had spent the night in the Jeep, were unpacked and I had showered and changed into my blue pin-striped suit.

The dining hall went silent when I appeared. I stood like a sleepwalker in the open French doors as the faces one by one turned back to their breakfast plates. A door flew open to my right, crashing against the near wall, and a tall, black-haired teenager emerged, balancing with one hand a huge tray of food. I stepped aside and was instantly lost in time.

This tall pretty girl was Erin and I was eighteen and we were here for another carefree summer. I watched her, feeling protective jealousy, as she delivered breakfast to a table full of men at the other end of the long room. Any second now she'd see me and smile the special loving smile that shared the secrets of the time we spent out among the rolling dunes.

Then a startling thought brought me back. Could this be my daughter? She looked nothing like me, but she shared traits with Erin, her long legs, her graceful neck, something in the way she thrust out her chin and squared her shoulders. The truth was, though, that for ten years now, all tall, pretty teenage girls have looked like Erin. And Little Dot, I realized, would have been much older than this girl. My daughter was, I decided after some quick calculations, twenty-six. Twenty-six! Sweet Jesus. Time certainly was relentless, wasn't she? He? It?

I was, I realized, sounding more like Dotty McConkle all the time. Expletives like *Sweet Jesus* and *Good Christ on the Cross* were springing to mind or even from my mouth now instead of *holy shit*, or just plain *Jesus* or *Christ*, which had served me well enough until now. By next week I'd have great sagging tits and I'd show a preference for kelly green knit shawls.

The dining hall was crowded, which was curious. Who were these people? Were they paying guests, or more owners like the old man I met last night? Had that been a bad dream, or was this? Maybe this whole experience was being sponsored by dying brain cells while I slowly strangled at the end of my Christmas rope. Men in drab, shabby jackets, jeans and mud-caked boots dominated the room with their smoke and noise. Two women ate together over against the back wall, in the corner, bending their heads in quiet conversation. Another woman sat across from Jimmy McCaffery—so he was real!—at a table beside a wall of casement windows. In all, there were twelve Formica-topped square tables, each with four chairs with molded plastic seats and metal legs. In the middle of each table there was a lace doily where an alabaster vase, holding a single plastic rose, stood in the midst of sugar, salt and pepper dispensers.

"Bring dining hall into the present century."

I headed for one of the vacant places at McCaffery's table, and as I approached, the woman with McCaffery looked up and smiled. She was in her late fourties, pale and trim; she had no doubt once been pretty. Red, or strawberry blonde hair was piled high, with brown roots, going gray. Her eyes were hooded and her mouth naturally downcast.

"'Morning," I said, pulling out a chair. "Mind if I ... ?"

"Hello, Mr. McWilly," the woman said. "Please."

The young waitress appeared at my side almost as soon as I was seated. Her eyes were so blue, in contrast to her ebony hair and brows, that they seemed to bore deep inside me. It felt as if she was memorizing me, or searching for something.

"Coffee, Mr. McWilly?" she asked, as she filled my water glass. If she was a relative of mine—why couldn't I get away from that idea?—she'd escaped any noticeable contribution from me, I thought as I nodded to her and noticed how beautiful she was. "And to eat?" she asked, with the most sensuous mouth I'd ever seen.

"Toast will be fine, thank you."

Her eyes sparkled, seductively I thought; this was no ordinary child. "You can't run your engine on toast alone," she said, dropping the line as she spun away.

That was exactly what Dot would have said, I thought, watching her go. She had quite a body on her. Shannon McGideon. What a handle! In ten seconds she was back with a stainless steel coffee pitcher.

"If you want coffee mornings, yes or no," she instructed, "leave your cup up or turn it down." She poured deftly as she spoke. "Saves me steps. We serve a mean poached egg." This last seemed charged with irony. She had to fight to hold back a smile, it seemed, and her eyes sparkled playfully.

"And a spicy bowl of milque toast, too, I'll bet," I said.

"What?" Her exquisite face wrinkled in confusion.

"Toast will be fine," I told her. I'd missed dinner, but my stomach was too tight to deal with food.

"Your loss," she told me, and turned away in response to someone's call.

As she crossed the room I saw how the men watched her, and I forced my eyes elsewhere. I heard a chorus of pig snorts, and I think I may have smiled.

"Isn't she a pip?" McCaffery whispered.

"Who are all these people, Jimmy?" I asked, and found that my stomach had steeled itself to receive another stiletto thrust.

"Workmen, most of them. Lots of building and repair work this time of year. A few natives. We're the only kitchen open up this way."

"And they're staying here? They're paying guests?"

"Some."

"Then the place is still functioning as an inn?"

"What did you expect?" asked the woman to my left.

I shrugged. "If anything I expected the place to be empty."

"As you can see, Mr. McWilly," she said, "nothing's changed since Dot left us. We're a self-sufficient little nation here. We all hoped you'd understand that. Dotty led us to believe–"

"But who runs things? The inn? And the restaurant?"

"I suppose that's me." She finished chewing a tiny bite of scrambled egg, then smiled, revealing large, perfect white teeth, as she set down her fork and extended her hand. "I'm Francine McCohen."

"Where are my manners?" McCaffery asked, rolling his eyes. Then he prattled on for two minutes about how easy it was to presume everyone here knew everyone else. Now and then Francine smiled and patted his liver-spotted hand.

"Dotty was ill for so long I just naturally took over to help out," Francine explained, when Jimmy paused for a breath. "But it's actually Heather McMittleman who does the work." She spread strawberry jam on a corner of golden toast. The color of the jam was darker red then her hair.

"Then what is it you do?" I asked.

She smiled at my bluntness. "Well, I suppose I do more or less what Dot did before she grew too weak and addled, which is mainly to oversee Heather's efforts, and Shannon's, and perhaps lend their work a certain, shall we say, dignity."

"A manager?" I asked, simply for something to say as my combative mind filed away the word "addled." Had Dotty McConkle been sane when she signed all those deeds? Then again, had she ever been sane? Had she been playing with a full deck, she certainly wouldn't have willed her beloved inn to me.

"I suppose you could call me a manager," agreed Francine. "Heather and Shannon are fully capable of running the place, but Heather's a little, well, *simple* might be the kindest word, and they're both such basic women that they need to feel the security of working under somebody's direction, which is all the same to me since I'm downstairs anyway, keeping my husband's business on track."

"And Heather and Shannon trade kitchen work for their room and board?"

Francine glanced suspiciously at Jimmy. "My goodness, if Heather heard you say such a thing you'd never talk her into staying."

Jimmy coughed. "If I led you to believe they were working to pay rent, I badly misspoke myself, Mr. McWilly, why ..."

Francine hushed him, leaned close and explained to me that Heather and her husband Marty owned their little room, free and clear, but because Marty was chronically unemployed, they had no money for common charges. Shannon used to live with them but once she hit fifteen, Dotty became worried that Marty McMittleman might not be strong enough to resist her, especially since he called Shannon his home-grown girl, and liked to brag about how he owned two beautiful women instead of just one.

"Anyhow," Francine said, "those two make Ireland hum. Of course, if Heather and Shannon are relatives, I'm Princess Di. But that, as they say, is none of my concern. Here at Ireland, we let anyone be what they need to be, for better or for worse. Heather helps me with the phone, the reservations, the money, and handles the kitchen, changes the linen, cleans, buys the supplies—"

"—Do we pay you?" I asked.

The swinging kitchen door banged against the wall again, and Shannon backed through bearing another over-loaded tray.

"Yeah, well, just because I like her," she shouted back through the closing door, "doesn't mean I'm queer for her."

There was a rumble of laughter from the men, and Shannon looked around and smiled. If she was embarrassed she managed not to change color as she delivered plates piled high with hot cakes or eggs and home fries and toast. I caught her glancing at me, twice, and the looks she sent my way were the kind men only get in their dreams, or in movies. It was easier to look at Shannon and enjoy her now that I was fairly certain she was not my daughter, although I still couldn't escape a new suspicion, that Erin, my first love, was slaving away behind those swinging kitchen doors.

Out of curiosity, or perhaps to get my mind off Erin, my attention drifted to the women in the corner against the back wall, one of whom attacked her plate as if the eggs had enraged her. Meanwhile her companion, a woman in her late fifties, or older, beamed at the pretty girl darting from table to table, and ate delicate bites from an egg perched high on a china cup.

"I take it one of those ladies is our famous lesbian," I whispered to McCaffery.

"Irma McCreedy," said Francine. "The one with the wolfish smile and the delicate spoon."

Francine's tone was curiously bitter, and although I looked again, I could see nothing wolfish in Irma's smile. She was attractive, with a square, pleasant face and soft, healthy-looking skin. Her companion, however, was long and bony, dark and homely, with wiry, unruly black hair and an angry sullen face. There was something immediately familiar about this woman, although I was certain I'd never met her before.

"The younger one who looks like she wishes her fork were a snow shovel is our Miss McJustice," said Francine. "She's forty-one but pretends to be older so as not to embarrass Irma, who has to be pushing sixty-five. They've been lovers for years. You can expect trouble from McJustice, and maybe from both of them, although Irma will hate you lovingly. Dot thought they were using black magic against her, and I can't say she was wrong."

"I see," I said, and wondered if maybe I should just call Ireland a freak show and sell tickets. "What's her problem?"

"At the moment, you."

"Me? What'd I do to her?"

"You arrived. Look at the two of them! Poor Shannon. Every morning she has to pass out food and pour juice and coffee to a room full of people who undress her with their eyes, all but me, that is, and Jimmy here."

"I have my days," McCaffery said.

I laughed, and noticed with some surprise how good it felt.

"I'm not dead yet," McCaffery added, pushing back his chair. He climbed awkwardly, painfully it seemed, to his feet. "Time's money," he commented. "And treasures abound."

After he had shuffled off, Francine explained that Jimmy McCaffery was a professional beachcomber. "Been at it nearly two decades now, from what I hear. Nearly broke his old heart when they outlawed metal detectors up by Old Barney. Jimmy thinks it's because they have a line on a second treasure chest left by Captain Kidd or the Mooncussers. Get him to tell you his stories some time."

"I'll do that," I said, even though I had no intention. I couldn't imagine the depth of boredom I'd need to feel before I turned to Jimmy McCaffery for stimulating conversation. Besides, I probably knew all the LBI legends from my time here before. At least I knew enough to know what "Mooncussers" were; I even knew that The Mooncusser had been this inn's name before Dot changed it to Ireland by the Sea.

Shannon was in constant motion, passing out food here, a bill there, taking money, making change, pouring coffee, shouting food orders through the kitchen door. She had a smile and something to say to everyone, and everyone seemed to like whatever she told them; at least she always left her customers smiling as she moved on to fulfill the next demand.

"When does she go to school?" I asked, looking at my watch.

Francine explained that Shannon usually found a ride to school with one of the regular men heading to work on the mainland. If not, Francine or Heather drove her over in O'*Woody*, the inn's station wagon.

Francine was an attractive woman, and there was an assertive strength in her that I liked, although she spoke as if hers was the last necessary word on any subject and that was already beginning to irritate me.

"Poor kid has several mothers but none at all," she commented, then paused long enough to sip the last of what looked to be grapefruit juice. "May I presume my services are no longer needed now that you've arrived, Mr. McWilly?" she asked.

"I think that's safe to say," I told her, "but let me take a day or two to get acquainted with everyone and see how things work. When I know what I'm talking about, we'll talk."

"I must say you haven't blown in like the storm we expected. Dot had us believing you'd arrive like a knight in shining armor, a regular King Arthur, and in a matter of hours have Ireland sparkling like a magic castle." She giggled.

"A magic castle, huh?" I found myself looking at Francine across what seemed a great distance. Suddenly I couldn't tell who she was or why I was sitting with her and yet in that instant I felt as if I had been sitting here without knowing it for a span more properly measured in years than minutes. I felt drunk. Maybe drugged. Was there something in the coffee? The water? The air? "I haven't made up my mind about anything," was the phrase I offered Francine McCohen, although my words seemed to wander like strays down an echoing tunnel, arriving at the other end in no particular order, until, unsure of what I had said or to what I was responding, I changed the subject and asked Francine what it was her husband did in my basement.

Francine laughed, although there was more mockery than mirth in the sound. Her lips, which suddenly became the center of my focus, were set in a vicious smile. Was the mockery aimed at her husband, as I first assumed, or at me?

"What does Bernie do? Well, among other things, he sells sea shells by the seashore."

I laughed at the phrase, and the way she said it, but I knew this exchange wasn't really happening. I laughed the way you laugh in a dream. Any minute now, I told myself, there'd be a scene shift to prove I was dreaming. I'd be back in my Manhattan cubby, killing time until lunch. Or I'd wake up dead in my attic. "I won't pretend I understand what that means," I admitted.

"Then I'll have to take you downstairs and show you. Sometime when Bernie's in an approachable mood. You have a great deal in common, it seems to me."

"I'll look forward to that," I said. "Also, when you get a chance, could you show me the inn's books?"

"Of course."

We stood and politely thanked each other for being such good breakfast company. Then Francine headed over to the table where Irma McCreedy and her friend, the brooding Miss McJustice, sat sipping coffee. They spoke, laughing now and then and glancing over at me when they thought I might not notice.

I floated towards the French doors that would take me into the lobby, but before I got there I had to peek into the kitchen. The woman at the stove, who turned to face me, was not yet out of her twenties, with dull brown hair, cut very short. If she was five-feet tall I'd have been surprised. Ache had left its mark on her face, along with worry and hard work. She had a faint mustache and arms with exceptionally thick, dark hair. No Erin here. That left Miss McX. Still, there was something vaguely familiar about Heather McMittleman. It was as if she and Shannon and even bony McJustice, all reminded me of others I had known.

Back in Dot's sitting room, I wrote my list of chores, knowing I was forgetting some of the important ideas I'd had last night and out on the beach this morning. I considered calling Bill Kern, but decided to put that off until I had a few positives to balance the bad news.

Maybe Heather was my daughter, I thought. She was more the age that Little Dot would have been by now, although with Little Dot's gene pool it didn't seem likely she'd have turned out so scrawny. Little Dot was eight months old the last time I saw her, so there was no way I'd recognize her now. Was this how parents felt a few decades after they've given up a child for adoption? Every stranger of the right gender and a certain age could be the one. Maybe Erin had changed our daughter's name from Dot to Heather; names, after all, were not permanent fixtures, especially here at Ireland.

I still felt drugged, and the sea gulls kept drawing me to them, so finally I went and stood by the window. My mind drifted between memories and fantasies involving Erin and Little Dot, and the next thing I knew they were ringing the bell for lunch.

I ate alone at a table by the window. Tomato soup and grilled cheese sandwiches, served by Heather McMittleman, who introduced herself to me with a cute little curtsey but could not meet my eyes. When she spoke she muttered as if trying not to show her teeth. There was absolutely nothing about her to support the notion that she was my daughter, and I was greatly relieved and at the same time disappointed because it confirmed that Little Dot was probably out of my life for good. Still, something about Heather fascinated me, almost as if I was on the brink of remembering her from another time. And twice, while I watched her serve lunch, I found myself toying with the notion of reincarnation, an idea I'd mocked since it had been introduced to me by my second wife after we'd lost our second daughter.

Lunch left me more dazed than I had been this morning, so I went into Dot's bedroom for a nap. The groaning of beams and pipes was louder back here, and as I drifted I was sure there were words concealed inside the sounds. The spread, the pillows, even the air had a smell that was Dot's, and the bed was far too soft. I'd have to somehow claim this space as my own, I promised myself, without knowing how. I dreamed I was hiding among boulders, with archers stalking me and shooting arrows at me each time I peered out. The archers were dressed like Robin Hood, but each wore a different colored outfit. Their arrows clattered against the rocks and I was more afraid of them than I had ever been of anything or anyone in my life.

Chapter Twelve

I pulled myself from sleep around three and changed into running shoes and sweats, thinking a long, brisk walk on the beach might blow away these druggy cobwebs. As I crossed the lobby, someone called my name.

"Welcome home, Mr. McWilly," said Irma McCreedy, sitting on the love seat and holding the house phone to her ear.

"Thank you," I said, and went to her. For a moment I was tempted not to know her name, for some reason needing to withhold whatever advantage or satisfaction recognition might give her. "Nice to meet you, Irma," I said, as we shook hands.

"We all hope you'll be exactly the medicine Ireland needs," she said.

"Francine said as much this morning," I told her.

"That was what Dotty promised. But Ireland has ways of testing people, if you didn't know." Her green eyes widened and I felt myself grow drowsy. I saw the archers again and felt besieged, the way I had in my dream. "Take care," Irma was saying when I tuned back in, "because Ireland will bring out your best and your worst, both the sinner and the saint hidden in you."

"I'm afraid I don't understand," I said.

"Then you have a lot ahead of you."

She smiled, lovingly and sympathetically, patted my hand, then put the phone back on its cradle and stood.

"And be careful whom you trust," she warned. "There are some who had hopes Ireland would fall to them."

She smiled, but sadly, then walked away; it was as if the mention of greed had made her heart weary. It occurred to me, watching her, that since I arrived here less than twenty-four hours ago I'd been almost constantly on the verge of *deja vu*. I had also felt, I realized, starting out on my walk, as if I was being constantly watched. It was good to breathe the cold salt air, and to stir my blood, so good in fact that after ten minutes I broke into a trot, then a run. I ran for perhaps two miles, until it seemed as if everything in me was making me run as far from Ireland as I could. I was hardly winded when I forced myself to stop; I could have kept going all the way to Cape May.

Going north was tougher, not because I was fighting a head wind, although that's how it felt, but because I was going back to Ireland. There was a strange energy in the place that sapped my strength and will and seemed to want to take over my mind, not that my mind was such valuable property or that there was much left to take. I moved slowly, amazed how far I'd run, and the moment Ireland came back into view, the feeling that I was being watched returned. The small hairs on my neck stirred. There was nobody in sight, no movement in any of the windows, but still there was this watching presence.

I felt lonely and a little scared, like a kid on his first day in a new school, and like that kid, I had a powerful urge to make sure all the people here liked me. But that, I warned myself, was precisely what I must not do. These people were my enemies, which of course left me more alone than I'd ever been. I sat on one of the rotting front steps, breathing hard and watching the sea, trying to let it soothe me. My insides were jumping and my temples throbbed. I was full of feelings that crashed against each other like powerful waves.

There was a thump below and in back of me, followed by a soft, whispered curse. I looked back between my legs into the dark space beneath the verandah and I thought I saw something move. I heard a scurrying sound and another thump.

"Hello," I said. "Is anyone there?"

There was no answer. I sat up, looked at the ocean for a few seconds, then quickly bent over, hoping to catch whoever had been under the verandah; I saw only shadows and sand.

Inside, as I headed for the shower, the plastic gulls called me to the window, and I paused there long enough to see a jogger run past. She was tall, blonde and attractive, at least from a distance, and I glanced at my watch. It was going on four thirty. Tomorrow I'd go for my run around this same time, and hope our paths crossed. I thought about Erin and about who Little Dot might be today as I looked out from boulders across an open plain to a forest where I knew there were archers hiding and waiting for a chance to shoot me. The dinner bell rang. I was in my pin-striped suit, my hair wet from a recent shower, yet I stood by the bay window as if I had never moved. The antique lantern was lit—it was the faint smell of burning kerosene that had brought me back just before I heard the bell. I had a clipboard in hand. It carried a pad that was a remnant from my former life. The pad said, "From the desk of C William Shackleton." And on it I had written the word "Wreckmaster."

I thought about Erin. I thought about Little Dot. And I wondered if I had really gone for that run.

Dinner was a fish fry, a feast that had become, I soon learned, one of Ireland's traditions. Platter after platter of a local favorite called tile fish arrived at the tables, and white wine by the jug. After dinner there was a movie on the big screen TV in the parlor. The movie crowd included Heather, Shannon, Jimmy, Francine, a shy young couple who had checked in around five, and three of the older construction workers. McJustice was there, but she left when I sat down. Some of the other guests had organized an excursion to Atlantic City for some serious drinking and gambling. The movie was *The Third Man*, starring Orson Wells, who, toward the end, delivers a wonderful diatribe about good and evil, peace and war, and the fringe benefits they generate. The Wells character, haughty and quite mad, asks us to compare the gifts made to the world by bellicose Italy's renaissance masters against the one contribution made by perpetually neutral Switzerland, the Cuckoo clock.

That movie, and an occasional run on the beach, were the only recreation I allowed myself. The rest of the time, when I wasn't sleeping or drifting off to places I didn't remember going, I was busy inspecting the inn's unoccupied rooms to see what each might need in the way of repair and refurnishing, then adding these to my growing list of projects and purchases. I paced distances in rooms and between doors with my feet, even though I had with me a perfectly adequate tape measure, and drew crude floor plans on the pages of the pad on my clipboard. Now and then, as I worked, I would encounter one of Ireland's residents, and while the greetings were always pleasant enough—except for the one time I ran into McJustice—I could tell these people regarded me with suspicion. And still, wherever I went I felt watched.

The dark back hall of the second floor had been, for many decades, a photo gallery, with enlarged and framed black-and-whites that told the history of both LBI and this building. The first showed two men, one of whom, in countenance and dress, looked like John Brown (of moldering in his grave fame) and the other brought Wyatt Earp to mind. They stood before a rather large cottage in their black frock coats and big-brimmed hats and untrimmed white beards. Each man held a double-barreled shotgun, at ready, and from the number of geese and ducks hanging on the porch rails and piled on the ground, these two had just attempted a species wipe-out.

I knew that Ireland by the Sea, without a name and less than a third its present size, had been built in the 1850s as a private hunting and fishing cottage. And from the stories Dotty McConkle used to tell, I knew that what had become of the building since then had been determined by war, even though for her first half century she stood virtually alone on the unpopulated northern quarter of this quiet barrier island "six miles at sea." A wealthy Philadelphia shipping family, the McMurtries, were the original owners. Since the early 1700s their chief imports had been spices, rum and slaves, and so Lincoln's Civil War proved bad for business. Three months before Abe was assassinated, David McMurtrie was forced to sell the family's LBI holdings, and the second owner, Jonas Greene, expanded the cottage into a twelve-room hotel, which he called The Harvest. World War I put The Harvest out of business, a year after Greene's daughter and her husband took out loans to add the rear wing, and the third owner, Caleb North, changed the name to Harvest Cedars before he went off to die in the trenches of Belgium. North's wife sold the hotel, but its ownership wasn't well recorded through the Roaring Twenties. Known from Washington to Manhattan as the Mooncusser, the place, foreshadowing Atlantic City, served the decadent wealthy of the era as a speakeasy, gambling parlor and, for a few months at the end, a whorehouse. During the thirties, ownership shifted to the First Federal Bank of Tuckertown, and the building was allowed to crumble nearly beyond repair.

The name Mooncusser seemed perfect to me, since men skulking in and out of the place probably preferred the obscurity of the dark. But the original Mooncussers had been more evil by far than any gambler, drinker or whoremonger, which is probably why Dot changed the name. Mooncussers were land pirates who used trickery to lure unwary captains onto the treacherous Barnegat shoals, then picked clean the wreckage that washed ashore. On dark or foggy nights, they would hang a ship's lantern, like the one in Dotty's bay window, around the neck of a horse or mule and create the look of a vessel riding at anchor by walking the animal slowly back and forth on the beach. Ships on an Atlantic crossing, bound for New York to the north or the Delaware harbor to the south, would try to hug this shore, but the captain who let himself be guided by the Wrecker's Light would find himself aground and breaking up in the vicious surf before he knew it. A few such incidents were all it took to start the legends, which explains why land pirates left their mark from Cape Cod—where the word Mooncusser was first used—down to Cape Hatteras, where their lantern trick inspired the town name of Nag's Head.

My favorite among the Mooncusser legends Dot used to tell involved a young woman whose father was head of a band of Barnegat Wreckers. Charming girl that she was, she enjoyed helping dear old dad strip the rings and watches and money belts off the corpses as they washed ashore, that is, until the night she rolled over a body and found herself looking into the face of her fiancé, who had gone to sea the year before. A ghost story was soon built on that legend, and over the years several dozen otherwise stable people had claimed encounters with this broken-hearted young woman, who was said to wander the beach wailing for her lost love. Indeed, when I was here last, there were some who claimed she made her home in the building I now owned, starting back in the days when it had been called The Mooncusser, and that it was her presence that attracted evil men to this shore.

A dozen grainy photographs captured the inn's history prior to the McConkle era, and these took me only a short way down the back corridor. Then came a series of pictures of 1920s-era baseball teams, with players in baggy flannel uniforms, with stubby, flimsy leather gloves on their hands and silly-looking striped hats that made their heads seem small. These photographs, interesting as they were, seemed out-of-place here, until the last of the sequence, which showed a team with the initials "BH" over the hearts of all the players. This photo was covered with illegible signatures, some of which said, "To Fred."

After the bank in Tuckertown took the Mooncusser, the inn was occupied only by beach bums and, according to legend, ghosts, until Fred McConkle bought the place in 1940. McConkle was a popular local boy, born on the southern tip of LBI in 1905 down in Holgate, and raised in Beach Haven. At sixteen he went to work as a parker at the largest indoor garage on the east coast, which was called Ostendorff's and was located at the corner of Pearl and Bay, not far from where Fred grew up. He would work there for twenty-four years, until the day he died, rising to the rank of Shift Manager by the time he married Dotty. But Fred's real work was baseball, and until he broke his throwing arm in 1941, three days after his wedding, McConkle played semi-pro ball in the stadium next to the garage. In that era, the Beach Haven team had entertained opponents such as the Bacharach Giants, the Black Yankees and an all Jewish club, coached by Grover Cleveland Alexander, called the House of David. That explained the pictures here in my hall.

Being gainfully employed, and a local baseball hero, Fred had no trouble talking the Tuckertown banking people into selling him the Mooncusser and loaning enough for a few structural and cosmetic repairs. And being a romantic Irishman whose best ideas came from a bottle, Fred put a ribbon around the partially refurbished Mooncusser and presented it to his fiancée as a surprise on the day of their wedding.

Dotty O'Brien had met Fred McConkle the summer before, when Dotty and her widow aunt passed through Beach Haven during a visit to America, and of course from the start her love for a tobacco-spewing, baseball-playing, goose-shooting parking lot attendant was opposed by her moderately well-to-do kin. She was disowned when she left Ireland to marry—although from time to time her mother sent her money on the sly—and she arrived from Dublin two days before her wedding, with only the possessions she could carry in her oversized twin carpetbags. And the only person at her wedding who wasn't a stranger, as she liked to tell it, was the man about to become her husband.

Over the next four years, Fred and Dotty poured their hearts, their life savings and all they could borrow into the inn, but World War II—with its blackout curtains and rationing stamps—and then Fred's death in a bizarre hunting accident at the age of forty, destroyed their dreams. After her husband was gone, Dotty McConkle surprised everyone by hanging on, but other than change the linen and sweep the rooms from time to time, she never tried to make a go of it. And I could understand why.

After a few days, my list of projects was so long that I lived on the verge of feeling hopelessly overwhelmed. I kept remembering one of the clichés used by overworked executives back at The Company, after the middle management purge had been under way for a few years and those of us who survived found ourselves doing the work of a half dozen. "How do you eat an elephant?" we'd ask one another, knowing what we meant. Then, in chorus, we'd answer: "One bite at a time." As I worked on my plans and lists, or called contractors from the Yellow Pages, I took frequent short breaks to look out the window at the ocean or to remember Erin. And I jogged on the beach around four o'clock each afternoon, hoping to meet the tall blonde.

One morning at breakfast, at the end of my first week, Francine McCohen handed me a manila file folder that was fat but not very heavy. "I thought I'd make myself useful," she said, and smiled. "Jimmy told me you didn't know about the deeds."

She had collected as many deeds as she could and had run down to the library to make copies. There were only five.

"They're all here?" I asked.

"All except for Miss McX's. She has the tower room on Two. I left a note, but it may be weeks before she responds, if ever."

"Because she's seldom here?"

Francine spread her arms and shrugged. "We never know."

"Well, I'll go knock, and if she doesn't answer, I'll use my master key and have a look."

"Can't," said Francine. "McX changed her lock the year she moved in. In fact, she has seven locks on her door now."

"Hmmm," I said, feeling challenged. "Well, thank you again for these." I shook the folder.

Shannon, who had become blatant about the crush she had on me, took our orders and Jimmy joined us in time to tell her what he wanted for breakfast. He spoke endlessly about a treasure chest he knew was waiting for the taking beneath the dunes up near Old Barney.

Later, as I was heading back to Dotty's sitting room, Francine caught up with me.

"I never got the chance to tell you what I wanted to say," she said, touching my arm as I opened the door to Dot's suite. "We're very fine folk here. At least most of us. We mean well. We all hope you'll feel the same. Mostly we hope life can go on as it always has."

"It may not be possible to keep things the same," I said. "See, I ..."

"We're like a family here, for better and for worse," she said. "And there's a sort of magic. I don't know how to tell you about us so you'll feel it. It's like getting stoned on grass. Remember? You're about the same age as me so you probably at least tried grass back in your twenties. At first you had to learn what to look for, remember?" I nodded, stupidly, because stoned was precisely how Ireland made me feel. "To tell you the truth," she went on, "it broke my heart when Bernie struck it rich. I liked it better when all we had was our place on the second floor."

"You no longer live here?"

"Not for three years," she said. "Bernie had Dotty change his deed to cover space in the basement. First we bought a four-unit condo down in Surf City, which we rent out for outrageous amounts during the season. Then we built a big modern place up with the millionaires of Loveladies, all very nice and clean, modern and booorrring, with way more room than two people need. Everything Bernie touches turns to gold, just the way Irma told him it would. People say he owns half of Long Beach Island, which isn't true. Just the five coin laundries and Cinemus Maximus One, Two and Three. Listen, I should get going."

"Thanks again for this," I said. "Jimmy thought there might be eight deeds."

"He's probably counting Shannon, who has a room but no deed, and McJustice, who claims to have a deed for Room Twenty-nine."

I nodded. "And I see that Heather's last name is McShea? I thought it was McMiddleman or McMittleman or something."

"She was McShea until she married Marty Mittleman and they became Heather and Marty McMittleman. Clear as mud, right?"

I smiled.

"There's one more thing I need to tell you," Francine said, taking a step closer. My heart sank. More bad news, I thought. "I think we're going to get along very well," she said. "I'd be pleased to be your assistant. Or to manage the place for you the way I did for Dot. I'm guessing a man like you has more important things to do. You'll find I'm very competent."

"I'm sure."

"And I'm wonderful in the sack."

I blinked. "I see," I said. "Then Bernie's a lucky man."

"Bernie hasn't been interested in that sort of activity since he was booted out of Harvard. Before you showed up, Mr. McWilly, Jimmy McCaffery was starting to look good. Do you find me attractive?"

"Of course. A bit forward, perhaps. But attractive."

She laughed. "You'll find," she said, "that Ireland has a strange effect on people. One thing it does is make you more aware of time, how slippery it is, and how precious. After a day or two, people start to let you know exactly what's on their minds."

"I've noticed."

"At first the bluntness is startling, but after a while you count on it. Also, people who can't stand it tend to leave, which is nice. So what do you say?"

I found myself smiling like an idiot, which Francine took as acceptance, but as she reached for me I stepped away.

"What?" she asked, disappointed and hurt.

"I appreciate the offer," I said, "but let me knock on your door, okay?"

"Fair enough," she said. "As long as you promise to tell me the moment you decide not to knock. I don't want to sit around anticipating what's never going to happen."

"Deal," I said, and of course the moment she was gone I began to wish I'd let her have her way with me.

I studied the deeds, although I was too distracted to find anything I might exploit, and after a few minutes I set the folder aside and turned to the Yellow Pages. I spent the rest of the morning calling carpenters and electricians and roofing companies and masons, and by lunch time I had six eager-sounding men lined up to drop by over the next few days to take measurements and prepare bids.

That afternoon a man from the phone company arrived and installed a pushbutton phone with two lines.

I spent a half hour telling Jill Rouse up in New York about Ireland and its residents and while she laughed and moaned in all the right places she wasn't really present somehow. When I asked if anything was wrong, she sighed and said, "Oh, nothing and everything. But how can I talk to you about it when you're half the problem?"

I laughed. "Then talk to me about the other half."

I asked if she wanted to come down to Ireland next weekend. She said she thought she needed more time on her own and I didn't press, even though I sensed she wanted me to. She invited me to stay in touch and wished me good luck with my inn.

Before it was time for my run, I made more calls to contractors, and at about three, while I held the phone hook down with my finger and tried to find the next number to dial, Brian Cox called me from St. Thomas. He and his crew had searched all day yesterday, he reported, until they had finally found a great place to film. It was out on Trunk Bay, and they were pretty sure if they set up the shot just right they wouldn't get palm trees or tropical islands in the background.

"That'd be good," I told him. "While you're at it, try not to make the ad look too luxurious, okay?"

"Oh? Does that mean I should worry about my investment?"

"Not really. It's just that we got rustic here. Not luxurious. And film on an overcast day so the aqua color is dampened down. And try for waves."

I really wanted to tell him to come home, but I didn't dare.

"The lab will handle the color," he explained. "These takes are just to introduce me. I come out of the water into a tight shot and I say, 'Hi! I'm Brian Cox and I've found a wonderful place to unwind right in my own back yard. Everything I need is right here.' On the word *here* I put my arm around this slinky string bikini and pull her against my side. 'Sun. Ocean. Sports. Great things to eat.' Right then the second string bikini snuggles into my other side. Get it? We three walk up the beach, and while I say more about all there is to do they'll cut in with the sports shots and the schmaltz with couples dining by candle light and strolling in the sunset. Then, as I stretch out on a beach towel with three string bikinis kneeling around me, I say, 'You can have it all, and only an hour or two from home, at Ireland by the Sea'. Then the girls converge on me and there's giggling as we go to black. And in voiceover, but laughing as if I'm being wonderfully distracted, I say, 'Pamper yourself. Spend the weekend in Ireland. Ireland by the Sea, on the New Jersey seashore'."

He had already been to bed with one of the three models, he told me, and he intended to bed down all three by the end of the week. The trick would be getting them all in bed with him at once, but he was working on that. For old times sake, I gave him a half-hearted pig snort.

Chapter Thirteen

The morning after my talk with Brian Cox, Francine took me by the hand and led me down a wide, rickety stairwell into the basement. I had been avoiding the place, I realized then, the same way I had avoided the other rooms occupied by the deedholders. There were stone walls, metal columns, a monstrous furnace with a hydra of ducts and pipes, a cracked cement floor with decades of ground-in grime. We walked along a narrow hall with hooded lights suspended from floor joists every ten feet. I counted five doors, one at the far end and two on either side. Francine stopped at the first door and opened it for me.

Bernie McCohen turned out to be a burley man in his early to mid-sixties, with more hair on his arms than on his head. He came to attention behind a generous blonde-wood desk, the surface of which had been scared and gouged with initials and curse words. When his wife introduced us, he shook my hand with a crushing grip, and said all the appropriate things one says, but his hard brown eyes never seemed to rest anywhere long enough to focus. With his hairless dome, his wild eyes, and his huge grin, he looked like a manic Humpty Dumpty, and I hadn't been in the man's presence a full minute before I knew beyond doubt that Bernie McCohen was several bubbles shy of plumb.

Apart from the scarred desk, which looked to be a refugee from some public school long since sacrificed to the wrecking ball, and a couple of wood side-chairs, similarly defaced, the office was unfurnished. There was a gooseneck lamp which bathed the desk in stark white light and cast strange jagged shadows throughout the rest of the cell. Gray sunlight pushed in through a small, fly-specked window up near the ceiling, illuminating a tangle of electrical and telephone wiring and copper pipes.

"Sit, please, Mr. McWilly," said Francine. "Bernie, Mr. McWilly is Ireland's new owner. Remember I told you he was coming." She spoke to her husband the way nurses and relatives speak to the addled, the ancient or the very young.

"And Dotty?" McCohen asked, absently, as I sat and looked up at them like a child listening to his parents.

Bernie stood behind his desk, a hulking, twitching figure with hunched shoulders and hands and eyes that could not find peace. He tried to focus, but other forces prevailed.

"Dead for months now, darling," said Francine.

"Oh, yes. Well, yes, I suppose."

"I'll leave you two to get acquainted," Francine said, patting my shoulder.

"Was it the sludge that got her?"

"No, honey. It was Alzheimer's. I'm sure you two have a great deal in common, so you boys enjoy yourselves now, okay?"

I wanted to protest her leaving, but watched her go without a word. McCohen sat down and began to talk about his business. He never spoke to me, exactly, but, addressing the desk, the pipes, the jar of pencils, he recited a speech which I assumed had been delivered many times to this same audience. His company, which he called McC Corp, made millions from his LBI holdings, and millions more, he claimed, by selling colorful pebbles through the mail to people who believed his stones possessed healing and spiritual powers. It was a belief, he said, created by testimonials Bernie paid some New York hack to write and perpetuated now by letters from satisfied customers whose lives had been turned around and whose bodies had been healed. Each week he paid close to a hundred thousand dollars to have these "letters" printed in various national magazines and tabloids. The trick was, he told me, to make the presentation look exactly like the other articles, except for the small print at the bottom which said "advertisement," as required by law.

"People see that word but they don't let themselves believe it," he said. "Not where it counts." He thumped his chest.

The pebbles he sold—the same as those I had seen on the beach—had been rounded and polished to a high sheen for having been tumbled against one another in the surf, although those with especially interesting colors or patterns were treated to extra time in one of Bernie McCohen's huge electric rock tumblers, four of which, now that he mentioned them, I could dimly hear rumbling away somewhere behind me. After that, the stones were soaked for a week in a liquid—"purely organic," Bernie assured me—produced by a formula he had developed while doing research at Harvard.

With perfect timing, Francine returned and the McCohens proudly showed me their "Rock Room," which was behind a door that had no doubt governed access to a bank vault in its former incarnation. In addition to the four noisy rock tumblers, there was a huge trough brimming with some acrid-smelling fluid and divided by screens into bins in which rocks from the beach, separated into color groups to which various body parts and their respective ills were supposed to be responsive, soaked in final preparation for mailing.

The Rock Room was located across the hall from Bernie's "executive office," and had mattresses, picked up at some dump from the looks of them, nailed to the walls and the ceiling to muffle the rumble of the tumblers. Further down the narrow hall, there was a large room where two women and a man, sad-looking folk who reminded me immediately of mushrooms, opened envelopes, typed mailing labels, wrapped jewelers boxes in which they had laid one of the magic pebbles upon a bed of snowy cotton, and piled those boxes ready for mailing upon plastic trays provided by the postal service. It was here, also, in the so-called "Fulfillment Room," at a small rolltop desk in the corner, that Francine logged in the checks and cash and kept the books and made sure each day that the number of boxes headed for the post office matched the amount of money headed for the bank.

Beside her desk was a bookcase that ran from floor to ceiling, and the volumes on the third shelf up, Francine told me, were Ireland's books. (She said she'd have one of the mushroom people transfer the contents of that shelf to Dot's sitting room, and I told her to hold off awhile until I knew what I was going to do.)

It also fell to her, she explained, in full hearing of her crew, to search the pockets and purses of the McC Corp employees, a ritual which took place in the room across the hall. All employees had to leave their street clothes in this locker area, and don pale green smocks with no hems or pockets. At day's end, Francine patted her people down as they went to change, and after that, they had to exit through a tall rectangular frame with rows of blinking lights—invented and constructed by Bernie—while Francine sat off to one side watching a television screen. Her employees believed this device would detect any stones, checks or cash they attempted to secrete, even in body cavities; of course it did nothing of the sort. It simply blinked and beeped.

As far as I could tell, the only thing Bernie did to make his business go was stroll the beach once a day with a burlap sack, gathering pebbles deposited by the shifting tide. But this, Bernie assured me, was no small matter. "Only I," he crowed, "possess the power to separate stones that heal from the ordinary. It's my gift. Lavinia told me so." Lavinia, I knew by now, was the spook who spoke through Irma McCreedy, the famous lesbian trance-channeler. The rest of the time Bernie devoted himself to what he called "my true calling."

"Which is?" I inquired, but Bernie wasn't tuned-in well enough to catch my question. He looked at his watch, a man worried about being late for something, grabbed my arm and, reaching for a burlap sack, invited me to the beach. I began to offer an excuse, but Francine cut me off, saying that her husband must have taken a shine to me since it was rare for him to invite anyone along when he went for the stones.

"You boys have fun," she called, settling at her rolltop.

"What's the fifth door?" I asked.

"The McC lab," said Francine. "Nobody goes in there except Bernie. Not even I can go there."

Bernie and I went out a side basement door at the end of the Fulfillment Room. It opened onto the public beach access, which was marked off on both sides by a sagging, wandering snow fence made of weathered red slats. With McCohen setting the pace, we walked rapidly over the shifting sand until we found more solid footing down beside the ocean.

Having recently been under water, the sand here was darker and decorated with uneven lines of foam and shards of clam shells. The air was cold, but the sun was warm. I was almost oblivious now to common sources of discomfort like hunger and cold, so I may as well have been munching popcorn and watching myself up on the big screen for all it mattered. Yet beneath my numbness, I felt happier than I had been in months. Go figure, I kept saying to myself, as I walked along beside my nutty new friend, striding hard to keep up. I would never have been able to explain what it was about Ireland that had caused something new and pleasant to be born inside me, but it was there. And I didn't want to examine it for fear of discovering that it was my own madness finally laying claim.

According to Bernie McCohen, the richer deposits of pebbles were found to the north, so we trudged with the sun and ocean to our right, and when we were out of sight of Ireland, McCohen began to speak in what I took to be a conspiratorial whisper.

"In the land of the rich and home of the greedy," he said, "we have shown an ingenuity for creating new and even more horrible ways to die. Isn't this so?"

"I suppose," I said, guardedly, because I had no idea what he was talking about or why he'd raised this subject.

"Do you realize that better than ninety percent of the scientists and inventors and engineers who have ever been alive in all of history are alive today?"

"So I've heard," I said. "Amazing, isn't it?"

"And that the vast majority have directly or indirectly, at one time or another, contributed their knowledge and labor to the invention or production of something that kills."

According to McCohen, our society had created a stupendous array of weaponry and war technology so that by now there was probably a bomb or a nuclear warhead or a canister of nerve gas or a tin of deadly germs for every ten square miles of American soil. And, he explained, if you considered also the barrels and barges and caskets of toxic waste and sludge, it was easy to see, in his words, "that we've got ourselves in a deadly pickle. We've got a smart bomb, a dumb bomb, a warhead or toxic waste canister, a zot of nerve gas, a sneeze worth of killer microbes for every man, woman and child in the nation," Bernie told me as we walked beside the waves. "We've got ground radiation, oil spills, EMFs, ozone breakdown, ice cap melt down, poisoned rivers, inedible snow, chewable air." He sighed as if the list had exhausted him before he could exhaust it. "The point is, there's more than enough death to go around, wouldn't you say?"

"What's an EMF?" I asked.

"Electromagnetic Field. Brain tumors in the making."

"None of this is exactly what you'd call hot news, McCohen," I said, startling myself. My alternative, I decided, would have been to say, "Bernie, I think you're nuts." And that was probably not hot news either.

McCohen said more, but my focus slipped because I caught sight of a familiar-looking spot where years before Erin Henry and I had done everything imaginable to one another. My mind fuzzed over and I was back with her on that ratty, checkerboard bedspread we opened under us to protect ourselves from the sand and the prickly dune grass. "Going for a walk," we called it, and no one ever asked us why we had to take her bedspread along.

"All this being the case," McCohen was saying when I came back, "I think we should insist on direct control over the things that can kill us. Have the bomb or warhead or can of gas or goo with our name on it located right in our own backyard. Give us the red buttons. Since the nation's weaponry and deadly by-products all belong to us, they're ours to control as we see fit, right? But when was the last time you were consulted on the placement of a missile launcher? Never, right? Did anyone ever ask you if you wanted all this death-dealing stuff around? No. They didn't even ask me, and I helped invent some of this shit. So now we want control over all the missile sites and dump sites, too, and all the support technology. We want our own little red buttons. And listen to this. We want the missile sites photographed and documented and mapped so that everyone knows precisely where each weapon is located. Right now you and I don't know any more about our defensive or offensive weapons than Saddam or the Soviets. Probably a lot less. So we're going to change all that by getting it all out in the open."

"Now that last part doesn't make sense," I said, as if the rest did. "First, there is no more Soviet Union."

"That's what you think."

"Okay. But even if some fragment of what used to be the USSR remains our enemy, or some Third World dictator develops a nuclear capacity to go along with his hatred, it sounds like what you're advocating here is global suicide."

"Ah. Now you've got it. Except I'm not *advocating* global suicide. That's there without help from me. I'm advocating getting the urge out in the open, waking up, noticing the gun we're holding to our head. Give us the red buttons. If you're going to poison my water, look me in the eye as you hand me the glass. If we're hell-bent on species suicide, let's at least be honest about it. Let's do it and leave our suicide note. What would we want to say to the galaxy just before we die?"

I laughed at this. "'We seemed like a good idea at the time?'" I suggested.

"Ha!" he said. "That's good. It's a mad world we live in and getting crazier by the minute."

"And you've decided to lead the way."

"Better to die in an assault aimed directly against us by someone we know," he went on, ignoring me, but flashing me a look. "Better to be killed by someone who hates us, personally, for irrational reasons we understand, than it is to be accidentally and anonymously vaporized in a fireball meant for somebody else. And if it is indifference and greed that does us in, better to be pureed or choked or incinerated or poisoned on purpose than to go with only a cosmic *oops* as our epitaph. Let the bastards responsible for producing all the toxic goo and sludge can it and ship it directly to me. Let them paste a picture of my smiling children and my golden retriever on the side of the can."

"Wait a minute!" I said. "Are you telling me you have kids and a dog living in my basement?"

"That was a figure of speech, McWilly. Christ! And of course death, anonymous or personal, is preferable to being among those unlucky few left to clean up the mess we're presently making of things, which is another reason to spread the targets and the deadly stuff of our progress around with greater equality. I mean, why should those people who happen to live near some plant that makes jets or warheads have all the luck?"

"You're quite mad. You know that don't you?"

"I am, aren't I?" he said, as if it was a wonderful new awareness and a compliment.

"I'm catching on now," I said, closing my eyes and shaking my head at such an overwhelming serving of insanity.

He looked at me strangely again, unable to determine, it seemed, if I was one of the rare creatures who understood him or just another person mocking him; had he asked, I would not have been able to say.

"Good," he said. "I thought you might. What I'm saying here is, let's take death out of the hands of the politicians and generals and big-wig corporate executives and give it back to the people." He raised his voice, and then, too late, his fist, an ungifted orator botching his big line. I imagined him at the lectern, with a hundred Harvard undergrads trying to decide if he was brilliant or mad, just as I was. In the presence of such madness, what was there to say? I pictured McCohen holding forth to the paying guests lured down here by Brian Cox's televised images of lusty living, and it was so absurd it made me laugh.

"Given our choice," he went on, ignoring me, "we opt for annihilation with a personal touch."

"I see," I said, regaining a straight face. For the first time since news of my inheritance reached me, I longed for my rented cubby back in Manhattan, and for the endless hours leading to lunch, and, after lunch, for those sluggish hours which accumulated through the afternoon until it was time for the train home. They had been, in hindsight, hours that had effortlessly blended into strings of uneventful days which, since they had counted for nothing, couldn't possibly be taken off my allotted time on earth. I longed for Jill. I glanced at McCohen one last time to see if the man was smiling. Maybe all this time he'd been putting me on, I thought, but he was intent, gone, and frighteningly sincere.

"That's another of our slogans," McCohen explained. "'Annihilation with a personal touch.' Ahhh! Here we go."

He knelt beside a moist, triangular-shaped depression in the sand that had been carved by two rivulets escaping back to the ocean from a pool where the water had been stranded when the tide went out. He began to scoop handfuls of rocks into his sack. They clattered deliciously.

"If the movement should spread," McCohen said, looking up at me as he worked, "and if I and my millions have anything to say about it, it certainly will, then in time each small town, each neighborhood, each rural county will have ..."

A solitary figure emerged from around a curve, walking slowly toward us on a serpentine path, head bent to one side, the flat disc of a metal detector sweeping the space before him, its long, chrome shaft glinting in the sun. Every now and then the man would stop, bend and scoop sand into a large silver cup that must have had some sort of screen on the bottom through which the sand slowly rained back upon the beach. I recognized Jimmy McCaffery, and, brightening, I was about to call out when McCohen silenced me.

"See those things on his head making him look like Mickey Mouse? Well those are earphones, and he's lost inside them. You might give him heart failure." McCohen stood and hoisted his sack over his shoulder. "Come along," he ordered.

I looked to the horizon, a vague line drawn by two shades of blue, and found myself wishing, with everything superstitious inside me, that I had never heard of Dotty McConkle or her niece, Erin Henry, a.k.a. Erin McClinch, a.k.a. Erin McWilly, a.k.a. Erin Whatever. My life still might not have turned out to be worth much, I thought, but at least I wouldn't be pressing against all this madness. Still, I was glad inside, and I realized that there was nowhere on Earth I'd rather be.

Chapter Fourteen

We passed McCaffery, and if the old man recognized us, even when he looked right at me, he did not let on.

"It's quite simple, really, as ideas of genius usually are," Bernie told me. "It's based on the philosophy that once you really get to know your fellow man you inevitably love or hate him, which pretty much boils down to the same thing. Nobody owns up to that, but it's true, mostly because when we get to know another human being well enough, we see those parts of him that we both love and hate in ourselves, the parts we'd just as soon obliterate, although of course it is far easier to obliterate them when we find them in our neighbor then it is to obliterate them in ourselves. My ad campaign is being mapped out even as we speak, at one of the biggest and best agencies on Madison Avenue, and once we hire the right rock star and pick the best TV programs to sponsor, we'll be ready to launch. Next year at this time we'll have a missile silo or a toxic waste container right in Ireland's front yard."

"Wouldn't that be wonderful," I said, unable to restrain myself, although if McCohen recognized my sarcasm he didn't respond to it. "What a tourist attraction that'll be. I can see the slug line now. 'Come end it all at Ireland By the Sea.'"

McCohen gave me another sidelong glance.

"We won't quietly shuffle off as an unfortunate sacrifice to someone's greed or madness. We refuse to be collateral damage or a statistical afterthought on some profit and loss statement or war map.

We'll go out making noise, making waves, making trouble. We want our little red buttons."

"How much is all this costing you?" I asked, deciding in that instant that, mad as he was, McCohen fully intended to squander his fortune on this insane quest.

Was there such a thing as a sane quest? Was it possible that all quests, all dreams, including my recent obsession with what Ireland could become, were built on at least a little madness? Madness of purpose and power enough to defeat the opposition, these seemed the essential tools of success.

"I've already sunk twenty million into the initial campaign," Bernie said. "Twenty million dollars worth of healing stones from the sea." He rattled his sack.

I laughed and choked at the same time.

"But that's just a beginning. A bucketful of pocket change, tossed against the tide. I'm putting everything I have into this because I see it as my chance to make a significant contribution to life aboard Spaceship Earth. And isn't that what it's all about? Making a difference. Once others join and start sending in their donations, we'll have billions to put behind the cause. We'll be unstoppable!"

I shuddered to think about the resort I could create with a tiny portion of what this lunatic intended to squander on his quest to put death under every nose. And I vowed to myself that from this day on, one of my missions would be to bring Bernie McCohen back to his senses—if he'd ever had any—and to enlist his help in the revitalization of Ireland. And the key to Bernie McCohen, I thought—if there was one—was Francine.

"I have a dream, too," I began, watching as once again Bernie knelt beside a pile of pebbles and began to scoop stones into his sack. "My dream is to turn Ireland into a resort."

"Oh?" McCohen looked up suspiciously.

Without giving it much thought, I decided to talk about my quest in an effort to support the idea, already proposed by Francine, that Bernie and I were kindred spirits, just a couple of little lunatics in the same pod, even though our imaginations were attached, for the time being anyway, to different balloons.

"It'll be a place where affluent young men and women from Philadelphia and Manhattan come to play," I explained, my hand sweeping across the ocean as if I could make my dream come true with a wave. "Ireland will be a rustic resort spa, complete with hot tubs and saunas and steam baths and exercise equipment and shapely instructors in skimpy outfits to teach fitness and wind surfing and water skiing and sunfish sailing and jet skiing and parasailing and plain old surfboard surfing and belly boarding and body surfing and sun tanning."

Of course there'd be lots of uninhibited sex, or the intimation there of, to be enjoyed by all the young single guests and, as a perk, the resort's four owners, although I didn't mention that part to McCohen. Ireland—or, more accurately, my dream of what she could become—represented my best and last chance to make something of a life that since I was sixteen had been on the wrong track. But I kept that to myself, too.

"I'll bring in a real chef. Maybe change the name back to the Mooncusser. By summer the place will be jumping."

"Mr. McWilly," said McCohen, standing to face me, his burgeoning sack over his shoulder. "Do you think the ocean is a hamburger?" The man's imperious tone left me stunned, but even if that hadn't been the case, I still wouldn't have known what to say to this *non sequitur*. "A hamburger to be packaged in a Styrofoam clam box with some clown's picture on it?"

"Of course not."

McCohen glared at me for a full ten seconds. "Good," he said, then bent back to his work. He indiscriminately scooped three rapid palmfuls of pebbles into his sack, which must have been quite heavy by now. "Because if you did I'd have to devote all my resources to opposing you, which would be a shame since that would set my mission back by several weeks."

"Don't worry," I told him. "I plan to proceed with taste."

"But wait!" McCohen said, standing to face me again, his face eager. "I have a great idea. What if we made signing up for my movement a requirement for every guest, with a donation of, say, fifty, no, a hundred dollars. Or better yet, we'll do a premium tie-in. Get a free night in Ireland for two with every two-hundred dollar donation! We'll make it a status thing, with pins to be worn by the elite so that your staff knows who deserves special treatment." With his free right hand he placed his next words in a line in front of him, at eye level. "'I faced annihilation at Ireland by the Sea.' It's a natural!"

I coughed into my hand and glanced toward the horizon again, wishing I was aboard the boat, a speck, really, that was about to vanish over that line. But in the second it took to wish myself somewhere else, something shifted inside me again and, standing outside myself, where I could only watch and listen in gathering alarm, I spoke again without calculation or guile.

"Your idea is brilliant, Mr. McCohen," I heard myself say, "but only as satire."

"I beg your ..."

"And unfortunately, I can't tell if that's the spirit behind it or not, and if not, then your idea is, in a word, bonkers."

"Oh?" McCohen said, bristling but trying not to sound defensive. "Please go on."

"It's shear madness. Total insanity. And for one simple reason and one not so simple reason."

"And just what would those two reasons be, Mr. Pimp for the Sea, Mr. Market-the-ocean-like-a-cheeseburger?"

"The not so simple reason is this, Mr. Only-I-can-pick-the-pebbles. Right now we've got one guy with the power in his fingertip to blow up the world. And even he has certain checks on his power, unless it's clear we're under attack. There used to be a guy like him in Russia, but not anymore. Now all the guys with red buttons are good guys. Or so we hope. And it so happens that most of these people got their jobs through some kind of political process that tested their ability to think rationally about the consequences of everything they say and do. So with the present system, haphazard as it is, the odds are still slightly in our favor. I say *slightly*, because of the possibility that some psychopath like Saddam will get himself a little red button, but still it's likely that no one nuts enough to press the button will get into a position to do it. Unless you have your way. With your plan, once you spread everything around the way you want, there's bound to be someone bonkers enough to do something crazy, so your plan virtually guarantees the destruction of the planet and everyone on it, and that, I suspect, is your secret intent. You're suicidal, but you can't face death on your own so you put together a plan to take everyone with you."

"Not true!" he said, his voice soaring by two octaves. "I only want more honesty. More old-fashioned democratic honesty, that's all."

"Maybe that's all you want. And maybe you want death. But some things can't be managed democratically." I was hot now, in stride, making it up as I went, which was the way I used to do business all the time when I was at my best. "Bad as it is, when it comes to managing all those deadly things on your list, the plan that's evolved over the last forty some years still tilts slightly in favor of survival."

McCohen's face had turned red as he listened to me, and now he seemed to draw-in way too much air for his body, large as it was. "And the simple reason?" he said, squeezing out the words.

"The simple reason is that nobody cares about toxic waste or any of that other stuff, as long as it's in someone else's back yard. Only a few people really understand the danger the planet's in. Why do you think, after millions of dollars worth of sophisticated marketing analysis, new products still get packaged in polyethylene and polypropylene? Things are the way they are because people don't believe in death, don't want to believe in it, and what they don't see can't hurt them. They're not sure what they *do* believe in, but they don't believe in death, which is why our politicians don't do as much as they should about the environmental issues. Politicians can pretty easily persuade the majority of us to go to war against some imaginary ill or some evil empire, and yet they don't bother to mass our resources against an enemy that is leading almost certainly to our destruction. And why? Because it won't play well in the voting booth, that's why."

McCohen, still holding his breath, seemed to be building up to a nuclear explosion of his own. But then, quite suddenly, all the air rushed out of him and he seemed to diminish in size.

"Fact is," I went on, "hardly anyone gives a thought any more to nuclear destruction. The cold war's over and most people realize we probably aren't going to blow ourselves off the planet, so they've gotten on with the more important business of greed and exploitation and the search for love and meaning. And the environment will take care of itself, as it always has."

I was employing the same spin-doctor skills I'd used in my prime as a public relations executive, and it felt wonderful. It had once been said of me that with the right budget, I could get the ASPCA to buy stock in U.S. Surgical. Poor Bernie didn't stand a chance. He looked to the ocean and a single tear ran down his cheek and shimmered in the sun.

"But look. It's not the end of the world," I said, softening a bit. "I mean, it was just a thought."

"Oh, what do you know?"

McCohen let his sack of pebbles fall from his shoulder, and I had to step lively to keep my toes from being crushed. Sensing movement behind him, McCohen turned. And when he did, it almost seemed he was surprised to find me standing there.

"Why didn't you show up before I put every cent I had into the ad campaign?" he asked. "I mean, what the hell am I supposed to do with ten thousand gross of little red buttons that say 'I want my little red button'?" He walked away muttering. He seemed to be heading back toward Ireland.

"Don't you want your pebbles?" I called, picking up the heavy burlap sack.

"What for?" He didn't turn.

"Listen," I said, rushing to catch up, bringing his sack. "We'll think of something you can do with those buttons. I'll bet there's a way to make them fit into my plans. Why not come in with me? Why not help me turn Ireland into the Club Med of the Jersey Shore?"

McCohen turned on me in sudden fury. His face went from pink to crimson as he grabbed my shirt and began to shout.

"You think you're so smart!" he said, foam accumulating at the corners of his mouth. "You think you're so creative and wise! Well let me tell you something, Mr. Hot Shot New York Business Executive. That idea of yours has been tried up and down this beach for years and it can't be done. You can't market the sea. On a tropical island, maybe, where you market the sun and the palms, but the ocean won't let herself be sold, not for any price, and better men than you have tried. You think I'm crazy. You're the crazy one."

"What about Atlantic City," I said. "That's just a few miles south of here."

"Oh sure. I should have known you'd have an answer. Guys like you always have answers for guys like me. I've dealt with you my entire life, and you always end up laughing at my ideas because you think I'm crazy and because the girls all like you because you're good at sports. But guess what? I'm not so crazy that I don't know right reason when it confronts me the way you confronted me just now. What you said confirms that I'm right but that my aim is faulty. So who's the crazy one, after all, Mr. Know-all-about-everything. Just throw Atlantic City in my face so you don't have to believe me. Break your heart. See if I care. But I'm telling you, friend, this is one ocean who won't let herself be exploited."

"What about your scam?" I shouted at him, our faces only two inches apart. Suddenly, below, beyond, above my rage, I was overcome with love for Bernie McCohen. There was something about the guy that let you—made you—say what came to mind, with all emotions attached. You just didn't pull your punches with McCohen, and that was so refreshing I found myself hoping this fight beside the rolling waves would last forever. "What the hell do you call this?" I shook the sack of pebbles.

"I honor the sea with what I do," McCohen said, softly. "I send its magical healing powers to those in need."

"Bull, McCohen. I watched you select your pebbles. I've seen bulldozers more selective than you."

"That part comes later," McCohen said, and turned toward Ireland again. "At least I don't make the ocean my whore."

We walked rapidly beside the crashing waves, side-by-side, our pace increasing every few yards because McCohen kept trying to storm off from me.

"So what about these other guys?" I asked him, shouting to be heard above the surf.

"Why should I tell you?" He stopped suddenly and turned on me again.

I took a moment to catch my breath. "Because if you don't, I'm not going to believe you. If you don't, I'll think you just said what you did because I popped your bubble."

McCohen sighed and looked past me at the ocean. I stood, waiting, staring down at his bald head, where I could see the dull reflection of the sun.

"Guy came down here with big ideas back in eighty-five," he told me. "Mort something-or-other. Sharp fellow from Newark. Put four million into an old place he bought for a million-and-a-half, and the night before he opened, as they were putting up the streamers and balloons and getting set for the first bunch of suckers they'd lured over from Philadelphia, the place got destroyed in a freak storm. One house south, one house north, everything was fine, but his place was torn apart board for board."

"Was he insured?"

"Sure. But it didn't do him any good."

"Why?"

"Because he was also dead. And there was another guy before him, this one down in Beach Haven. He had big plans like yours. Got them cooking, too. Had ads running in all kinds of slick magazines, a summer's worth of bookings. Went swimming one day and never came back. Ocean just swallowed him up. Like that." He snapped his fingers, but with bad timing.

"So it's a superstition, is that what you're telling me?"

"Call it what you want, McWilly, but the bottom line is that I wouldn't join you for all the money in the world. Crazy as I am, I'm not that crazy."

"That's saying a mouthful."

"Ireland'll get done in by a hurricane or tidal wave before the ocean lets you turn her into the whore you want her to be. She's survived all the worst storms so far, thanks to her magic charm, but you'll destroy all that, the way you're going."

I stared at McCohen for perhaps ten seconds, not knowing what to say, until finally he turned south again, and, moving along together more slowly now, we started for home.

After ten minutes, as Ireland came into view, we caught up with Jimmy McCaffery, who was still working the beach with his metal detector. We approached the old man from behind, and as we did, McCohen leaned close and suddenly lifted the round earphone from McCaffery's left ear.

"Time for lunch, Jimmy," he shouted.

Startled, McCaffery did a jump-step to his right, like a vaudevillian double-clicking his heels.

"Gonna kill him one of these days," McCohen said to me, grinning as he set off for Ireland across the dry, loose sand above the tide line.

"Find anything worthwhile?" I asked, as McCaffery patted his chest and caught his breath. For now at least I wanted to put distance between me and McCohen.

"Oh, just the usual. A couple of coins. A ring. Did you and Bernie have a pleasant talk?"

"Nothing out of the ordinary," I said, and smiled to myself.

It had been a long time since I felt this jazzed.

Chapter Fifteen

The first carpenter who came out to Ireland had hair like Jesus Christ's, but otherwise he was too muscular for the part, with too many hard edges. I walked him around the inn for two hours, and I don't think he spoke more than a dozen words, although he did treat me to an expansive repertoire of grunts. An hour after Jesus drove off in his ancient blue pickup, I was with a red-headed electrician who looked and sounded like a juvenile delinquent and who seemed to disapprove of everything he saw. These two men, and a half dozen others, promised estimates within twenty-four hours, but at the end of my second week at Ireland, I still hadn't heard from anyone.

I'd worked my way through the Yellow Pages' entire supply of electricians, plumbers, masons, wallpaperers, exterior and interior painters, contractors, handymen and companies that specialized in pools or kitchens or bathrooms or roofs. (And in the process, incidentally, I began to suspect that the materials these people worked with had shaped or distorted their characters; either that, or it was character that had cast the deciding vote when each guy chose his profession. Electricians were jumpy and easily irritated. Plumbers were moody but pleasant enough as long as I let them get where I wanted them to go in their own way. Carpenters were steadfast and unforgiving, but capable of artistic thought, and beneath all their macho bluster, quite warm and mellow. I told Jill my theory one night on the phone, just for something to say, and without missing a beat she wondered what that might suggest about proctologists?)

In spite of my frustrations, I remained tireless and undefeated as I sketched, measured, phoned, made lists, studied catalogues and wallpaper samples and paint chips. I took my meals alone in Dotty's sitting room—working as I ate—or in the dining room with Jimmy McCaffery or Francine or both. While I listened far more than I spoke, I said enough about my plans for the inn to get the word out to the population of Ireland. Except for McJustice, who played her role of resident witch with grim determination, the residents remained friendly enough, even as they learned of my plans. At most, they regarded me with what I took to be suspicion, and I could hardly blame them for that, since it was my desire to either drive them out or assign them to tiny unused corners of the inn and then alter their home beyond recognition. Manifest destiny. Indeed, as word spread, I expected them to rise up in opposition, but they never did.

Ever helpful in tiny ways, Francine worked hard to appear an ally, and implied that her husband was on my side too, "unlike the dikes," she said one evening over coffee. According to Francine, who leaned close and held my forearm when she delivered this news, Irma McCreedy and McJustice had for years attempted to employ their contacts with the spirit world to gain control of Dot's mind, and this inn, which for years had been one and the same. They'd used spiritual intimidation and mind control, Francine told me, "but fortunately it didn't work, because even in her decline old Dot was too gritty for them. That's why, in case you didn't notice, the dikes are your sworn enemies."

Francine was seldom this expressive. While eager to please and chipper by nature, she seemed frequently on edge, snappish, and I presumed it was because she was impatiently awaiting my knock. Meanwhile, Jimmy McCaffery babbled on about the pirate legends of Long Beach Island or the wreck of the *Powhatan* and the ghosts from that ship who had taken up residence at a certain hotel down in Surf City. He didn't appear to mind that no one paid attention; he talked, it seemed, more for his own amusement or perhaps to verify or catalogue the stuff that filled his mind during his solitary walks on the beach.

Having been over the entire island many times, Jimmy knew every nook and cove and swamp. He knew which buildings contained ghosts and which buildings were constructed from the beams and boards of LBI's many shipwrecks or from hotels long since dismantled or destroyed by storm or by the sea. He was a font of information, but he droned on so, it was impossible to sit with him without soon turning him into background noise.

Francine came to me one day as I was working and asked that I tell her exactly what I had said to her husband when we took our walk. Some new project had Bernie's blood boiling, she reported, but he wouldn't say what it was. "He's on the phone constantly," Francine said, "wheeling and dealing. And, best of all, he has stopped all his nonsense about warheads and canisters of nerve gas and killer germs and toxic waste."

"I told him he was bonkers," I said.

She shrugged. "I've been telling him that for years, but it's never done any good. There are even signs his libido has been jump-started."

"That's wonderful news," I said.

"Is it?"

"Yes," I said, and, without thinking, I found myself telling Francine that nothing was ever going to happen between us.

"All work and no play makes Jack a dull nerd," she said. "There's someone else, isn't there? That Jill person who calls."

"I don't know yet," I said. "Probably not, because for the first time in my life I'm not doing anything to make it happen. But possibly."

My calls to Jill had fallen off because I sensed her waiting for me to give up on this crazy dream and return to Manhattan and a "normal" job. It was nothing she said. Outwardly she was as supportive as ever, but there was a new tension between us, and a lack of warmth which I took as disapproval, or at least impatience. Still, each time I let more than forty-eight hours pass without leaving a greeting on her answering machine, she called to tell me, in hurt tones, how much she missed me. The last time we talked she asked if I was dating anyone, and I laughed until I was blind with tears. She didn't seem to think it was funny.

Estimates finally started to come in and I was being paged by Francine or Heather every half hour or so; after a day of this, to my delight, Francine suggested I consider a beeper. I hadn't dealt with these kinds of people in years, and I was surprised to find out how much harder inflation had hit this segment of the work force. One electrician wanted four thousand dollars just to fire up the chandelier. Jesus the carpenter, for "around twenty or thirty grand," would repair the verandah and the steps to the beach, but not the verandah's sagging roof. The same guy wanted thirty-five to forty thousand to put a civilized staircase down to the basement, and three times that to convert space down there into a spa, plumbing and tile work to be jobbed out and paid for separately. The only roofer to come in so far wanted nearly two hundred thousand. And nobody would up-date the bathrooms or take on my plans for the courtyard pool and Jacuzzi for less than three hundred grand. One contractor wanted a quarter of a million to bring Heather's kitchen into the 1990s, appliances extra.

"You must have more work than you can handle," I told him.

"Sorry," he said. "My hands are tied."

That seemed an odd comment, and five minutes after I had hung up on the kitchen man whose hands were tied I called him back and asked him to explain.

"I got nothing against you," he said. "It's just that I like my knee caps. And my wife and kids are kinda fond of eating and having a roof over their heads."

"Sweet Jesus," I said, my mind reeling. "What does *that* mean?"

"I've said too much already. Listen. It's nothing personal, okay? I've always loved that old place and wouldn't mind working on her. And if it was just me, well I don't care if you *do* turn her back into the Mooncusser."

Someone was working against me, making it so I couldn't get fair bids, and of course Bernie McCohen immediately came to mind. I went looking for him, but he wasn't in any of the unlocked rooms down in my basement and there was no response when I pounded on the locked doors of his Rock Room or his lab.

I thought it best to have some work underway, or at least some estimates and contracts in hand, before I made my first report to my partners. But the estimates I'd received so far would cause a panic. What would I do if Bill Kern got it into his head to write off the whole idea of Ireland by the Sea? He could easily sway my other two friends to vote with him, and the next I knew I'd be forced to sell. Considerable money had already been spent on the ad campaign, more than I could hope to raise and still keep my inn. So I put off calling Bill and spent even more time standing in the window watching the ocean and the silver gulls. I knew Kern would be angry because I'd waited so long to inform him of the deedholders, and, as usual, the anger I anticipated provoked an even stronger anger in me. Now, as I walked around Ireland or ran on the beach, I told Bill Kern off and cursed him for his failure to think beyond the bottom line, sometimes out loud. I knew what Kern would say; he'd demand to see the deeds, and when he got his hands on them, he'd find loopholes which he would instruct me to exploit. So by putting off my call, was I protecting the residents of Ireland from my pet shark? If so, that seemed strange, since they were the ones killing my dream. Kern would say I was going soft, but all I knew was that I now had as much to fear from my supposed ally as I did from my enemies. Still, sooner or later I had to call.

And so what? It would take Kern a week or two, I figured, to arrange a meeting with the entire partnership, and if in that time I could get some progress started, I'd be able to mix good news with the bad. The trouble was, Kern would want a summary over the phone, and he wasn't going to like what he heard. I had no problem with the idea of lying—for years I'd made my living bending the truth—but I knew if I lied now I'd have to go on lying until Ireland was a success or a failure. Liars, I realized then, are the loneliest people on the planet.

Each day that I put off calling Kern, I sank deeper into numbness. Now and then I'd shake off my paralysis enough to call a contractor in one of the inland towns, but these people rarely called me back and the few who did, refused to come all the way to Long Beach Island for an estimate. I knew I should do something to help myself, but I was only modestly handy and each time I thought to take on a project, the magnitude of all that had to be done overwhelmed me and sent me back to the bay window to watch the waves.

There is no way for me to tally the number of hours I wasted at Dotty's bay window during this phase, and I would not have mustered much of an argument had someone told me I'd been living at Ireland for years instead of weeks. From somewhere just beyond my awareness, Ireland spoke to me in whispered creaks and groans. And in the air there was a scent so faint that it vanished the moment I tried to identify what it might be or where I'd smelled it before. The silver-plated gulls went around and around and the sun glinted off each pair of wings as they floated through a certain point of brightness. Most mornings, if there was no cloud cover, the sun to the southeast spread a green-gold stain toward shore until it reached the broken lines of froth that topped the waves. There it turned to pure gold for the few seconds it took each wave to play out on the sand. And as each golden wave rolled in, I would hear Bernie McCohen telling me that the ocean could not be marketed like a cheeseburger in a Styrofoam clam box with some clown's picture on it. No matter how many times I remembered it, that line always made me smile and also filled me with a dread and an emptiness I'd never known before. It also reminded me how angry I was at Bernie for having sabotaged me, and it sent me out in search of him again. He must have known I was looking for him, because he had dropped out of sight; even Francine never knew where he might be.

The silver gulls slowed sometimes, but were never at rest. They sped forward, but they were never in a rush. And they took my mind away from all my concerns.

So far I hadn't drifted away in anyone's company; publicly telling off an invisible Bill Kern was bad enough. But I was doing less to help myself now, making fewer calls, pulling myself away from the window less often, and that, I knew, but without appropriate concern, would mean my defeat. I could predict with precision the instant sunlight would be flashed in my eyes by the gull wings, and it was this flashing, along with the sun on the ocean and that faint indescribable scent and the voices of Ireland all around that finally carried me over the line into what seemed a much deeper level of insanity.

During one of my drifty sessions by the window I suddenly found myself back in that place with the boulders I'd first visited in a dream— at least I had assumed it a dream. I peeked out across a barren plain, and beyond, where ocean met beach, I saw a dark forest. I knew there was danger in that distant green wall, even though the whole scene seemed, on its surface, tranquil enough. I also knew that in reality I was standing in Dotty McConkle's bay window, that the plain was the beach, the forest the ocean. But this other was real, too, or almost real, and it seemed to draw me in with a will. Several times I thought I saw something red move among the trees, but when I looked harder there would be nothing but ocean and I would be back under the silver gulls with the inn looming around me, needing enough work to break the bank. I'd pick up where I left off, worrying about the deedholders who were killing my dreams and the contractors I couldn't afford to hire and Bernie McCohen's treachery or my partners who would soon pull the plug on my life. I'd watch the waves and the circling gulls as I ruminated, and the next thing I knew I'd be back among the boulders.

One day, knowing that my paralysis was more an enemy than Bernie or Ireland's sorry state, I pulled myself away from the window and drove down to Ship Bottom, to the office of Asp, Brinkhoff and Bernbaum. Horace Asp, a big friendly man with only a few strands of white hair combed meticulously across his head, had been Dotty's lawyer for the last twenty years of her life and was now executor of her will. He had called me over a week ago, when he and his partners had returned from their golf vacation in Florida, to tell me there were forms that had to be completed and signed before he could initiate the process that would eventually put Ireland in my name.

"So how have you found the old place?" Asp asked, as he spread the half dozen forms before me.

"It's about what I expected," I told him.

We exchanged Dotty stories while I wrote, and eventually I found myself summarizing my plans for the inn, glancing up from the paper work to see his response, which seemed positive enough.

"Have you considered incorporating?" he asked.

I told him about OU Inc. and our funding structure, but he still thought incorporating Ireland would be a good idea. "Make the inn a legal entity," he explained, "then make contractual links between the two corporations."

Clearly he was looking for business. I told him I'd think it over. Disappointed, he sat back and let me do more work on the forms.

"So did you move your family down here?" he asked, just for something to say.

"No," I said. "I'm in the process of getting a divorce."

His pale brows shot up as he leaned forward suddenly and yanked the pen from my hand. Then he quickly gathered up the forms I hadn't quite completed. "It might be best," he said, "to postpone the transfer of Ireland until after your divorce. Wouldn't want the inn to be part of the marital pie, would we?"

I thought that advice worth a great deal and told him he had just won himself a new client. He'd be Ireland's attorney, at least here in New Jersey. And if he wanted to draw up papers of incorporation, that was fine with me.

After that, we went through Dotty's file and, with a laugh like Deputy Dog's, he showed me a separate deed that made me owner of Dotty's suite on the first floor. Probably in response to my curious look—but maybe because he was a born lecturer, as are most lawyers I've known—he explained that he had urged Dotty to use this separate deed to satisfy her pledge to me. "I never understood why she felt so obligated, seeing what happened and that it was all so long ago. But she did. Now, of course, this little deed is redundant."

"But valid?"

"Oh, yes. Sign that sucker and file it with the Town Clerk and it's binding as crazy glue. And this!" he said, handing me another deed. "There was no reason Dot had to include this deed with the other, but she did."

"What is it?" I asked, reading but not finding the point amid all the legal jargon.

"Deed to the bay side land. Across Long Beach Boulevard."

There was, I knew, a vacant lot over there that ran all the way back to the bay. And visible among the weeds and bramble and cedar saplings were a few mangled beach chairs and umbrellas, some beer cans, a couple of TVs with cracked picture tubes, and a sink. There was also a sign that said, "Available," and gave the name of a realtor down in Beach Haven. I had it on my list to call that number and demand that the lot's owner cart all that unsightly junk away, but had I done so I would have ended up talking to myself since the entire parcel belonged to me. There were four building lots, one of them directly on Barnegat Bay, with a huge wood dock reaching into the water. The plot had been put on the market three years ago by Dotty McConkle, and there had been five good offers, according to the realtor, all within a hundred thousand dollars of Dotty's asking price of one million; Dot was, if nothing else, a stubborn lady.

When I got back to Ireland, I called the realtor and pulled the entire plot off the market. And once that was done, I picked up the phone to call Bill Kern, thinking this was the piece of good news I needed to make the deeds easier to swallow. Then I stopped myself. This ace, I decided, belonged up my sleeve.

A few more calls were all it took to learn that the bay side plot had not been part of the appraisal I'd commissioned back in January. So if the time came to buy out my partners, in order to save Ireland, I'd have some hope of managing it.

I first spotted the red archer the day after I met with Horace Asp. He stepped from the woods, and even from a distance I could see how large and powerfully built he was. And of course he was armed with his red bow and a quiver full of red arrows, although had I been armed, I still would not have been a match for him, unless of course I was carrying a semi-automatic. Worse still, I knew—the way an old fighter can tell such things—that even if he put us on equal footing by throwing down his bow, he would quite easily clean my clock. He seemed to know it, too. He also seemed to know precisely where I was hiding. He came directly at me, striding confidently across the plain, like an enemy in one of my son's bloody video games. His pants and boots and shirt and hat were red. The feather in his hat was red. His face and arms and hands were red. His eyes were red.

He stopped mid-way between the forest and the boulders, took a sideways stance and reached over his shoulder. With an easy, deliberate motion, he fit an arrow to his bow string and fired, seemingly without aim.

The red arrow came right at my eye and I jumped back, tripped over Dotty's wing-back and tumbled to the floor. I blinked, trying to reorient myself. The gulls circled, flashing sunlight in my eyes. There was nothing to do but laugh. Pain radiated up my arm from my left wrist. That wasn't so funny. There was someone knocking on my door.

"Yes?" I called.

"Mr. McWilly," said Jimmy McCaffery. "There's a man here to see you about a pool."

"Okay, Jimmy," I said. "I'll be right out."

I stood and as I did I peeked over the sill, taking care in case the archer was still there, ready to let fly with another arrow. A wave tumbled upon the beach. My jogger in blue ran past. Had she been in red I'm not sure I'd have managed to keep it together. She was tall and shapely and she brought me back to the more solid footing of lust. I disrobed her in a flash, then, feeling more sane, went to the door.

The man waiting for me in the lobby was obese and filthy, which of course did nothing to instill confidence in the pool company he represented. He wore sagging jeans with black grease stains left by weeks, maybe months of wiping dirty hands upon his bloated thighs. His black satin jacket said "Ace Pools" across the back and over the breast in red script stitching, and he identified himself as "Ace" Morgan, as he shook my hand. His wrists and hands looked as if he'd come to me straight from a break and lube job. I, on the other hand, had just nearly been killed by a figment of my imagination, but he couldn't tell that. I expected to find that some of his grime had transferred to me, but all that came away when I withdrew my hand was a gritty odor that reminded me of ancient fireplace ash.

"This way, Ace," I said, and led him across the lobby and down the back stairs to the courtyard formed by the inside-out L of Ireland's wings. I gestured with a sweep of my arm. "I want a swimming pool and a Jacuzzi out here, and a privacy fence down there by the Boulevard."

"How big?" he said, and stuffed a well-chewed, unlit cigar in his mouth.

"Oh," I said. "About like this."

Having tried unsuccessfully to describe over the phone what I wanted to three other prospective bidders, I decided this time simply to draw lines in the big gold pebbles with the heel of my running shoe. That way, my design could be refined as I collected ideas, and be here for each pool company that came to bid on the job, if any more did.

Ace the pool man followed me as I moved around the court, drawing with my heel and doing my best to work around the two vehicles parked here. Once he even grunted appreciatively as I made a graceful turn. There would be no sharp corners in my pool, I told him, and the two pools would blend gracefully with one another, and with the landscape. And there would be plenty of room on the deck for lying in the sun.

The courtyard was now an expanse of dusty pebbles with tufts of grass poking up. Out near the Boulevard was a garage with a sagging roof and a broken window. That building, refurbished, would become the pool house. Beside it would be a volleyball court.

"So where will you park then?" Ace asked me, in a sharp Jersey twang.

I pointed to the vacant land across the four lanes of Long Beach Boulevard. "Part of the contract," I explained, "will be to clear the front section over there, edge it with Belgian Block and fill it in with this big gravel." I kicked the stuff on which we were standing and in which my pool and Jacuzzi were now etched. "That'll be Ireland's parking lot, and I'll see what I can do to get a foot bridge built over the road."

"We don't do landscaping," Ace told me, walking away along the line I'd drawn, measuring with his feet. "We just do pools."

"Do you sub-contract the landscaping?"

"Naw. Making it pretty is your problem. We just do pools."

Chapter Sixteen

An orange Allied van drove past on the Boulevard. It stopped with a hiss down the way to my right, behind Ireland's neighbors to the north. Gears ground, then came a staccato horn that tooted incessantly as the van slowly reversed.

"Okay," I said to Ace. "So take your measurements."

"What do you think I'm doing?" he said, pointing to his feet. "Perfect size twelves. I was built for this job."

"Swimming pool here," I said. "Jacuzzi over here."

"Separate? Like you got it drawn?"

"Just as I've drawn it. Separated by, what's that, about ten feet of deck?"

"Eight and three-quarters. So you want to make people haul their asses up outta one pool and walk over eight and three-quarters feet of hot concrete to get to the other."

"Only if they're in string bikinis," I said.

He didn't smile.

"I can make it so they're separated by just a little tile wall," he said. "Then all you got to do is slip a leg over."

"Two pools," I said. "As drawn."

The van, having reversed past again, shifted gears and pulled into the courtyard, finally coming to a stop between my old Jeep and the Inn's vintage woody wagon. (Legend had it that Dotty McConkle had taken the woody to settle a long outstanding account—taken, that is, in the middle of the night from a driveway up in Morristown. The wagon's metal had been painted kelly green, and across each of its front doors was written, in neat yellow script, the word, "O'Woody.") There were three men in the cab of the truck. And movement behind them. A dog, maybe. The driver climbed down. He stretched his back. The engine rumbled. He was a tall, skinny man with a two-day growth on his jaw and a prominent Adam's apple. He wore a down vest over a Grateful Dead T-shirt, jeans and motorcycle boots. His black hair was slicked back and pulled into a six-inch pony tail.

"Is there a Mr. Shackleton in residence?" he asked, in a voice that might have spent time at Oxford.

It had been a while since I'd responded to that name, and before I could answer, a child's voice cried, "Dad! Dad!"

Ryan clamored out of the driver's side door of the cab. I only got a glimpse of him because he was quickly in my arms and kissing and hugging me and I was staggering backwards to keep my footing.

"That's confirmation enough," the driver said. He climbed back behind the wheel, gunned the engine, and backed out, again under protection of his little tooting horn.

"Wait!" I called, thinking he was leaving. I wanted to ask who he was and how he happened to be delivering my boy to me. The least I could do was thank him. But he ignored me, if he heard me at all. He backed out of the lot, pulled forward, then backed in again, somehow placing the big van perfectly, first try, in the narrow space between O'Woody and my Jeep.

The great engine went silent. The driver and the other two men, one short and muscular, the other tall and skinny, but with an alcoholic's pot and arms covered by tattoos, climbed out of the cab and threw open the wide side door of the van, then the double doors in back. The driver handed me a clipboard with several documents attached, all in need of signing. Ryan hugged and kissed me and kept saying "Dad, Dad," over and over. Meanwhile, the man from Ace Pools paced along the lines I'd drawn, even though there was now a moving van parked in my swimming pool.

My Connecticut lawyer had taken me at my word when I told him to accept any settlement Glady and her lawyer offered. Their proposal, probably an opening gambit, gave me sole custody of Ryan, along with stingy monthly child-support payments and almost all the furnishings from the house Glady and I had shared. Of course it gave Glady the house and all the bank accounts except my pension, and visitation rights that included all major holidays until Ryan turned 21. It wasn't binding until we had our day in court, but I knew I wouldn't fight or request the slightest modification. Ryan was with me and that was all that mattered, even if this was just a bluff by Glady.

I had not let myself think about him, except in passing, but somewhere inside I had missed him terribly, and the moment he was in my arms I was flooded with feelings of sorrow and longing and loss and joy and relief. Beyond my will, tears started to roll, and to avoid a total melt-down, I concentrated on the paperwork the driver had handed me. I knew at once what had happened, and later Ryan confirmed it. Unable to tolerate anything that reminded her of me, and unhampered by funding limits, Glady had refurnished, redecorated and here and there rebuilt her entire house. Her giving up Ryan surprised me at first, but I began to understand when he told me how he had carried on each evening about how much he missed me and how badly he wanted to live with me, and how he had started to "act out", as the shrink Glady had taken him to called it. Glady had little tolerance for tension and believed to her bones she was entitled to live without it. Her big mistake, I suspect, was attempting to make Ryan forget about me. Against that pressure he had done the opposite.

Out of the truck came pieces of furniture I thought I'd never see again: sofas and beds and chairs and lamps and tables, televisions and stereos and radios, even the old grandfather clock I'd given Glady for our fifth anniversary. I was surprised to discover that I'd been mourning these small losses ever since I left Connecticut. So what else had I been mourning, all my life, beyond my knowing?

With Ryan in my arms, or occasionally on my shoulders, I directed the off-loading, and what I couldn't take into Dot's suite, I spread around the inn. The men from the van were kind enough to shift about some of the furniture already in place, and when we were through, the lobby, my apartment, and several guest rooms had been considerably improved.

Ryan stayed glued to me for a time after we unpacked his boxes and trunks in the extra room of my suite—mine now, not Dot's, thanks to the new furniture and the presence of my son. Finally assured I wasn't going to vanish—or hang myself—he ran off to investigate his new home, returning in ten minutes to report on his discoveries, and make certain I was still here, then venturing out for a slightly longer exploration.

The people in the dining room made a fuss over my son that first night. He had never been so outgoing back in Connecticut, and as I watched him smile and chat with all these strangers, it occurred to me—self-serving thought—that my boy was thriving here, in just the brief time he'd been away from his mother.

After dinner, Ryan went off exploring again, and discovered a secret stairwell in the rear wing. He had me locate two flashlights and, pulling at my arm, led me back past the suite shared by McJustice and Irma McCreedy to the broom closet at the end of their hall. Inside, behind the brooms and mops and the Bathroom Buddy, in the shadows of the lowest shelf, there was a missing board beside a second board that could easily be swung aside.

"Throw a light in there, Dad," Ryan said. I was bent almost double, my beam joining his as I peered into a narrow passage at what looked to be the start of a small staircase. Ryan easily squeezed through the opening, but I knew I'd never make it.

"Don't worry," he said, his face peering out at me now from behind the swinging board. "Just go into the next room." He pointed to his right, my left. "And close the broom closet door. We don't want the secret getting around, do we?"

I rapped softly on the door to Room Three, and when there was no response, I tried the handle. The door was unlocked—all the unoccupied rooms were—and as I stepped inside I felt for the light cord. The hanging bulb came on, a stark white light that did not flatter the room's shabby decor. There was a highboy in need of paint and a sagging double bed with wooden head and foot boards that were badly scarred. The closet door opened and out stepped Ryan.

"Right this way, Sir," he said, bowing.

The closet was deep, and the lower half of the back wall was a removable panel which Ryan had already pushed aside. I bent low and followed Ryan into a narrow chamber.

We were soon climbing steps that, while too narrow for my shoulders, seemed solid enough underfoot. The staircase made a one-hundred-and-eighty-degree turn at a small landing which I guessed was mid-way between the first and second floors. Five more steps brought us to a larger landing, this one perhaps six feet square. Two dark corridors angled left and right from here, and behind us there was the start of another set of stairs.

"This is as far as I got," Ryan whispered. "It was too scary to go on."

I was surprised he'd made it this far. Back in Connecticut he'd been reluctant to stay alone in his second floor bedroom and more often than not fell asleep on the living room sofa while he waited for Glady or me to go to bed. On the other hand, there was nothing really spooky about this space, except for the sense that we were the first to set foot here in years.

"Let's go down this way," I said, and pointed to the corridor on our left. Even though what we were doing wasn't scary, it seemed appropriate to whisper.

Ryan sent a beam of light into the dark and we saw at once that the corridor was only ten feet long. I think we were both disappointed. I had to crouch and squeeze through, but the space was made for Ryan. The hall turned to the right and ended after only three more feet. I was about to edge my way back to the landing when I noticed a panel like the one in the closet of Room Three. I tried to visualize the layout of the second floor and decided we were about to enter Room Twenty-eight, which was in the back north corner of the rear wing.

"Go ahead," I told Ryan. "See if it opens."

He pushed, but nothing happened.

"With the one downstairs I had to push and lift and slide," he said, grunting as he did all three.

The panel came open and I helped Ryan set it aside. He stepped through; I crawled through, then stood beside him. We were in a closet, and Ryan's light played on the door knob.

I opened the door, carefully, determined that the room was vacant, then we both stepped out. We were in Room Twenty-eight and, after a quick glance around, we both started to laugh and give high-fives as if we had achieved a thing of greatness. It was silly to be so delighted by something so inconsequential. We had found a secret passage into a vacant room of the inn I owned. *Big Whoop*, as Ryan might have said. But it felt important, somehow, and I didn't bother to question the joy.

We peered out into the second floor corridor, like cat burglars, then silently closed the door and slipped back into the closet. The other corridor in Ryan's secret passage took us to the closet of Room Twenty-nine, a huge room in the other back corner, the one that McJustice claimed had been deeded to her. Three windows looked out onto the gravel courtyard where my Jeep and the inn's old station wagon were parked. Because of the view, this was one of the inn's least desirable rooms, except perhaps for those directly above on Three, where we found ourselves in another ten minutes, after we had gone back down the secret passage and up another narrow flight of stairs.

A somewhat longer corridor brought us out into what I guessed was Room Thirty-four, across the hall from the McMittleman's room and just down the corridor from Shannon's. We weren't as giddy about our adventure now. We just glanced around from the open closet door and didn't say a word or even smile.

We were about to slip back into our secret passage when I noticed the teddy bear. It was lying under the covers of the room's single bed, it's head on the pillow. We stepped out of the closet and looked around again, alert for other signs that this narrow room was occupied. Something wasn't quite right in here.

The last thing I wanted was to allow our adventure to intrude on a guest, and I was about to suggest we make a quick and quiet exit. There was no luggage in sight, and that was a relief. But there was a toothbrush on the shelf above the sink in the cramped john, and a dirty towel on the towel rack above the tub. In one of the bureau drawers there was a child's soiled, striped shirt and a pair of well-worn blue jeans, sandy in the knees, that would not have fit Ryan.

"Must have been left by a guest," I said, and wondered why I hadn't noticed this stuff when I visited all the vacant rooms while sketching my floor plans.

"Where's the door?" asked Ryan, turning from one direction to the next. "There's no door, Dad."

He was right. There was a tiny window that looked out onto the courtyard, but no door. The only way into this room seemed to be the way we had come, which meant, judging by the presence of the bear, toothbrush and clothing, that we weren't the only ones who knew about the hidden passage.

"Check under the bed," I told Ryan, as I went down the wall opposite the closet, rapping lightly but hearing nothing.

Ryan pulled out a cardboard box full of clothing. There was underwear for a little girl, more jeans and shirts, a sweater. None of it was new; all of it was clean and neatly folded.

"No door gives me the creeps," said Ryan, and he started for the closet.

I grabbed the teddy bear, then followed the beam of Ryan's light back along the narrow corridor to the secret stairs.

"Should we try down here?" he asked, pointing his light down another passage, which seemed to lead us toward Shannon's room.

"Why not?" I said, but a few seconds later, when I heard a voice, I grabbed Ryan's shoulder and stopped him. We stood still and listened.

"Who's that?" he asked.

"Shannon. I don't want to intrude on her."

I couldn't hear what Shannon was saying. Now and then she paused and another, softer voice answered, but it was too faint to hear. I signaled Ryan to follow me and we retreated.

"Maybe she's naked," Ryan said.

"Don't be so precocious," I told him.

"I'm not precocious," he said, then he smiled knowingly. "But if I know what precocious means then maybe I am. Then again, I got a father who walks around holding the paw of a teddy bear, so how would he know?"

I looked down, surprised to find the bear in my hand. I gave it to him. He gave it back.

We went up another half flight of stairs, which led to a small passage under the eaves, hardly big enough for me to crawl through. It seemed to run the entire length of the third, or attic floor's rear wing, opening, mid-way, into a storage space full of trunks and picture frames and pieces of furniture under dusty sheets and racks of clothing and stacks of boxes. There was nothing spooky about the place. It was just an attic full of someone else's junk, in places piled right to the ceiling.

"Neat," said Ryan, peering out.

Crawling further through cobwebs and dust, we finally came out in the peaked roof of the front turret. This was the room immediately above McX's room on Two, and after we'd lowered ourselves into the closet and stepped into the room with its commanding view of the ocean, I went searching for another secret door. This room was part of a three-room suite up here on Three, furnished with two easy chairs and an antique rolltop desk. The back wall had a built-in bookcase, and that held some promise, although no matter where I pushed or knocked, nothing gave way or slid open, and I was badly disappointed. If I could have found a secret way to get a look into McX's room, I'd have done it without a second's hesitation.

We decided to return to the first floor the conventional way, and so we started down the front corridor, poking our heads into each room we came to. These rooms were under the front gables and featured fantastic ocean views. Fixed up even slightly, they'd be worth a fortune, I told myself, and realized with a rush of longing that what was needed was a woman's touch.

Harmless as it seemed, our adventure in the secret passages and stairwells spooked Ryan more than he let on, and that night he woke up screaming. I held him until he was calm. He tried to tell me about a soaking wet little girl with the back of her white dress torn away, who had walked into the waves and had not come out again, but he upset himself and began to gasp. I lay with him and stroked his head and his cheeks—amazed at the softness of him and the warmth—and told him over and over that it was only a dream. But as we both drifted off I heard him mutter, "that's what you think."

Before breakfast, Ryan made me take him for a walk. Poor deprived rich kid, his ocean visits had all taken place in the Caribbean, and he was in awe of the roaring waves. It seemed he had to be out of sight of Ireland before he dared deliver his news, which was that something fishy was going on at my inn.

"I mean, there's someone just beyond the corner of your eye," he said. I knew that feeling, but decided not to tell him so. "And there's that stuff we found in the room without a door. And my dream." I hadn't put those three together but it made sense to me that Ryan had. "I think you got a ghost on your hands, Dad," he said, earnestly. He wasn't alarmed, not here on the beach, with the sun glistening on the ocean. He was simply drawing a conclusion and delivering the news.

If anything, he was delighted to be the one to tell me.

"Maybe we should ask Shannon who she was talking with last night," I suggested.

Ryan shrugged, that topic forgotten. "Do I gotta go to school?" he asked.

"Of course," I told him.

"Bummer. Seems like it ought to be vacation. Can't I get educated right at Ireland?"

"Nobody there is smart enough to teach you."

"You are."

"No I'm not. I make things up as I go along. You could get away with that once, but now you really have to know stuff."

"Bummer," he said again. "So what's with this Mc and O stuff they got going on?"

"It's something the lady who owned the place started. Dotty McConkle her name was. She was a little dinggy."

"No duh! So when do I get one? A Mc or an O?"

"You want to change your name?"

"Sure. I mean, why would I go on being Ryan Shackleton when my father's name is McWilly and my mother's gone back to being Glady Anderson?"

"That's a good point. So be Ryan McWilly."

"Naaa. That doesn't have anything to do with me. I was thinking I might like to be Ryan O'Boy."

"My boy Ryan O'Boy," I said.

Chapter Seventeen

The next day at breakfast, Ryan packed away three times the food I did. He ate the way the construction workers ate, shoveling in eggs, bacon, potatoes, a side of flapjacks, three glasses of orange juice, milk laced with Hershey's Chocolate. Then, properly refueled, he took off to resume his explorations.

I started back to my room, thinking the time had come to face Bill Kern, but halfway across the lobby I was hit by a more powerful urge. I turned and went through the Staff Only door to the kitchen. Shannon wasn't there, as I'd hoped, but Heather was working at the griddle, an oversized spatula in hand.

"Did you know my daughter?" I asked as I approached down the galley, thinking the element of surprise might gain me something.

Her expression went blank. Then she looked down and put her limited concentration into her work. With a single deft flick she flipped four eggs, sunnyside down. That done, she set her spatula aside and picked up a large mixing bowl and cradled it in her left arm. With her back to me, she went to work with a long-handled wooden spoon.

"Did you?"

She turned but did not look at me. Her face scowled in concentration as she watched the muscles strain under the black hair on her arm. "I ...I'm not sure, Mr. McWilly. I don't think I ever knew anyone named that name. The only Dot I ever met in my life I think was Dotty McConkle."

"So then you wouldn't know if my daughter had a daughter?"

Her hand flew to her mouth and left a white smudge. Clearly that question hit some mark. Then again, a heated episode of *The Love Connection* made Heather McMittleman nervous. She was too shy or dim, or both, to answer my questions, but Shannon wasn't, and when she came in with a tray of dirty dishes, I began to question her as she loaded the dishwasher. These two, I knew, were on the receiving end of more of my frustration than they deserved, but I still couldn't find Bernie McCohen, and somehow, in that moment, word of my daughter was more important to me than Ireland by the Sea or my partners and all their money.

Shannon claimed not to know anything about a secret passage behind her room, or a room nearby that had no door, or a little girl who might be missing her teddy bear. She knew who Little Dot was, she said, because Dotty McConkle had spoken of her, but she had no idea what had become of my daughter or my ex-wife. And as I questioned her, her answers became shorter.

"I saw clothing in that room that belonged to a little girl," I said. "Four, five, maybe six years old. Smaller than my son. What do you make of that?"

"Well," Shannon said, glancing at Heather, who was filling clean plates with eggs and home fries, "maybe all that stuff was left by someone last season." She moved past me and began loading a tray. "Or maybe a family with a kid just checked in."

"Right," I said, sarcastically. "And stuck their child in a room with no door."

"What else could it be, Mr. McWilly? And besides, what makes you think I know? And why would you suppose, if there was such a child, she was related to you?"

"I don't know," I said, because I was wondering the same, "but I do know you know more than you're saying." She was not a masterful liar, but she was a teenager, and teens can stonewall better than Republicans. She met my stare and tried for a hard look, but just when it seemed she might soften or break, I was called to the phone by Francine. Shannon shrugged, hefted her tray and walked away through the swinging door. I took the call from Brian Cox in my room.

"Well, I did it," he began. "I got all three models into bed at the same time. What a romp."

"Good for you," I said indifferently, then asked about our ad.

"We're looping end of the week," he told me, disappointed because I hadn't awarded him an oink. "How's it going there? Thought I might come down this weekend and take a look where my money's going. If there's room in the inn."

"More than enough," I said, in a tone that might have worried anyone else. I gave him directions off the Garden State, and as I did the gulls started to pull at my mind.

The red archer was waiting where I left him. He stood mid-way across the plain, still two or three hundred yards off, his bow string stretched to the right corner of his mouth. He'd been standing that way for almost twenty four hours, and, absurdly, the first thing I thought, even as his red arrow came flying at me, was how strong someone had to be to manage that.

The arrow ricocheted off the rock immediately behind me, then clattered away among the boulders. When I looked again the red archer was ready with another arrow. And another. He was also striding toward me in the interval between each shot. I tried to bring back the beach, the ocean, the silver gulls, the Wrecker's Light, but these, visible beyond the more solid reality of what I knew to be my hallucination, refused to solidify. This time my projectionist had gone too far, I thought, and I saw a Cuckcoo's Nest future in store if I didn't somehow manage to turn away from the window. I thought it might help to focus on the furnishings of my apartment, but, like the beach, that reality was only a watery presence within the boulders.

Behind me I saw the opening of a passage that I somehow knew led back through a maze to an invulnerable rocky fortress, and in my urgency to escape the red archer I decided to follow it. In a few seconds, though, I found myself in a confusing labyrinth, and everything in me warned against venturing further. To go on, I seemed to know, was to give up hard-won ground. Reluctantly, fearfully, I returned to my post and peered out.

The archer had closed to within a hundred yards, his arrows arriving almost instantaneously with the twang of their release. There was, I knew then, no avoiding him, and I realized exactly what I had to do. It scared me so badly I began to tremble, even as I reminded myself that the archer was just a product of my imagination, or my psychosis. All this was a dream, I kept telling myself. An hallucination. The archer wasn't real and his arrows, I told myself, could not hurt me.

I stood and stepped into the open. It was the bravest act of my life, and I hoped the archer would be impressed. I faced him, my unprotected chest an open target.

He shot me.

He didn't pause to admire my bravery. He didn't offer battle on equal terms. The bastard simply shot me. Twang!

And contrary to my pep talk, the red arrow that pierced the center of my chest hurt beyond telling. I bellowed and fell backward, kicking and flailing in wretched agony. I knew it was a mortal wound, and I even took time to consider how sad this was for Ryan and how mysterious it was going to be when they found me with a red arrow sticking from my chest. Then I realized that the arrow should have already killed me, but instead of fading, my thoughts raced and the sounds I made gathered strength. A surge of red-hot emotion rose up and faded and rose up in me again. I wasn't hurt, I was enraged. And there was no red arrow protruding from my chest. I had somehow absorbed it. I got to my feet and was surprised to find that the archer had retreated.

No! He had shrunk.

He fired, and again his aim was deadly. The shaft pierced my sternum and sent me writhing to the ground and bellowing out with a rage my body wasn't large enough to contain. Far off behind me, back among the rocks, way inside that labyrinth, there was the sound of knocking on hollow wood. I pulled myself to my feet the way you do when you have to beat the count. The archer was half my size now.

"You bastard," I shouted, and with more strength than I've felt in years, I charged him. I felt like a bull in a cartoon, fury bursting from my nostrils, but the archer stood his ground, plucky little shit, and hit me with three more arrows before I could close the distance. Each shot made me stagger and clench my fists and strain my throat as I screamed out my rage. But these last arrows, I realized with a surge of ebullient confidence, didn't knock me down the way the others had.

Each one did less damage than the one before, and by the time I'd survived the last of these shots the red archer was too small to be seen.

I stomped around like Godzilla in the space where he'd been standing, and when I stepped back, my tantrum over, I noticed a tiny red stain on the ground. But then I blinked and it was gone. The ocean was back. The beach. The rotating gulls on their invisible strings. The Wrecker's Light.

"Dad," Ryan called through the door. "Dad, are you okay?"

All the people of Ireland were in the lobby, drawn by the terrible noises I'd been making. I must have looked awful because they retreated a step when I came out, all except Irma McCreedy, who stood off to one side, smiling that doped-up smile of hers, and McJustice, who seemed to delight in my discomfort. The rest gaped as if I was a ghost, and I realized then how I must have scared them with my struggle. Later Ryan said I was bright red and my hair was up like I'd been electrocuted.

"Are you all right?" Francine asked.

"Fine," I said, and found that my voice was a hoarse whisper. I was embarrassed, but deeper than that superficial emotion, I was perfectly calm and immensely proud of myself. I'm not sure I've ever felt such a combination of power and peace.

"What in the world happened in there?" asked Bernie, trying to see past me into my sitting room.

"Sounded like you were wrestling with the devil himself," said Jimmy McCaffery. "Why, you were groaning and shouting and bashing about. I haven't heard such sounds since ..."

I noticed that Ryan was standing beside a dirty-faced little girl, who held Shannon's hand and looked at me with no expression at all. Other than Irma and McJustice, she was the only one in the crowd who didn't appear to be scared or curious.

"Bad dream," I said. "I'm okay now. Thanks for being worried about me."

"I wasn't the least bit worried," muttered McJustice. "I was hoping it was terminal."

Irma, the spaced-out, trance-channeling lesbian, smiled at her companion as if she'd said something clever.

When it finally dawned on me that I'd just seen Bernie in the crowd and turned to look for him again, he was gone. The others began to drift away, too, all except Irma, Shannon, Ryan and the dirty-faced little girl, but the younger ones held back, waiting, it seemed, while Irma stepped close.

"It appears you passed your first test," she whispered, and patted my arm. "Amazingly well, it seems." Then she walked away.

"Come on in," I said to the others, looking curiously at Irma's retreating form. "And who is this?"

Shannon brought the two children into my apartment. They didn't seem to notice as, in spite of myself, I glanced fearfully about for the red archer or one of his friends.

"It's my fault," Shannon said. "So don't blame Chelsey."

"I take it this is Chelsey?"

"I should have told you the truth when you asked," Shannon went on, "but, well, you get used to mistrusting and I still wasn't sure about you, so ..."

"Chelsey lives in that secret room?"

Shannon nodded. "Heather and I have been hiding her," she explained, which of course was no explanation at all, and I let my expression convey that. "Dot was the only thing standing between Chelsey and an orphanage," Shannon added. "And I'm just a kid and Heather's, well, Heather's Heather."

"And?"

For the first time since I met her, Shannon seemed flustered. For the first time she seemed her age.

"Well, see, it's ... I've been telling Chelsey I didn't think you'd let them take her. Haven't I, Chelse? But she's been waiting to see. Dot told us we shouldn't trust anyone else and we should check you out to make sure you weren't nutty about some skirt. Dot's words, not mine. She said if you weren't, you'd put the magic back in Ireland."

I knelt down in front of Chelsey. "So then it must be your teddy bear whose taken over my TV," I said, pointing.

Chelsey didn't speak, and she didn't hurry as she retrieved her bear, but from the way she held it as she returned, you could tell that bear was her whole world.

"So who is she?" I asked Shannon, standing.

"She's ..." Shannon turned red and looked away. "It's a long story," she said.

"Does she go to school?" asked Ryan.

"We couldn't chance that," Shannon said. "I've been teaching her. She's very smart."

"And does she always look so, so shabby?" he asked.

"Hey!" Chelsey said to him, "you wouldn't look so hot if you lived in the walls. In fact, you *don't* look so hot." She shifted her gray-eyed gaze from my son to me. "And you look terrible."

I laughed. "I imagine I do. How long have you been living like this, Chelsey?"

She shrugged. I looked at Shannon.

"Since Dotty got really bad. Maybe a year now. Not quite."

"And where are your parents?"

Chelsey looked at Shannon, then back at me.

"She doesn't remember her parents," Shannon said. "You might say she's a child of Ireland."

"Okay," I said. "Then what's your last name, honey?"

As before, she looked at Shannon, who nodded at her.

"Shay," the little girl said, without inflection and without taking her eyes off Shannon.

"And you don't have to go to school?" asked Ryan.

"Nope."

Ryan smacked his forehead. "I think maybe tracking you down was a big mistake," he said.

"Too late now," said Chelsey. "You dummy."

I decided to press Shannon for details about Chelsey Shay when we could find some time alone, even though I would have loved to explore the implications of Chelsey's last name. Instead, I gave Shannon all the cash in my pocket, maybe two hundred dollars worth of twenties, and told her to buy Chelsey some new clothes and whatever supplies she needed.

"Get her settled in," I said. "Get her cleaned up. Then you and I will talk. If you run into problems, see me. Take my Jeep. The keys are under the mat."

"Can I go with them?" Ryan asked.

"Of course."

As they started away, Shannon glanced back at me, and now her expression wasn't seductive, which was a bit disappointing. The crush she'd had on me had been, I realized now that it was gone, delightful. But now her feelings were much deeper. She was relieved, I could tell, and I suspected also that she might have just appointed me her honorary father; if so, my family was growing so fast it left my head spinning.

When I looked at Shannon I saw Erin, and I had to keep remembering how old I was—and how young she was—in order not to fall in love. And looking into Chelsey's eyes just now had been, I was alarmed to realize, a little like looking at Ryan and a whole lot like looking in the mirror. Everything in me said she was Little Dot's daughter, but of course by now I was suspicious of my suspicions.

"Maybe you two should move down to Twenty-nine," I called, realizing that Shannon's room up on Three was too small for them both and that I couldn't have Chelsey spend another night in that tiny cell with no door. Twenty-nine was a huge room and it offered access to the secret passages and stairwells, which I thought might make Chelsey feel at home.

"Great," said Shannon. "We'll do it soon as we get back."

When the children were gone, I dialed Bill Kern's office in Manhattan. There was no hesitation or dread, but before the connection could go through, my call-waiting signal sounded, so I disconnected my New York call and flashed to the other line. The call was from Ace, the guy who had been here when Ryan arrived.

"You got major problems," he told me, without bothering with a more conventional greeting.

"Tell me about it," I said. "Major problems and I are old buddies. What is it? Zoning? What?"

"Naw. That part's a piece of cake. I can probably do what you want done for around eighty grand, but word's going around to triple bids on Ireland."

Paranoia was bad enough, but finding out my worst fears were real stunned me.

"Are you there?" he asked.

"Say that again."

"Word's out that you're going to bring whores to Long Beach Island. Triple the bids on Ireland, if you bid at all. That's the word, and it's got teeth in it. Atlantic City teeth. Anyone who doesn't jack up his prices won't be getting subcontracts. A few guys even got paid off pretty good not to bid."

"But you're willing to work?"

"I don't know. I hate this shit. And you seem like a pretty good guy, with your boy and all. Check with me when everything else's lined up, and if I still got a set a balls, I'll put in your pools for you and fuck 'em."

I sat for a few minutes looking out the window. Atlantic City teeth, I thought. That probably meant organized crime.

Absently, I dialed Kern again. His sexy-sounding secretary, whose name was Helen, said she'd beep him out on Shelter Island.

It had to be Bernie McCohen doing this to me, I thought, while I waited for Kern's call. Who else would care? And who else would have that kind of clout? But why? What had made him turn against me?

On the other hand, did it make sense for me to expect things at Ireland to make sense? Bernie McCohen was crazy, I told myself as the phone rang, and crazy men respond to a logic all their own.

"Hey," said Kern. "I thought you died."

"Many deaths," I told him.

He laughed. "How's it going?" he asked, but then, before I could answer, he said, "hold on," and I had to listen to muffled voices for a full minute. "I gotta warn you," he said, coming back, "I can only take a second. There's three million dollars on the table here and I should get back to it pretty quick."

"Sounds like a poker game."

"Sort of is. What's up?"

"We have big problems."

"Figures. Otherwise I'd have heard from you."

I told him about the deedholders and about the conspiracy among the contractors, and without seeming to give it a second's thought Kern told me to fax him the deeds and the names and numbers of the contractors who had tripled their bids.

"I'll take care of it," he said.

"Okay. But I think we need a meeting."

"Fine. A week from Monday. My office. Nine. I'll have my girl set it up."

He hung up.

What a guy. I could still take lessons from him, I told myself and remembered how I had invoked the stern, take-charge personality of Bill Kern in order to get rid of Tonya Angione. And I seemed not to have progressed much since then; I still needed Bill Kern to solve my problems.

I called Brian Cox back, but he was taping his show. The NBC switchboard operator put me through to Brian's secretary, and I was telling her to tell her boss to cancel his visit when suddenly I was pulled back in among the boulders.

This time it was a pink archer shooting pink arrows.

"How sweet," I said, as I closed my eyes and shook my head in resignation and made myself step out from behind my rock.

The first arrow went deep into the center of my chest, but it didn't knock me over and I felt elated, triumphant. I think I may even have laughed in jubilation. Then the shivering began. I dropped the phone and collapsed to my knees. Some vital part, some structural beam, had turned to liquid. I flopped onto my stomach as if my bones had melted.

"Hello? Hello?" said the NBC secretary, but she was far away, in another world.

Slither, I told myself. Crawl. It didn't matter where. If I didn't get away I would die. Or worse.

Someone was groaning and someone else was laughing and someone else was saying hello and asking if I was still there, which seemed a damn good question. There was no place to go, and I was too limp to move. The pink arrow, or the hole it poked in me, was about to drain off all that I was. My whole being seemed liquid now, ready to pour from my wound in a flood of tears and blood and semen until there was nothing left of me but a stain.

But that wasn't what happened, and after a moment or two, surprised to find myself still intact, I forced my legs to give movement a try. I got to my knees, then I stood and wobbled toward the pink archer the way I had the red one.

Each pink arrow that struck, although not nearly as potent as the first, left me so limp it was all I could do to stay upright. I sagged like the scarecrow in *The Wizard of Oz* as I staggered forward. His arrows were no bigger than pencils now, and although they jolted me, they no longer melted me, and as I absorbed each one, I could see the pink archer shrinking. But I was still pouring out of myself, and since there was no way to stop the flow, I wasn't certain which of us would be the first to vanish. I forced myself closer, and after a parting shot, the pink archer blew me a kiss and disappeared.

I looked out at the beach and the ocean, and found myself weeping for Erin and Carol and Gail and Glady and Jill and every woman I'd gone to bed with but had failed to love, or love enough, even the on-the-road one-nighters. Looking down at me from the clouds was a woman's face, radiant and beautiful, and I was sure I was seeing the Virgin Mary. For a second I had a vision of hosts of pilgrims making their way to Ireland by the Sea to be healed, but then the face above the ocean became Erin's, then Gail's, they Glady's. Then Glady's face became Jill's face and Jill's face became Erin's face again. These four women looked nothing alike, and yet they shared the same face, made from the same clouds, and I wept for the loss of all of them. And of course for the loss of my mind.

"Hello? Hello? Should I call Nine-One-One? Hello?"

I picked up the dangling receiver and as calmly as I could told Cox's secretary that I had dropped the phone out the window. The sounds she'd heard, I explained, were the surf and the wind and the banging of the phone against the side of the building as I was struggling to retrieve it.

"Jeeze," she said.

I made her repeat my message to Brian before saying goodbye.

Jill wasn't home the first few times I called, and for some reason I didn't want to talk to her machine. I drove over to the mainland, faxed the deeds to Kern's office, drove back and dialed Jill again. Still no answer. Finally, just after I heard the kids start up the stairs to begin their move to the second floor, Jill picked up.

"Oh, Hi," she said. "I was just thinking about you."

"I was thinking about you, too," I said. I was going to tell her I'd seen her face in the clouds above the ocean, but restrained myself. "I'm coming up Sunday after next. Can I stay at your place?"

"Of course," she said, but she wasn't as glad as I thought she should be. "You still have your key?"

"Right."

"Good," she said. "Because I won't be here. I'm going skiing in Vermont that weekend. With my new friend, Ben."

"They still have snow?" That was all I could think to say.

"You haven't lived until you've done April skiing in Vermont. So listen. Just let yourself in and enjoy, okay?"

"Okay, thanks," I said. "You too. Have a good time."

"Oh, I will. I will."

Her old boyfriend was history, I knew, and I guessed as I hung up that since I hadn't fought to win her, Jill had decided to put herself back in circulation. So why, I wondered, didn't this new guy spark possessive or jealous feelings? Maybe I was shell-shocked by all that had happened. Or maybe I didn't care about Jill as much as I thought.

It seemed, for a few seconds, that when a woman I liked got away from me it might be cause for celebration, as when one of Dracula's intended brides escaped his spell. I would use Jill's key, I decided, then slide it back under her door when I locked up. And that would be that.

Chapter Eighteen

Chelsey and Ryan bickered like siblings as we worked to move Shannon and the little girl to their new room. And they looked the part as well. And Shannon, I kept thinking, could easily have been their older sister. If I stopped lusting after this girl I could probably adopt her, which I knew, in spite of myself, would create a more solid love.

The next day, after tossing and turning all night about my bouts with the archers and about what Ace had confirmed for me, I went down to Bernie's lair in my basement. I was looking for a fight, but, as before, he wasn't around and I found myself alone in his office. On his desk was a mound of small red buttons, with pins on their backs. The red buttons said *I want my little red button*. There were thousands on the desk, thousands on the floor. There was also a typed manuscript, maybe four inches high, the title of which was *God's Windows*. The by-line was shared by the unlikely team of Bernie McCohen, PhD., and Irma McCreedy. The subtitle said: *Amazing Scientific Evidence Confirming the Existence of God and the Accuracy of Astrological Theory*. Beside the manuscript was a stack of 8x10 color photographs, with caption strips glued to their bottom edges. They looked to be works of abstract art, with odd swirls and shapes of various shades and colors. The captions said things like "Libra Sun Energy," "Pisces Moon Energy," "Energy from Virgo in Pluto."

I went down to the fulfillment room, where Francine ruled from behind her rolltop desk, but encountered only the three mushroom people, in their shapeless smocks. They labored away on Bernie's stones, and only glanced up at me in stunned silence when I asked if they'd seen their boss.

I looked in the Rock Room, where the tumblers grumbled away, but Bernie wasn't there, either.

I tried the door of his lab and was surprised when the knob turned. Immediately in front of me was a white-walled chamber with strange blue lights in its ceiling, and along its floor a dozen rows of glistening white planter boxes where hundreds of mushrooms were growing. On another table there were containers that appeared to be made out of some sort of transparent membrane, each one containing a viscous fluid in which tiny colored specks, iron filings from the looks of them, were suspended. Above each container was a video camera, with cables running into the wall behind. These were, I realized, the sources of the photographs on Bernie's desk. But Bernie wasn't here, so I gave up my search, my rage somewhat spent, or displaced, perhaps, by my curiosity about what I'd found.

As I went back down the hall I happened to glance into Bernie's office and caught sight of his bald head behind the mound of red buttons.

"You sneaky bastard," I said, startling him.

He lifted his head like a turtle.

"Is there a problem?"

"You've been avoiding me."

"Have not."

"You have too."

"That would place me in front of you, while in truth I've simply moved about behind you. And I've been very busy. Did you understand anything you found in my lab?"

"Not really."

"I gave you a glimpse into the meeting place of science and magic, and you didn't even know it."

"You've made it impossible for me to get fair bids, you bastard." He smiled at me, the way he had probably smiled at his less gifted students. "So what do you want?"

"Well," he said, as if I'd asked him a philosophical question, "when I bought off those first yah-hoos, all I wanted was for you to go away. Back to where you came. And I didn't think it'd take much. You were the enemy, and anything goes in love and war."

"But now?" prompted Francine, who had come in behind me.

In response to his wife's presence, Bernie stood up behind his desk and started to fidget. He looked at his feet, at the ceiling, at his fingernails. He picked up a handful of buttons, which caused a small avalanche. He shifted about, twitching, jiggling, fidgeting. It was exhausting to watch him, and I wondered if a psychiatric disorder had caused him to be invited to leave Harvard.

"But now I see that you are far stronger than I imagined," he said.

I was sure this is not what I'd have heard if Francine hadn't been standing beside me.

"And?" she prompted.

"And ... and for a long time I wanted it to be me who led Ireland into the future. But I have no magic, except for making money. And designing experiments. But you're different. You're an idealist. You're like Dot, although not half as daffy. And you've got the magic."

"Don't be too sure," I said, referring to the daffy part.

"See," said Francine. "See how honest he is. That's the honesty that will save Ireland. The one thing black magic can't abide is the magic of honesty."

"Yeah, yeah," said Bernie, glancing at his wife, then at me, then back at the floor. He dropped his handful of buttons, causing another avalanche. The space in front of his desk was entirely covered by little red buttons now.

"And so," Francine prompted.

"Anyhow, I want to see if we can start off on another foot."

"Dot promised us," said Francine, "that you'd take care of Ireland the way Saint Patrick took care of the snakes."

"Ahh," I said.

"That's why some of us were so upset to learn that greed brought you here. Tell him the next part, Bernie."

"I'm not sure this is the right time, Fran."

"Tell him."

Bernie took a long breath. "I want the spa franchise," he said, and then, in response to my quizzical look, added, "I already got the basement."

"Yeah. So?"

"You'll have less trouble with me if you franchise me the spa and fitness center."

"Wait a minute. Wait a minute. Aren't you the one who said you weren't crazy enough to join me? You look like that same guy to me."

McCohen grinned, ready to play. "You said yourself I was suicidal. And, as I say, I already got the basement."

"Not for long."

His face hardened. "Oh? And why's that, Mr. Arrive from Nowhere and Lead Us From the Darkness?" He glanced sheepishly at his wife.

I laughed. God, I loved this guy.

"No way am I required to give you all this room. One room, at most, and for residential purposes only. And Ireland should probably get a percentage of your operation, too. If I have to, Bernie, I'll build my spa around you and give you a room too small and dirty for a cockroach."

"Not bad," Bernie said, "assuming you can find someone to do the work."

"Oh, I'll find someone. I'll find someone if I have to import workers from Japan."

"Or you could get me on a zoning violation, or drug charges. Or immigration violations. But all that would take time, which you don't have. So at least listen to my proposal, okay? What can it cost you to listen?"

"Go ahead," I said, looking at my watch as if I had somewhere to go. "Tell me why I should let you handle my spa?"

"For one very obvious and simple reason," he said.

"Which is?"

"Because I know what mankind's next evolutionary step is going to be."

I closed my eyes and shook my head. "I'm glad it's just a simple reason."

"Being Enhancement."

"Enhancement?"

"Not just *Enhance*ment. *Being* Enhancement."

"I see."

"There is already a superior intelligence among us," Bernie explained, looking past me with a rapt and pious expression. "An intelligence in chemical form whose molecular structure fits our DNA like a key. A reverse key, actually, but never mind. This superior intelligence is passively spreading itself among us, even as we speak, leading to a whole new level of awareness among those who open themselves to it. It is the link between the god energy, which comes to us through the windows of alignment caused by the earth's rotation and the orbital movements of the planets and the moon against the fixed positions of the sun and the stars and the constellations and the far off galaxies. And this god energy tells me that the self-improvement, recreational, educational, personal growth and mind distraction industries will soon become man's essential occupation, all leading to what I call *Being Enhancement*, a name chosen because organized religions and New Age simpletons have taken over all the other best words and phrases and left them void of meaning. I'm telling you, McWilly, Being Enhancement is our destiny, that is if the technology bringing us into the future doesn't kill us first. It really is quite simple."

"So you said."

"The work force needed to provide essential goods and services will continue to shrink, so there'll be nothing for the rest of us to do except entertain, distract, teach and improve one another. More people realize every day that they are only pretending to usefulness. More and more people are waking up to the fact that their energy is being devoted to nothing more than a protect-your-ass mentality. In a phrase, there simply aren't enough real challenges and goals left to go around."

"Isn't he brilliant?" said Francine.

"Don't you imagine," Bernie went on, "if you had insider information on the cultural shift that took mankind from hunting to herding, or from gathering to planting, you'd have made a killing?"

"So to speak."

"Or if you had predicted the industrial revolution? Well that's where we stand today, you and me, and Ireland can lead the way by becoming an all purpose, self-contained enrichment center. It's the way of the future, McWilly. You, of all people, should be able to see that. You're the one who got me to see it."

I closed my eyes and nodded. My own madness was hard enough to contend with, but Bernie's madness entirely fogged my mind.

"So here's what I propose. I'll move my pebble operation and my lab down to the far end, then I'll have the rest of the basement converted into the most beautiful fitness center on the East Coast. I'll hire the staff and when they aren't busy making people fit, they'll do pebbles, which I'll give to guests and patrons of the spa. I'll buy a fleet of wind surfers and sun fish and rollerblades and mountain bikes and sea kayaks and I'll hire instructors. I'll want a break on rent, of course, and the right to sell memberships to non-guests, but other than ..."

"Ah," I said. "I knew there had to be a catch."

"No catch. It's right out in the open. No point letting all that equipment and staff go to waste during the slower seasons. This way, we'll keep the spa busy all year, and make the investment pay. And of course make more converts."

I told Bernie, on the spot, that I liked his proposal, but that if we did the spa his way, Ireland, the corporation, would have to get a percentage.

"Anything you say," he told me, absently, having found something of interest in the pile of photos on his desk.

"Of your entire operation."

"Whatever."

"Including your pebbles. And anything else you peddle."

"Sure, sure. Anything."

"Glad to have you with me, Bernie. Mostly because you're a pain in the ass to have anywhere else."

"I am, aren't I?" he said.

Francine went behind her husband's desk, crunching little red buttons underfoot, and put her arm around Bernie. With her free hand, she squeezed his cheeks and squealed with joy.

"So then this means you'll put the word out that I'm to get fair bids from now on, right?"

"We'll see," Bernie said.

"Bernie!" said Francine.

"Hey, babe. I can't change all my spots." He slipped his arm around his wife and squeezed her left bun.

"If you don't," I said, "it's no deal. If there's no inn, there's no spa. Look at it that way."

Bernie appeared to agree, but still nothing seemed to change among the contractors during the week leading to my meeting with my partners. I began to sand and scrape the weathered siding myself, but the inn was so huge, the job so overwhelming, that each hour of work left me feeling more hopeless.

I would have pestered Bernie, but I rarely saw him.

Now and then, because my curiosity made it impossible to restrain myself, I questioned Shannon and Chelsey about Chelsey's identity, but I didn't really push and they always wiggled out of each encounter. Chelsey's last name was Shay, I'd learned that first day, but she and Shannon insisted that Heather, whose name before it became McMittleman had been McShay, was not Chelsey's mother. They wouldn't say who or where Chelsey's parents were, or why Chelsey was here. I kept suggesting Shannon and Chelsey had to be sisters, but Chelsey would look at me blankly and Shannon would look away and shrug. It was a look I'd gotten often from Erin.

I got Chelsey and Ryan enrolled in the local elementary school, identifying Chelsey as a niece whom I was in the process of adopting. That went unchallenged, but the principal, a reasonable and kind woman, wanted Chelsey to enter kindergarten. There weren't very many weeks left in the school year, she reasoned, and Chelsey, who was so small and frail-looking, had never before been to school. But the two kids put up such a stink that I finally talked the principal into giving Chelsey a trial run in first grade.

I ran into Bernie out on the verandah the day after the business of school was settled, and reminded him that it was time he helped me get fair bids on the work I needed to have done. He looked at me blankly.

"You remember our deal, don't you?"

"Deal?"

"You're going to handle my spa."

"Did we settle that?" He seemed more distracted than usual.

"All except for setting the percentage Ireland gets."

"God wasn't looking," he told me, as if this was news that should have caused me great alarm.

"What?"

"God wasn't looking through the window when it clicked into place this morning. It means my theory needs revision. How's five percent sound?"

"I was thinking of something more like twenty five percent," I said, starting five points higher than I had planned. I expected a counter-offer but Bernie walked away.

That night at dinner Bernie suggested eight percent, so I dropped to twnety. After that, each time we crossed paths, one of us would throw a new number at the other, slowly narrowing the difference between us, and finally, on Friday morning, as I was returning from my run on the beach, we agreed on fourteen and a half percent. I had suggested he could deduct any rent paid during the period in question, and that seemed to tip the balance. So right there on the steps of Ireland, the spa deal was decided on a hand shake.

At last I had something positive to report to my partners.

"Listen, Bernie," I said, "it's in your best interest now to tell people I'm not going to turn Ireland into a whore house."

He coughed. "That wasn't my dirty work," he said. "It saved me a great deal of money, and I think it was a stroke of genius, but I can't take credit for it."

"Then who?"

"My guess would be McJustice, but I have no proof."

I wasn't out of the woods yet, I thought, as Bernie climbed the steps and went inside.

The ocean was rolling and foamy, and the most amazing shade of green, and I watched it for ten minutes, without really thinking. I heard that same scurrying sound I'd heard once before, and this time, when I bent over to see back between my legs, I found myself looking upside-down at Chelsey.

"Hi," I said. "What are you doing under there?"

There was a sigh of frustrated resignation, then a whispered, "I'm hiding."

"Oh? Who are you hiding from."

"You."

The blood was rushing to my head and I was starting to see spots. "Well," I said, laughing a little, "then you're not doing a very good job, are you? How come you're not in school?"

"Because I don't know how."

"You don't know how to be in school?"

"I don't know how to be anywhere but here."

"Ah. I see. Well, why don't you come on out of there and we'll talk."

"That's okay. I like it where I am."

"That's great, Chelsey," I said, "but I can't sit like this forever. I feel like a bradypus."

"A what?"

"A bradypus? That's a furry animal with a long nose and three toes who hangs around upside-down from trees all day and nibbles leaves and takes naps. Also known as a sloth."

"Oh, I've heard of them."

"Ryan saw one on a school field trip to the Bronx Zoo once. Have you been to a zoo?"

"I haven't been anywhere."

"We'll have to do something about that. I have another question for you."

"What?"

"Are you my granddaughter?"

She snorted. "I was going to ask you the same thing."

She scrambled from under the stairs and sat next to me, her elbow on her knee and her chin in her palm as she looked at the water. "Dot told me you were my grandpa," she said. "'You wait till your grandpa gets here. Everything will be different then and the magic will come back.' She used to tell me that all the time."

"Dotty would be the one to know if we're related," I said.

Little Dot, I thought, could have given birth to Chelsey when she was about twenty. But it made no sense. Certainly the child wouldn't be here without her mother, unless of course Little Dot was dead. That thought knocked the wind out of me.

"Dot would know," Chelsey agreed. "Except she was a ding dong. How come you don't know?"

I coughed. "I guess because I lost track of my daughter."

Chelsey nodded, gravely. "Easy to do," she said, and then we sat together without speaking for a full minute, maybe two.

"Listen," she said, making me jump. "A few weeks ago as I was crawling around inside the walls, I heard two of the women talking about you. They said ..."

The child's soft voice was lost in the crash of a wave.

"I'm sorry. What did they say about me?"

"They were saying maybe you'll get so crazy you'll just go away. Then they laughed like a couple of witches. You aren't going away, are you?"

"Who were they? Could you tell?"

"Not for sure. I think it was the one with the pet spook, or her friend, but I know the other one was the lady who never leaves her room."

"McX?"

Chelsey nodded. "That's what they call her."

"Interesting," I said.

Chelsey had just crushed one of my favorite theories. All along, I had anticipated an encounter with Erin or Little Dot, and I still caught myself looking to find my daughter in Shannon, in spite of having proved she was too young for the part. The only hope I had left was that Miss McX would turn out to be Erin, and now that seemed unlikely. Nobody, not even Jimmy McCaffery, knew who Miss McX was; nobody had set eyes on her, or so it seemed. Dot rarely spoke of her to Jimmy or Francine or Shannon, the ones I had asked so far. Still, someone was in residence up in Twenty Four, at least some of the time. Even though there had never once, in all these years, been a response to a knock, there was, according to Francine, a monthly envelope full of money and an occasional note left as evidence of McX's existence. And Shannon told me she sometimes found a pile of dirty linen or bag of trash outside the door of the room in the north front corner of Two. But if Heather was my granddaughter, and if she had overheard a conversation between someone and Miss McX, then McX couldn't possibly be Erin because McX was clearly not someone the child knew. McX was therefore not related to Chelsey nor, by extension, to me. Elementary, my dear McWatson.

As I reached this conclusion I looked at the sky and bellowed a laugh that probably sounded mad to anyone who heard, although if it rattled the child beside me she didn't let on. After all, she had seen me red, with my hair electrified. And I had stolen her teddy bear. She had also watched me sleepwalk my way around Ireland and across the beach for weeks. Besides, what was a little mad laughter between relatives? It was all so crazy, I thought, as I stood. If there was a plot to drive me mad, then my only hope was that nobody but me knew how well it was working.

Who cares who Miss McX is? I thought. Who cares who any of these people are? Bottom line was, they stood between me and my goals, my dreams, so no matter who they were, they were my enemies, and enemies were to be disposed of, any way possible. It was, in the end, as simple as that.

"Let's go in," I said, offering Chelsey my hand. "I'm getting cold."

"You go ahead, Grandpa," she said.

"That's McGrandpa to you," I told her, and earned my first genuine smile.

She took my hand, but instead of letting me take her in, she led me under the porch and into the opening of another secret passage where the wood and the stone foundation met. We climbed through the dark, Chelsey knowing the way and offering comments like a tour guide. "Right through there's your sitting room," she'd say. "Down that crawl way is the kitchen. You come out into the laundry chute." We crawled and climbed up past the second floor and finally stepped into the storage space under the eves. "You have to see this," she said, still holding my hand. "I watched Mr. McCohen build it." She giggled. "That man talks to himself more than you do."

Ahead of us, the way was blocked by what appeared to be attic junk stacked to the ceiling and covered by sheets. But Chelsey lifted up a corner of one of the bottom sheets, and, using a numerical code, caused a five-foot-tall metal hatch, rounded on top and at least a foot thick, to swing open.

We stepped into a small square chamber that was illuminated like a darkroom, with an eerie red glow. Twelve plastic tubes, wider on top than at the bottom, reached up to and through the ceiling, which I realized was really the roof of Ireland. The bottoms of these tubes entered an elaborate-looking machine that was unlike anything I'd ever seen but that appeared to contain several video cameras, their lenses aimed every which way. And below this contraption, through a window, I saw a set-up exactly like the one in Bernie's lab, with more video cameras aimed down into membrane bins where colored iron filings hung suspended in a clear, viscous-looking fluid.

"What is this thing, Chelsey?" I asked.

"The God Machine," she said, with no detectable reverence.

"Do you know what it does?"

She nodded. "It looks back at God," she said, again with no inflection. "Through his window. It ought to be called the Peeping Tom Machine."

I began to laugh. What an education in madness this child had received. And now, God help her, she had somehow slipped into my hands.

Chapter Nineteen

I kept telling myself to focus my attention on Monday's meeting, even though when I did, there seemed to be nothing I could do to prepare, and I found that somewhat disturbing. I had my deal with Bernie, and I intended to exaggerate my confidence that Ace would put in my pools, but there was nothing I could do about the rumor going around that I was a big time Manhattan pimp, or about the deeds Dotty had given away, or the strange people who owned them, and these were my main problems.

All weekend I successfully avoided the bay window and the gulls, because I wasn't up for another battle, but after I packed for my trip on Sunday, while Shannon was out back warming up my Jeep, I made the mistake of stepping over near the Wrecker's Light for a last look at the ocean. In the next instant I found myself facing the most vicious foe my hallucinations had sent me up against so far, and when the yellow archer's first arrow struck, the fear that erupted in me nearly loosened my bladder.

This scrawny bastard, such a sickly shade of yellow, turned out to be the Gattling gun of archers; arrow after arrow after arrow pierced my chest and all I could do was moan and squeeze with all my might to keep from pissing in my pants. With the first arrows of his volley I went to my knees, like one suddenly inspired to repent. My head was full of bugs that produced a noisy electric fuzz which seemed to hide an echoing female voice. Words hung beyond my awareness. And of course beyond all this there was the terrifying certainty that I had lost my mind. Bernie was in my attic playing with his God Machine while

I was at my window doing battle with color-coded archers. And we two were Ireland's last and best hope for the future.

Even under this vicious fusillade, I somehow managed to stagger forward, walking on my knees like an actor playing Toulouse-Lautrec. I knew from experience that my only hope was to absorb his shots, take the best he had to give, but even so, it required all my will not to give in to the terror and turn away. I already looked like I was hugging a yellow porcupine. How much easier it would have been simply to keel over, curl into a ball and sleep. And what would happen if I let myself? After all, this was only my imagination at work. Or my psychosis. Would the archer take my scalp? Chop off my head? And if he did, so what? Would my hair or head be gone when the hallucination ended? I doubted it, and that gave me courage, although in the next instant I became aware of an even worse fate. The yellow archer wouldn't scalp or decapitate me. No. He'd suck away all that remained of my will. That's what he'd do. I'd be left one of those lifeless hulks you see lying in doorways or living in cardboard boxes.

I knew this the same mysterious way I almost always know the points of the compass, and of course my certainty did nothing to ease my fears. Had my enemy not been less than a foot tall and shrinking with each arrow he fired, I don't think I'd have found the will to go on. I was trembling and starting to topple, but I told myself that if I could walk on my knees just a little closer, then maybe I'd squash him into a tiny yellow blob when I let go, or drown him in urine when my muscles became too week to hold back the flow; maybe then he wouldn't be able to suck away what was left of my vitality.

He was now the size of a PlayMobile person, his arrows no bigger than shirt pins, so I scooped him up and held him in my open palm, trying to decide what to do with him. The other archers had vanished when I got this close, but this fellow was made of sterner stuff. Should I clap my hands and see what that did to him? Or make a fist and squish him like a grape? While I was thinking, the little shit shot me between the eyes, and I almost dropped him as a bolt of pain cracked my skull and tunneled my vision.

"You little fuck!" I screamed, and curled the index finger of my free hand, intending to flick him into oblivion. But something stopped me and as he got ready to shoot again, I picked him up by his head so that he hung suspended between my thumb and index finger. He kicked at me with his little yellow legs and feet, and, squirming about, tried to line up another shot. So I ate him. Without an instant's thought, I popped him in my mouth and crunched his bow and quiver and squirmy little legs to mush. Then I swallowed.

He was better than the most powerful drug. My headache vanished and my chest swelled with the most profound sense of courage I've ever known. Bring on King Kong. Bring on the devil himself. Bring on Bill Kern, I thought, turning away from my window. I grabbed my suitcase and headed for the door.

Shannon was waiting for me in the driver's seat of my Jeep, Chelsey and Ryan in back, battling away on linked Gameboy units. The two kids liked each other, although neither would own up to it. And they both adored Shannon, who called herself their big sister but was each day acting more like a young mother. (They were all moving into my suite while I was away, mostly because Ryan had refused to spend the night in what he called "The Lady's Room.")

I crammed my bag into the narrow space between the rear seat and the tail gate, then snapped the flap back in place.

The Jeep lurched forward, spraying gravel, before I'd closed the canvas door and we bounced out onto the Boulevard, then sped south. After the causeway, as we approached the station, Shannon cleared her throat, started to say my name, stopped herself, then cleared her throat again.

"Yes?" I asked.

She sighed, and seemed to give up. "I'll tell you when you get home," she whispered.

"Tell me what?"

She looked at me. "About Chelsey. And me."

"Good," I said. "I'm not the enemy, Shannon."

"I'm starting to believe that," she said, then she drove in silence.

She seemed to be fighting back a grin as she put on her turn signal to enter the parking lot on the north-bound side of the station.

"Can I ask you something?" she said, then raced through an opening in the traffic only a teenager would have found.

"Sure. What?"

"It's very personal," she warned.

"Go on," I said, but felt something tighten in my stomach.

"How come you have a yellow tongue?"

I laughed.

"Something I ate," I said, then immediately wished I'd said *someone* instead of *something*.

Shannon pulled the Jeep to a stop in front of the station, leaned over and gave me a kiss on the cheek that was too moist to be daughterly but too chaste to be anything else.

"See you guys tomorrow night," I called as I climbed out.

For the first time I felt like a real dad. These were my kids, and that seemed both strange and wonderful and frightening. During the first six years of Ryan's life, he had been Glady's child. And of course I was so young when Little Dot vanished that I had barely begun to realize I was a father. I unsnapped the back flap, leaned in and kissed Ryan, but when I turned to kiss Chelsey, she made a sour face and pulled back.

I slept most of the way up the coast, but roused myself in time to watch the burnt-out slums and refinery tanks of Elizabeth and Port Newark slide past my window. An hour and a half later, after arriving in Penn Station and flagging a cab, I was slipping Jill's key into her lock. And still I hadn't let myself focus on the significance of what Shannon had asked me.

Jill watched me come in. She sat motionless on her black leather sofa, and it took a moment before I noticed her. She sat with her knees to her chest, dressed in fuzzy pink socks with eyes and pointy cat ears on their toes, old jeans and a sweatshirt that said "Men Suck" across the front, in Greek-style lettering. She watched me without speaking.

"Hi," I said. "Ski trip fall through?"

"No ski trip," she said.

"Too bad. You were looking forward to it."

"Never was a ski trip."

"No?" I left the living room and opened my suitcase on her bed, thinking I should hang up my suit.

"It was," she called, "purely a Fig Newton of my imagination, as my mother used to say."

I laughed, but it was phony. I slipped my suit into her closet, then went back to the living room and stood behind the couch, looking down at her. "You invented a ski trip for the first weekend I was coming back to the city?"

"Worked like a dream, didn't it?"

I looked at her and, too late, felt myself shake my head. The movement was slight, but it was enough to make Jill uncoil and erupt.

"Don't you judge me!" she screamed, face to face with me, the sofa between us. "Don't you dare! And don't pity me. Or be mystified by my irrational womanly ways. Just don't!"

I took hold of her shoulders, gently, without giving much thought to what I was doing or what I wanted to tell her.

"Stop this!" I said. "Stop this and listen to me."

She stopped, but her jaw was set, her lips a pale line, her eyes hard. She waited, but I didn't have anything to say. I had only wanted her to stop yelling.

"If you want something from me," I heard myself tell her, "say so." I let go of her shoulders and went around the couch. "If you want to know something, ask. If you want to be with me, tell me." I took hold of her hands. "If you want to know where I stand, how I feel, anything, ask."

"Oh, sure." She pulled her hands away. "Easy as that." She snapped her fingers. "Where do you live, la la land?"

"All I can do is say 'yes' or 'no' or 'maybe'. And if you aren't ready for one of those, you aren't ready to ask."

"Right. Right. All that hyper-logical bull you men use in place of feelings." She turned away. "Haven't you learned anything in your half century on the planet?"

"Probably not."

"Love isn't logical."

"Love is neither logical or illogical," I said. "It's women who aren't logical."

"I could have pulled it off," she said, after flashing me a look that said she was letting my quip slip for the sake of a more important topic. "I could have been gone. But I decided you were the one I was going to stop playing games with."

"Great. So when do you intend to stop?"

"It just isn't possible, is it? The more in love they are, the more at odds with one another men and women get."

"Are you saying you're in love with me?"

"Shut up. I'm making a speech."

"Oh. Excuse me."

"Men and women who fall in love are at odds because we want different things. Even if we want the same things, we want them at different times, in different ways. And we each think our survival is at stake."

"Women may think their survival depends on a relationship," I said. "But men don't. Not real men. Men only get that serious over their careers or their dreams or ..."

"Or professional football," said Jill. "The point is, the worst part of how we are is that we want each other to be what it's not very good for us to be."

"I think I follow that."

"When a women designs herself to please men, easy as that is, she gives up some vital part of being female. On the other side, women are drawn to men who seem so powerful and so secure that they're invulnerable, but if a man has to live up constantly to those qualities, he'll miss out on being human. And he'll probably turn out to be a mean SOB."

"Okay, fine," I said. "You're right. Men and women are impossible for one another. But just between us, don't pull this topsy-turvy shit anymore, okay?"

She turned away, so I took hold of her shoulders again and made her look at me.

"What," she said.

"Don't say one thing and mean another," I told her. "Don't want one thing and say the opposite. I'm tired of strategy, Jill. I don't want to waste time trying to figure out what everything means. I'm sick of second- guessing. Life's complicated enough. I mean, if that's what it takes to have a relationship, then I'd rather be alone. And I'm sick to death of always having to fight."

I thought this a pretty good speech, and I waited for the combative set of her jaw to relax, and the hardness in her eyes to melt. I let go of her shoulders, the way you might release a wild animal.

"You sleep on the couch," she said, softly, then turned and went striding into her room.

I watched her go. I watched her slam her door. The sudden sound the door made, even though I saw it coming, made me wince.

"Fine," I called after her, "but if this is another test, I'll flunk it like I did the last one."

"No test!" she said, opening her door and shoving out my open suitcase with her foot. The door slammed again.

"Don't tell me to sleep on the couch, then get bent out of shape because I haven't knocked on your door."

"Don't worry," she yelled. The door opened again and out flew my suit, pants leaving the hanger in mid-air.

After that, the apartment was silent, except for the bubbling of Jill's aquarium. A school of electric blue neons swarmed about a pirate's treasure chest. The lid of the chest kept opening to release a big bubble of air, which would wobble to the surface as the lid fell closed. I thought about packing my suit and leaving. It was what I would have done a year ago, but now the idea of retreat felt wrong, and I had my archers to thank for that. Inside the pirate chest there was a pile of tiny gold coins, and draped over this booty was a skeleton. Nice touch. The slow rise and sudden fall of the lid, along with the drifty movements of the fish and the incessant bubbling of the filter, were nearly as hypnotic as the gulls in my bay window back at Ireland. But the noises of Ireland, its strange hidden voices, were missing and so I did not slip away. Just the opposite. Right then, when I should have been thinking of something to do about Jill, I finally let myself wonder how my archer hallucination could have produced an actual yellow stain. After a few moments, I bent down until I could see my reflection in the aquarium and stuck out my tongue.

"Who's Francine?" Jill asked, her door open only enough to allow her nose to stick out. "And why are you sticking your tongue out at my fish?"

"Francine McCohen," I said, straightening, looking back at her. "She's a woman who works at Ireland. Do I have a yellow stain on my tongue?"

"Let's see."

She came to me and I stuck my tongue out at her; it was precisely what I wanted to do, and I made that clear by adding a burst of raspberries.

"You sure do," she said. "Right in the middle. Like you ate a big yellow Gob-stopper. What *did* you eat?"

"If I told you, you'd thing I was bat shit."

We stood side-by-side in front of her aquarium. The treasure chest opened and closed three times. Jill lifted the aquarium's hinged lid. The fish became excited, thinking it was feeding time. She used a net to remove a partially eaten corpse, its electric blue color a meaty gray. An orange cat appeared and rubbed against Jill's legs until she held the net down to him. He sniffed the fish, cautiously, before he took it in his mouth and trotted off.

"What the hell kind of a name is Francine McCohen?"

"Jewish-Irish," I said. "Her husband is Bernie McCohen."

"I see. Well that certainly clears everything up."

"And he sells sea shells by the sea shore. Among other things."

"You *are* bat shit."

"I know. The place is driving me nuts."

"So when are you coming back?"

"Actually, Bernie sells beach pebbles. Makes a mint. People think they help you find love or grant you everlasting life or regular bowel movements."

"Oh, yeah," she said. "I got one of those once. It arrived the day you rented your cubby. Got it through an ad in the National Enquirer. Damn thing was coated with something that made my hands stink and had the most bitter taste."

"For a while," I said, "Francine wanted to be my lover."

"That explains the possessiveness on the phone."

I told Jill more about the rooms Dotty McConkle had deeded away and the people who held those deeds and the trouble I'd had with Bernie and how I had resolved it and how Dotty had made everyone who came to live at her inn change his or her name to something Irish. I told her about Ryan's arrival, and the secret passages and stairs and Bernie's God Machine. But, along with things too trivial to mention, I left out Chelsey and the archers. Maybe later.

"So I'd be Jill McRouse," she said. "Is that how it works?"

"You'd be anything you like. There's something almost magic about Ireland that makes you more of what you are. If you're a mad genius like Bernie, you become a world-class mad genius. And if you have a touch of altruism mixed in, that starts to show up. If you're a mystic or a frustrated leader or a hopeless romantic or a budding psychotic, all that starts to bubble inside because there doesn't seem to be any way to hide it, or at least no point trying. I know how New-Agey all that sounds, but it's true."

As I spoke, she took my hand and led me to her sofa. We curled up together, Jill half on top of me.

"Why didn't you tell me not to go skiing?"

"Because it never occurred to me," I said, and waited for her to start yelling again.

"Nice. Is that supposed to make me feel better?"

"It's the truth," I said. "It's not meant to hurt you. How it makes you feel is up to you."

"Aren't we the little philosopher all of a sudden."

"The reason it didn't occur to me is because you sounded so happy to be going."

"And I suppose next you'll tell me the only thing that matters to you is my happiness? Lines like that have probably gotten you into a few dozen panties over the years."

"No."

"No?"

"Well, you're right about where those kinds of lines have gotten me. But the truth is, my happiness matters to me more than yours. And my son's. And my granddaughter's."

"You didn't tell me you had a granddaughter."

"I didn't know it until a few days ago. We'd probably find a few more in line ahead of you if we forced this."

"Great!" She rolled away and sat up. "Listen, I've never had to be number one, but I can't let myself get lost in the crowd."

"Then don't."

"And just how do I stop that from happening? Especially if you don't care enough to fight for me."

"Fight for you against who? Whom? Against you? If it made you happy to go skiing with someone, that was something I had to live with. There was nobody to fight. I mean, if you were being abducted by King Kong I'd stomp his toes. I'd kick his shins. I'd rent a World War One fighter and machine gun him to kingdom come or get crunched into matchsticks trying, but ..."

She giggled. "Weren't you even a little jealous?"

I shook my head. The glib gladhander had returned for a moment there, with that King Kong business, but he didn't follow through enough to give Jill what she wanted. And she wasn't asking for much. Just a show of possessive love.

"I felt one of those tugs of loss," I admitted, because this was true. "You know?"

"That's something, anyway." She looked at me for a long time, then touched my face. "God, you're so different."

I laughed, and pulled her on top of me. "I feel different," I told her.

"Did I tell you how great you look?" she asked. "You look like a well-rested Clint Eastwood or somebody."

"I've always thought of myself as more the Tom Cruise sort," I said.

She snorted. "Don't push your luck," she said. "Not with your yellow tongue and this nose." She gently pinched the break left by some guy's lucky right hook. Then she kissed my nose, and of course that got us started. We made love on the sofa, then down on the floor, directly beneath her aquarium, where I treated her to my yellow spot until I wasn't the only bat-shit person in the room. This time there was more play and laughter in our loving, and far more juice. And after, we held each other and listened to the bubbling of her aquarium.

Later we went to dinner, and as we ate I told her about the archers I'd vanquished and how crazy my visions made me feel.

"You really ought to see someone," she said.

"But what if it's real? Like the yellow stain."

"Then you *really* ought to see someone."

"I am bat shit, aren't I?"

"You are. But I wouldn't want you to change too much more. I feel like I'm with an entirely new man and that it's like love at first sight."

I looked at her for a long time without knowing what to say. "It's like Ireland has done something to me," I told her, as a way of explaining my changes. "Or maybe it's the ocean."

"If it does this for everyone," said Jill, "I think you've got yourself a gold mine."

"It's so strange to look back on the way I've been," I told her. "I've been this totally selfish shit, you know? Everything boiled down to what I owned, who I owned, what I earned and how much people liked me. And when that fell apart I tried to kill myself. And when you think about it, what's more selfish than suicide? But you want to hear something strange? Since I was a kid, the one thing I never dared say to anyone was 'I want'. Isn't that a bitch?"

"Poor baby," she said, and reached across the small table to stroke my cheek.

"Think about what a curse that is. A totally selfish person who can't utter the two simple words I *want*."

She sipped her wine, looking at me over the rim with soft eyes. "If he's so selfish, you'd think that'd be all he could say."

"He can't say I *want* because then people will know what to withhold."

She put her hand on my hand and looked at me with an expression so full of love it made me nervous. There was no way I'd be able to handle that much love and give it back. No way on earth, no matter how much I changed. I looked away.

"I devised all sorts of twisted methods to get what I wanted without letting on I needed anything," I told her. "Or anyone."

"Doesn't everyone do that, a little?"

"Maybe. But if that's true, it's pretty sad. Maybe if it was okay to say I *want* we wouldn't have to be so selfish."

We pondered that bit of heaviness for a moment, sipping wine, looking into each other's eyes.

"Maybe this is why so many women have left you," she said. "Women find it hard to be with a man who doesn't need them. He can't be a weak wimp, but he's got to need me. He's got to need me to survive and at the same time be up to a fight with King Kong."

We walked back to Jill's apartment holding hands, taking our time.

"When you're ready," I told her, "I want you to come to the shore."

She sighed. "Are we talking visit or what?"

"Stay as long as you want."

"I see. Well, that takes care of my side. So how long do you want me there?"

"Forever," I said.

"We hardly know one another," she said, teasing.

"We know enough."

"You're crazy."

"Right. Are you?"

"Maybe not enough." Her sigh made this a serious comment.

"Too bad," I said, without inflection.

"So you're positive you want me with you forever."

"Or until one of us says I quit."

"Ah, I see," she said, suddenly all business-like. "Fair enough." She stepped in front of me and held out her hand. "Nice doing business with you," she said.

We shook hands, then started to walk again, and nothing more was said until we were in the elevator.

"What if I need to stay here?" she asked. "What about you coming back to New York and getting a normal job?"

I didn't answer until we were back inside her apartment. Jill poured us each a small glass of red wine, which we sipped on her sofa as we watched the neons swim about in her aquarium.

"I won't be coming back to New York, Jill," I told her. "I've found my home. However it all turns out."

"Then bat shit or not," she said, and clicked her glass to mine, "you're a lucky man."

Book III
Appearing Now
For The First Time
In America

Chapter Twenty

Jason Sargent was waiting for me in the hall outside the door to Bill Kern's office.

"You look splendid," he said, his voice a little reedy and a pitch too high. "All trim and tan." His eyes darted about. His hands were clammy and his smile was forced. "Suppose it'd be all right if we just walked in?"

"Seems like the best plan," I said, not wanting to add to his tension with anything as weighty as, "Hello, Jason, how are you?"

How odd, I thought. This guy could jigsaw his way into a cranium and calmly muck around in someone's brain, yet here he was, all ajitter in anticipation of our meeting. My heart went out to him, even as I wondered what he knew that I did not.

We went in and introduced ourselves to Kern's secretary, Helen, with whom I'd spoken on the phone dozens of times but had never met. Compared to the reality I now faced, I much preferred the image I'd developed in my mind. She had forearms as big as my thighs and a face like a Nazi storm trooper. She also had the voice of a sexy young angel and the disposition of a saint, and flirting with her over her orderly desk meant I didn't have to deal with Jason.

Cox came in about five minutes behind us. He grunted some kind of greeting at me then asked, as always, if Jason had gotten into any good head lately. Cox had an even harder time making eye contact with me than Jason had. Clearly I was in for a bumpy ride here this morning.

Kern's secretary led us to the door of a narrow kitchenette, where she stepped aside, gesturing graciously, and invited us to help ourselves; she did not, her body language claimed, do coffee. I took orders and went in to make regulars for Cox and me and a herbal tea for Jason. Once we were each armed with a steaming, white, cardboard cup, Helen led the way into a conference room that had a large, round glass table, a wet bar, and a wall of north-facing windows full of Central Park.

"Mr. Kern will be with you as soon as he's off the phone," Helen explained, then smiled, bowed slightly, and pulled the door closed as she backed from the room.

"Must be a great secretary," said Cox.

I had been disappointed by Helen, but not surprised. Kern had told me that an extra thirty pounds and a face that could stop a fleet of trucks were job requirements here, just ahead of typing speed, computer know-how and organizational skill. "Never get your meat where you get your bread," Kern liked to say.

There would be none of that sort of banter today, though. Kern threw open the great double doors to his office, revealing a huge glass desk and a leather throne, and breezed into the conference room as if in a hurry to get somewhere else. He tossed a manila folder onto the table, then sat in the room's only chair with arms. Somehow, without thinking about it, without even noticing, the rest of us hadn't considered that chair. It occurred to me then that this meeting represented a first for the four of us. We had been friends forever, or so it seemed. Cox and I went back to 1958. I had met Kern in the mid-sixties. And fifteen years ago we three had pulled Jason in because he had the sexiest wife at our country club and we needed a fourth for paddle tennis and golf. In all that time, though, we'd never come together in a formal meeting to deal with anything that mattered. Even at the start of the year, when we had launched OU Inc., we had arrived at our agreements and made our ideas and requirements known through a series of one-on-one phone conversations or during discussions that took place while we were busy doing something more important such as drinking in the bar car on the way home or chasing a spongy green paddle tennis ball around a wire cage. We had gotten together as a quartet only when the work was done, to celebrate. Of the four at this conference table, only Kern seemed at home in his role, and of course that made perfect sense. He opened his folder, read for a few seconds, then said:

"The only question I have is how do we cut our losses?"

I knew I had to take control of this meeting away from him, but more forceful men than I am had gone down in flames trying.

"That may be what we need to discuss," I said, speaking to all of them, "but there'll be time enough for that after I've given you a more complete picture of where things stand. And of course that way our discussion will be better informed."

Kern's eyes unlocked from mine long enough to dart to my tongue as I started to say more, which made me clamp my mouth closed. "How much more do we need to know?" he asked. "I mean, if there's brown stuff mushed all over the bottom of your shoe and you stink, chances are real good you stepped in shit. You don't need to send your shoe to the fucking crime lab."

Bill Kern had already provided Cox and Jason with photocopies of the deeds I'd faxed to him, and he'd exaggerated the difficulties I was having with the contractors. He had, it became clear, painted a hopeless picture of Ireland's future, and nothing I reported over the next fifteen minutes made much difference, even the deal I'd negotiated with Bernie. I tried to convince these three that I'd get reasonable bids now, but they were reluctant to spend any more of our funds. I told them I was confident I could work around the deedholders, even incorporate some of them into our plans, the way I had Bernie McCohen. But that wasn't good enough for Kern. He wanted the deedholders evicted, if not stoned to death. They were the enemy and had to be vanquished. But since, having reviewed the deeds, he knew this couldn't be accomplished in time for the tourist season, he thought it best to, in his words, "fold our tent."

"No matter how you cut it," Kern said, "this baby's heading south. So how long will it take to sell the place?"

"I'm not going to sell," I said, evenly.

"I'm not aware that you have a choice."

"I'm not selling Ireland."

"I see." He sat back and folded his arms. "Well I have news. If we vote for you to sell, you'll sell. Or we will."

"No, Bill, I won't," I said, still without emotion.

"You have no choice, McWilly," said Cox. "Wise up."

"I hold the deed," I told them. "I own Ireland. Not this corporation. You can vote to sell the corporation but not the property."

I wasn't about to tell them that the deed had not yet been officially transferred from Dotty McConkle's estate to me, but sitting here, I was glad Horace Asp had urged the delay.

"Bullshit!" Kern erupted. "That's just a technicality. And what the fuck's wrong with your tongue?"

"A technicality you'd exploit if you were in my shoes," I said. "Besides, our partnership papers contain a provision governing how we liquidate our holdings. You wrote it, Bill."

"I don't understand," said Jason, upset by the escalating confrontation.

"It's like this," I said. "I haven't transferred the deed over to the corporation yet, and of course now that I see what my partners are made of, I'm not about to."

"Meaning he's going to screw his friends," said Kern.

"Friends who have pulled together to screw me. If you guys were going to crumble at the first sign of trouble, you shouldn't have come into this deal. Nobody starts a resort without set-backs. What's wrong with you?"

"We just don't see the wisdom in losing money on your dream, that's all," said Kern.

"Because your fucking dream is turning into a nightmare," said Cox. "As always."

That hurt, and I had to take a couple of breaths before I went on. I had no idea Cox was so bitter. And his bitterness clearly had history.

"You said there was a provision for selling shares," said Jason. "How does that work?"

"The guy who wants to sell sets the price," I explained, "but he must be willing to buy at the price he sets. Right Bill?"

"We want the place liquidated," shouted Kern, slamming his palm on the folder for emphasis. "Don't fight me on this. You're way out of your league. I'll eat you alive, McWilly."

"Then your tongue might change color too."

"What is it with your tongue?" asked Cox. "Every time he talks he flashes yellow."

Jason turned to look, his medical curiosity aroused. I ignored them. So far I hadn't been combative, in tone at least, but now I stood, knocking back my chair, and suddenly there was fear in all three pairs of eyes. They knew my background, and they realized that if I got out of control they'd be in trouble. They sat perfectly still.

"Take your best shot, Kern," I said. "But make it count, because you won't get a second chance."

"Wait a minute," said Jason, rattled. Cox looked strained around the eyes, but he was employing his show-biz skills to cover it. Kern was ice. I had my cocky Steve McQueen smile working because, oddly enough, I was enjoying this, even though I knew I wouldn't like where it would take me. But Jason seemed about to cry. "We've been friends for too long to let this happen," he whined. "Isn't there some way to give the project more time? Or some other way for us to get our investments back?" He glanced from face to face, eager for a sign of hope, but found only stubborn resolution in Kern and nobody home in Cox. I shrugged as if to say: *That's all I'm asking.*

"The deed was promised as collateral," said Kern, glaring at me. "Now he's withholding. That's actionable, McWilly."

"Then take action," I said, calmly.

"I can't believe you're going to screw your best friends," Cox said.

"As far as I can tell, my best friends are walking out on me. You two have let Kern scare you." I glared at Cox, then at Jason. "But listen," I added, thinking my only hope was to give Jason something to hang onto. "Why don't you each come down to the shore and spend some time with me?"

"Unless the property belongs to the corporation," said Kern, "there's nothing to do but figure out how much money is left, divide that by three, let the corporation die and bring action against you for damages."

"Don't be such a hard ass, Bill," I said. "Ease up. You'll live longer. Why not come spend some time with me? What do you have to lose?" In the back of my mind I thought that Ireland might contain the necessary magic to save herself, but I dismissed that idea as a desperate fantasy.

"He's got a point," said Jason. "What's lost is already lost. What can a few more weeks matter?"

"If you come down and get a feel for the place," I told them, leaning on the back of my chair, "then I'll find some way to make sure you each get back your two hundred and fifty thousand, if you still want out."

"Plus interest," said Kern.

"Plus interest," I said.

"We've already spent three hundred grand on advertising," said Cox.

"Assuming McWilly hasn't spent a dime, that cuts us damn near in half," said Kern.

"Or," I said, "looked at another way, it means I only have to come up with three hundred thousand and change to buy you guys out, assuming that's where you set the price. And I can get a mortgage for that amount. But remember, I have the right to sell or buy your shares in the corporation at whatever price you each set."

Kern looked at me with hatred. "You're more of a bastard than I am," he told me.

"Thank you," I said, with a slight bow in his direction.

"I say we give it more time," offered Jason.

"With my forty percent," I said, moving toward the door, "and Jason's twenty, that's sixty percent of the vote." I grabbed the door knob then turned to face them. "Gentlemen," I said, "call me to arrange a visit at your earliest convenience. I don't think we have anything more to discuss."

"Not so fast," said Kern. "Unless you let us close on your deed, you don't have any vote here at all, because you don't have any shares in the corporation. You were to buy your forty percent with the deed you inherited. By withholding, you violate a verbal contract, and nothing in the papers of incorporation pertains to you, only to the three of us who have lived up to the original agreement. That gives us each a one-third vote, so Cox and I represent a majority. And we, not you, will decide what to do."

"Good," I said, still without heat. "Then I'll tell you what. I'll call Helen when I get back to the shore this afternoon to see what you've decided. If you want to liquidate, set a price. I'll see what I can do to match it. In the meantime, I have a resort to build."

The trembling started before I was out on the street. Things had happened too fast for thought, but now, as I replayed the meeting, each phrase I had said made me wince, and I wondered if it was too late to run back and beg my friends not to take Ireland away from me. Kern was right. I *had* promised to put up my inheritance as my contribution to the corporation. And my withholding the deed now was a violation of a verbal contract.

All the way across town in the cab I called myself a fool for the way I'd acted, and by the time I was collecting my things at Jill's, I was on the verge of a depression to rival the one that almost killed me on the last day of last year. I felt cursed and befuddled, and I packed my belongings as if I meant them harm. *Here you go again,* I kept telling myself, employing my mother's admonishing tones. *Here you go again, fucking things up.* (That, of course, was not how Mom would have phrased it, but it's what she'd meant, more often than not.)

I watched the ragged homeless come and go as I waited in Penn Station for the next shuttle to Hoboken. An old woman picked meticulously through the trash. A skinny, stubble-faced man who looked ancient but was probably no older than I, asked for spare change, the sour stench of alcohol radiating from every pour. I shook my head at him—hard-hearted New Yorker to the core—and with a shrug he shuffled away, asking others as he went. After ten minutes of arduous panhandling, he stretched out for a cat-nap on the bench across from me, a rolled up *Times* for his pillow, another for his blanket. Pay attention, I kept telling myself. You'll soon be glad you know how it's done.

As I rode south down the coast I imagined my three friends—my three ex-friends—still hard at work at Bill Kern's round conference table, deciding what to do about their McWilly problem, and I hoped pragmatism would prevail. Without me there to antagonize him, I thought, perhaps Kern's need to beat me in battle would eventually be replaced by the group's need to win their war against me. Maybe Jason had gotten Bill back on track, I told myself as my train made another of its endless stops. Being the smart, bottom-liners they were, perhaps they would realize that while they could eventually beat me, they'd tie us up in court for several years. But if they pretended to go along with me, even made efforts to heal the friendship, they could—behind my back—take steps to strengthen their legal position while weakening mine, in the long run saving themselves money and time. Worse still, I thought, by taking a reasonable position Kern, Cox and Sargent could make me look like a total asshole and miscreant if I continued to withhold my deed.

I had lost my three best friends, I thought as I left the train. And I was entirely in the wrong. But what could I do? Once I had taken the position that Ireland still belonged to me, not to OU Inc., the only thing left was to walk out. I'd gone against all my corporate training, but I had done the only thing I could to protect Ireland, emotional and irrational as that urge might have been. In the long run I'd lose, I knew, but had I stayed at Kern's table, I'd have lost everything then and there. So at the very least I had bought myself a month or two. Still, I felt horrible about my friends, and worse still because I had no idea how to make use of this time I'd won.

Then I realized, as my cab crossed the causeway, that by now all three of my friends were doing more important things. Cox was getting made up for his afternoon taping. Jason was poking about in someone's brain. Kern was buying another skyscraper or maneuvering to leverage the bank papers that allowed him to wipe out another land-poor slob on Shelter Island. They were a threesome of winners, and they had no doubt settled their McWilly Problem before I'd finished packing my bag at Jill's.

There was a Town Car, with a driver waiting behind the wheel, parked behind my Jeep, but I gave it no thought and so I was taken by surprise when I found Bill Kern in my lobby. He was sitting on the love seat with Irma McCreedy, who was holding both his hands. Their knees were pressed together and their eyes were closed. Irma opened her eyes when she heard my footsteps, and shook her head at me, warning me off. I stopped in the middle of the lobby and listened.

"You were speaking of a place called Manchonake," she whispered to Bill, and in response he muttered a few words I couldn't decipher. "Yes, yes," soothed Irma. "The place where many have died."

Kern nodded and grunted. "I," he said, "am a *great* Montaukett chief."
I saw his mouth move, but I didn't recognize his voice.
"I know," whispered Irma, and her tone made me drifty.
"But I let myself be cheated by ..."

The rest of Kern's sentence was incoherent because of the way he mumbled and sputtered, but it sounded as if he'd said ..."by a lion." Kern's face was hard. If I thought he had been angry at me this morning, I hadn't seen anything.

"One gun," he grumbled. "Some cheap cloth and ammunition that misfired. A jug of watered down rum and one black dog."

"Payment in full for your beloved Manchonake," said Irma, doing a much better job than I was of understanding Bill.

"And the fucking dog ran off," Kern said. He looked at the ceiling and moaned. Then he actually cried. My model for impervious and invincible maleness leaned his face into Irma's bosom and sobbed. She patted the back of his head until he suddenly sat up and bellowed, "Lion, you son of a bitch! I'll get you if it's the last thing I do on earth."

What was happening made no sense, but I was back in Ireland now, and even with Dot long gone, you learned not to expect things to make sense here. I hauled my suitcase into my apartment and, without letting myself look at the silver gulls in the bay window, went to my room and unpacked. Now and then I heard Kern bellowing through the walls, but I paid no attention.

I wished Ryan, Chelsey and Shannon were home from school. I needed to feel my family around me—since in a sense they were the ones I was doing all this for. Beyond that, there were some things I needed to know, and the two girls were the only ones who could tell me. And Shannon had promised me the truth when I got home.

I was about to have a major confrontation with Bill Kern, but strangely enough I felt no anxiety. I knew also that I would soon have to confront the entire population of Ireland by the Sea and intimidate or persuade them into support, or, failing that, neutrality, and that made me more nervous than facing Bill. I went into the apartment's living room and watched the gulls in the bay window, almost willing another archer to come out and do battle. The mood I was in, I was ready to kick some butt, no matter what color. I blurred my eyes, but the boulders and the forest never materialized. The tall lady jogger in blue came by, long blonde hair and full breasts bounding with her stride. I thought of Jill and wondered what it would be like to have her join me here, perhaps even as wife Number Four. And I wondered what had become of Ireland's creaks and groans and the voices they concealed. Then I remembered the yellow archer and the stain he'd left on my tongue, and stepped away from the window.

I went into the bathroom and brushed my tongue, hard, for a full five minutes, without success. The yellow stain seemed to go deep below the nubby pink surface. It was now part of my tongue, and I'd just have to get used to the way people's eyes darted into my mouth and the way they pretended not to notice or fought the urge to ask. I decided to tell people the stain was my yellow badge of courage, which was as good as anything else I might say.

Bill Kern went away without a confrontation. I had no idea what had gone on in the lobby between Irma and Bill, but whatever it was, it changed his mind about dealing with me, and he drove off without attempting to complete the mission that had brought him all the way down here. I heard a car start up and went into the suite's back room, now Ryan's, and watched out the window as the Town Car pulled away. His helicopter was no doubt waiting at the nearest airport.

It took me ten minutes to track Irma down. I finally found her having tea in the dining room with McJustice, although that was the first place I'd looked and they hadn't been sitting there ten minutes before. I almost turned away at the door, but instead forced myself to walk in. I sat at their table without being asked, which got me started on the wrong foot. Then I compounded my difficulties by bluntly asking what Irma had talked about with my friend.

"That is strictly confidential," Irma said, pleasantly.

"And you," snarled McJustice, "are interrupting a moment of quiet intimacy."

Of all the people I had living here, McJustice was the only one who made no attempt to conceal her loathing. Whenever I came close, I could see hate harden her eyes, and from a distance I saw the way her body stiffened when she heard my voice or caught sight of me. More importantly, I was convinced she had spread word that I intended to take Ireland by the Sea back to the days of the Mooncusser.

"I wasn't really speaking to you," I said, in a charming tone, "so would you please kindly fuck off?"

She stiffened and glared. "Well!" she said.

Irma smiled and closed her eyes as if she was enjoying some quiet, exquisite pleasure.

"I'm sorry," I said to McJustice, "but you've been glaring daggers at me ever since I arrived, so there's no way I could have begun this conversation that would have been acceptable. If I had said, 'Excuse me ladies, but would you mind if I joined you for a moment?' you'd have said 'No way' or you'd have looked at me as if you wanted to cut my balls off."

"Possibly," McJustice said, with a brief, grim smile, probably at the thought of mutilating me. "Still, it would have been nice of you to ask."

"You live under my roof and yet you treat me like scum," I said, surprised that there was no heat in my tone. "So if we're going to be rude to each other, let's just get it out in the open and take the gloves off. Why not start with you telling me what you've got against me?"

"I have my reasons," she said, all superior and nasty. "And I need not share them, if I so choose."

"Is that so," I said, mimicking her tone. "Then as I said before, fuck off, sister."

McJustice cackled a laugh and Irma smiled at me as if I'd said something clever. I smiled back as I stood.

"I'd like to have a private talk with you, Irma," I said. "At your convenience. But let's get one thing straight. If someone comes here to see me, and if you waylay them in the lobby and as a result they go away without seeing me, then you better consider what you talked about my business."

"That's clear enough," she said, tranquil as a sleepwalker.

"So don't do it again."

"I won't. Unless, of course, they ask."

"Of course."

I walked away, wondering if I had won.

Chapter
Twenty-One

As I waited for Shannon and the children, I put in a call to Ace the pool man. His machine answered, as I'd anticipated, and I told his tape, being purposefully vague, that I had a proposition I thought he'd find interesting. That done, I watched the ocean until I heard the kids on the back steps.

"Bring your snacks in here," I called, as they crossed the lobby, heading for the kitchen. "And get something for me."

Shannon brightened. So did Ryan. But Chelsey looked at me without expression. The little girl's face, boyishly cute, seemed to be covered by a plastic mask, and I supposed that her time in hiding, and whatever other horrors of abuse and abandonment she may have suffered, had forced her emotions underground.

In about ten minutes they came into my suite, carrying two plates piled high with freshly baked Tollhouse chocolate chip cookies, a stack of Dixie cups and a pitcher of chilled milk. Shannon poured while Ryan passed out napkins and talked excitedly about some ghost story Jimmy McCaffery had told the children while I was away. Chelsey sat on the chair opposite mine, her feet no where near the floor.

"And it happened right out on this beach, Dad," Ryan said.

I didn't want to hear a ghost story. I wanted to learn the truth about Erin and Little Dot and how Chelsey came to be here alone at Ireland by the Sea, but I didn't have the heart to stifle Ryan's exuberance.

"See, there was this guy," Ryan was saying, "who ran this big hotel back in the olden days who got himself appointed Wreckmaster, which meant he was the guy in charge when all the bodies and stuff washed up from shipwrecks. He was supposed to keep the land pirates away and see the cargo and the valuables from the dead guys got where it should. And ships crashed here practically all the time. A couple a week."

"Not that much," said Chelsey.

"More than a hundred a year," argued Ryan. "Anyhow, one time these two boats crashed, bim-bam, one after the other, and there were all these Germans lying all over the beach and the Wreckmaster and his crew went out to take care of them. But instead of doing their job, they stole all the money from the bodies and all the jewelry too and they buried the money belts in the sand, but then another big storm came and unburied the money belts and the Wreckmaster was driven off the island forever. Isn't that a neat story, Dad?"

"It is," I said, a little rattled because *Wreckmaster* was a word I'd found written in my own hand on the clipboard I'd been holding during one of my early window trances. "It is, but where are the ghosts?"

"Oh, well they all moved into the hotel from the beach where they were robbed."

"I see. That makes sense, doesn't it? If there are such thing as ghosts that's probably what they'd do."

"You don't believe in ghosts?" asked Chelsey.

"No."

"I do," she said, without inflection. "I've seen one. Three times. And I know she's a ghost because she comes out of the waves and goes back in. She's older than me but not much, and she's drowned dead. She lived way back in another time because she wears this long white dress nobody would be caught dead in today, and it's all torn away in the back from what happened to her when she died."

"I've seen her!" said Ryan. "Remember, Dad? Remember the dream I had the night before we found Chelsey?"

"I remember," I said. I had already thought of that while Chelsey was talking, and it spooked me a little, in the same way the word *Wreckmaster* had, although with the things that had happened recently, a common haunting seemed pretty harmless. After all, I was still trying to figure out how a hallucination could have left a yellow stain on my tongue. "The next time anyone here sees a ghost," I instructed, "come get me."

"He's being sarcastic," said Ryan. "I can always tell by the way his nostrils get bigger."

"Okay," I said, looking over at Shannon. "Enough ghost stories. It's time for some truth."

Shannon seemed torn between her urge to tell the truth, as promised, and her urge to protect me from the truth. And the truth was that my first love, Erin Henry McClinch McWilly, was dead. The words caused Shannon to weep and they poked a hole through the center of me that would probably never be filled. Even Ryan, who had no idea who Erin was, seemed touched, if not by the news then by my distress and Shannon's tears. Only Chelsey remained impassive. She munched on cookies and sipped milk as if she were watching TV.

Erin had died ten years ago, just shy of her fortieth birthday, and I wondered why the world hadn't felt like a different place once she was no longer in it. But there was more shocking news, which Shannon withheld until we had both recovered a little.

"Erin," she said, "died with Tonya Brice."

In my stunned state, I didn't recognize the name. "Tonya Brice," I repeated. It was there, a name from another life, but ...

"You know," Shannon prompted. "Tonya Angione."

"Oh my God!" I said. "Tonya and Erin? How could ..."

Tonya Angione, my pubescent, South Philadelphia girl friend from the fifties, who had chased me around New England back in the midsixties, had died with Erin Henry, my first wife and the mother of my first-born child. It made me feel drunk and heartsick.

The last time I'd encountered Tonya's name, outside my own private wandering thoughts, was when Erin had written her hateful letter to me a year or so after she'd run off with our infant daughter.

Tonya and Erin, Shannon explained, were crushed when the roof of their mountain cabin collapsed on them as a result of a fire started by the ancient wood stove they used for heat.

"It was late," Shannon said. "They were asleep in their bed and never knew what hit them."

"Were they lovers?" I asked, in spite of the presence of the two six-year-olds, who seemed to become far more attentive.

"Of course," Shannon said. "For more than five years."

I asked her to tell me that story. She gave me a warning look. I insisted.

"Well," she began, "Tonya was married to a creep named Bill Brice, and they had three kids before they divorced, which was the year Erin and her baby showed up. Tonya's youngest, Billy, was the same age as Erin's daughter, or maybe a year older."

"My daughter."

"Right. Your daughter. All this happened way before I was born. It's only what I've heard."

"I understand."

"Anyhow, the next year Tonya married Gary Shay, the lawyer who got her divorced from Billy Brice. They had Jesse in nineteen seventy-two."

I glanced at Chelsey when Shannon said the name *Gary Shay*, but she had no reaction. A few names and connections began to fall into place, but raised more questions than they answered.

"By then Erin had married a local resort owner named Michael Gideon, and ..."

"Gideon," I said. "As in McGideon?"

"Right."

"Good Lord! Erin was your mother! No wonder you ..."

She beamed at me as tears ran down her cheeks.

"Then Heather's not your older sister," I said. "She's Tonya's youngest daughter."

"Right."

My mind flashed to a New England motel bed where an infant was having her diaper changed.

"I was only five when they died. Billy and Deirdre were sixteen and Jesse was ten. Heather was eighteen."

"And Deirdre is ...?"

"I'm sorry. Your daughter. Erin changed Dot's name to Deirdre Gideon."

"So you all moved in together. What about Tonya's oldest girl. What was her name?"

"Justine. I never knew her. She ran off with her boyfriend before I was born. She'd have been twenty-one or so when her mother died, but we never heard from her. She may not even know, after all these years."

"What happened to the little boy?"

"Jesse died in the fire," she said softly. "Heather got us out, but he ran back in after his ..."

"And Little Dot?" I asked, everything in me tightening. "Deirdre? Did she die, too?"

"Of course not," said Chelsey. "She's my mommy."

"God, it must have been awful for you," I said to Shannon, relief flooding through me, even though I felt foolish for having asked. Of course she'd survived. Chelsey was only six and the fire had occurred a decade ago.

"It was awful," Shannon said. "But I was young, you know. It was worse for Heather and Billy and Deir ... little Dot."

Heather had heard Erin's stories about Ireland by the Sea, and Little Dot had been told by her mother that if anything ever happened to separate them, she should go to Aunt Dot. So Heather brought the combined brood here to the inn, where Dot took them in and passed them off as three nieces and a nephew. Billy and Little Dot became lovers the way Erin and I had, sneaking out to the dunes with a blanket. But Billy ran off the moment he found out Little Dot was pregnant and was never heard from again. A year after Chelsey was born, Heather married Marty Mittleman and as a wedding present, Dot deeded them a room, where they lived with Shannon, eleven at the time, whom they passed off as Heather's sister. Little Dot went a little nuts with the loss of Billy and the birth of her child. She stayed in bed after Chelsey was born, and started to have what Shannon called "fits of agitation." Twice she nearly drowned her child, and finally she ran away from Ireland just as her mother had two decades earlier. Supposedly she went to find Billy. She took Chelsey with her, but six months later Chelsey mysteriously showed up in the lobby.

Chelsey told me then that her mother and father would come for her one day soon, and Shannon stroked the little girl's hair and nodded as if she agreed, even as she shot me a miserable look.

As far as the outside world was concerned, Chelsey was Heather's daughter. Dot, Heather, and later Shannon, all feared that State authorities might take Chelsey away, and after Jimmy McCaffery let something slip one night at dinner in front of Irma McCreedy, McJustice began to make threats. That was how, according to Shannon, McJustice had gotten Dot to deed Irma a room. And later, when Dot became ill, McJustice's threats began again. This time she demanded ownership of the inn. So Heather and Shannon, fearing for Chelsey, put the child in hiding and claimed that her parents had come for her.

The last thing I learned, as Shannon lingered at my door, Heather calling to her from the kitchen, was that Tonya and Erin had lived in what they used to call *a pure, man-free state*. "They hated all grown men," Shannon said, "and you were at the head of their list."

Shannon went to help Heather with dinner. Chelsey and Ryan went out to fly combat kites on the beach. And I sat staring at the gulls and thinking about Erin.

Not for a second did it seem extraordinary that my sixth-grade love and my first wife had gotten together as lovers, or that Tonya's son had impregnated my daughter or that all this history had gathered here at Ireland prior to Dot's death, as if in anticipation of my arrival. I was numb to fate's surprises now. I even decided, without emotion, that grumpy Miss McJustice had to be Tonya's oldest girl, Heather's sister, and I persisted in that belief even after I calculated the years and realized that McJustice was a decade too old.

I had lost Erin more than twenty-five years ago, yet news of her death brought a new grief. It was one thing for her to detach from me. Somehow, beyond my awareness, it had been important that Erin was still living life out there somewhere in the world; I even took delight in the idea that she devoted time and energy to contacting women I had known to tell them how lucky they were to be free of me. It was another thing to think that by now there wasn't even flesh on her bones. It changed the world, and left me more alone and grief-stricken than I felt when my parents died.

It took away my past. Even the tangible evidence of my history, accumulated around me here at Ireland, was swallowed by my numbness. I suddenly longed to have Jill with me, but at the same time my grief made me feel as if I'd never let myself fall in love again. Wasn't it enough for Erin to break my heart when I was a callow young man, full of faith in love and life? Did she plan on haunting me forever? And Tonya Angione! Christ, the woman kept showing up, didn't she? Even in death she had attached herself to my life. What were a few adolescent hand jobs worth, anyway?

I came here in the hope that a man might actually be able to make a fresh start. And if anyone could, I had thought, it would be me, since I arrived with little of the usual baggage that fifty years accumulates. Indeed, at first I sometimes felt as if I had been set down here by a space ship, and that seemed good. I had wanted to be entirely free of my past, with only the dilemmas, mysteries and complications of today to worry about, since these were quite enough. Yet life stuck to me like flypaper. Look what had happened in only a few weeks: I now had full-time custody of my six-year-old son, and I had, it seemed, acquired a six-year-old granddaughter as well. Shannon was becoming attached to me, even though we hadn't quite figured out where we fit. Beyond that, I had an inn full of people who expected me to be their savior or their invader—I seemed to be Saint Patrick to some, King Arthur to others, and to at least one I was the Antichrist. I had lost my third wife and I had failed to give Jill the meager encouragement she needed to join her life to mine. Now I had lost my three best friends, as well, because it was more important to me to protect the dream this crazy place on the shore had inspired in me, even if this new dream was rapidly turning, as Brian Cox so cruelly informed me, into a nightmare. So was all that had happened to me a consequence of random fate, or did I bring it on myself with my attitudes, or the way I lived? Or was someone else pulling the strings? That I was author of this fate simply did not compute, but after I got past the grief and wonder, there was little to do but dream and trudge after the dream no matter where it took me. What else made life worth living?

Ace's return call caught me in this shell-shocked state, and it took me a moment to remember why I'd left word on his machine.

"Where are you living?" I finally asked him, and he was silent for a few seconds, probably considering telling me this was none of my business.

"Got a room on the boulevard in Surf City," he said. "Why?"

"You happy there?"

"What's happy? I'm here maybe eight hours out of twenty-four, and most of those I'm snoring. It's cheap. Year 'round rentals are hard to find."

"It's just you?"

"Just me."

"I may have a better deal for you. Can you come up?"

"Sure. What the hell? I'll be right over."

When Ace arrived, I ushered him into my Jeep and we drove slowly north and parked in the lot below Barnegat Light, beside a plaque commemorating what was called "The Barnegat Massacre."

"Why are we here?" he asked me.

"I'm never sure who's listening at the inn," I told him.

During the drive I had asked about his general handyman skills and he'd told me he could handle most carpentry projects and that his pool work had brought his plumbing and electrician know-how up to speed. Now I outlined my plan to rent Ace a room on the third floor of Ireland in return for ten hours a week labor. I'd get him a crew, somehow, somewhere, and he'd be my foreman. He'd be free to carry on his other work.

"What's with your tongue?" he asked me.

"Birthmark," I said.

"Funny," he said, "but I didn't notice it last time."

"So do we have a deal? If you give me more time than we've bargained for, we'll apply it to any meals you take. And if you give me more than that, I'll repay you with cash and stock in my operation."

"Would my room have a view of the ocean?" asked Ace.

"If you position your chair right."

"And I can keep my pool business?"

"We'll put in your phone."

"I'll need to think this over, of course" he said, and turned to look at the lighthouse. "Okay, enough thinking," he said. "Deal." He held out his big, rough hand.

"Great!" I said, as we shook. Finally something had gone the way I'd hoped.

"Seems to me," said Ace, "the first thing we got to do is debug the place so we don't have to hold meetings in your Jeep."

"That might be a good idea," I said. "But I don't think the problem is electronic."

"Like what then? You got spooks?"

"In a manner of speaking," I said, thinking about Irma and her spirit guide Lavinia. It may have been nothing more than dedicated antispiritualism, or it may have had something to do with Irma's affiliation with McJustice, but I was still suspicious of her.

"So okay then. When do I move in?"

"That depends on what your commitments are."

It turned out that whatever commitments Ace had were easily broken; he was lugging his possessions up the stairs the next evening. And by then I'd taken a few more steps in my quest to save Ireland.

I had contacted the realtor who handled the listing for the land on the other side of the boulevard and told her she would find me more reasonable than Dotty McConkle. We'd start, I said, by selling off separate building lots near the Boulevard, but we'd keep a small plot on the bay. We'd give "serious consideration to all reasonable offers," I said, and as a bargaining chip, to be tossed in only if needed, we'd offer free use of Ireland's spa facilities. She, of course, was delighted.

That done, I invited Francine McCohen to stay on as Ireland's manager, on a deferred salary that would be based on a percentage of net. And the moment she accepted my offer, I assigned her the task of setting up a meeting of Ireland's residents.

That same morning, on my way down to Ship Bottom to see Horace Asp, I stopped at the bank where I now had my checking and savings accounts, and where Ireland's accounts had been for years. I spoke to a loan officer about my need for a mortgage, and, encouraged by his response, I left with all the necessary forms. Asp and I filed papers to incorporate the inn, and more papers to transfer the property from Dotty McConkle's estate to me and then, almost instantly, from me to the new corporate entity. After that, I went into Dotty's file to look at the paper work supporting each of the deeds Dot had given away. There was, I noticed, a separate deed granting McJustice ownership of Room Twenty-nine, just as Francine had suspected. That was bad news, especially since Room Twenty-nine was where I had parked Chelsey and Shannon. The good news was that nothing in Asp's file identified Miss McX, and I asked him if that might be a loop hole I could use to reclaim at least one room.

"Maybe," he said. "Until someone steps forward and claims to be McX, which just about any woman over forty-four years old could do."

"Does it give you any trouble," I asked him, as I worked to figure out why it had to be a woman over forty-four, "being the one to write these deeds and then working for me to break them?"

"Of course not," he said. "It's all in a day's work."

The deed to McJustice had been issued in 1968, a few months after the first deed was ever issued, which went to Jimmy McCaffery. Next came the McCohen deed for the south corner suite on Two. McX's deed was written in 1969, and in order to be a legal document, McX at the time had to be at least twenty-one years old. In 1986 McCaffery's deed was altered when he turned in his room on Three and was given his present space off the lobby. The deed to Irma McCreedy for Room Five, a suite on the first floor, was written in 1989; it was the last. There was paperwork begun on a deed for Shannon McGideon, but it had never been completed. As far as I could tell, Dotty had never separately deeded the suite on Two to Cyrus McCohen, nor had she done anything of a formal nature to deed space in the basement to Bernie McCohen or his McC Corp.

I asked, but Asp knew nothing of these transactions, and back in Dotty's suite, when I studied the deed with Cyrus McCohen's name on it, I discovered that Dotty McConkle's scrawled signature did not match her signature on the other deeds. It did, however, match the one on Bernie McCohen's deed for "office and work space in the basement."

Now that's interesting, I thought, as I drifted over to the bay window. And it raised a perplexing question. If the McCohen deeds were forged, then Bernie or Francine, or both, had to be the guilty parties. Failing that, the forgery had to have been done with their knowledge. So why would Francine so eagerly provide me with copies?

I yanked my mind away from the pull of the window. I had important things to do, and powerful enemies lined up against me, so I could not let myself be distracted, even by insanity.

Chapter Twenty-Two

It was a bright afternoon, and the sun finally offered some warmth. Shannon wore electric-blue lycra tights and a pink thong, and I wished again that either I was years younger or this girl years older, and that we were not in some moral way related.

I was running harder than usual, but she still had to restrain herself to stay with me.

"I talked to the kids, like you asked," she said. "Everyone thinks it's a totally awesome idea. The only problem you'll have is keeping kids away."

"Did you talk to anyone ... with experience?" I asked, trying not to sound winded.

"One guy worked last summer as a carpenter. Another guy and two girls did some house painting. And one guy said he's taken total care of his parent's cottages since he was thirteen."

"Then let's do it," I said.

Ace thought the idea was insane, but I insisted he at least give it a chance. Shannon put the word out, and at nine the following Saturday, we had a small army of teenagers assembled on Ireland's verandah. They were a lively, good-looking crew, but once they got their hands on the sanding machines and scrapers, the hammers and saws, it was clear even to me that they had far more energy than skill. Ace and I went around with clipboards and pens, taking names, making notes, and asking questions about work experience. After a couple of hours of this, we walked out toward the ocean to talk, the kids watching us, knowing, as kids usually do, that we were deciding their fate.

"Get rid of them," Ace grumbled.

"They're not so bad," I said. "And I think their energy might be just what we need around here."

"I'm telling you, they'll be nothing but fucking trouble."

"The tall redhead's pretty sexy," I said, glancing at my clipboard for the star I'd drawn. "Tammy McIntyre."

"What's that got to do with anything?" asked Ace, failing to see the humor.

"Well, for one, she won't have to change her name. That's a plus, don't you think?"

"Listen. If you want her for decoration, fine, but get some people who can get the job done."

I liked his intensity, but not his thinking. "We'll give them a shot," I said. "For two weeks."

The kids worked all that day with electric sanders, caulking guns and putty knives, and they returned for more of the same on Sunday. Ace watched and shouted at them like a disgruntled football coach and wrote notes on his clipboard. I had made it clear to the kids that this was a paid audition and that by the end of the week we'd be selecting only a dozen, so they worked especially hard and refused to take breaks, even when invited. They came back after school on Monday, and again on Tuesday; during the mornings, Ace went around repairing their mistakes and cursing. He insisted I let him do the final screening, knowing I'd pick the twelve best-looking girls, and I agreed, although I told him to hire, if possible, an equal number of girls as boys.

We intended to post a final list on Friday, but that turned out not to be necessary. During the week the ones who couldn't stand being told what to do, or those who had no feel for the work, stopped showing up, so we were left with eight guys and six girls, not counting Shannon, Chelsey and Ryan, who so far had worked as hard and as well as the others. Ace wanted to drop one of the guys and three of the girls, including Tammy, the tall redhead, but I decided to keep all fourteen. We should, I told him, anticipate absences.

That settled, Ace divided the workers into two teams, each with a captain and a co-captain, and under his supervision, Shannon's friends went to work. They were contagiously high-spirited, and soon, as I walked around the inn, I began to see signs of progress. They were also gorgeous young animals who on occasion left me dazed and wallowing in useless sentiment as I stood looking at the ocean and longing for Erin. I envied them the freedom of their innocence, although when I thought about all they had in store I would not have traded places.

I worked as many hours as anyone, except perhaps Ace, and so it was that on one of the first days of May I was three steps from the top of a wobbly stepladder, gingerly replacing bulbs in the chandelier Ace had risked his life to re-wire, when three gorgeous women sauntered into the lobby. From my perch I saw them a few seconds before they saw me, and my eyes leapt from cleavage to cleavage until I'd found the most attractive of the three. This was a woman in her early thirties with short black hair, full glistening red lips and a jaw line like an arrow. She was willowy, dressed in tight designer jeans, mid-calf leather boots that were buckskin-colored, with hot pink laces, and a silk blouse the color of port wine open to mid-sternum. The drape of a half dozen gold chains filled the space between her throat and the pale flesh of her breasts.

"'Excuse me, Bud," the tallest of the three called, her hands on her hips. "Can you tell me, where do we find the boss?"

The last thing I wanted was to forsake my perch, but I told her I was the boss and started down.

The other two women were blondes, although clearly not by genetic blessing. They were in their early forties—great bods, hard faces—and decked out in animal: leopard for one, tiger for the other. They wore spiked heels and gaudy clattering jewelry made of sea shells. One of them had aqua eyes and the other, the evident leader, was taller than I am by an inch, a fact I didn't realize until I stepped off the ladder. Of course she had on spiked heels, but still ...

"Is there a place we can talk?" this woman asked, after looking me up and down and deciding I wasn't putting her on about being the boss. "In private like."

"Sure," I said. "What about?"

I caught her staring at my tongue. All handicapped or deformed people, I'd recently decided, know the precise instant when the thing which makes them different registers, and it becomes something of a game to see how each person will respond.

(I'd been to a dermatologist, twice, who had scraped and cultured and analyzed and consulted. To his credit, he admitted from the start that he'd never seen anything like my yellow spot, and after all his tests and consults, he still had no idea what it might be or how to treat it. I didn't tell him I'd eaten a yellow archer because I didn't want to be referred to a psychiatrist. As it was, he wanted me to see an oncologist, and that was frightening enough. Irma McCreedy told me a while back, without so much as a hint of a smile, that I should think of my stain as a "New Age stigmata." And another time she called my yellow tongue "the mark of the emerging shaman," but all that sounded like crap to me; as far as I was concerned I had been scarred by an hallucination, and while it made no sense, I was trying to live with my deformity, or, to be more politically correct, my physical challenge. Fortunately, there was no pain, and so I was able to forget my tongue for long periods, except when I caught someone gawking, or when I encountered the stain in the mirror and ended up gawking at myself.)

"Business," answered the other blonde, the one with the startling eyes. And as she spoke this single word, she tried for a significant flash of aqua.

"Right this way, ladies," I said.

Spiked heals clomped on the newly sanded parquet floor of the lobby, and, now that they were behind me, I began to grin, because I had a pretty good idea what was going on here. Once I had my visitors seated at a table by the windows in the dining room, I poked my head in the kitchen and asked Heather to put on some coffee, and maybe bring out a basket of sticky buns. Then I went back, enjoying the view into the wine-colored blouse once again as I sat down.

The youngest woman sat across from me and when I looked at her eyes I found myself sinking into the deepest brown I'd ever seen. "So what can I do for you?" I asked, pulling free.

"And you are?" asked the lady to my left, Miss Aqua Eyes.

"McWilly," I said.

"Is that a first name or a last one?" asked their leader.

"Interchangeable," I said, as the younger woman tipped back her chair and craned her long neck for a view of the ocean.

"Well, okay, *McWilly*," said the tallest blonde. "I'm Connie, this here's Pat, and that there is Pearline. Never Pearl, understand. Pearline. We heard you were about to open for business, and so we naturally considered there might be openings for us. We've been talking about making a move for, how long has it been, Pat?"

"For fucking ever and ever, amen," said Miss Aqua Eyes.

"So we figured," Connie said, putting a hand briefly on my hand, "that we'd consider jumping."

"That is," said Pat, "if you can make us comfortable. And guarantee our minimum. And keep us safe."

"Safe's good," said Connie, and looked around the dining room. "This isn't exactly what I expected."

"It's a fucking dump," said Pat. "Let's call a spade a spade here. Health department tests this place half as often as it does me, this guy's looking for work."

That made Connie giggle.

"I think it's lovely," said Pearline, tilting her chair forward. Her voice was almost a whisper. "I could live here forever," she added, leaning across the table, showing lots of flesh in the opening of her blouse while her brown eyes pulled me in like quicksand.

"I intend to," I said, absently, then blinked myself free. "I intend to overhaul Ireland, top-to-bottom," I explained. "It'll still be rustic, but by the time ..."

"Hey, yeah. That's right," cried Pat. "They call this dump Ireland. I heard that somewhere. Just like the country with the shamrocks and leprechauns and bombings."

Just then Heather came bounding from the kitchen with a tray of cups and a basket of sticky buns and a pot of coffee. "Can I make anyone eggs?" she asked, as I passed out cups and plates, napkins and silverware, working off her tray.

"I already ate," said Connie.

"I'll have two poached eggs," said Pat. "A side of bacon. Well done. Home fries if you got any."

"Could I have orange juice?" breathed Pearline, making it sound like the sexiest thing on earth.

"Sure thing," said Heather. "And for you?" she asked, looking down at me. She seemed to be fighting a smile, and I wondered if maybe little Heather was a bit more aware than she let people think.

"Nothing for me," I said, as I poured coffee all around. "I have work to do."

When Heather went back to the kitchen, I started to go into detail about my refurbishing plans, but Connie cut me off.

"So where are you bringing your girls in from?" she asked.

"Are we talking New York talent here," asked Pat, "or what?"

I knew what these women were, but I guess I just didn't want to believe it of my true love there across the table. But there could be no ducking the truth now. Next, I thought, I'd be facing some smarmy, pissed off Atlantic City pimp and his eight-foot goon, come to collect their missing property. A perverse part of me wanted to play this misunderstanding out as far as it would go, but, keeping a straight face, more or less, I explained the misunderstanding.

Connie looked at Pat as if to say, *You dumb shit.*

"You mean we drove up here for nothing?" Pat demanded, as if it was my fault.

"Looks that way," I said.

The blondes on either side of me abruptly pushed back their chairs and stood, but Pearline just looked at me. "Any chance you might change your mind, Mr. McWilly?" she asked.

"He's not set up," said Connie.

"We'd get blown away," said Pat. "Or worse."

"Too bad," sighed Pearline. "I could get real used to this." She tipped her chair back again for a last look at the ocean. Then she stood and, with glances back at me, followed her friends out the door.

As they made their exit, Heather came from the kitchen with Pat's breakfast order, which I sat and ate as my lunch. The swine in me wouldn't have minded spending time with Pearline, and she had seemed to feel the same, I told myself. And of course for the right price ...

Twice that week, as the work on my inn progressed at an unbelievable pace, I caught myself day-dreaming about saving Pearline by giving her a respectable job. And one night, I almost drove my Jeep to Atlantic City to find her.

Working always on Ireland's sunny side, the kids relentlessly scraped and sanded and caulked and primed and painted, while others labored inside, moving through the unoccupied rooms and the halls. In spite of the cool spring air, the guys wore cut-offs and went bare-backed and the girls did the same, peeling off layers until they were down to skimpy bikini or halter tops. Each hour and a half, the interior workers traded places with the exterior crews, except for the two guys and one girl who had carpentry and plumbing experience. These three had become Ace's crew, and, because it gave them special status, they followed him around like puppies. They wore tool belts identical to his, and if they giggled sometimes at the way his crack peeked up from above the belt of his Levi's, they still jumped to accomplish each of his orders and were hungry to be told they'd done a good job.

This SWAT team, as they came to be known, did the structural repair work, having set up a command post out back in the garage with Ace's power equipment. The high scream of circular and skill saws, routers, drills and jigsaws, became a constant background music, punctuated occasionally by the staccato reports of a .22 caliber nail gun or the machine gun bursts from a pneumatic hammer. And all this was played against the sound of young people enjoying themselves, and further off, the splash of the surf.

One afternoon, a week after the three hookers visited me, my vision of dealing with an Atlantic City pimp came true, although it wasn't anything like I'd imagined. The kids had just arrived from school and were getting to work. Ace and the SWAT team were down in the basement framing out the spa. And I was waiting by the phone in my apartment for a response to my counter-offer on a bid for one of Ireland's bay side building lots.

"Two gentlemen to see you," Francine told me. "They prefer to wait on the verandah."

The pimp, if that's what he really did for a living, was a refined-sounding man in his early forties who might have been a Wall Street trader. He was well-dressed, although not the least bit flashy, and his manner, while intense, was business-like and polite. He introduced himself as "a salesman and consultant." His name, he said, wasn't important, and that was my first clue I wasn't going to be offered a vacuum cleaner. His companion, instead of the eight-foot gorilla who spoke single syllables through a crushed nose, was a handsome, solid-looking kid in his early twenties who could easily have won a modeling assignment with Dockers.

"So you're here to sell me something?" I asked.

"In a sense," he said. "I'm here to sell you what we might think of as health insurance. Or perhaps even life insurance."

I was about to tell him I had all the insurance I needed when the kid shifted his stance, slightly, and the street fighter still dormant inside me went on full alert. The movement was subtle, not the kind of thing most people would have paid attention to, but to me he seemed ready to strike, as if he'd heard a cue in his master's voice. My muscles tensed and I balanced myself, which is why I was able to take him by surprise when his boss said, "Show him!"

The kid lunged, and he was fast, but I caught him with a quick combination that sent him tumbling down the newly repaired front steps and into the sand. My left jab had altered his nose—I felt it go under my knuckles—to the point where Dockers was now out of the question. And I was pretty sure the right cross had broken his jaw. The street fighter, having awakened like a puppy, was ready to romp; it was all I could do to keep from bounding down the stairs for more.

The four kids who were working on the verandah gathered to watch, the boys stepping forward as if ready to help, which was brave of them, but also safe since the kid in the sand was in no shape to do any damage. He was pouring blood all over his Izod.

"You have no idea what you're getting into, friend," the well-dressed man said, and it bothered me that he wasn't afraid. "Action along this shore is under tight control, and there are some people you don't want to cross who prefer it that way."

"Then tell those people," I said, "that I'm not a threat to them, unless they've gone into the seaside inn and fitness spa business."

"They'll want proof," he said. "Especially now." He nodded at his bleeding friend, who kept touching his nose, then looking in amazement at his bloody hands.

"Come back and check us out after Memorial Day," I said. "Bring your young friend and I'll give him a rematch."

That little adventure made me a hero among the kids, and I noticed that when her friends were around, Shannon found reasons to touch me. She'd take my arm or touch my leg when she talked to me, sending a possessive message to the others.

An exuberant, infectious spirit drove our young workers, and after the second weekend, even Ace had stopped grumbling about them, except in the mornings when he went around touching up their mistakes. In spite of persistent financial worries, my spirits began to rise as I watched Ireland's face-lift progress. Now, if only a couple of my bay side lots would sell, or if my application for a mortgage would go through, I'd be soaring.

On school days the crew would arrive at three in a fleet of funky cars, topless Jeeps and noisy motorcycles, and on Saturdays and Sundays they'd straggle in between nine and ten, sluggish from partying the night before. Of course they mixed play with work, but we soon learned that more was accomplished if we did not pit ourselves against that urge. There was loud music, lots of laughter, an occasional water fight, time out for tickling and chasing and dabbing noses and butts with caulk or paint. And now and then, when the surf was up, a shift of three or four would go "off the clock," slip into wet suits and catch some waves. When they worked, though, they worked with far more zeal than pros accustomed to an hourly wage.

Once the patching, sanding and painting blitz was going full tilt, McJustice, who until now had been content to watch and scowl at me and my workers, took to shrieking hideously at the kids several times each day. One afternoon she so badly surprised a burly boy with a blond stubble on his face that he fell backward off his ladder into a sand dune from a height that might have done serious damage. Fortunately he only had the wind knocked out of him, and a sprain, although for a while it seemed certain he had broken his wrist, and I drove him across the bay for x-rays. Without warning, the ugly face of McJustice would pop out of a window or through a door or around a corner, and you could hear her shriek from anywhere in the inn. She'd point her finger as if casting a spell and in a piercing voice she would call my kids "invaders" or "rapists," or "whores" or "devil's helpers," then she'd lapse into an angry word-salad which the kids came to call "speaking in tongues." At first she spooked the crew, but after a few days they began to talk back to her in a gibberish of their own, which only stoked her madness.

"Go get your broom and fly away," Tammy McIntyre told her one morning, after McJustice called the tall redhead a whore.

"You think I'm a witch?" McJustice responded, as if this was the last thing anyone might imagine.

"No duh!" said Tammy, and McJustice wandered off muttering.

McJustice refused to let the kids touch the walls outside the suite she shared with Irma McCreedy, threatening to get a court injunction against me, if necessary. And while that was absurd—according to Horace Asp—for the time being, I told Ace to have the kids work around her. So on one side of Ireland now there was this dingy rectangle of shingles, with two sad windows looking north, and I sensed that it may have started a rift between McJustice and Irma, which made the battler in me happy.

In the evenings, the kids would linger on the verandah and eat pizza and sneak beers which they hid in a tub full of ice buried in the sand beneath the steps. Sometimes Jimmy McCaffery would sit with them and tell his Long Beach Island ghost stories or tales of pirate treasures yet to be found. Now and then a couple would head down the beach to the privacy of the dunes. And I was jealous as hell.

Things, I knew, were going too well, and of course the moment I had that thought there was trouble.

Kern's secretary called, and I noticed that her sweet voice had lost its appeal after my encounter with the reality of her. She told me, indifferently, that Mr. Kern had decided to support "The Ireland Project" through the first tourist season, provided I sign a letter of intent which would arrive shortly by registered mail. I would have forty-eight hours to sign the letter and fax it back to her.

The letter turned out to be far more reasonable than I had any right to hope for, after what I'd pulled up in Kern's office. In two terse paragraphs, I, "the undersigned," pledged that if, "contrary to previous agreements, pledges and promises," I elected to withhold from the corporation the deed "to real estate holdings known as Ireland by the Sea," then I relinquished my place in the partnership and "any claim pertaining there to." And should I elect to take that position, then "I further acknowledged" that all corporation funds "expended to date" be considered a loan, "collateralized by said real estate holdings and other personal assets, including pension funds, savings accounts, stock holdings ..." to be repaid with interest computed and compounded at an Annual Percentage Rate of twelve percent, plus two points. "Payable in full on demand."

The last line, of course, was the crusher, but I could ink that out, along with that bit about "contrary to my previous promises," or I could rewrite the entire letter more in my favor and see what Bill did. Or I could ignore it and hope the mortgage I'd applied for came through in time.

That same afternoon, two girls and one of the more responsible guys failed to show up for work, and Shannon told me the next day that they had been forbidden to return to Ireland, even to collect their pay. It seemed that parents of crew members were being contacted by anonymous callers and told distorted stories about what went on here at the inn, and about the kind of place the kids were helping me open. Most of my crew's parents ignored these calls, or had told the caller to mind his or her own business, while some had responded with understandable concern, only to be ignored by their kids. I called all the parents to express my side of the story, and that seemed to work. One father drove up to see me and when I was finished with him he had volunteered to work here himself. But the three sets of parents who had pulled their kids from my crew were unwilling to speak with me.

I asked Shannon to find out at school if there had been more than one caller, but that proved difficult to determine. One kid said her parents were sure that two different women had called, and Tammy said her mother had been contacted by a man. "Then again," she added, "my mom makes love with Elvis, so that doesn't prove anything."

In spite of this setback, we didn't go short-handed for more than a few days. Word had spread through Shannon's high school about how much fun the Ireland crew was having, and there were ten kids waiting to fill each vacancy. I let Ace do the hiring, and so the three replacements we took on were selected on the basis of proven skill, which meant that in the end, according to Ace, we had come out way ahead in the deal.

Chapter Twenty-Three

Kern's letter of intent turned OU Inc. funds into an equity line of credit, with Ireland and everything else I owned as collateral. And that was fine, except Bill had put conditions into the letter that were unacceptable. For a while I considered inking out certain phrases and adding others, but in the end it was easier to draft a letter of my own. With Francine capturing my words on a steno pad, I wrote terms that were, I thought, fair to all concerned, most of them plagiarized from a few boilerplate paragraphs I found on the Equity Credit Contract I had picked up at the bank where I applied for a mortgage.

I faxed this revision to Kern, who called me at Ireland three hours later.

"You should have been a lawyer," he told me. "This looks pretty good, except you didn't sign it."

"I wanted you to see it first," I said.

"Listen, McWilly. I don't understand why you're fighting so hard for that dump, but I'm impressed by your grit. You probably don't know I flew down there to see the place. I figured it must really be something if you were willing to screw your friends like this."

"I knew you were here," I said. "What went on between you and Irma McCreedy?"

"Who?" His tone was distracted, and I pictured him at his big glass desk, reading something that had nothing to do with Ireland or me.

"The old gal you were holding hands with in my lobby."

"McWilly, are you okay? You've been really strange ever since you started this Ireland business."

I laughed. "One of the deedholders here is this trance-channeler named Irma McCreedy, and when I came in you two were holding hands and sitting kneecap-to-kneecap."

"You've lost it, McWilly. I wandered around your place then I sat alone in the lobby for maybe a half hour or so, waiting for you to show, but you never did so I left."

"Bill, I'm telling you, when I came in you were talking to Irma about a black dog who ran away from you, probably when you were a kid. You cried about it. Irma signaled me not to disturb you, so I waited in my apartment, but you just got in your car and drove off."

"Bullshit!"

"Why would I lie about something like this?"

"To psych me out. I do remember having some strange thoughts while I was waiting for you, but I was alone. Don't you think I'd remember if I held hands with some woman? I sat in your lobby and I had this idea that was so amazing it changed my entire approach to the Shelter Island project. In fact, if it works it'll be the biggest thing I've ever done. My life's work. But it's a gamble. And a big risk. In fact, I may want you in on it with me."

"I thought we were enemies."

"Only where Ireland is concerned. I've gained a new respect for you, McWilly, and I want you on my side with this next venture. I'll get back down there one of these days and tell you about it. You'll love it. It's right up your alley."

"I'm glad someone knows what my alley is."

"You sound down," Kern said, and his concern seemed real. It must have been his legal training that let him be friend and enemy simultaneously, a kindly total bastard.

"Well, as you know, I do have some problems on my hands at the moment."

"Don't sweat the small stuff, McWilly," he told me. "It's only money."

Bill Kern's re-revised letter of intent arrived the next day, which also happened to be the day the bank tentatively approved my mortgage application. Kern had incorporated most of my changes, but he had cleaned up my language, and, shocking but true, he had inserted no new shark tricks, at least none I could detect after ten readings with my amateur eye. This, of course, made me suspicious, so I fired back a request for an audited statement of OU Inc.'s books, in a tone that was anything but contrite, and the next day Kern dropped his bomb.

According to his unaudited figures, which arrived by registered mail, all that remained of the original $750,000 was thirty-two thousand and change. I faxed back a demand for an audited line-item accounting, and Kern phoned two hours later to tell me that my request might take a while.

"In fact," he said, "it might take until after you sign your letter of intent. Or after a court decides what to do with you."

"Where did the money go, Bill?"

"Here and there. Advertising costs, mostly. It takes big bucks to attract top talent. And of course there were legal fees. We had to develop and print a prospectus in order to bring the corporation into being."

I closed my eyes and shuddered. My pulse hammered under the hinge of my jaw and I understood better than ever the origin of that cliché about "seeing red." I wanted to reach through the phone and strangle him.

"This hurts, Bill" I said, in a voice that seemed on the verge of tears. "All the money went to you and Cox, is that what you're saying?"

"In a manner of speaking," he said, and from his restricted and irritated tone I could tell he was surprised by my display of unmanly emotion.

I was surprised, too, and tried to move my feelings from sadness and betrayal to rage. My mouth formed the word "Scum," which would not have been an inappropriate thing to call him, but what came out was a wretched moan which embarrassed me and left Bill speechless. "Now I know what it feels like to be raped," I managed to say.

There was a moment of stunned silence, and then, in a subdued tone, Kern said, "You're the one wanted to play hardball, McWilly. I told you you were in the wrong league." Then he caught himself and turned hard and haughty again. "There is, however, one ray of hope."

"Oh? As if I'd trust anything you told me."

He laughed, and his delight, or relief, was genuine.

I slammed down the phone and sat looking at the gulls until Tammy McIntyre began to paint my window lights. Her breasts were in my face, great firm quarter spheres pressed over the top of her bikini. Knowing I was watching, she seemed to work more vigorously. At first she pretended not to see me, but then she smiled and shook free her tangle of wild red hair.

All around me I heard the sounds of work in progress, and I knew the time would soon come when I'd run out of funds. These kids weren't working for free, in spite of all the fun they were having. I had my savings and my stock option and my pension to draw on, and of course I'd be receiving my salary for another few months, thanks to the "bridge" I was on. I was all right, at least for a while, although I'd take a big tax hit if I went into my pension. Still, the work that needed to be done here required serious money, at least $300,000, Ace and I estimated, and for that kind of cash I needed either a loan or for the bay side lots to sell.

I turned away from the breasts in my window and dialed the bank. It was time to put on some Bill Kern-type pressure and set up a closing. They had already appraised Ireland and reviewed my financials, so all that remained was a title search, and that, I had learned from previous real estate transactions, was a mere formality. Ireland was now incorporated, and Horace Asp was in the process of transferring the deed. He'd sent a letter to the bank informing them of the legitimacy of my ownership and the creation of Ireland Incorporated. How long could it take to send a law clerk to town hall to pour through the microfilms?

I couldn't sign Kern's letter now because it exposed me to debt that would sink me before I had a chance to see what Ireland might become. So I'd have to fund Ireland's face lift with this mortgage, and, if that didn't come through fast enough, with bridge loans, my own funds and my percentage of Bernie McCohen's operation. I'd fund the work any way I could, of course, and hope to hell Kern's suit against me for breach of promise and pain and suffering or whatever he concocted would take forever to come to court.

My contact at the bank, a Loan Officer named Bert Manning, was in a meeting, and that, I decided, was not a good sign. I waited for his return call, pacing while the tall red-head flirted with me through my window. I knew in my gut that something had gone wrong, and as usual, when it came to foreseeing in-coming shit, I was right.

Manning's secretary called back, catching me as I was going out the door. She was obviously young, nervous, very polite, very sympathetic, and totally unyielding. There was, she said, a lean against my deed that had been filed by a New York attorney named Kern on behalf of a corporation called OU Inc., and also there were seven deeds of ownership on record, six of which had been validated by the Records Clerk, which meant that those deedholders would have to approve of and become co-signatories on any mortgage granted by the bank. Five of the deedholders had been contacted, Irma McCreedy, Miss McJustice, Bernie McCohen, James J. McCaffery, and Cyrus McCohen, and all five had refused to let their deeds become part of the mortgage. The sixth deedholder, Heather McMittleman, hadn't understood what was being asked and had promised to have her husband call back; so far Mr. McMittleman hadn't been heard from.

"What about Ms. McX?"

"The Clerk of Records hasn't been able to determine that such a person exists," the secretary said, "so that deed hasn't been certified. If that was the only hold-out we'd let it pass, but as it is, well, I'm sure you can see the position we're in."

"What about the lots I have up for sale? Over on bay side?"

"Those are on a separate deed, but we can't grant you a mortgage on the land. You might get a small development loan."

"I see."

"If I can be of any further help, please don't hesitate to call. Remember, we're LBI's bank with a heart."

"I'll remember," I told her.

I was so furious with Bernie McCohen I could have beaten his fleshy face to a pulp, and so I didn't dare go near him. He and I had hammered out a deal. We were partners now. And still he had undermined me with the bank. It made no sense, and yet, as I kept learning, nothing at Ireland made sense.

A day after my conversation with the bank secretary, desperate to be doing something, I called Jason Sargent at his hospital. He was in surgery, and I had to wait almost four hours before he returned my call.

"I wasn't sure I'd ever speak with you again," he began.

"I'm not going to beat around the bush," I told him. "I want to know what you got out of the swindle Kern and Cox are pulling. I know what they got, but what was your cut?"

"I'm not sure I know what you mean," he said, in a tone that told me he knew exactly what I meant and that he'd been dreading this moment. By the time I hung up I was pretty sure the $385,000 dollars had been distributed equally among my partners, which meant I owed each one less than $122,000. And while I might never be able to prove what had become of the funds, I was almost certain Jason would not be able to lie under oath.

My next move was to fax Bill Kern an offer to pay the corporation $150,000 to wipe the slate clean. It was just an opening bid, an invitation to a negotiation, but to my surprise, Bill phoned that afternoon and with no detectable hostility told me he would talk my offer over with Brian and Jason.

I said "Thanks," as sincerely as I could, then hung up.

Work on Ireland progressed, even though I had no idea how I'd pay for it. I tried other banks, but everywhere I turned I ran into the deeds Dotty had given away. So I pressed Francine about arranging a meeting of Ireland's deedholders, but arranging that meeting turned out to be nearly as hard as getting a loan. Irma McCreedy and McJustice always claimed to have made previous plans for each proposed evening, even though evening after evening they never went anywhere. Even Bernie had given Francine a difficult time. And of course there was no way to contact Miss McX.

Twice I went with Francine to knock on the door with seven locks up in the north front corner of Two, but there was only silence on the other side. On the second visit I even pounded like a pissed-off police officer.

"This is Mr. McWilly," I boomed, feeling foolish but not knowing what else to do. "Ireland's new owner. I demand you open this door."

Nothing.

That afternoon, I had one of Shannon's friends go up the turret on a ladder to peer in McX's window, but he came back down quickly and reported that there was some weird coating on the glass that made everything blurry. He seemed spooked.

"Could you see anything?" I asked him.

"Yeah," he said. "It looked like a skinny lady all in white was sitting near the window in a big chair with books and jars of shit piled around her."

"Alive?"

He shook his head and shaped his mouth into an expression that said, "I don't think so."

"Jimmy says she's a ghost," said Tammy, who'd come up behind me. "He says she was a girl from long ago who went out with her father to take the valuables off some corpses that washed up from a shipwreck and when she rolled one over to see if he had any rings or money, she recognized him as her true love, lying there drowned. So now she stays up in the turret watching the ocean and on stormy nights she walks the length of the island, moaning and crying. Isn't that the most touching thing you ever heard?"

After that, of course, I couldn't get any of the crew to work on the turret, and even Ace found more important things to do when I suggested we ought to break into McX's room through one of the windows. So I went up myself, with a hammer, and as I approached the top of the ladder, moving carefully because of both the height and a certain dread of what I might see, I heard a voice whisper, "Don't. Please." So I stopped. There were eight kids below, looking up at me, but the voice had come from above, and closer. I could see over the sill and I thought I saw something pale move through the dimness beyond the blurred glass. "Don't. Please," the voice said again.

Confused, a little spooked, I backed down and found Ace and the entire crew waiting for me.

"Well?" asked the boy who'd gone up the ladder before me.

"I don't know," I said. "I heard something and I thought I saw movement."

"How come you didn't break the window?" asked Ace.

"I can't break in if there's someone actually in the room."

"Or some *thing*," said Tammy.

"Maybe it's the ghost mother from the Old Mansion," said one of the kids.

"Yeah, maybe," said another.

"That's got to be who it is," said a third.

Later, lingering over coffee in the dining room, I asked Jimmy McCaffery to tell me about the ghost mother; I'd heard it from Ryan, second hand, but now I wanted it from the master. And so, while everyone else rushed for the door, I endured McCaffery's tedious rendition of the *Powhatan's* Atlantic crossing, which had ended in a blizzard on the Barnegat shoals five miles south of us, on Sunday, April 18, 1854. None of the three hundred on board was saved, and the corpses that came ashore were stripped of all their papers and valuables by the Wreckmaster, a man named Jennings whose job it was to prevent such violations.

"Jennings ran a place that in its more prosperous days had been called the Mansion of Health," Jimmy explained, "where people stayed four to a room for the outrageous sum of five dollars a night so as to enjoy the healing of the sea and salt air. It stood between Central and Barnegat, on what was later turned into West Seventh, and when Jennings the Wreckmaster was in charge it was called the Old Mansion."

After that, Jimmy's narrative abruptly shifted to August, 1861, and to seven young men who had sailed over from Manahawkin to cut salt hay in what they still called "The Great Swamp." "They were camped out in the Old Mansion," he said, "which had stood abandoned for a few years." And during some late night horseplay on the widow's walk, five of the boys encountered a young woman who stood holding her baby and looking out to sea. "She didn't threaten them," Jimmy assured me. "She didn't even look at them. She just stood there sort of radiating a powerful sense of longing. And then she vanished."

That had been the main sighting, but there had been others dating back to the *Powhatan* wreck.

"Of course after what those boys saw, hardly anyone set foot inside Old Mansion again, certainly not upstairs. In eighteen seventy-four the place was destroyed by fire, but ten years later the Mansion House was built on its foundation, right where houses two-four-three, two-two-nine and two-two-three are today on West Seventh. And a few years later on they up and moved the whole place to where Crane's Surf City Hotel is."

Jimmy's story went on for another half hour, and this, in condensed form, is what he said. Jennings, who was never arrested, was long gone by the time the empty money belts and papers were uncovered by another storm. They'd been hidden behind the hotel under a cedar stump. Some said Jennings opened a big plantation down south, others said he struck it rich in the California gold rush, but most believe he was shot dead in a barroom disagreement down south or out west. Jimmy told me that a mass grave could be found over in the Manahawkin Baptist churchyard with a marker that says "To the Unknown from the Sea," and, according to him, the cemetery records show that among the fifty bodies in that grave are the remains of a woman and "the child the sea couldn't pull from her arms." And of the boys who came to cut hay that August, "all seven went off within a few years to fight the Civil War. The two who hadn't seen the ghost fell at Gettysburg, but the five who did returned without a scratch."

When it was clear he had finally finished, I asked if Jimmy thought the ghost mother, or any other, had moved into Ireland and was living here now—so to speak—under the name McX.

"Not really," he told me, chuckling at my question, "but it sure makes a good story to scare the youngsters with. By the by, when did your tongue change back to normal?"

"What?"

"Your tongue. It's not yellow any more."

I rushed to the window, which was dark enough now to serve as a mirror. My tongue was pink again, and I wondered if—no, it was more like I knew—that this was McX's way of thanking me for not smashing her window. Stunned, I wandered off, absently thanking

Jimmy as I passed the table where I had been sitting.

There wasn't much that I could do now to help myself except work on Ireland with the crew and hope for a break with the bank or for the sale of one of my bay side lots. I told Francine once again to let it be known that I needed to meet with the deedholders to discuss the possible liquidation of Ireland, but only Heather responded. She brought me a saving pass book worth almost two thousand dollars and what looked to be about fifty dollars worth of singles and loose change in a tin tub.

My next move was to have Francine take a letter in which I spelled out our situation as clearly as I could.

"Dear Deedholders of Ireland," I began. "We are about to lose our home."

"Really," Francine asked me.

"Francine, please."

"Sorry."

"Some of you are fighting my efforts to save Ireland and this is a self-defeating battle. Paragraph. I could dispute some of your claims, and if it comes to that I will, but one thing I've realized since coming here is that fighting doesn't do much except perpetuate conflict. I never knew that before. Paragraph. On the other hand, turning the other cheek is a good way to get both sides of your face bashed in."

Francine giggled. "That's good," she said. "A nice touch."

"Paragraph. If you work against me," I said, closing my eyes as I composed, "and if I work against you, we will succeed only in destroying Ireland. If you don't have time to meet with me, please take time to call or write. If I don't hear from you, I'll have no choice but to work around or against you any way necessary."

I paused to think up a last line.

"Ireland asks this of you," I dictated, "in return for all she has given you."

"Great," said Francine.

I'd arrived, I told myself. I was finally the voice of an inanimate entity. Or was I? Ireland sometimes seemed anything but.

"Scratch that last," I told Francine.

Francine typed, corrected, duplicated and distributed my letter, putting one in the mail to her son and slipping the rest under the appropriate doors. The first to respond was Cyrus McCohen, even though he was furthest away. He called me to ask what compensation I might offer those who turned in their deeds.

"How about the same compensation you gave Dot," I shot back.

"I see," he said. He was clearly unhappy with me. "Well then, what's in this for me?"

"What do you want?"

"I want to keep my nice big suite."

"And if that's impossible?"

"Then I want a different room, with a view."

"How about a room with bars? I'm pretty sure I can prove someone forged Dot's signature on your deed."

"Wasn't me. That'd be my mother. Put her in jail, why don't you? She's no friend of yours, in spite of how she acts. She's been trying to get control of Ireland for years. It's always seemed to me that Ireland was a war zone, spirit versus cash. That's part of what made it a fun place to visit and a shitty place to grow up."

"So what makes you so entitled to space here now?"

"Because the place ate my childhood. How'd you like to grow up in a musty old inn full of dusty-musty folk who won't even let you keep your own name and force you to give up your heritage? How'd you like to have mad Bern as your dad, and sexy Francine as your mom? If that was in your history, don't you think you'd feel entitled?"

"I guess. But I can't let you keep your suite. Come meet with me and we'll decide what to do."

"Okay," he said, and sighed. "Tell my dear sweet mother to let me know when the meeting's being held."

The next response came from McJustice. In the middle of dinner one night she stood on her chair and, pointing at me, shouted to the entire room, "This evil one is trying to make us turn Ireland back into the Mooncusser." There was rumbling, the dying words of a few conversations, then silence. "He wants to make us responsible for his duplicities and all his financial miscalculations."

The dining room wasn't crowded, but at least half the people eating dinner had no idea what she was talking about.

"He squandered three-quarters of a million dollars, and now wants us to pay for it," McJustice raged, still glaring at me down her extended arm and pointed finger.

(The only one who knew that information was Francine, so now I understood that I really couldn't trust anyone here over twenty, other than Ace, and maybe Jimmy.)

"He says he doesn't want to fight us, yet he threatened Bernie into building his spa."

"Is that true?" asked Heather, frozen in place as she'd been carrying a tray back to the kitchen.

"Poor Bernie has to give the evil one here almost fifteen percent of his pebble operation," explained McJustice, "or else McWilly will convert Bernie's space in the basement into a dungeon."

"Did you do that to Bernie?" asked Heather, after handing her tray to Shannon.

"Yes," I said.

"Shame on you," she said. "I thought you were a nice man."

"And next he intends to challenge our deeds," said McJustice. "Before long he'll probably get around to you, Heather, and you, too, Jimmy."

I wasn't about to make a scene in front of a room full of dinner customers, so I set my fork and napkin aside and, with everyone watching, and with Heather looking at me as if I had slapped her, I left.

It amazed me that I wasn't more angry or depressed.

Shannon, then Francine, and finally Ace, came by my apartment to see how I was doing. Shannon's wisdom, spread out over ten minutes and spoken guardedly, without profanity, boiled down to "fuck 'em!" Francine wanted to know if I regretted having been so honest in my letter.

"No," I told her, "but I regret being so honest with you."

That, of course, took her by surprise and she seemed genuinely insulted.

"How else would McJustice know about the funding amounts?" I asked.

"How do those spooks know anything they know?" she shot back. "Does this mean you won't be honoring your deal with Bernie?"

"That depends whose side he ends up taking," I told her.

Ace poked his head in to say we could work around the deed owners no sweat, and have a successful season in spite of them.

Except for Francine, I told each of my visitors that I wasn't worried and that, in fact, we were no worse off than before McJustice's outburst, which may not have been true but it sounded good.

Brian Cox called as I was getting ready for bed that night, but he didn't identify himself. He started out whistling a Paul Simon tune, that one with all the "Li, li, li's" in it.

Being whistled at made me smile, and somehow, before Brian spoke, I knew it was his whistle; maybe I even recognized his humor behind the song selection.

Brian invited himself for a visit, and arrived the next day in time for lunch. We shook hands in the lobby as if the meeting in Manhattan had never happened and as if he and Kern weren't trying to screw me.

I'd made up my mind not to raise any issues about OU Inc., or ask about how my settlement proposal had been received, but it was difficult to stick with this as I led him to an ocean-front room on the second floor. Brian babbled about the great weather and the wonderful smell of ocean air, so I guessed he didn't want to get into anything controversial, either.

Most of the people in the dining room recognized my friend the TV star, although except for Heather, they were too proud to stare or otherwise let on. Heather dropped an entire table's worth of soup and sandwiches and gasped:

"My God, it's you. And you're old."

Chapter Twenty-Four

"Any point running the ad?" I asked, casually.

We sat side-by-side in wicker rockers, watching the ocean.

"Only if we don't mind getting sued for false advertising," Brian said.

The crew arrived as we spoke about the shape Ireland was in and how soon the tourist season would arrive. They stripped down and got to work, and as they did I could feel Cox's attitude shift. By four the old fool was down on his knees beside Tammy McIntyre, painting the verandah's patched floor.

With my friend happily occupied, I went inside to call Horace Asp. In a recent conversation, my New Jersey lawyer had told me I'd have to make application for condo status before I could get a mortgage, but now, the moment I told him to go ahead with that paperwork, he said I wouldn't be allowed to "condo-ize" until all the deeds were verified and appropriately filed. "It'd be just as easy," he explained, "or just as difficult, to evict them all."

"So then let's do that," I said.

"Are you sure?"

"What else can I do?"

"It'll be like declaring war."

"Then war it is," I said. "I've given them every chance to cooperate. I've invited them to join my efforts. And they keep stabbing me in the back."

Asp proceeded to ask questions about each of the deedholders, and I could hear him making notes and filling out the proper forms, all "on the clock," of course. It took nearly an hour, but when we were done, I'd initiated eviction proceedings against Cyrus McCohen, Bernie McCohen, Irma McCreedy, McJustice and McX. I'd spared, at least temporarily, both Heather and Jimmy, even though doing so, Horace warned, would weaken my case against the others.

I instructed my attorney, over his strenuous objections, to start the process that would grant a deed to Ace MacDonald, and to reactivate the paperwork that would deed a room to Shannon McGideon. I also told him to certify and register the deed that made me owner of the suite where Ryan and I were now living.

That done, I went down to the basement and found Bernie in the Rock Room, where he was transferring pebbles from the tumbler into the soaking bins. In a large vat to my left, several thousand red buttons were soaking in the same acrid, bluish solution as was used on the stones, with several thousand more awaiting their turn. The air was thick with a musty smell that was mixed with something sharply acidic. It made my eyes burn and my head light, but it also let me identify, finally, what the nearly constant faint scent of Ireland was. The vapors of Bernie's magic formula wafted up from the tubs in wavering lines, like heat from a highway, then melted just below the ceiling. But the fumes, I realized, probably seeped through floor boards and walls and permeated the inn.

"If you want out of our agreement, it's fine with me," I told Bernie, after I had studied the vapors a moment. "Just say the word. That's all I need." I had expected to feel the kind of angry energy that surges inside you in a fight, but all I felt was a lightheaded driftiness, a slight sadness and a powerful need to confront the truth, no matter what the result.

"Who said anything about wanting out?" Bernie asked.

"The way you act says you want out."

"There's a hopeless bean counter living inside you, Mr. McWilly. Did you know that?"

"You may want out when you find out I'm attacking your deed. And your son's deed."

I watched these words reach him across the vapor-filled space, but it seemed then that we were both floating away in some uncharted galaxy and babbling unrelated nursery rhymes at one another. The image made me grin.

"The deeds are nothing," Bernie said, and grinned back at me. "The franchise is everything. That and the God Window." He came around his row of soaking tubs, took my arm and led me out of the room. We went down the long corridor, and by the time we were out in the sun I already felt my mind beginning to clear. "I'm telling you, McWilly," Bernie was saying, "we're ahead of our time, you and me. We'll spread our truth like mushrooms."

"Like mushrooms."

"Like mushrooms. But next we got to make some educational and self-improvement stuff happen here. Seminars. Workshops. Marriage enrichment. Men's groups. Spiritual awakening without all the mumbo-jumbo. Keep the place filled all winter."

"I don't get you, Bernie. One minute you sound like you're with me. The next I know I got stab wounds in my back."

"As Francine likes to say, life's never dull when I'm around." He was beaming at me, but suddenly his brows fell and his expression became serious. "You're not backing out on our deal, are you?"

"No."

"Good."

"I just don't get you."

"That makes us even."

"You don't get me either?"

"Oh, I get you. I don't get me."

My talk with Bernie left me dazed for hours—or was it the air in his tumbler room? And Cox's presence, along with his escalating flirtations with one of Shannon's friends, made me want to get as far from this madhouse as I could.

I took Chelsey and Ryan crabbing over in the bay for an hour, sitting on a weathered wood dock which I owned, and where three large cruisers were tied up. Later I spent two hours boiling and cleaning the crabs we caught, while the kids flew their battle kites out on the beach. My body was tense and my mind was racing, but I wasn't actually thinking, which was a bad sign. Now and then I'd make myself wonder about those three boats, who they belonged to and who had given away the docking rights, but nothing came of these thoughts.

I went for a run and crossed paths with the tall lady jogger in blue.

She was even more beautiful up close, and she smiled at me. I smiled back. Neither of us broke stride.

After my shower, I sat alone on the verandah. Tired of thinking and even more tired of working hard not to think, I watched the ocean and felt it calm me. Shannon came out and sat with me for a few minutes, telling me a story about something that had happened to her at school.

Funny, I thought, the way days could slide past when I wouldn't even notice the ocean. Like everything else in life, like all the women I'd loved, I had come to take the sea for granted.

"Atlantic is pacific today," Irma said. I had thought Shannon was beside me, but somehow she had turned into Irma. "I'm sorry. Did I disturb you?"

"It's all right," I said.

"What were you thinking just now?"

"Nothing."

"For a man with nothing on his mind, you wore a powerful look of longing."

I laughed. "I was thinking how sad it is that we take things for granted. Like the ocean."

"Or a rose. Or perhaps a yellow archer?"

I looked at her curiously, then stuck out my tongue to show that my stain was gone.

"It means you've faced and embraced your worst fears. Especially your fears of needing and being needed, of giving and receiving both anger and love. The struggle is to learn to balance between contradictions, between your own goodness and badness, between life and death. You're the only man I've known who could survive the journey, which doesn't mean you will." As she spoke I felt my mind become drifty, the way it had down in the basement with Bernie, the way it did each time I stood in the bay window and watched the gulls. She said a whole lot more, but her voice was now a wordless melody, with tones rising and falling.

"What's next?" I heard myself ask, as if my voice and my watching mind were separated by a great distance. "Are there more archers?"

"No more archers," she assured me. "It's time to seek truth inside a rose."

"What will that do for me?"

"You are presently being pulled apart from two directions. The future and the past might be one way to think of it. Good-Bad. The masculine and the feminine. But these are just inadequate words. The spiritual world pulls you one way, the material world the other, and the rose will help you know where to find your balance. Find the rose and go inside."

Brian Cox's voice cut into Irma's spell. He said something about youth being only in one's mind. He was directly below me, under the verandah. I heard Tammy giggle.

"He's thirty two years older than she is," I told Irma, who looked at me as though I'd just told her that Gaul was divided into three parts.

"Here at Ireland," Irma said, "things unfold on their own and, now that you're our energizing catalyst, always precisely as they should. Years and bodies and names and plots and plans mean less here than truth and time and dreams. For you there is only this bombardment of worries and problems and frustrations and fears, because that is how you live. Your problems blend into the throbbing headache of daily self-doubt, and yet they are your own creation. You make the reality that besieges you. Let go, McWilly. Let go and go into the rose. Let go and find the peaceful powerful balance point between contradictions and opposites. You'll lose yourself in the rose and find yourself and you'll leave the battle behind."

"You'd like that, wouldn't you, you dike bitch," said Bernie McCohen, speaking from immediately behind us, through the dark screen of the bay window in the front parlor. And as he spoke, I heard Tammy sigh below me, and Brian moan, and across the beach the ocean surged and above me the gulls cried.

"Bernie!" said Irma, as I fought to hold onto my mind. "Have you been spying on us? How typical of you."

Irma stood and walked away, but as she did she turned to me and smiled. And her smile was full of kindness and love. She paused at the door.

"Why not take a rose and a candle with you into your shower," she said. "That can sometimes be a shortcut. Travel into the rose, McWilly, and see what happens."

"Great idea," I said, but with less sarcasm than I intended.

"What'd she say?" Bernie asked me.

"She said to tell you to mind your own business," I said.

"What does she think I'm doing?"

Cox didn't show up for dinner, so I guessed he was still rolling about under the verandah with Tammy. Old geezer would probably have a heart attack, I thought, trying to keep up with an eighteen-year-old.

As I was eating a piece of Heather's homemade apple pie, with a slice of cheese, a messenger arrived with a dozen long-stem roses. Someone must have pointed me out because he marched straight across the dining room to the table where I sat with Ryan, Chelsey and Jimmy McCaffery, and, with a stiff bow, placed the long rectangular box in my arms.

"From a secret admirer," the card said, in a neat, loopy feminine script. "See you on the beach?"

Dreamer that I am, I thought my secret admirer might be Pearline from Atlantic City, or maybe the blue jogger who had smiled at me, or Jill, who had indicated in our last phone conversation that she was still trying to decide what to do about her new friend and me. Those three women's faces flashed before my eyes in less than a second, but I knew the roses were from Irma, and my deflated fantasies made it impossible for me to give her gesture the thought it deserved.

After dinner I was too restless to sit with the little kids and the teenagers on the verandah to hear more of Jimmy's ghost and treasure stories, so I went for a walk in the gathering dusk. I walked for probably an hour, but no secret admirer stepped from the shadows. Later I tried to watch television, but ten minutes of switching channels told me this wasn't going to work. And because I had nothing better to do, and since otherwise I'd have worried myself dizzy about how I was going to fight off Bill Kern or what would happen here when the legal action I'd taken against some of the deedholders came to light, I lit a candle, stuffed one of the roses into a Coke bottle, stripped and went into my shower. I put the candle on the soap tray, then cranked up the hot water until I was engulfed in steam.

Almost immediately the wispy gray cloud got inside me and caused my legs, my arms, the back of my neck and my shoulders to release their tension. After about three minutes, I decided I had done the right thing by coming in here, even though a part of me still felt foolish and there remained in me an urge to resist Irma's strange suggestion, simply because it had come from her. The rush of the shower became an insistent noise that urged me to float away, and the candle was now a distant glow, miles off through the fog. I soon felt myself beginning to disappear into the endless folds of the rose pedals.

The walls around me were red, but further on, deeper into the pudenda folds, there were other layers and other colors, and from the start I sensed their presence with an uneasiness that was a step away from panic. The red zone was an angry space. Near the top, the color was dull and dirt-streaked, and as I moved through I became aware of a number of irritations too petty to even bring to mind. Then the color around me became a more sanguine red, and my mind suddenly started to time-travel through phases of my life, and from setting to setting. In the same dizzy second I went from South Philadelphia to Bryn Mawr to college, to all the motel rooms where General Motors had sent me, to New York City, and then to my various homes in Connecticut. I also jumped from person to person, marriage to marriage to marriage, as I made this journey. I was a scared kid acting tough in order to survive the brutality of his relatives and friends and a young college man keeping himself stewed on beer so he could pretend the loss of love wasn't sitting in his stomach like poison and a washed-up executive riding the train to nowhere. I remembered feeling like a freak at sixteen, a foreign species transplanted to a place where great value was placed on charm and wardrobe and athletic prowess and next to none on toughness, endurance, or grit. I remembered finding Erin Henry again just as I was convincing myself I could marry Carol Zeller, the thrill of loving her with my entire being and at the same time facing the awfulness of our incompatibility, measuring that against the obligations of parenthood and marriage. I felt again the shock when Erin ran out on me and took our daughter with her. And of course I remembered how foolish and useless I felt when the company I had dedicated myself to tossed me aside. All these and more came as pictures flashed rapidly on the screen in my mind. Then, in the next instant, I confronted today's angers: having my best friend use legal and financial skullduggery to murder my last chance to make something of my life; Erin's relationship with Tonya Angione and their deaths; the deedholders; Bernie's betrayal; Jill. I was so full of rage and hate now that my fists were clenched and I knew that had I come face to face with Bernie McCohen or Bill Kern in that moment, they would not have survived. Same with Erin Henry, who was already dead. Oddly enough, McJustice never put in an appearance.

Rattled, I shut off the shower and dried myself as if I meant to rub away my skin. I was pulsating inside with a strange new energy, although I can't say that I felt particularly angry anymore, once I was dressed. I had grabbed a pair of light, cotton draw-string pants from my drawer, which were creamy white, and without paying attention to how I looked, I slipped on a pure white oversized T-shirt. I went out on the porch and stood looking at the ocean. There was a three-quarter moon, with thin clouds sliding across its face, and it gave the sand a waxy glow. Jimmy and the kids were gone and for a few moments I had the verandah, and the beach, all to myself.

There was movement behind me and the door softly closed.

"You look good enough to eat," a soft female voice whispered. Then Erin slipped her hand into mine and we went together down the stairs and onto the cool sand. She had her checkered bedspread over her arm. We were both barefoot and we made the dry sand squeak as we walked.

"Did you get my roses?" she asked.

"Yes. Thank you. I'm not sure anyone has ever sent me flowers before."

"If you were mine, really mine, I'd send you flowers every day."

We passed Brian and Tammy. They were walking with their arms around each other, leaning close and staggering like drunks.

"They make a nice-looking couple."

"I think they look absurd," I said.

"Love always looks good on people."

We were back among the dunes now, spreading our bedspread on the sand as if we'd done it many times. I was on my knees, smoothing out the lumps, but something nagged me about having seen Brian and Tammy. Erin let her shorts fall, stepped out of them and unbuttoned her shirt.

"He's so old," I said. "And she's so young."

"He and you are the same age, right?"

"Just about."

"But you look so much younger."

She wore skimpy, nearly transparent panties, pink if they were any color at all. She lay down beside me and let her fingers tickle the hair on my left arm. Her body was long and lovely, and it made me melt inside, but the panties, instead of turning me on, provoked the question, "Why bother?" which, even as it came to mind, I realized was something only a jaded old fart would think at a time like this.

"I guess I'm in better shape than Brian," I said.

"He's all cosmetically handsome. Not natural, like you. And of course I look so much older than Tammy, so maybe you and I aren't as absurd-looking as they are."

I blinked as the implications of this sentence registered, and my blink broke the spell. Shannon lay practically naked in the moonlight beside me, looking just the way Erin had more than thirty years ago. My mind reeled away, and from a distance I saw myself kneeling in my all-white costume beside this girl; I looked like a priest about to sacrifice a virgin, and the horror I felt must have registered on my face.

"What's wrong?" Shannon asked.

"What are we doing?" was all I could gasp out.

"We're becoming lovers," she answered, simply enough. "The energy's been there for weeks and weeks. It's only been a matter of time. And we've both known it."

"But you ... you're ..."

"In love."

"This doesn't feel wrong to you?"

"Not at all. I'm in love with you."

"It sure does to me," I said, standing and turning my back. I looked at the ocean and felt crazier than ever.

How could I have let myself come so far under the illusion that Shannon was Erin? And what if I had gone a little further? What if Shannon and I had made love? What if I had tuned back in right in the middle of sharing an orgasm with this child? I'd have gone right over the edge and never come back. They'd have had to carry me off this beach on a stretcher and put me in some home.

But Erin was dead, I told myself, and Shannon was here. And maybe her love was what I needed.

Was I really going to throw that kind of love away again? After all, I was here to make a new beginning, and maybe to get it right this time. How many fifty-year-old men get another chance at this kind of pure love? And wasn't it this longing that ate away at our aging souls? Perhaps loving Shannon and being loved by her might let me reclaim the life I'd squandered. Wasn't that, after all, what my dreams of Ireland were all about?

"Why'd you meet me then?" Shannon asked.

I looked back and found that she was sitting up and covering herself with folded arms. Her pretty face showed anger and hurt.

"I didn't."

"Sure you did. You were there exactly when we said."

"We said?"

"At dinner. After the roses arrived. Remember? I went, 'See you later?' making it, like, a question. And you went, 'Sure. I'll probably go for a walk around ten'. Then you said, 'Want to come?' and I flashed you a look that you flashed back and we both smiled about the double meaning."

"Get dressed, okay?"

"You think I'm a slut now, don't you?"

I shook my head. "I'm crazy, Shannon. I had no idea the roses were from you and when you took my hand, and then the whole time we were walking up the beach and spreading out this blanket, I was with your mother, for crying out loud."

In silence she finished buttoning her blouse, and then, without bothering to stand, by rocking back and lifting her legs, she wiggled into her shorts.

"Why *did* you send me the roses?"

"Because it was time to stop all this flirting and dreaming and make something real happen. I was telling Irma how in love with you I was and I think she gave me the idea about the roses."

"She didn't try to tell you I was too old?"

"No way. She told me that it was a gift to know what's in your heart, but that once you do know, you have to reach for it with all your might because you might not ever know so clearly again and these chances can easily be lost."

"I agree with all that. But ..."

"I know." She held up her hand. "Spare me the lecture. I don't want to hear about how you'll be in your seventies before I'm finished with my thirties and how a girl like me will end up feeling tied down by an old fart like you and how I'll resent not having babies and start to run around and in the end make your life a living hell."

"I wasn't going to say any of that." I found that tears were streaming now and, after a moment's embarrassed shame, I became comfortable letting them flow. "What I was going to say is that you're the closest thing I've got to a daughter, and I don't want to lose you the way ..." My throat closed and I strained to finish, then gave up.

"What," she asked, gently.

"I've lost all my daughters, Shannon," I managed to say, before I shocked us both by sinking to my knees beside her and starting to sob.

Shannon held me and stroked the back of my head and it was a good ten minutes before I could speak again. When I did, I spoke first, but only briefly, about Little Dot, then I told Shannon how my second wife had lost two babies, both girls, and how any pain I had felt had to be set aside for Gail's sake.

"In each case," I said, "the miscarriage occurred on the day we learned our child's gender, so I got it into my head that there was a curse on me making it so I could never have a daughter. I think I've believed deep down that if a female knew what was good for her she'd stay miles away from me. I was so relieved when Ryan turned out a boy I embarrassed myself in the doctor's office the way I shouted and carried on. Everyone thought I was the worst male chauvinist pig on the planet, but I was only reacting to the curse."

We sat together and held each other for probably a half hour, watching the moon and the ocean, and had anyone seen us they would have been certain they'd come upon lovers in after-glow. But they'd have been wrong because in that time we were silently becoming something far more intimate.

Finally I stood and, offering Shannon both my hands, I pulled her to her feet. I hugged her and told her I loved her.

"I love you," she said. "Trouble is, I never had a father so I don't know more than one way to love a man."

"I know," I said, folding up the spread. "So we'll make it up as we go."

Chapter Twenty-Five

I went to bed expecting to feel shame or guilt or regret over what had nearly happened with Shannon, but those familiar feelings never attacked, even in my dreams, and I awoke with a surge of hopeful energy. I was flowing and alive inside, and while I didn't stop to analyze what was happening—doing so, I felt, would ruin it—I suspected the changes had to do with my experiences with the rose and with Shannon. So that afternoon, my work done, I took my candle and my rose back into the shower.

The water whispered on the tile and soon enveloped me in steam. The red around me this time was so vibrant it shimmered, and even before I became aware of any specific event from my past, I knew that the stored rage here was many times more powerful than the rage I felt last night. Waiting here to grab me were feelings attached to injustices and wounds that were, or so I'd thought, too big to matter to any one person: the global victory of greed and evil over kindness, both in me and around me; the fact that so many of my generation died for a bad idea in Vietnam while I remained exempt; the impossibility of dealing with a woman I loved without the protection of guile, power or indifference; the death of love; the death of youth; the death of friendship; the death of purpose or possibility; the death of a valid masculinity. I recognized all these as the stuff of serious depression, and to dwell here, I knew, was to be immobilized and to risk becoming suicidal again. So I hurried on until I finally stepped from beneath a fold of a rose petal into the yellow zone, and this was, I knew instantly, the realm of fear. As bad as the last part of the red zone had been, I wanted to turn back.

"Fear is the foundation of anger," I heard someone say, and at first it didn't seem strange to me that I'd hear a voice inside my shower; that's how far gone I was. I was hiking inside a rose the way thousands of tourists each year hike into Grand Canyon, so why would a disembodied voice bother me? I was, however, dimly aware both that the voice sounded like Irma's, only younger, richer, softer, and that somehow it was part of the steam around me. I was aware, but too entranced to attach any significance to my awareness. I'm not certain what part of what came next came from my mind or from the voice, but it went like this:

"The mother of fear is loss, which at its heart is the fear of abandonment, every child's most terrifying nightmare. And the fear of abandonment is a nightmare because it invokes the fear of annihilation. When you know fear, you are not in the present. Fear is an emotion attached by anticipation to the future and through regret to the past. In the moment, in the present, even in the face of danger, there is no fear."

What wisdom the woman possessed, I thought. Why hadn't I realized until now how wise Irma was? And what the fuck was she doing in my shower?

I snapped off the water and threw open the glass door, half expecting to find Irma standing in my bathroom. But the room was empty, although that was hard to tell at first since it was full of steam. I stood there holding my burning candle in my right hand, the Coke bottle with the rose sticking from its neck in my left. In the distance I heard a thumping sound but it took a minute before I recognized that someone was pounding on the door of my apartment. There had to be a hidden speaker around here somewhere, I thought, but the fog was too dense to allow a decent inspection, and so I opened the bathroom door.

I came from the bath shrouded in steam, still holding my Coke bottle vase and my candle, and nearly collided with Francine, who was coming down my hall. She giggled at the sight of me, but it took a moment for me to realize that I was soaking wet and naked. I jumped back into the bathroom.

"There is a large gathering of women in the lobby," Francine informed me. "And I think you should greet them just as you are."

"What do they want?" I stuck my head out. Steam swirled around me and, seeing myself from Francine's perspective, I began to laugh.

"Your head, it would seem. They won't leave until they've seen you, and if you go out there with your candle and your rose, you won't have a thing to worry about from now on. Are you all alone in there?"

"I'm afraid so."

"God, you have a rich imagination. Too bad nothing came up between us."

"Would you tell the nice ladies that I'm getting dressed, and will be with them shortly."

"I'd be please to."

"Thank you."

"But only if I can have one more peek."

"What the hell," I said, and jumped into the hall, paused a moment, then jumped back into the bathroom.

I heard Francine giggle.

The bathroom was less foggy now, and as I dried I glanced about for a speaker. Irma had found a way to insinuate herself into my mind, I now firmly believed. She had caused me to have hallucinations and had no doubt implanted hypnotic suggestions meant to serve her best interests, including an amnesia message that had probably erased any memory of her presence. After all, she had erased herself completely from Bill Kern's memory. So did this mean she was responsible for the archers and the sleepwalking that had left me down by the surf on my first morning here? I decided the answer was yes, and that Irma had also nearly succeeded in turning Shannon into my lover, which she and McJustice would no doubt have exploited as evidence of my corruption. In the supposed war that pitted me against the greedy McCohens on one side and the New Age lesbians on the other, Irma was by far my most dangerous enemy. And the worst of this awareness was that it meant I could no longer trust the thoughts and inclination that emerged from my own mind.

I felt relaxed as I dried myself and thought about Irma's treachery, and that seemed strange. Why wasn't I tense and angry, the way I usually get in response to betrayal and conflict? I felt a new lightness of being, and a self-contained power that had nothing to do with fists, and I knew instinctively that these feelings, like those I'd awakened with this morning, were due to my having strolled down into that rose, crazy as that seemed. And facing down the archers had done me no harm, either, now that my yellow stain was gone. And Shannon and I had gotten past our crazy lust, mine for the love of youth, hers for a loving father, and had found something in each other that we each had desperately needed. So if Irma's purpose was to drive me crazy, as the comment overheard by Chelsey suggested, then something in me had turned her black magic to good use, although I had no idea how I'd managed to do that or if I'd be able to do it again.

Waiting for me in the lobby was a crowd of about fifty women, and when I stepped through the door, they began to shout questions and accusations at me in a way that made me want to cover my head and retreat. I could make no sense of their words, although the placards carried by some made their mission clear. The group seemed to go by the name "Mothers Against Decadence," or so a half dozen placards proclaimed, although one woman's sign said she was a "Mom Opposed to Perversion," which made her a MOP instead of a MAD, and I liked that.

"Keep LBI safe for children," said another sign. "Burn Ireland."

I counted five signs that said, simply enough, "McWilly Go Home."

Had I been awarding a prize for best sign, though, it would have hands down gone to the one that said:

"We don't want the (@#*@)%# Mooncusser back."

Brian Cox, wearing an alarmed expression, and Tammy, wearing the world's skimpiest bikini, watched from just inside the front door, and in a flash I imagined what Cox would soon report to Bill Kern and Jason Sargent. Way in back, part-way up the stairs, I saw McJustice, and there was more pleasure on her face than I would have thought possible. This was probably how she looked during orgasm, I thought, then wished I hadn't. Irma was not in sight, and as I made note of this, a crazed voice in my mind told me, "Of course not, because she's still in your shower."

I held up my hands for quiet, but that only caused the women to turn up the volume. I said, "Ladies, please," several times, but only those closest to me heard. Finally I bellowed, "Will you all please shut the fuck up!"

"Well!" said someone in back, as the rest settled down.

"What more do we need?" said someone else.

"The proof's in the pudding," said someone to my right.

"If you'll speak one at a time," I told them, "I'll be happy to answer your questions."

A dozen voices shouted at me.

"If not," I bellowed, "then I'll have to ask you to leave."

That provoked more angry shouts.

"And if you don't leave," I told them, when they were quiet again, "I'll have no choice but to call the police and press charges against you for trespassing."

"They can't be trespassing if they're my guests," said McJustice.

"Okay," I said, without rancor. "Then please take your guests into your suite, because if they clog my lobby and interfere with the operation of my inn, then I'll have you arrested along with them."

"Is it true you plan to hire whores?" someone shouted.

"No."

"Then why were hookers seen leaving the inn?"

"When you tell a lie," I said, glancing up at McJustice, "you create a reality."

"Is it true you plan to open a spa here?"

"Yes."

"How can you let children live in such a place?"

"It'll be a health spa. Not a massage parlor."

"How can you let high school children work here?"

"They need the work. We need the work done. They seem to like the work. I like what they've accomplished."

"Why did my son lose his virginity here last weekend?"

"I don't know. Probably for the same reason someone's daughter lost hers. Probably for the same reason you lost yours and I lost mine."

"How do we know the whole island won't be infected with AIDS because of you?"

"Because I'm not HIV Positive," I said. That caused a few heads to nod, I think, and made me feel that maybe I'd managed to change the climate a little. "Let me say a few things and maybe I can ease your fears," I said.

There was a reluctant quieting. Francine and Bernie squeezed up from the basement and took a place against the back wall. Heather and Shannon and Shannon's friends on our crew watched the show, some through the open front windows, some from the French doors to the dining area, a few from the stairs above McJustice. The blueberry blue door of Jimmy McCaffery's room was open a crack, so I figured he was in there listening. Then I noticed Bill Kern standing beside Brian Cox. And somehow Jill was there, too, looking in from the verandah. And Pearline, the Atlantic City hooker, stood beside the blue jogger, expectant expressions on both their faces. And I realized in that instant, that, glib as I am, I have all my life dreaded the moment when I would have to make a speech that actually mattered.

Back in my twenties, when I had traveled about giving ten assembly programs a week for General Motors, I thought nothing of standing in front of one packed auditorium or gymnasium after another and mindlessly spouting off about the dazzling future promised to us all by democracy, capitalism and modern technology. It had been so easy then to be confidently articulate about life and will and dedication and the importance of education and curiosity and creativity and the indomitable spirit and imagination of man. After GM, and for the rest of my career, sound-bite pearls and quotable quotes were my stock in trade, and it became frighteningly easy to toss out propaganda candy-coated by eloquence. I had years of experience to prepare me for this moment, but I froze now because I knew my tricks would work against me, and that all I really had to offer was a handful of truths this audience wasn't going to like.

I looked for inspiration to Bill Kern but he was gone. So was Jill. So were Pearline and the nameless blue jogger. This wasn't a terrific time to start hallucinating, I told myself, half-expecting an attack from one of my Technicolor archers, or maybe all of them at once.

"I don't know what you've been told," I said, "but it is true that when I came here I planned to hire a young attractive staff so that the place would have a certain sex appeal. But according to the rumors that got you here, you'd think I intended to turn Dot's old place into some sort of Roman-Greco spa, with people running around in togas or nothing at all. 'Eat peeled grapes 'til you puke.' That sort of thing. I was really thinking of it more as a kind of North Atlantic Club Med, with maybe a touch of Canyon Ranch. Lots of water sports and fitness activities. Great food. But strictly BYOD."

"What's BYOD?" someone asked, as I hoped.

"Bring Your Own Decadence."

There were a few smiles, a ripple of laughter.

"Anyhow, there was never going to be prostitution, but if my guests wanted to fuck each other's brains out, that was more than fine with me."

The women murmured in response to my language and Brian shook his head and looked away. The kids hooted and applauded.

"But now," I added, "I have all I can handle just to keep Ireland from being sold off to developers, so there's been what you might call a change of plans."

Someone suggested that developers would be better than having the inn go back to what it was when it was called The Mooncusser. And someone in back, probably a realtor, told me I could be a multimillionaire overnight if I leveled the inn and put five homes in its place. Someone else, a hopeless prude with a puckered face down front, asked again about my idea for a spa, and so I explained my arrangement with Bernie McCohen, and ticked off the equipment we intended to install.

"The spa will be open to all of you," I said. "Not just to guests. And appropriate attire will be required. I hope to attract couples and families, not hot-to-trot singles. This is my home. I have a six-year-old son and a six-year-old granddaughter to raise here. I'm not about to turn my home into a whorehouse."

"Isn't your language proof you are what everyone says?"

That earned some shouts of agreement.

"If everyone who uses the word fuck for emphasis, or calls fucking fucking, was banned from your island, the place would go broke and the ban would apply, I suspect, to some of you."

They grumbled, but I saw a few smiles, a couple of nods, and one blatant wink. Meanwhile, the crew of teens cheered and laughed and slapped palms, which of course did me no good at all.

"He's just a pimp with a good line of bull," said someone in back, and the crowd seemed to be in general agreement with that.

"I could select words to please you," I said. "But then I'd be controlling what you think." I was amazed at how focused and calm I was. I didn't have to struggle to control my anger because it never put in an appearance, and I realized that being forceful without rage was a far more powerful way to be. "It's funny," I told them, "but I've spent my life controlling what people think. So now I'm just going to give you the truth and let you do what you want to with it. Trouble is, it's tempting to control what you think because it seems like someone's going to."

There was angry muttering, and I let it roll from the front to the back, then back to me again.

"You didn't come here looking for truth. You came as a lynch mob because of someone else's hatred of me. Stop thinking like a bunch of sheep. If you'd think, even a little, then nobody, not me, not my enemies, nobody, could control you."

There was more muttering, but I could tell I was getting to some of them.

"Now go away. Come back as individuals, with your own concerns and questions. I'll give you all the time you need. We'll sit on my porch. We'll look at the ocean. We'll have a cup of tea. We'll talk about what is real and what isn't real and what matters and what doesn't matter. But there's not much I can say to a mob of sheep. Other than, Baaaaaaaaa."

I turned, thinking this was a great exit line, but McJustice's voice rose above the insulted grumbling and the cheering of my teenage crew, and froze me before I could reach my door.

"DO NOT TRUST THIS MAN!" she bellowed, her voice surprisingly powerful. I thought I heard South Philadelphia in her shout, and that seemed odd.

Everyone turned to her, including me.

"Dot never intended Ireland to be a splashy resort," she said. "All you residents know that. Dot intended Ireland to be a refuge for a select few, a haven for souls misunderstood and battered by life."

"That's right," said Bernie, like a Baptist saying his *Amen*, and hearing him, my heart sank.

"This man blackmailed Dotty into leaving her home to him."

"Like you blackmailed Dot," Shannon shouted, "to get Irma her deed, you witch."

"Shannon!" said Heather.

"I'm proud to admit that I'm the one who spread the word about what this black-hearted pimp intends to do to Dot's beloved Ireland," McJustice said, speaking to the chandelier. "I did it and I'd do it again, because what he intends to do here is a perversion. I know this man better than any of you and I can tell you he has the morals of an alley cat."

"What have you got against alley cats?" asked Tammy McIntyre, still standing beside Brian Cox, although I noticed him start to sidle away when Tammy's comment drew the crowd's attention. Francine and Shannon and the kids laughed, as did Ace, who had come up from the basement where he'd been working on the spa, but the rest had given their attention to McJustice and simply glared menacingly at the tall redheaded teen with her breasts pushing over the top of her bikini.

"This man is evil, I tell you. He has a black heart, like his father before him."

"Isn't that a bit strong?" asked Francine, speaking before I could ask what in the world my father had to do with anything.

"More than anyone in the world I am entitled to call him evil. And the reason is because he is my brother."

"Oh, shit," I said.

"You mean he's your brother in the spiritual sense, don't you?" asked Francine.

"No. Ashamed as I am to admit it, this evil one and I were sired by the same man."

McJustice's revelation caused a wave of murmuring to roll through the mob of moms and the kids. They were certainly getting their money's worth here at Ireland by the Sea. Too bad nobody had sold tickets. They were all startled and amazed, it seemed, although why they should have cared about the sordid doings of Ireland was beyond me.

"His blood flows in my veins," McJustice was saying, having thrown the back of her right hand to her forehead, a bad actress reciting hackneyed lines. "Slightly diluted, praise the Lord. Difficult though it is to acknowledge, I am the linkage here."

"The missing linkage," said Shannon, which gave everyone except McJustice a laugh.

Rattled, McJustice glared at Shannon, took a breath, then forced herself to go on.

"I share blood," she said, "with Heather and with Chelsey and with the boy, Ryan, too, and more directly with this creature who would lead us back into the ways of the flesh. Even now his friend the movie star is seducing a mere child." She pointed an accusing finger at Brian, who seemed to shrink into the wall beside the front door.

"Yeah, right!" said Tammy. "Like you haven't been giving me the eye."

"One of us is evil," I said to McJustice, surprised that I was still without even a hint of anger. "Maybe we have both been evil," I suggested, amicably. "At different times."

"Glibness!" she shouted, as if she had caught me jacking off. "See what he is. He's as glib as the devil. Life has always come easily for this one. He and his kind always end up on top. What you don't know," she said directly to me, "what reveals your depravity, is that one is either evil or not. Evil doesn't come and go like the flu. And one does not acquire it. It's in your bones. It comes from the soil which bares your roots."

"I don't know what program you've been watching—" I said, and I would have gone on if Heather's voice hadn't cut me off.

"—You," Heather shouted at McJustice, her voice quavering, "forced Dot to give your friend a room here to keep you from getting the state to take little Chelsey, your own niece, or whatever she is to you. You're my aunt," she sobbed, "and you did that to me."

"And by then," I added, to let Heather off the hook, "Dot was an addled old woman who was scared she might lose the only family she had left. I'd say that was a pretty evil thing to do, wouldn't you?"

"You intend to use women's bodies for their sales appeal," McJustice shrieked back at me, as if this somehow answered my charge. Spittle flew from her mouth and her face was twisted in rage. I could see the crowd pull back from her, so of course I let her go on. "All your life you have used women for the comforts and pleasures their bodies could provide, then you've discarded them like squeezed out orange rinds. My sister Tonya. Dotty's niece, Erin. Carol Zeller. Your two other wives, I'd bet. Now you want to do the same on a grand scale by turning our home and sanctuary into the next Sodom. Well, you'll do so over my dead body, *brother*. Over my dead body." McJustice looked around as if she was surprised to find herself standing on the stairs above this crowd and issuing such an impassioned speech, surprised also at having spilled her gorge so completely.

Irma McCreedy, who had come down from upstairs and sat now on the step beside McJustice, patted her thigh.

"Ask him where he was late last night," McJustice told the crowd, too exhausted to ask me herself. "Go on. Ask him."

The women looked at me.

"He had an eighteen-year-old girl naked on a lover's blanket out among the dunes," McJustice said. "A girl who trusted him and thinks of him as her father."

An angry grumbling started somewhere in the middle of the crowd and spread rapidly to its edges as it gathered both rage and volume. In their eyes I was every incestuous father and brother and uncle and trusted family friend who ever lived, and for a second I actually feared for my life. It would not have taken much, just then, for this mob of moms to claw me into tiny pieces.

"I was with him last night," Shannon said, so softly it broke through as no shout could have. "But I tried to seduce him. I knew sometimes in his head he confused me with my mother and I used that. I wore some of her things. I put on the kind of perfume she used to use. He wanted Erin back and I tried to be Erin so I could be his special love. But he made me get dressed and he showed me what it means to be loved by a father." She was crying so hard now she was almost unable to speak, but she managed to say, "You should all be so lucky," before she turned away and went into the kitchen, Heather and one of her friends following.

There didn't seem to be anything more to say, and I knew that without me here, there'd be no reason for the crowd to remain in my lobby. So I went back into my apartment, undressed, retrieved my rose and my candle, and resumed my shower.

Chapter Twenty-Six

The candle burned through the fog like a distant lighthouse, and the floor shifted beneath me. I looked down at my bare feet, planted squarely on either side of the drain where the shower water whirlpooled away. The floor shifted again, even as I was watching. According to my eyes nothing had happened, but the shift felt more violent this time, and when I looked into the fog again I found myself on the pitching deck of a huge sailing ship. Lightening flashed across a dark sky and waves crested above me. It had to be the same ship I had sailed on back in my Manhattan cubby, only it was damaged now beyond recognition and breaking up in a pounding surf.

I saw parts of the rigging fall. I saw a man crushed under a spar. I saw women and children by the dozens slide down the tipped deck and vanish into the frothing ocean. Suddenly I was with them, being tossed about in the numbing water, rolling and tumbling, gasping for air. I was too stunned to protect myself each time my body was scraped along the sand, and too frozen to breathe during the seconds my head broke the surface. Salt water clogged my nose, my throat, my lungs, even my mind.

For a moment there was sand under my knees, and I almost managed to stand, but a wave hit me from behind, driving me down and I tumbled into darkness.

Hands pulled at me. A man's voice called my name.

I had slipped to the tile floor of my shower stall and Brian Cox was trying to haul my slippery wet carcass out of there.

"Wake up," he shouted. "What the fuck, McWilly, wake up."

I focused on his face. "Don't take my money belt, you bastard," I yelled.

"Your money belt?" he said. "You're buck naked."

I pushed off his hands and stood.

"It's you," I said.

He tossed me a towel.

"I'm getting you out of here, buddy. You've lost it. What is this?" He looked into the shower stall at my flower and candle. "Are you into some sort of witchcraft or devil worship or what?"

I looked back at him, half here, half drowned on some long ago beach. I was terrified by him, and enraged, so I turned away and started to dry myself.

"Your zanies are pulling together a meeting," he said. "That's what I came to tell you. I had to break in the door." He rubbed his right shoulder. "I thought it was a heart attack."

"No," I said. "Just a shipwreck."

"You've really lost it, McWilly."

"Who's pulling together a meeting?"

"All your nuts and fruits. They're waiting in the cafeteria for you. Seriously, man. Let's get out of this place."

"Hang around, Brian," I said. "The fun's just starting."

I dressed. Brian waited in the sitting room, pacing, muttering.

"You want me to go with you?" he called.

"No," I said. "I have to handle this on my own."

"If you handle it like you did your showdown in the lobby, I may as well pack your bag."

"Don't worry," I said. "I know what I'm doing."

"Yeah, right," he said. "Just like I do."

"No wonder it never bothered me to take from you," I called.

"You don't make sense anymore, McWilly. Take what from me?"

"Erin, for one."

There was a long silence. "I see," he grunted, and then he was silent again.

I came from the bedroom, tucking a purple sport shirt into my white, draw-string pants from the night before. I had no shoes on, and probably wouldn't bother to find any.

"I never think about that anymore," Brian said, absently, as he stared out my bay window.

"Right. Same here."

"I don't."

"Good. Because it's even now anyhow. It's all over."

"It was over years ago," he said.

"I don't know how we got through it," I said.

"I'm falling in love, McWilly. I'm so fucked."

"Tammy?"

He nodded and looked out the window. Then his handsome face became curious and intent and he stepped closer, his head among the gulls.

"You staying in here?" I asked.

"If you don't mind. There's something interesting out there. It's almost as if I can see into another ... I don't know. It's interesting."

"I know. But if you get caught up in something, finish it. Don't give up, no matter what."

"Finish what? Christ, McWilly! I'm standing at a fucking window, that's all. And I'm thinking how the water I'm seeing has been all around the world and maybe all over the universe and how insignificant that makes our little worries."

"Have fun," I told him.

I went across the lobby to the dining hall and found Irma and McJustice at one table, Francine and Bernie at another, Jimmy and Heather at a third. Shannon and the two children were on the window sill, sharing a tub of Sour Patch Kids. Everyone looked at me as I sat down near Shannon and the children.

"So," I said, "is it finally time to talk?"

"It is," said Francine. She sighed nervously and looked down at a page of notes in her lap. "And I'm supposed to start."

"Shoot," I said.

"You hinted in your letter," she began, "that there were deeds you intended to challenge and you told Bernie you were challenging our deed and our son's. We'd all like to know more about that."

I explained, simply, that I questioned both McCohen deeds because of forgery, McX's deed because the person named might not exist and the deeds held by Irma and McJustice because they were won by duress from a woman functioning with diminished capacity.

"And those are the only deeds you're challenging?" asked Heather.

"Right."

McJustice scowled and muttered. Irma patted her hand while at the same time she asked me if things were really as critical for Ireland as I'd been saying. I explained, as if addressing a class of freshmen taking their first course in business school, that while the inn had been superficially self-sufficient, no funds generated by rent or by Heather's kitchen, or by common charges, had ever been set aside for upkeep or capital improvement. "That's why Ireland has deteriorated to the point where she can no longer compete. And by occupying some of the most valuable rental space, and obstructing the commercial operation of the inn, you have over time drained Ireland of capital necessary for her survival."

"Exactly what do you mean by *obstructing?*" asked Bernie.

"I've made calls to some of the people who have stayed here," I told them, "and nobody I spoke with will come back because some of you were so hostile. Other descriptive words I heard were *crazy, spooky, intrusive and tedious.*"

Everyone looked at McJustice, who glowered at me.

"As some of you know," I went on, "I have partners who want me to sell Ireland so they can get their money back, and if the matter goes to court, I have no doubt their claim will prevail. As deedholders, you have a say in what becomes of Ireland. But as things are structured, all of you together do not own as much of Ireland as I own, or as much of Ireland as my three friends will own once the court forces me to sign over my deed. And bad as I might seem, you are better off with me than you are with my friends, or at least with one of them. So our only hope is to work together and make Ireland's survival our goal."

"How do we do that?" asked Heather.

"First, we make Ireland competitive in the vacation market. Second, we raise rental and common charges so that the cost of Ireland's maintenance is amortized over the next five years. That way Ireland really will become a self-sufficient little nation, as the inn was described to me once by one of you. Mostly," I said, concluding, "I want you to realize that if we don't change how we treat this place and one another, our home will be history. I give her a year, two at the most."

"But what can we *do*?" asked Heather, who looked as if she might cry.

"Do? You can convert your deeds into shares of stock in the Ireland Corporation. Either that, or relinquish your deeds altogether and move out. If you stay, I want you to agree to higher common charges. And I want you to put your rooms into a rental pool. If you'll do that, you'll earn a percentage of everything Ireland earns. If not, we'll eventually condo-ize and you'll have your room and little more."

One of my ideas was to convert the garage, or maybe some of the storage space in the attic, into dorms where we could all move during the season, and I explained this, ignoring a groan from McJustice and pained expressions from everyone except Bernie and Francine, who wouldn't be affected.

"I've figured that rent on the owner's suite alone would add six to ten thousand dollars to Ireland's balance sheet," I said.

"If we convert our deeds to stock you'll just out-vote us every time," said Bernie.

"I have a better idea," said McJustice. "Why don't you just sign Ireland over to us and go away."

Irma beamed. Bernie nodded.

"All those in favor of McWilly's immediate departure say *Aye*," called McJustice.

"Aye," said Bernie, Irma and McJustice, without hesitation.

"And opposed?" I asked.

"Nay," shouted Francine, Shannon and the two children, none of whom, it was immediately determined, had a vote.

"Bernie's already spoken for the McCohen deed," argued McJustice, "and Shannon has no deed. All those opposed."

This time there was silence. I waited for Heather or Jimmy to say something, but they both studied the table top between their hands.

"Sounds to me," said Irma, "that you're pretty much on your own."

"And that you have just voted yourself out of a home," I said, standing and walking away.

Brian Cox sat sprawled in one of the leather easy chairs that had once flanked the hearth in my Connecticut home. He looked like a boxer on his stool, about mid-way through a fight that wasn't going well. But I was too distracted to pay much attention to him, having just come from a losing bout of my own. I said something about being fucked and he muttered a phrase that sounded like "why does it matter?" although it seemed as though he was pushing out his words through a sudden case of lockjaw.

"The child of my father's indiscretion is my sworn enemy and my oldest friend is the Wreckmaster," I said. "That's enough to make one's head spin. Now and again life certainly takes a funny bounce, doesn't it?"

He muttered something that might have either been "You bet," or "You butt."

I stood by the window, my back to him, wondering what I should do next. I was sick of the way life kept interfering with my dreams, and I said so. Brian muttered that he was leaving and that I should come back to New York with him if I knew what was good for me. After ten minutes or so, when I didn't respond, he got up and left, quietly shutting my door behind him. He went up to his room to pack and I waited for him to say goodbye but he never did. He simply drove away.

As I worked on Ireland over the next few days, I marveled at the perversity that had placed my half-sister here with me, along with the others linked to my life through Tonya Angione. I kept hearing Tonya say to me that she and I were joined by karma, and the memory never failed to make me shiver.

Brian Cox reported to Bill Kern that I had popped my cork, and that if they didn't get me out of the inn soon I'd be lost forever. After that, Bill called almost daily to beg me to put Ireland up for sale and return to New York and my friends.

"Come home, McWilly," he kept saying. "Come back to a normal life. Come back and be what you were meant to be."

"Have you decided what to do about my offer?" I'd ask him each time we talked.

"Not yet. Sell the place and come home. Brian says it's haunted."

"I am home, Bill. You sound like you're talking to Lassie."

Jason called now and again to say the same thing to me, prompted, in all likelihood, by Kern.

"Come home, McWilly," he would beg. "Get out of there before the place drives you insane or kills you."

"How's it going to kill me?" I asked.

"It ruined Cox, I can tell you that. Who wants a game-show host who can't move his tongue?"

"What's wrong with Brian's tongue?"

"He can't move it. At least not much. And there's no good medical reason. He sounds like he's got the world's worst impediment."

"And they fired him?"

"Not yet. They've given him a medical leave, but he thinks he's washed up because his replacement's getting better ratings. And he blames it all on Ireland, although he won't say why."

"I'll call him," I said.

"He won't take your call. He won't talk to anyone these days. He's a total hermit. He's filed for divorce and he's living in my basement. He doesn't want anyone to know that, so forget I told you."

Jill weighed in with her own version of "Come home, McWilly." She had finally decided that having children was her true calling and that she would marry the next man she met who wanted to be a father. "Come back to New York and make babies with me," she said.

"To have a child," I told her, "a person needs more innocence and faith than I have left. Sorry."

"That's kind of what I thought you'd say. Friends?"

"You bet."

Meanwhile, Horace Asp had moved the eviction paperwork along, and it seemed there wasn't anything more I could do about the deedholders until we went to court. Ace and I worked on the building with our young crew, and I spent the rest of my time either on the verandah or playing with Ryan and Chelsey.

One day we were crabbing over on the dock, using a long-handled net and a chicken drumstick tied to a kite string. The trick to crabbing was to ever-so-slowly draw up the string after you felt something tug at the chicken. If you were careful enough, the crabs would stay attached to the meat until they were in range of the net. Then the catch, often two or three crabs at a time, could be transferred from the net into a covered bucket, although sometimes the prehistoric-looking critters held on and had to be pulled free, at considerable risk. And sometimes they missed the bucket and fell on the dock, where they scurried sideways, their two claws lifted and ready to pinch, their legs clattering on the wood. When this happened, the children would squeal and skip about to protect their toes while, with sheep dog tactics, they tried to keep the escapees from dropping back into the bay. Chelsey and Ryan took turns with the line and the net, while Shannon and I sat nearby like tranquil parents, hoping we wouldn't have to help, and sometimes rooting for the crabs.

As we watched, a good-sized boat pulled to the dock and a woman on the bow threw me a rope.

"Tie us up," said the man on the flybridge. "That's a good fellow." He was the picture of leisure wealth: tan, with long, silver-gray, windblown hair and expensive sunglasses. Had he been wearing a blue blazer and an ascot he'd have looked more the part, but he destroyed the image with his electric blue shorts and a red tank top. The woman who had thrown me the rope was dressed the same, and was equally well-tanned.

I intended to challenge their right to this dock, once they stepped from their boat, but the man beat me to it. "This is a private dock," he told me. "I don't allow people to crab here."

"I see," I said. "And I don't allow people to dock here." I smiled. "Seems we have something of a problem. Do you have anything to prove ownership or rental?"

"We've been tying up here for years. We live right over there." He pointed to a cluster of modern homes to the south. "Residents of those three houses own this dock."

"Not according to my deed," I said.

"You're the fellow owns Ireland?"

I nodded and explained that according to my deed I owned from here at the breakwater back to the boulevard. "Maybe there was an easement or some arrangement," I suggested. "I'll have my lawyer do a title search." I was being amicable because I felt no ire, and because I had battles going on too many fronts as it was.

"You do that," the man said, all puffed up and pissed off.

"That won't be necessary," said his wife. "We knew this day might come."

"Alice, shut up."

I smiled. "Women are so damn honest, aren't they? Life would be much easier if they'd just learn to be assholes like us. How many years did you say you've been tying up here?"

"Fuck you."

"Well, if it turns out you and your neighbors have been using my dock without paying for it for years and years, there's probably a good-sized bill headed your way."

"We'll see about this," the man said, and turned away, cursing at his wife as they headed for home.

"I'll have my lawyer get in touch," I called.

"You jerk," shouted Ryan, and for a moment I thought he was being fresh to the man from the boat. I turned to reprimand him, but saw that he was talking to Chelsey. "You jigged him off. Let me do it."

He grabbed the crab line and pushed the net into Chelsey's hand. She pulled back, hurt, and watched as Ryan lowered the bait, waited, then began to draw up the line.

"Catching that crab's pretty important to you?" I asked him.

He glanced back at me, irritated by my distraction.

"More important than Chelsey's feelings, right?"

He looked back at me again, curiosity mixed with his irritation. Then his line went slack.

"YOU IDIOT!" he shouted. "Look what you made me do."

"Or my feelings?" I added. "Pretty important crab."

"Catching crabs is what we're doing here," he said.

"It's our purpose, right?" I said. "It's the goal that has us out here. And it's far more important than Chelsey or me and how we feel. Forget that stuff. Get the crab! No matter what, get the crab."

He looked at me while Chelsey took her turn with the line.

"Jeeze you're strange sometimes," he said.

We went home with nearly two dozen crabs, which I boiled and cleaned. And as I worked in Heather's kitchen, I thought about the brief exchange I'd had with Ryan and I realized I'd been talking to myself more than to him. All my life I had pretty much treated the people I loved like necessary, even precious, appendages, which meant that until I'd injured them or lost them, I gave them little thought. Instead, my life was energized by tangible goals, things worth having or achieving. Lowering my golf handicap, owning a certain car, getting a special someone into bed, winning a paddle tennis tournament, earning that next promotion, catching that crab. I focused on these tangible objectives and let the messy emotions that are the stuff of relationships take care of themselves. When I spoke with friends and wives and lovers, I came to rely on a supply of tested topics and phrases, and so over time my encounters took on a ritualized or scripted quality. "Hey, how's it going? Heat spell finally broke. How's business? Man, that Clinton! How 'bout them Mets?" And after fifty years of this, my goals and dreams were piled around me like fossils, and most of the people were gone. What was this fool's bargain I kept buying into? And where had I gotten the idea that some accomplishment would finally satisfy me or identify me, or prove my right to be? The chase seemed both sad and absurd now.

I had started out a wild colt, head-strong and full of nature's power, but by the time my mother, the suburbs, college, Corporate America and marriage were finished with me, I was a sagging dray, with blinders that kept my focus on the carrot. There had been no joy in all my plodding, I realized, and less in the occasional attainment, but still, it was what I knew and I was doing it all again, here at Ireland.

I took a shower to wash off the crab smell, but I left my rose and my candle in the living room and I didn't make steam because I was determined never again to re-live that shipwreck. Now and then I'd hear the voice in the hiss of the water on the tile, and I wondered if it was Irma's voice or a chorus of Long Beach Island's various shipwrecked or love-starved ghosts. I thought it might be fun to devise some means of direct encounter with the source of that voice—if there was a source—but my mind kept drifting off before I could give that plan any real thought.

As I dried myself I realized that I was probably one of the few otherwise healthy people on the planet who had to rest up after his shower. But it beat worrying and fighting. And if what I was embarked on here was actually a journey into insanity, then I had no choice but to enjoy the ride.

Ireland had begun to sparkle now under her new roof and in her new coat of stain. She was the color of exceedingly rich vanilla ice cream, with blueberry blue shutters and doors. All the unoccupied rooms had been refurbished, along with the corridors, the dining room, the lounge and the lobby. The chandelier sparkled, and when you hit the wall switch, one hundred and sixty seven candle-shaped bulbs ignited. The lobby floor had been stripped and refinished, as had all the corridor floors. The bathrooms had new tile, paper and paint, and fixtures that did not look like they had been stolen from a dump. There was a whole new feeling about the place, and a clean new smell.

We had a sign painted and when we took down the old driftwood plank that had been nailed to the shingles just above the verandah roof we found that, woodburned into the side that had faced the building was the inn's old name, "The Mooncusser." So we hung this plank from chains in the dining hall, and put the new sign in its place above the verandah.

I had given the deedholders the right to determine how they wanted their rooms repaired and painted, but held them responsible for shouldering the cost, unless, of course, they wanted to reconsider the stand they had taken. Knowing I was moving against him, and perhaps thinking he could win me over, Cyrus McCohen phoned to give me *carte blanche*, but the illusive Miss McX never responded to my memo and the abrasive McJustice sent word through Irma that she'd sue if I so much as touched anything that belonged to her. To my surprise, Jimmy McCaffery told me he wanted to keep his room as it was. Too much change, he said, wasn't good for a person.

Chapter Twenty-Seven

Two of Ireland's bay side lots finally sold, for a total of $212,000, and Bernie McCohen presented me with a check for $23,250, my fourteen and a half percent of his pebble business from the day we shook hands on our deal. And, as an added little windfall, the three dock squatters over on the bay settled out of court for fifteen thousand dollars. These funds came to reside in a new corporate bank account, less what I'd paid in wages and bonuses to Francine, Ace, Shannon and her friend, and less my expenses.

I had urged Heather to design the kitchen of her dreams, and then blocked each of her efforts to shift her various decisions to Francine or Shannon. With Bernie handling the spa and the water sports, the kitchen was both my hardest job and my greatest expense, and while I had a selfish interest in the project, I was really doing it, I soon realized, for Heather. As work on the kitchen had progressed, Heather and I revised her prices so that she stood a chance to turn a profit, and I promised her twenty five percent of what she earned, in addition to her salary. (Her husband had yet to put in an appearance, and everyone but Heather seemed to know he was gone for good.)

As Memorial Day Weekend approached, a newspaper ad campaign with the headline "Enjoy the magic of Ireland by the Sea" ran in the Philadelphia and Manhattan papers, along with a few local New Jersey, New York and Connecticut weeklies. The fee for that, and for a few radio spots and the creation and printing of a colorful brochure to be supplied to travel agents and tourist bureaus, took my account down to a few thousand.

Now, all I could do was wait and pray for bookings, and great weather.

To my immense relief, the phone started to ring the day the ads came out, and, sooner than even I had dreamed, Francine and Heather were telling callers, "I'm sorry, but we're booked solid that week. Please try us again."

The old place came to life at noon on Friday, May 28th, with families and couples arriving in a steady parade. Three of Shannon's crew, now employed as bell hops, lugged luggage up to the rooms, while three of the girls hustled around making things beautiful and neat. (I had found places for the rest of Shannon's friends as water sport coaches and fitness instructors.)

The season was finally underway, and Ireland had become a whole different place now that it was full of strangers. We were booked solid. I moved with Ryan to one of the back attic rooms and rented the owner's suite for three hundred a night. The ocean was still too cold for swimming, although the surfers were out in their wet suits, but the sun was bright and by Saturday afternoon that first weekend there were many red faces in the dining room. The staff and I were kept hopping by guest requests and an occasional complaint, and I was treated to a crash course in the difficulties of hotel management. I'd never worked so hard in my life, but, disappointingly, it was not the kind of labor that fulfilled me. Just the opposite. I felt like a servant in my own home and I labored with the sense that I had somehow let myself be demoted. At the same time, I also felt as if I was where I belonged, doing what I was meant to do, which seemed strange.

The spa in the basement, ready only hours before the guests checked in on Friday, was a hit with the under-fifty crowd, although some complaints were registered because some favorite apparatus or another was missing. Bernie passed out little red buttons which said *I want my little red button*, and these pins, each with a microchip on the back, served to identify spa members and automatically triggered a computer log when worn by someone stepping through the door. And each person to finish a workout was awarded a healing pebble from the sea.

McJustice did her best to glower and snarl at the guests when they encountered her in the hall or dining room, but she was for the most part ignored. Jimmy told all the standard LBI ghost stories, which most people found more quaint than scary, and Irma entertained the guests every other evening with readings by Lavinia. It was not uncommon in the first weeks of June, as the crew and I worked out the bugs and settled into harness, to find a small crowd gathered around Jimmy or Irma in the lobby or the dining room or in the evenings out on the verandah, and after a while I quit worrying that these two might be bothering my guests. They were part of Ireland's magic, I decided, for better or for worse.

One night, urged by Chelsey, Shannon, Tammy and Ryan, I went out to hear Irma, and as Lavinia spoke to us in Irma's soft, lulling voice, I watched the phosphorous in the waves and looked at the splash of stars in the indigo sky.

Life was pretty good, I decided, in spite of all its snags.

"Roll your eyes upward," Irma said, her voice slithery, like the voice I'd heard in my shower, only not quite identical, which was disappointing. "Roll them up as far as they will go and with your consciousness, reach upward further still and attach yourself to a beam of golden light pouring down through the crown of your head. Rise slowly up out of yourself on this beam of light and look back at the top of your head. Move slowly, leisurely. Take a moment to get comfortable with this new perspective. Play with it. Try out slightly different views."

"Neat," I heard Ryan say.

"Shhhh," said Chelsey.

"It's, like, mystical," said Tammy.

I zoomed away, and my head turned into a ball that looked very much like planet Earth, as shown in photos taken from the moon. And thinking that, I found I had ascended so far into space that I was no longer even in orbit. There was no telling where I would have gone had Irma's voice not pulled me back.

"See the light beam entering the crown of your head and ride it back inside yourself and let your eyes fall back into their normal position. Feel the light fill your mind, starting with the space inside your forehead and moving back from there until you find the exact point where consciousness begins. From there, let the light spread out to the temples and to the base of your skull, the very top of your spinal column and from there, downward, through your body, out your arms to your finger tips, through your stomach, your buttocks, down your legs to your toes. Feel the golden light's warmth and comfort. Feel the relaxation as you gaze down toward the core of you."

She paused for what seemed like ten minutes, and I saw my lungs, my heart, my kidneys, my bladder, my appendix, my prostate, my gonads, my intestines. I realized, even as I wandered inside myself, that I was entirely under Irma's power, and I wondered if maybe I hadn't been under her power ever since I arrived here. My eyes popped open. Had she programmed me with words like these? If so, how? I had to find out.

This, I decided, would be my new mission.

Just then some people who had gone gambling down in Atlantic City with Ace returned to the inn and disrupted the meditation session with their laughter.

"Shhhhh," one of them said. "It's flake time at Ireland."

"I forgot my tea leaves," said someone else.

"Shhhh," said Shannon. "Lavinia's teaching us to meditate."

"Oh! Sorry," said Ace, who was a little drunk. "Excuse me, Lavinia. I'll just pull up a toad stool and listen."

After that, the meditaters on the verandah could only be serious for a few seconds at a time, and finally Lavinia bade everyone a fond good night.

Day after day, the sun was hot and bright and the sky endlessly blue. The ocean behaved exactly as it should. All around me, everyone was having fun, except for McJustice.

School ended the second to last week of June, which meant Shannon and her friends could be here full time. Ryan and Chelsey, inseparable now, devoted themselves entirely to an exploration of the creatures of the bay and daily brought home new crustacean pets.

Calls from New York had fallen off, and while Kern and Jason hadn't entirely given up on me, they had realized, it seemed, that this latest dream of mine, like a fever, had to run its course. Brian Cox had dropped out of sight. He was no longer living at Jason's, and nobody knew where he was. According to the tabloids, Cox had lost his speech, and therefore his job, due to a sexually transmitted disease acquired through contact with aliens from space. He, of course, was not available for comment, but insiders reported that he had been taken aboard a mother ship and forced to demonstrate all forms of human sexual activity. Clippings about my friend kept showing up in my mail, with nothing to indicate who sent them.

Jill stopped calling, and when I called her to report on Ireland's success, the message on her machine said, "Hi. Jay and I can't come to the phone just now, but if you'll leave your name and number ..."

So Jill was history, I told myself, hanging up before the promised beep.

There was always Pearline to hope for. And the blue jogger.

My challenge to Cyrus McCohen's deed came to court and was decided in my favor in less than ten minutes. Francine sat beside her son, who was thirty five, give or take a year, and handsome, with a leading man's strong jaw and black mustache. She patted his leg as the judge read his decision, and I thought she fought back a smile. The same judge wiped out McX's deed in even less time. McJustice's deed and the one in Irma's name were scheduled to come to court in September, and I could tell that the rulings against Cyrus and McX had them worried. McJustice and I never spoke, although now and then we'd lock eyes and she'd zap me with a bolt of hate. She and Irma had been served with papers, but neither confronted me or discussed the court case or tried for a compromise.

Even with the court ruling in my favor, I didn't have the balls to attack the locks on the door of Room Twenty-four; I tried, but it was as if some force behind that door kept warding me off. Once I sent Ace to do it, but he broke a chisel while working on McX's hinges, returned with a power saw and renewed vigor, only to put a gash in the meaty side of his left hand that required eighteen stitches.

One night at dinner, Bernie and Francine McCohen, out of sympathy for their son, made a big show of shredding their deed to space in my basement and dumping the confetti onto my untouched dinner plate. Francine, I realized, was getting what she'd wanted all along, her boy Cyrus back in her big, luxurious home up in Loveladies.

Less than an hour after this display with the confetti, Francine and Bernie found me on the verandah and let me know that nothing had changed regarding our partnership.

"No?" I said, somewhat surprised, but without really caring one way or the other.

"No," said Francine, while Bernie twitched beside her. "The old relationship is dead. Long live the new relationship."

"For today," I said, without looking away from the ocean.

I was at times restless and at other times strangely at peace. My love life, usually both the source and the barometer of my well-being, was at an all-time low, but that didn't seem to bother me the way it would have in the past. I thought at least once each day about going down to Atlantic City to find Pearline the hooker and save her from her life of sin, and I kept looking for the blue jogger, although there were hundreds of heavenly bodies on the beach these days, and she had gotten lost in the crowd. I was lonely, but not enough to strike up a conversation with any of these ladies, even the ones who smiled at me, and for days on end it was enough to serve my guests and play with Ryan, Chelsey and Shannon.

We went crabbing in the bay or fishing for eels or flying kites beside the ocean or playing catch or just walking beside the waves and looking for especially odd or brightly-colored shells. We started a collection of sea horses and sea glass, and as the ocean warmed, we began to spend time riding the waves. Body surfing terrified me, but with a belly board I was fearless, that is if the waves weren't too huge.

Life pulsated around me and Ireland thrived. I was the perfect congenial host, anxious to please, ready to jump at each request, regardless how petty. Heather's kitchen, now calledThe Mooncusser Cafe, was a success. And Bernie's spa, called the Emerald Isle Health Club, was doing well, especially with the locals and the LBI renters. (Everywhere I went on the island I saw people wearing those little red buttons that said *I want my little red button.*) Things had come together better than I had dreamed, and yet I sometimes felt as stale as I'd been in the weeks after I was fired. I wasn't suicidal, far from it, and I could float through my days more-or-less content with life, but something seemed to be missing.

What, really, did I have to show for all my work and all my dreaming? I had this inn full of laughing, smiling, sunburned strangers, where I could raise my boy and my granddaughter and live alone and watch everyone else love and have fun. Other than that, I had my shower and my candle, now and then a fresh dying rose, and my campaign to catch Irma meddling with my mind. And the question was, was that enough?

Late one night, as I was sitting on the verandah, a man in a hooded sweatshirt angled toward me across the beach. He climbed the steps, and there was something about his body language that put the street fighter in me on alert.

Had the pimp's young enforcer returned for his rematch?

I stood and went to the top of the steps, ready to receive whatever might be coming. The man glanced up and down the verandah, as if to make certain we were alone, then he climbed closer.

"McWeelwee," he said.

"Yes?"

"Iss me. Calx."

It was Brian, and, with considerable difficulty, he let me know that he needed a place to hide. So I moved him into the attic with Ryan and me, and he was so grateful he cried.

He took his meals alone in his room, which was probably smaller than his clothes closet at home. When he went out, which he rarely did, he moved about in the obscurity of his oversized hooded sweatshirt. Only at night did he feel at peace. And of course he rarely spoke. It pained him to try, and his frozen tongue made articulation almost impossible. He had come to hate the word "What?" he told me in one of his rare notes. Usually he was far too proud to be reduced to frantic scribblings; better to be mute.

After a few days, Ireland by the Sea became his sanctuary, especially once Ryan and Chelsey introduced him to its secret passageways and stairwells. Nobody else knew he was living with us, not even Tammy, whose heart he had broken during his last visit, but who had recovered quickly, thanks to a lanky surfer named Suds.

Without his splendid voice, backed up by his looks, Brian was nothing, but being nothing for a time, agony though that must have been, seemed precisely what Brian Cox needed. Ireland, he soon came to see, was more than a sanctuary; "It is," he wrote to me, "the only place on earth where I can either heal myself or live with myself." He was, it turned out to my surprise, no trouble at all.

My cut of McCohen's operation for June came to $49,723.50, a bit more than ten percent of which was generated by the spa. Bernie's mailorder pebbles produced thirty two thousand and change, and the rest, more than twelve thousand, was generated in the last week of the month by Bernie's little red buttons.

The *I want my little red button* buttons were now being test-marketed in selected novelty stores and a dozen mail-order catalogues and magazine ads, and early signs indicated that Bernie had the next pet rock on his hands. Of course I felt guilty taking nearly fifty grand from Bernie, although not guilty enough to give back any money.

During that same time, Ireland made a $9,524 net profit, which did not include the $3,000 taken off the top for upkeep and future advertising. This was petty cash, in contrast to Bernie's numbers, but it represented a smashing victory for the inn. And for the first time in history, Heather's kitchen, The Mooncusser Cafe, showed a profit, generating an additional $2,543.73 dollars for the corporation, after a salary raise and generous bonus for both Heather and Shannon and Tammy McIntyre, who was almost as good a waitress as Shannon.

As the long Fourth of July weekend approached, a season high point on LBI, a call came through from Bill Kern. He hadn't phoned in nearly two weeks, so I thought it might be important. Summoned by Francine, I ran in from the beach where I'd been playing with the kids, and grabbed the phone in the lobby, dripping sea water on the refinished wood floor. Without greeting or pleasantries, Kern asked if I would have room in the inn for him for August first.

"No," I said. "But you can bunk in with the kids and me." I didn't tell him Brian Cox was here.

"I have two or three things to talk over with you," he said. "Is that a good time?" He sounded subdued.

"Good as any," I said. "Have you thought about my offer?"

"That's one of the things we need to discuss."

"Okay," I said, glad to have nearly a whole month before he dropped the ax. "See you in August. You shouldn't have tried to fuck me, Bill. Ireland's going great."

"I'm glad for you," he said. "But you're going to have a problem starting tomorrow or the next day, or the next at the very latest."

"Oh? What's that?"

"You'll see. It won't be pretty. See you in August."

I tossed and turned that night, trying to figure out what kind of dirty trick Kern had pulled, but there was no way I could have anticipated what would be waiting for me in the morning.

Sometime before dawn, as we slept, several hundred tons of medical waste washed up on our beach, with more coming in all the time. Later, as I walked among both the identifiable and unidentifiable refuse, I didn't even have enough spirit left to wonder how Bill Kern had known. What I saw spread around me said that defeat had come again, and this time there was nothing I could do about it.

The disgusting trash was scattered across the damp sand, from Barnegat Light down to Holgate, less plentiful than seaweed but more so than Bernie's polished stones. There were squares and long strips of bandages, wads of bloody cotton swabs, syringes of various sizes, plastic pill bottles and drinking cups, stained paper sheets and surgical gowns and caps and booties and masks, rubber gloves, blue Johnny coats, aqua bed pans and urine pitchers and water bottles, each with a half-life of ninety gazillion years. Rumor had it that a foot had been found down in Beach Haven, and a finger had rolled up in Loveladies. Our medical waste made all the news shows, all the papers. The hospitals blamed the carting companies, the carting companies feigned ignorance. And local health officials closed our beaches. Reservations were canceled. Deposit checks had to be returned. And each day, more medical waste arrived to decorate our shore. You rarely saw any of this stuff float in—we were told most of it was churning in thermal levels a few feet down—and so day after day the ocean looked as inviting as ever, as if to tantalize us. The worst of it by far was the way McJustice gloated; you'd have thought she had somehow made it happen, and I was now crazy enough to suspect maybe she had.

Locals and the more loyal cottage renters still ate at Heather's and still worked-out at Bernie's spa, but the inn remained less than half full through July.

Brian Cox took the turret room on Three, and since the owner's apartment was going vacant, Ryan and I moved back downstairs. If it hadn't been for Bernie's pebbles and his red buttons, I would not have been able to meet my month's expenses.

When Bill Kern arrived, Brian Cox went into hiding, moving into the doorless room and staying in the secret passageways, except late at night, when he would sneak out to the beach. Kern more or less had his choice of rooms, and he picked one of the big front suites on Two. He did not seem surprised at the number of vacancies, nor did he gloat. He shook my hand warmly when he arrived, then went to change.

When I saw him next, he was dressed in Hawaiian print swim trunks, a matching shirt and LL Bean boots, an odd ensemble, especially for one who was usually so splendidly out-fitted. He told me he wanted to inspect the damage on the beach, so we walked and watched the crews working to remove the refuse. They wore heavy gloves and where possible, they used shovels and spikes and pincers. Now and then a truck would roll past and the men would heave stuffed black plastic sacks aboard.

"People are scared to death some kid will step on an AIDS infected needle," I said.

"Couldn't happen," said Bill. "Stuff's been exposed to air and salt water."

"You can't blame them," I said. "I won't let Ryan and Chelsey play out here. They like the bay better anyhow."

"What a mess. Sorry this screwed you up."

"Not half as sorry as I am," I said.

"Funny thing is," said Kern, "it was probably my company."

I looked at him, not entirely understanding.

He nodded and chuckled at the irony of it. "That's right. It's about ninety percent likely."

"You own the company responsible for dumping all this stuff at sea?"

He nodded. "What a bitch, huh? Funny how things work out. I wanted to beat you, but not like this."

"Yeah, well, that's hardly the point." I felt rage and sadness crash together inside me, and my feelings must have registered on my face.

"Ocean dumping happens all the time, McWilly. Grow up."

"Yeah, well it still sucks. I mean, look at this mess. How can you face this and not feel ashamed?"

"So a couple of my barge guys decided not to go out as far as they're supposed to. You know. Cut expenses. Two dumps for the time and fuel of one. It's just smart business."

A tear ran down my cheek, and although I felt like the Native

American in that environmental ad they used to run on television, I was not ashamed.

"Shit, McWilly," said Kern, turning away from me.

We ate dinner with Francine, who flirted openly with Kern, then we went out and sat on the bottom step of the verandah. The rise of the beach blocked our view of the garbage and left a blue sweep of ocean with waves rolling in and white caps forming and melting all the way to the horizon.

"God it's gorgeous," said Kern. He had a cigar in his left hand, a brandy in his right.

"It always surprises me," I said.

"I envy you, McWilly. I wish I was the kind of guy who could just be. You know, just sit here and enjoy the view. But I'm driven. I can't even look at the ocean without half my mind cranking away on some big plan."

"I'm not so much like that anymore," I said.

He told me then that he was Attorney of Record for the Montaukett Indians, eleven of whom he had located so far.

"So?" I asked him, still angry and stunned about his role in bringing all this hideous refuse to our beach.

"Their blood's pretty diluted," he said, "and there's not a thinker in the bunch, let alone a leader."

"So what, Kern? Why are you telling me about Indians when you should be rolling on the sand begging me to forgive you for this plague of garbage?"

"They're the genuine article," Kern said, as if I wasn't there. "And they're pissed off about having had their heritage stolen. I deeded over fifty acres of Shelter Island to them, and now we're making a claim against the Gardiner family, for Gardiner's Island."

"Wait a minute. You gave away fifty acres of prime ocean-front real estate, and you're screwing me over a quarter-of-a-million dollars?"

He smiled but didn't comment. Instead, as if this was an answer, he explained that until it had been purchased from the Montauketts by a man named Lion Gardiner, Gardiner's Island had been called Manchonake. Kern was pretty sure he could prove that Gardiner had cheated the Indians, which rendered the Gardiner family claim void, if he could also prove an unbroken residence or consistent effort to regain residence.

"When did you find all this out?" I asked him. "Before or after your session with Irma?"

"I told you before, McWilly. I don't know any Irma. I've known about Gardiner for years."

Kern was in the process of getting the tribe recognized by the State of New York and the Federal Government. After that, once tribal land holdings were designated a reservation, the Montauketts would get busy building Manchonake Casino. And Bill Kern would receive fifteen percent of the take.

"With these reservation casinos," he said, laughing cynically, "the Indians have finally figured out how to deal with the white man's greed."

"And suddenly Bill Kern cares about the Indians?"

"Sure do. And they are now called Native Americans."

I sighed and shook my head. "I worry for your soul, Kern," I said. "And I worry for the planet with men like you running things."

"Got to care about something," he said.

"Is there anything you won't exploit?"

He seemed to give the question serious consideration. "I don't think so," he finally said.

"I don't think so either."

"It's all part of the game. What else makes life worth living?"

"Grace," I said, without thinking.

After that, Bill and I sat for a long time, saying nothing; to anyone who saw us we probably looked like two old friends, comfortable with our silence.

"What you did hurts," I told him, without really thinking or filtering what I said.

"Hurts? Hurts? McWilly, I swear I think maybe you've grown a snatch."

With that, he took his cigar and brandy and went to his room to use his cellular phone and his portable fax.

Chapter
Twenty-Eight

Kern and I went out to dinner the next night, his treat, to a place where the tile fish was white and tender and the wine list a thirty-page book.

"So listen," Kern said, after we had ordered enough food to run Ireland for a week. "I need you with me on this Manchonake Casino project. Lots of legal problems and PR problems."

I just looked at him.

"I see you as my CEO."

"I don't know," I told him, realizing then that no matter what happened to Ireland by the Sea, I never wanted to leave this beach, this ocean. "I have my hands full keeping Ireland alive."

"So I see," Kern said, sarcastically. "It's real hard work sitting out on your verandah counting the gulls."

"Whatever," I said, in the sarcastic way I'd learned from Shannon and her friends.

"I got the papers all drawn up," Kern said. "I've given you a whole new identity. A whole new history. And you're one guy who could use it. Your great grandmother was Millie Wind Voices, the eldest daughter of Chief Mashomac. And you are Carter Jameson who, by the way, is really in Potters Field up in the Bronx. After we bring you out of this small cave over on Gardiner's Island, where you've been living for twenty years and where an uncle and a great-grandfather and a great-great uncle of yours made their home, you'll be Chief Executive Officer and Chief Operating Officer of Manchonake Hotel and Casino, for a salary of two hundred and fifty thousand a year plus a percentage of net. And you can bet that any title with the word Chief in it takes on a whole different meaning when you're an Indian."

"You're nuts, Kern. And that's Native American."

"So you're not interested?"

"Am I interested in becoming some guy named Carter who lives in a cave? You're crazier than I am."

"At least give it some thought."

We dropped the subject, and talked about Brian Cox's mysterious disease and his recent disappearance.

"His tongue was his life," Kern said. "I wouldn't be surprised if he turns up dead somewhere."

"I doubt that," I said, without revealing that I had insider information.

While we ate, we spoke of our days with The Fish and then he began to talk about his recent sexual exploits. I disappointed him when I said I had nothing to report, that I'd been celibate for weeks. He just looked at me and shook his head.

We didn't pick up the subject of my becoming Millie WindVoices's long lost great-grandson from Potters Field until the next morning.

"What have you got to lose?" Kern asked me. We were having our morning coffee on Ireland's verandah. The air was still, the sun a shimmering glare on the ocean.

"Nothing," I said. "And everything."

"You don't even have a real name to give up. And this deal down here is driving you bat shit. Besides, Ireland's doomed. Your season's in the shit can."

"Thanks to you."

"You're in debt up the ying-yang."

"Thanks to you."

"So what have you got to lose?"

"Not much. It's just that I gave the business world my identity once, Kern. I didn't like it."

"You know, don't you, I could have squashed you with a court order anytime I wanted? Come into the casino with me and we'll write off the entire debt."

I looked at him suspiciously.

"What the hell. We'll all make out like bandits with the tax write-offs anyhow, and Cox, Sargent and I need paper write-offs a whole lot more than we need a few extra thousand. So don't thank us, McWilly. Thank the IRS for being so kindly disposed to the rich."

"You'd lift your lien and relinquish your claim against Ireland if I went in with you?"

"That's right. You ought to think about it. Don't be a fool. You'll go under here, then you'll come begging."

"No I won't."

"Sure you will."

"I've got more pride than that."

"Since when?"

"Since I came here. I wouldn't be like you now for anything on earth. You're cursed, Kern. If you can't fuck it or make a buck from it, it ain't worth your time, right? Your code. The code of the manly man. The code that's going to take us the way of the dinosaur."

He looked at me for almost thirty seconds, and I met his gaze.

"It's too late for you, isn't it?" he said. "You've lost it. Too bad, McWilly. You had such potential."

Kern stayed for two more days, and not once did he apologize or in any other way express regret over the medical waste problem which had wiped out the tourist season for the entire Jersey shore. His company would be sued, of course, and he would pay through the nose, he said, the implication being that fines and other financial penalties would be penance enough. And I suppose where he lived, this was true.

Other than summarize for Brian Cox Kern's Indian casino scam, I didn't give Kern's crazy offer a thought once he was gone, although I probably spent a dozen hours or more wondering how much longer the Earth could survive men like Kern. It was a new way to think, and I felt like I'd caught a case of Bernie McCohen's madness, and Irma's flakiness. It was a waste of brain time, although my meditations on what made men like Kern tick, and why I no longer needed to model myself after him, seemed to help in my efforts to catch Irma as she toyed with my mind.

It was not uncommon for me to hear voices in the hiss of my shower, but I could never quite tune them in before I was pulled under their spell. It was, I'd realized some time back, a Catch 22. If I listened to the voices, I fell instantly into a trance, but if I didn't, how could I ever learn how Irma worked her magic? Then one morning I discovered, by accident, that if I concentrated on trying to understand what drove Kern, and if I tried to appreciate instead of regret what was now so different about me, I found I could tune in on the voice for a few seconds at a time without slipping away.

The payoff came one night when I distinctly heard my shower spray whisper the word "Down." My mind started to go fuzzy but I got busy thinking about how Kern let nothing stand in his way, how for him winning, attaining his goals, was his only reason for living, how to men like Kern, the world, nature, life, was a thing to be controlled and exploited. And that was probably the only reason I heard what came next.

"Down and down and down and down," said a voice concealed in the rush of my shower.

Suddenly I was in a dark forest, running through branches with thorn spikes that tore at my eyes, my face, my bare arms. And when I forced myself back to my shower I saw, to my horror, that a thin red stain was swirling down the drain. I thought about how I used to force myself to be like Kern.

"You are one with the forest," Irma's voice told me, although it wasn't quite the same as the voice she used out on the verandah. She had, it seemed, a slightly different voice when she was appearing in my shower.

I felt angry and frightened and I wished, absurdly, that there was someone big nearby to protect me.

Just then the surrounding green turned darker and it was suddenly alive, fecund and dangerous, not because of what it contained but because of what it was.

"The forest pulsates with the indifferent power of nature to recreate herself," the voice said, and I felt myself, simply by my presence in my shower, be drawn into that drama like one more leaf. "Rebirth, life, death, decay. Every contradictory urge and trait is balanced, for every force, a counter-force."

These forces that created balance pulled my mind in different directions and made me dizzy. Somehow, beyond logic, it seemed natural now to be both cowardly and brave, selfish and generous, angry and loving, hard and soft, peaceful and aggressive, bad and good.

Down here, the voice seemed to imply, the only possible sin was a forced consistency, because consistency upset the natural balance.

"When you emerge from the forest you are holding two hearts, one black, the other deep pink and throbbing with life. As before, you must decide which heart to take into yourself. So set one heart aside now and as you step back into yourself, your heart pulses with life. You have named and owned your fear of rage and your fear of fear and your fear of love and your regret and your selfishness, which means these forces are yours to let go of now or use as you need them."

Naked, dripping, thinking about how different Bill Kern and I were, I silently stepped from the shower stall, leaving the water running behind me. All around me the water voice droned on. At first I thought it was coming from my toilet, and so I went to my knees; had anyone been there, they'd have seen a man about to toss his cookies.

"Your emotions, your dreams, your hopes, balanced by your goodness, and your warrior nature, balanced by gentleness, bring you to your rightful place in the cosmos. All these aspects of yourself make you who you are, and you are profoundly glad to be the one-of-a-kind being who is you. You are profound. You are unique. You are joy. You are love. You are life."

"And you," I said, "are a Stick-up."

The voice, suddenly silent, seemed to have come from a round plastic devise attached to the tile wall behind my toilet bowl, designed to emit a sanitary and slightly perfumed smell. There was, I had no doubt, a similar devise somewhere near the bay window in my living room, and probably one under my bed, installed so that my dreams could be guided.

"I found you Irma," I shouted.

"So you think," the voice said, and now it did not sound at all like Irma's voice, nor did it seem to come from the round devise on the wall. "But in truth, you found you."

I grabbed the piece of plastic and ripped it from the wall. There was no wire to break, and when I cracked into the slatted plastic cover, all I found was a waxy tablet.

I rushed from the bathroom, quickly got into my terry cloth robe and burst into the lobby, intending to find and confront Irma. But I didn't have far to look. She was sitting peacefully on the Victorian love seat beside the front desk, and she appeared to be chatting on the phone.

"How long have you been here?" I demanded.

She looked at me with that Buddha expression of hers, then said, "Just a moment, Bonnie."

"How long have you been talking on the phone?"

"I don't know. Twenty minutes. Why?"

"I don't believe you." I grabbed the phone. She smiled as she watched me lift it to my ear. "How long has this call been going on?" I demanded.

"Huh? A half hour. Who's this?"

I handed back the phone. I think I managed to say the word "Sorry," before I wandered away.

Stunned, I changed my clothes and looked in the bedroom and near the bay window for other Stick-ups. I found nothing, and I wandered outside because I needed fresh air and I wanted to see and feel the ocean.

Brian Cox was asleep in one of the verandah chairs and Jimmy McCaffery was beside him, also asleep. Chelsey and Ryan were sitting on the steps.

"Ocean's pretty sick," commented Ryan.

"Sure is," said Chelsey. "And with stuff we use to make ourselves better. Does that seem right?"

He shrugged.

"Isn't it, like, crazy?" she asked.

He shrugged again, as if to say it was no crazier than anything else adults did.

"It's crazy," I said. "It's greedy and stupid and crazy."

They both looked up at me. Their faces were tan and dirty, and tears had cut paths down their cheeks.

"Is that why you're crying?" I asked. "For the ocean?"

Chelsey shook her head.

"For Mr. McCaffery," Ryan said.

"Oh? What's wrong with Jimmy?"

"I think he's dead," said Chelsey.

"Let's go get crabs," said Ryan.

"Naw. We did that already."

"How 'bout the kites then?"

"Let's see what Heather's cooking," said Chelsey, and as she stood she put a hand tenderly on Ryan's shoulder.

Ryan stood and followed Chelsey past me to the door.

"It's true he won't wake up," Ryan said to me, as if making a huge concession.

"Because he's dead," said Chelsey.

"Is not," said Ryan, as the door slammed behind them. "He's taking a nap, like Mr. Cox."

"Is so dead," Chelsey said, as they crossed the lobby.

The slamming door awakened Brian Cox, who stretched, yawned, squinted at the ocean. He looked over at Jimmy McCaffery and shivered. Then he saw me standing a short distance away.

"Hey, Killer," he said, in his normal voice. "God, I had the strangest dream. I kept handing this old guy some sort of gem, like a diamond, only it had a goldish kind of light, you know, and he kept handing it back. It was almost like a fight. I wanted him to keep the gem and he wanted me to have it."

"Who ended up with it?" I asked.

He sat forward and squinted. "What happened to your face?" He seemed alarmed, and I wondered if the thorns in my shower had actually left scratches. "You look ancient. Like overnight you turned forty or something."

"That young, huh? I'd avoid mirrors, Cox. The sight might be bad for your heart. Who had the gem when your dream ended?"

"Me."

"And now you can move your tongue. You got your voice back."

"What are you talking about?"

"I'll explain some time," I said, stepping closer to Jimmy and wishing I'd see him breathe.

It turned out Chelsey was right. Jimmy McCaffery was dead. The paramedics didn't even bother to work on him because he had already stiffened; they just toppled him into a brown vinyl bag, his body holding the shape of the chair.

The death startled Brian Cox out of the time warp he had entered upon awakening from his nap. He remembered, vaguely, that for several weeks his tongue had been frozen and numb, but he couldn't or wouldn't tell me what had happened to him when he looked out my bay window.

Several times over the winter, in front of any number of people in the Mooncusser Cafe or out on Ireland's verandah, he made cryptic comments that seemed to support the rumor which had him enjoying unsafe sex with space aliens. But he always did it with a look in his eyes that contradicted him. If he regretted the loss of his job he hid it well, and made no move to reclaim his former life. He was a changed man. The posturing egoist was gone, and in his place was a person brimming with love. He loved the ocean and me and Ireland by the Sea and maybe a seventeen-year-old named Tammy McIntyre, with whom he started to spend time again as that first summer ended.

He didn't even say, "Gotten into any good head lately," when Jason Sargent showed up.

Jason arrived the same day Jimmy died. He walked into the Mooncusser Cafe around dinner time, and found Brian sitting with Irma and me.

"Cox!" he bellowed. "You're alive. Where have you been?"

"Right here," Brian said, calmly.

"You missed your brain transplant appointment," Jason said, with uncharacteristic brashness; he seemed surprised by the line, and didn't know what to do with the laughter it produced.

I introduced Jason to Irma and invited him to join us.

"What do you know," Irma said. "A physician who is also a healer. How unusual."

For the next few hours, out on the verandah, Cox tried to explain to Jason what he'd been through, and when I went off to bed Jason was examining Brian's tongue with a penlight.

The next morning after breakfast, Jason joined Francine, Brian and me when we went to search McCaffery's sparsely furnished apartment. We were looking for a will or some final instructions. The rooms beyond the blueberry blue door were cramped but neat. There was a narrow bed and an old oak bureau in the sleeping alcove beyond a sitting room with an easy chair and a writing desk. Cracks in the plaster ceiling formed what looked like a map of Ireland.

Francine began to open drawers in the desk while I leafed through some unopened mail and a ledger book. Brian went directly to the bed, as if he knew just where to look, slipped his hand under Jimmy's pillow, and came out with a large manila envelope. He unwrapped the red thread, lifted the flap and removed Jimmy's deed, which was now just a souvenir, since one of its conditions had been that it not become part of his estate.

Jimmy's will, officially notarized, was also in the envelope, along with certificates of birth, baptism, holy communion, and confirmation, all issued long ago in Dublin. The will contained, beyond the standard legal gibberish, two simple sentences:

"I hereby leave everything to Ireland by the Sea."

"I wish to be cremated and scattered on the beach."

While I was reading Jimmy's will, Brian Cox made an even more important discovery. Still moving about as if he'd been here many times before, Cox went into the closet and found that it contained six shirts, three sweaters, a winter coat, two pairs of pants, a pile of blankets, a box of baseball cards—which turned out to be worth nearly thirty-thousand dollars—a pair of LL Bean boots, and a large trunk. The trunk proved to be incredibly heavy, but working together, Brian, Jason and I managed to drag it from the dim closet. And once we had it out where we could see, we noticed it was padlocked.

"Nothing's ever easy," said Francine.

We were a turned-on bunch of voyeurs, I thought, picking through another man's private sanctuary. Even Sargent, who had explored the brains of his fellow man with all the tools of modern science, was enjoying this rummaging through the leavings of a life.

I wanted to find Ace and get a hammer and chisel or a hacksaw, but Francine, who had known Jimmy best, suggested that the key was probably hidden somewhere in the tiny apartment. She immediately began to search in the half-sized refrigerator, while Jason and I picked through desk and bureau drawers and pockets of pants and shirts in the closet.

Brian went into the bathroom and emerged in less than a minute with the key. It was in the medicine cabinet, under a cake of shaving soap stuck to the bottom of an old-fashioned mug behind a collection of medications and toothbrushes.

"What made you look in there?" Jason asked him.

"I don't know," said Cox. "Seemed logical."

I used the slippery key, but even with the padlock gone, the trunk lid still seemed locked. It was heavy, and the hinges, we decided, were in need of oil.

"So how the hell did old Jimmy open it?" I wondered.

"Probably didn't," said Francine. "Whatever's in there probably hasn't seen the light of day in a decade."

The hinges screeched as Brian, Jason and I, on a three count, lifted with all our collective strength.

There was treasure in the trunk. I don't know what we each expected, but what we found stunned us. We stood gaping, I can't guess for how long. There were gems and coins and gold chains, some delicate, some thick as a large man's finger. If we had been living in a cartoon, there would have been heavenly music and lots of those glinting stars popping from the trunk, and of course dollar signs in our eyes. There should have been a skeleton lying here as if on guard, I told myself, and that thought got me moving again. My alternative was to let myself be transported to Jill's apartment, and her aquarium, and I didn't want that. I was missing Jill less and less now, but still …

This, more than greed, was why I was the first to sink my hands in the treasure, followed by Brian, Francine, and then, long moments later, Jason. We played in this booty like children, like pirates, lifting it into the air in handfuls and letting it rain back into the trunk. Most of the coins were common quarters, dimes, nickels and pennies, but scattered about were a number of gold doubloons and pieces of Spanish silver. There was jewelry mixed with the coins, more rings and watches and bracelets and necklaces than I'd ever seen in one place, hundreds, maybe thousands; most of it, Francine said, was junk, costume jewelry and trinkets lost in the sand, probably by children. But some of what glittered here was gold, and many of the stones were real.

In less than a minute, four or five dozen diamonds, sapphires, opals and rubies had tumbled through my fingers, and if only a third of them was real, then this trunk was worth a fortune.

And it all belonged to Ireland.

Chapter Twenty-Nine

Other than Jimmy's metal detector and his baseball cards, there was little else of worth in his estate. We boxed his possessions, turned his will over to Horace Asp, and hauled his treasure trunk down to Bernie's vault in the basement, with help from Ace and the boys.

After the cremation, we had a memorial service on Ireland's verandah. There were brief eulogies by Francine and Irma. Ryan stood up and said he hoped that Jimmy was hanging with the Long Beach Island ghosts he'd loved. I said I thought Jimmy had been part of the soul of Ireland by the Sea and that I would miss him. Brian Cox tried to speak but became too choked up.

We had a moment of silent prayer and meditation then we all went for a walk.

As I sprinkled Jimmy on the beach he had so thoroughly explored, I found it comforting in a way a cemetery never is. Eternity in the sod, held down by a slab of granite, with not nearly enough information on it to matter, seemed a hideous fate, while the idea of spreading out here beside the ever-changing ocean felt like eternal freedom. I promised myself the same fate.

"What will you do with Jimmy's room?" asked Cox, once we had turned for home.

"I don't know," I said. "Nobody's going to rent it, it's so narrow, with only those two windows at the end."

"You could deed it to me," suggested Cox.

"Yeah, sure," I said. We climbed the verandah steps. "I just got the room back. Why would I want to give it away again?"

Jason joined us. He had on a neon blue T-shirt that said, in neon pink script, "The New Man Creeps In On Little Pig Fetus."

"Why would you want to deed Jimmy's room to me?" Cox asked.

"To get yourself out of debt, my friend. A simple swap."

We stood for a moment by the rail, Jason to my left, Cox to my right. It was a tempting deal, but there was something not quite right about it.

"I might have other plans for Jimmy's space," I said, "but it's okay with me if you make a second choice."

"You don't have to do that," Jason told me, before I'd finished my sentence. "Say the word and I'll give you a letter explaining what happened to your funds."

"The new Jason," said Cox, with surprisingly little hostility. "That would sure put Kern's nuts in a vise. Mine, too, I suppose. Oh, well. It was worth a try. So what the hell does your T-shirt mean, Jason?"

"It came to me in a dream my first night here," Jason said, puffing out his chest. "I had it made down in Surf City. It's kind of an in-joke that makes reference to the use of pig fetus tissue for brain implants."

Cox groaned, staggered down the steps and out onto the beach, where he turned to face the inn, fell to his knees, spread his arms wide and said, "You've given him a set of balls. Now could you please do something for his sense of humor?"

I spent the rest of the day getting Ryan and Chelsey ready to start school while Jason and Cox gave Atlantic City a try. We met for breakfast the next morning, and almost before he sat down, Jason announced that he'd had the most wonderful idea of his life while he was taking his shower.

"Here we go," said Cox. "Ireland strikes again."

Jason had been looking for ways to introduce his interns and residents to what he called "the human side of medicine," he explained, and the answer seemed to be Ireland by the Sea.

"It's the perfect setting," he said. "And it's magic."

"I suppose you want a deal, too," I said. "Well, at least with you guys I don't have to turn myself into an Indian Chief and live in a cave."

"I'd appreciate a break on room and board," Jason said. "But what I said yesterday goes. Either way, you owe me nothing."

"Done," I said. "Let's make it happen."

Jason went back to Connecticut two days after we scattered Jimmy, and with nothing else to do, Brian and I spent some time trying to get the hang of Jimmy's metal detector. I found it tedious and somewhat disorienting to walk the beach listening to the hum inside those big sweaty earphones, my eyes following the slow sweep of the disc at the end of the chrome shaft. Even the prospect of buried treasure couldn't lift my boredom. But Brian Cox was enraptured. He uncovered a Kennedy half dollar and an ornate silver ring in his first half hour, and the way he hooted you would have thought he was a pauper.

It only took a day for Ace and his crew to incorporate Jimmy's room into the parlor, and another day to wallpaper and decorate. Soon all traces of Jimmy were gone, and I was sad about that. There was something wrong with Ireland's symmetry now, or its mix. It seemed right that there be both youth and age in residence, and now age was gone.

I offered Cox the turret suite on Three, which was, to me, among the three best spaces Ireland had to offer, but Cox turned it down. If he couldn't have Jimmy's room off the lobby, he'd take Shannon's old room in the rear wing, which had been Jimmy's before he got too old for the stairs. Cox offered to use his own funds to restore the room downstairs—he was still wealthy by any sane standard—but everyone seemed to appreciate the expanded parlor so I stood firm and eventually we had Horace Asp start the paperwork to deed over Shannon's old room.

Shannon went off to college up in New Brunswick and was only home on weekends. On her third visit she brought with her a new boyfriend, whom I hated, of course, although I was glad to see that my possessive response was fatherly and nothing more. By the end of that first weekend visit, Ryan and Chelsey had tested and tormented the poor fellow in ways I would never have thought of, and he had survived at least enough to be invited back by this gruesome twosome.

Brian spent his time searching for treasure and trying to win Tammy away from Suds the Surfer, a hopeless cause, but no less consuming for that. What treasure Brian found he listed in the newspaper, making note of, but keeping to himself, any engraved initials or dates or identifying characteristics; twice already he had returned rings of untold sentimental value to their owners, and that seemed to do more for him than all the money NBC had paid him or all the trips or appliances or vehicles he had given away in his former career.

Following Brian's lead, I did the same with the jewelry from Jimmy's treasure chest, but nobody came forward to make a claim. With Francine's help, I hired coin and gem and baseball card appraisers and by October we were informed that the treasure in Jimmy's trunk was worth nearly two million dollars. There were tax complications, but I knew now that with this money and Ireland's percentage of Bernie's various operations, I'd be able to keep the inn afloat long enough to bring the tourists back. If necessary, I could even buy off Bill Kern, although I had switched my strategy where he was concerned.

I had sent Kern an invoice for $250,000 worth of "Past Life Vocational Guidance," along with a note informing him that he could pay this fee or agree to give Ireland ten percent of everything he made as a result of "images, insights and ideas" provided during his consultation. So far he hadn't responded.

Through agents in Manhattan I sold the baseball cards, some of the largest gems, and the ancient coins—except for the dozen I'd given to the museum here on Long Beach Island; the rest of the really valuable gems were in a bank vault, having been assayed and registered and insured. Money was no longer a problem, especially since Bernie's *I want my little red button* buttons were suddenly a novelty phenomenon that had already produced hundreds of thousands of dollars for the McC Corp, and thousands for Ireland. And a stroke of genius by Ryan turned the dead months of autumn and early winter into a profitable season.

"There's an old empty pirate's trunk in the attic," Ryan said one night, "so let's fill it with Jimmy's loot and hold a treasure hunt."

Jimmy's huge trunk in Bernie's vault was still half-full, and Ryan and Chelsey and I carried the pirate chest down to the basement one afternoon after school and filled it with a few dozen handfuls of jewelry and coins.

"Hey, neat," Ryan said. "Look at this."

He picked something out of the small chest we had all but filled and held out a gold charm, about the size and thickness of a Life Saver candy, with a claw etched on its side. I felt something push me back and my head went fuzzy.

"I got dibs," Ryan said.

"You okay?" asked Chelsey. "You look like you've seen a ghost."

"Turn that thing over," I told Ryan. "There's a balance scale on the other side."

Ryan did. "How did you know?" he asked.

"That used to belong to me," I told him. Then I looked at Chelsey. "I gave this to your grandmother instead of an engagement ring, a long, long time ago. I shouldn't have because someone else gave it to me. It was a rotten thing to do."

"Here," said Ryan. "Now the rotten thing is undone."

"Well, not really," I said. "But it's a nice thought."

We finished filling our small trunk, which looked as if it might have been around in the days of Captain Kidd, then lugged this upstairs, making sure we weren't seen. We hid the treasure chest under a loose board on the landing of the secret staircase, between the first and second floors, then we spent the next five hours making up clues, which we hid that night in each available room.

After that, all it took were a few well-worded, well-placed ads about Jimmy the Beachcomber's lost treasure, and we were booked almost solid on weekends for the rest of the year. That, of course, meant business for The Mooncusser Cafe and The Emerald Isle Spa, which had been doing fairly well as it was.

None of our clues gave enough information to matter, and that required our guests to find ways to work together; soon strangers were dealing with strangers as if they were old friends. Many of the same people returned each weekend to resume their hunt, and to get new clues, and these guests began to spend as much time walking the beach and talking about their hopes and dreams, what they'd do with the treasure if they found it, what they'd do with their lives if they didn't, as they spent hunting for treasure.

A single mother and her ten-year-old daughter, working together with a birder from Cape May, finally discovered a way into the secret passages and, with only two hours to go before their checkout time, located the treasure chest. The find made all the papers, and so of course we announced there'd be another hunt next year, featuring Brian the Beachcomber's treasure.

Christmas at the inn was quiet and a little lonely, since Ryan was with his mother in Saint John, but strangely enough my Bah-Humbug Blues never struck. Chelsey and Shannon were here, along with Brian and Tammy (and Suds and some of the others from our summer crew). We had a tree, and silly gifts, and Heather turned out a turkey feast, which we consumed at one long table under the old Mooncusser sign.

Ryan returned for a second Christmas on New Year's Eve day, and that night he and Chelsey and Shannon and I hugged and cheered out on Ireland's verandah as one year became another. It wasn't until I was in bed and almost asleep that I realized I'd have been dead a whole year by now had fate not untwisted the knot I had tied around that attic beam.

Following through on a resolution, I forced myself to go see Irma and McJustice in their suite, a move I'd been putting off because I wasn't sure I was ready for the answers I might get. Irma looked at me as if she was stoned, McJustice as if she'd have enjoyed stoning me.

"I have to know, Irma," I said, standing just inside their sitting room door. "I have to know how you got inside my head."

She smiled and looked at the wall to my right as if she was watching a television program nobody else could see.

"You did something to make me see the archers. What was it? Did you drug my food? Hypnotize me? What?"

She shook her head at each of my suggestions, but her distracted expression never changed.

"Please. It's driving me nuts. I'll drop the suit against you. I'll honor your deed."

"You'd do that?" McJustice asked.

"Not your deed, Sis. I have other plans for you."

"I can only imagine."

"I'd tell you if I could," Irma said, her voice soft and drifty. I strained to hear the voice from my shower, but it wasn't quite right. "The truth is, I don't know where those visions come from or how it is I know what I know sometimes. The only thing I can tell you is that I've been up against the archers myself, and I've been down inside the rose."

It brought a profound sense of comfort to learn that another human being—even a New Age flake like Irma—had experienced the same things I had. It explained nothing, but it indicated I might not be totally psychotic, or that if I was, I was not alone.

"Just wait until you get to the cliffs of final choice," Irma told me. "You're in for a real treat then."

"What did Brian Cox see?"

She looked up at me and giggled. To my surprise, so did McJustice. It was the first time I heard her laugh with delight, although I'd heard her nasty cackle often enough.

"What?"

"It's x-rated," McJustice said.

"Put it this way," said Irma. "You know that expression about living and dying by the sword? Well, in a manner of speaking, that's what happened to your friend."

"The revenge of the twat," said McJustice, and the two women giggled again while I stood there grinning.

"Does everyone see this stuff?" I asked. "Have you?" I addressed this last to McJustice, and I could tell by the way she dropped her smile that I'd hit a nerve.

"Not yet," she muttered. "And why it should come to you is quite beyond me."

"Because I'm pure of heart, Sis. So it's not something everyone who lives or visits here experiences?"

"I don't know why some do and some don't," Irma said. "Or why some of the ones who do run away, and others stick with it. Or why some get physical signs. We thought you'd run."

"We hoped you'd run," added McJustice.

"But you fooled us. In fact, you turned up the heat on the magic."

"Who else has visions?" I asked.

Irma looked at the ceiling. "Heather does, I'm pretty sure. And I think little Ryan may have started. Chelsey's too closed off. None of the McCohens were open enough, although I think Ireland touched Bernie on other channels. Jimmy never got it. I don't know about Shannon. The guests come and go, some do and some don't. You can usually tell by their eyes."

"But what is it?"

Irma shook her head as if to say, *don't ask.*

"You know more than you're telling me," I prompted.

"It's McX," she said, with trembling reverence. Then, shaking her head as if to clear it, she added, "Or one of the ghosts Jimmy used to tell about, or maybe the fumes from Bernie's mushroom solution. Who knows?"

Irma and I talked a while longer, McJustice sitting quietly by—without scowling, I noticed—but I learned nothing more.

Later that afternoon I had Horace Asp withdraw our action against Irma, and in the days that followed, she and I spoke often about our experiences with the archers and the rose. That same week, deeds were filed at town hall for Brian McCox, Shannon McGideon and Ace McMac, and the deed for the owner's suite on the south side of the first floor was awarded to one C McWilly. The rest of the inn now belonged to Ireland by the Sea, Inc., and I instructed Asp to divide corporate stock evenly among all the deedholders, as well as Ryan and Chelsey.

In February, Jason and his medical students started coming down for long weekends. They held meetings in the dining room mid-morning and mid-afternoon, and on sunny days they bundled up and walked the beach.

Jason became fascinated with Bernie McCohen's God Machine, and together they devised methods to bombard Bernie's membrane containers with brain waves, getting video images of the patterns a subject's waves made in the color-coded iron filings suspended in the viscous solution. They did the same experiments with various forms of music, by dropping submersible speakers into the vats. And they tested the brain wave output of subjects who were listening to music, arguing, sleeping, having sex, eating. Hour after hour Jason and his students hovered over Bernie's video monitors, comparing the images caused by human subjects—including me—against the images caused by the stars and planets in their various alignments. As far as I know nothing came of this work, except the joy of doing it.

As all this was going on around us, McJustice and I slowly let down our guards, until one day, in mid-March, I went to her with a proposal. She was sitting alone in the enlarged parlor, watching television.

"How about signing your deed to Twenty-nine over to Chelsey?" I said, sitting down beside her on a wicker love seat.

"What in heavens name would make me want to do that?" she asked, and squeezed herself as far from me as she could.

"You never use the room. And I've dropped my action against Irma, so you're safe there."

"But what if Irma decides to leave me?"

"If that happens," I told her, "we'll find you a room."

"You'd do that?"

I nodded. "What would we do without our resident witch?"

She glared at me, but I could tell she was fighting a smile.

"So what's your trick?" she asked.

"No trick."

"With you there's always a trick."

"As long as you want a place here there'll be a place for you. I promise."

"I think I'll take my chances in court."

I stood and began to leave.

"Why is it you haven't cleaned out Twenty-four?" she asked me. "I mean, you say you don't believe McX is in there, so why haven't you taken the door down and reclaimed the space?"

"There's been too much to do," I said, "with Jimmy and the treasure hunt and the holidays and now Jason's retreats. And gearing up for next summer has ..."

"So it's not because you're afraid of the ghost?"

"Maybe a little," I said, and my honesty made her smile.

"You know who McX is, don't you?" she said.

"I don't even know if she is."

"Well you should."

"Do you?"

"Of course."

"Is it Dotty?" Crazy as this was, the thought had occurred to me several times recently.

"Don't be absurd. Dot's dead. Although Dot certainly hand-picked McX, the same way she did you."

"And you know who she is?"

"You would too, if you weren't such a blockhead."

"Tell me."

"Not on your life."

"Tell me, or ..."

"Or what?" She smirked in a way that said, "Caught you!"

That conversation nagged at me, and soon, with all else settled into a comfortable routine, the discovery of who McX was became my quest. I considered plans for breaking into Room Twenty-four, but I knew I never would. Then one afternoon, a year to the day since my arrival here, as I showered after my run, an idea came to me that made me shiver, even there in the hot water and steam.

After Ryan fell asleep that night, I went up onto the second floor, and though I told myself the idea was absurd, the prospect of being right made my insides electric. There were young doctors everywhere, so having one more person wandering about meant nothing. Still, I wanted to be alone when I tested my idea, so I kept walking past the door of Room Twenty-four, with its seven locks. Finally, when the halls were empty, I stepped close and knocked, too softly for anyone, other than the person inside, to hear. If anyone was inside.

"It's me," I whispered. "Gregor."

There was no sound from beyond the door; I was greatly relieved, and a little disappointed.

A young couple moved past, and looked at me, curiously. I smiled and muttered something about "room service."

As I began to walk away, one of the locks snapped open.

Then another.

And a third.

After the seventh lock was released, the knob slowly turned, the door moved, and a voice, the soft voice of Ireland, whispered to me through the widening crack:

"It's about time."